The Gamma rover came bounced out. Each carried his weapon at the ready, and they spread out at a fast jog.

The LT steered their rover toward the right while Chief Harris kept his eyes on Sanders and his men. The fire team advanced in a leap-frog formation, one pair moving forward while the other covered it with their weapons. The chief kept the outboard multi-barreled machine gun ready to support them.

"Flash—got a flash out of the supply building!" Lt. Jackson barked.

The Foxtrot rover vanished in a silent blast, fire flashing for an instant as fuel and oxygen combusted with searing force. The explosion broke the vehicle in two, and left a mist of pulverized material—a vapor with a sickening tint of redness—slowly settling to the surface. One lone wheel rolled a short distance, wobbled, and fell onto its side.

The command rover heeled violently as the LT accelerated, veering unpredictably as he steered a zigzag course. Harris fired at the place where he had seen the flash, the rapid-fire weapon spraying so many tracers they looked like a fuzzy laser beam licking at the target.

Another flash brightened the gap in the supply shed's doorway, and their rover lurched hard. The depressurization warning flashed, shocking Harris into an instant of panic until he remembered he was wearing a suit.

"We're hit!" snapped Jackson. "Shit—I lost power!"

Chief Harris saw the hole in the cockpit dome where the shell had entered; it must have passed out through the body without exploding. Outside, the SEALS were pouring fire while still moving toward the barracks building. He glanced again at Foxtrot. The wreckage was scattered in a wide circle, dust still settling. There was no prospect of finding a survivor. But the SEALS never left one of their own behind, alive or dead. When they could, the squad would search the wreckage for their teammates.

Right now, they were in the fight of their lives on alien soil . . .

# STARSTRIKE

## TASK FORCE MARS

**Kevin Dockery and Douglas Niles**

BALLANTINE BOOKS • NEW YORK

*Starstrike: Task Force Mars* is a work of fiction. Names, characters, places, and incidents are the products of the author's imagination or are used fictitiously. Any resemblance to actual events, locales, or persons, living or dead, is entirely coincidental.

A Del Rey Books Mass Market Original

Copyright © 2007 by Kevin Dockery and Douglas Niles

Published in the United States by Del Rey Books, an imprint of The Random House Publishing Group, a division of Random House, Inc., New York.

DEL REY is a registered trademark and the Del Rey colophon is a trademark of Random House, Inc.

ISBN 978-0-345-49041-4

Printed in the United States of America

www.delreybooks.com

OPM 9 8 7 6 5 4 3 2 1

To all the men of the Teams—

past, present, and especially
future.

Hooyah!

# One: Weigh Out

Master Chief Petty Officer Rafael Ruiz was more than mildly irritated by the need to conduct another six-hour training regimen without even a break for a hot meal, let alone a catnap. After all, he had been outside the SAT-STAR1 station for the last ten hours, enclosed in his suit, breathing bottled air and watching his men go through the paces of a weightless/vacuum survival drill. The six SEALS had passed with flying colors and were floating toward the mess hall and then their bunks, but the chief had to take one more man outside and check him off the list.

But verbal displays of selfish displeasure were for lesser mortals than master chiefs, and so Ruiz carefully replenished the air supply for his breather and the mobility jets on his suit again, double-checking all the connections for his life support pod. The Mark III Survival Suit/Vacuum/Military was a marvel of engineering, but it wasn't exactly a pair of silk pajamas. It weighed more than a hundred pounds at 1 G—and though they were working in a weightless environment, the suit, like everything else up here, retained every ounce of mass when it came to moving it or stopping it from moving.

The suit was triple-lined with layers of rubber, plastic, and metal foil. Even so, it was thin and supple, riding close to the skin and not restrictive of movement. The gloves allowed the fingers an amazing degree of dexterity so that a man could flip a coin or—more to the point with SEALS training—operate the trigger and reload the magazine of a small handheld weapon without fumbling. A utility belt around the waist offered attachment points for a dozen tools and weapons, and the helmet was titanium around the back of the skull but had a full hemisphere of transparent Plexiglas at the front, allowing for complete peripheral vision.

The suit had plenty of high-tech augmentation, too. It had a self-contained breather, of course, with enough air for some twelve hours of sealed operation. Also, the air bottles could be changed easily without removing the suit; they could even be swapped out in a vacuum environment without danger to the wearer. There were several sensors built into the suit, including full life support readouts that provided the wearer's blood pressure, heart rate, and other vital signs. It could detect external radiation, analyze air quality and pressure (or the lack thereof), and provide all the data on a heads-up display (HUD) that projected onto the interior of the visor for easy reading. The data also could be accessed by someone else and was reported on a small LED on the chest. A full-function computer was worn on the wrist, with a link to the HUD and a small screen and keyboard on the unit.

An additional and innovative feature of the suit was the individual mobility system, which allowed the wearer to move through a weightless environment. The IMS consisted of small adjustable nozzles at the hips, shoulders, and feet. By bleeding off a very small amount of the air supply, the wearer could use that released pressure as propulsion. If he began to drift away from his ship, for example, he theoretically could shoot himself right back with a few bursts of air. Of course, an inherent liability of that system was the fact that the more moving around a SEALS did with the IMS, the less air he had to breathe. All SEALS needed to check out with this controlled personal space suit, but Ruiz was not a big fan of the system. Several times during training it had resulted in dangerous leaks that had required a trainee to make a quick return to the station air lock before his emergency backup tank ran out of air. Ten minutes may sound like a lot of time, but not when a SEALS was doing zero-G maneuvers with a faulty IMS.

The military suits were a new design and featured an innate autotourniquet feature at the ankles, knees, elbows, hips, and shoulders. That feature was intended to save the life of the wearer if the suit was breached by attack or other damage in one of the limbs. Though in a vaccum the cost was the loss of the isolated limb, it was hoped that a tight seal would allow the wounded SEALS to reach a pressurized environment while he was still alive.

Chief Ruiz was not entirely sure the thing would work as advertised, but he had seen enough near accidents in training that he was willing to give it a try. Space was full of tiny objects moving at very high speeds, and any one of them could puncture a suit before the wearer even had a clue that he was in danger.

The most important thing about his suit to Master Chief Ruiz and to any other of the few men who currently had the privilege of wearing it was the golden trident he was entitled to wear as his shoulder patch. Ruiz and his platoon commander, Lieutenant Jackson, had been the first to be awarded the new spacefaring SEALS trident. Ensign Sanders, if he completed the final drill regimen, would be the sixteenth.

After Ruiz was satisfied that his own suit checked out, he did the same for the young officer who was the cause of this inconvenient outing.

Ensign Dennis Sanders was a bright-eyed newbie to space, though—like all members of the elite SEALS Teams—he had been through the rigors of BUD/S training in Coronado. Also, he recently had completed the even more extreme program at McMurdo Station on Antarctica. The Alien Environment School was a requirement for any SEALS who aspired to add the newly coveted "S" to the end of his rating, and Ensign Sanders obviously had survived and completed that course.

After all, he was here, wasn't he? And it wasn't his fault that he'd arrived after Ruiz had checked out the rest of his Teammates in their vacuum suits and gone through the paces of the final exterior drill. In fact, he'd even offered to wait until Ruiz was ready to go, but the master chief had simply said, "Let's do it."

Sanders was so grateful, he looked almost giddy, an expression that seemed natural on his boyish features. With Sanders's dusting of freckles, sand-colored hair, and light blue eyes, Ruiz had no trouble imagining him as a twelve-year-old, though he was in fact twenty-five. At an avuncular thirty-five, the master chief was the old man of the outfit and a contrast to Sanders in every other way as well. Dark of complexion and black-haired, befitting his Puerto Rican ancestry, Ruiz was fond of saying, "I'm too old for this shit." But he and his Teammates knew it was a lie. In fact, here in space, with the unlimited vistas and the hostile but thrilling environment, Master Chief Rafael Ruiz was having the time of his life.

He paid particular attention to the back of the ensign's suit, visually confirming that all the connections were secure and that the helmet was properly seated in the collar, with no creases or obvious flaws in the material. He checked the LED on Sanders's chest while the ensign did the same with his HUD; both showed that his blood pressure and temperature were normal, with his heart rate only slightly elevated—just what one would expect from a guy about to make his first untethered space walk.

"All checked out, Enswine," Ruiz declared, his voice tinny and mechanical within the confines of his Plexiglas helmet.

"Thanks, Chief," Sanders replied. If he'd heard the mispronunciation of his rank, he knew better than to comment. Although ensigns technically outranked petty officers, even master chief petty officers, any young officer with a pretense of wisdom knew that he needed to earn the master chief's respect, not simply demand it by virtue of the single gold bar of rank he wore.

Ruiz turned and allowed Sanders to inspect the back of his suit; then they repeated the drill of comparing the LED and HUD data.

"Looks like we're good to go," the ensign finally concluded, giving the chief a pat on the shoulder.

The two SEALS moved down the passage to the air lock, using the handles in the bulkheads to pull themselves along. Quickly easing themselves into the spacious compartment—it could hold six suited SEALS in close quarters—they waited only a few minutes for the pumps to draw the air out. Checking his HUD, Ruiz watched the air pressure drop. In the first minute it went from the atmospheric pressure of Earth at sea level to that near the summit of Mount Everest. In another ninety seconds, the sensor read "0 PSI."

Each man attached a tether line to his utility belt. The thin filament would reel out as they moved and would keep them secured to the station until they determined that their IMS was working properly.

Only then did Ruiz nod toward the wheel on the exterior hatch. It was a design familiar to anyone who had ever served on a submarine or any other navy ship, which included all SEALS. "You want to do the honors, Enswine?"

Sanders nodded and quickly, even eagerly, spun the wheel.

When the outer hatch opened, they were confronted by the full infinite vastness of space. The sun was on the other side of the station, and Earth, half-illuminated, was brilliant and beautiful just "overhead." In shadow, they moved away from the air lock.

Ruiz, as he always did upon emerging from the air lock, took a second just to stare. He never got over the wonder of seeing the whole world in one look. The Atlantic Ocean was blue and dazzling except where the spidery outline of a tropical storm moved toward the Caribbean. Ruiz's wife was safe in Coronado, but he crossed himself and whispered a prayer for his mother's safety in San Juan. He could see England and the Bay of Biscay, but the east coast of the United States was obscured by clouds. Farther to the west, the Great Lakes stood out in vivid azure relief.

"It's really something, Chief," Sanders breathed in awe, floating nearby, the tiny transmitter and earpiece rendering his voice with remarkable clarity. "Kinda takes your breath away."

"Sure does, Enswine," Ruiz replied gruffly. "Now, are you ready to get to work?"

"Just tell me what to do," Sanders said cheerfully.

*Good answer,* Ruiz thought, still mildly disgruntled.

But it was hard to hold on to his anger out here, in this infinite playground. The two men remained tethered to the station as they drifted free of it. The training module that was their destination was a sphere located on a boom extending some hundred meters away from the air lock. Sanders activated his IMS, and Ruiz watched critically as the officer guided himself along, the thin line of his tether trailing behind. The fellow seemed to know what he was doing; he needed only a tiny adjustment to keep himself on a straight course toward the training module.

Once he reached it, Sanders took hold of a hand grip and turned around to watch Ruiz coming after him. The ensign's eyes immediately widened.

"Hey, Chief—take a look at that!"

Sanders's voice was as excited as a schoolboy's, and Ruiz sighed silently, pivoting to look at whatever had attracted the young officer's attention. And then he, too, whistled in amazement.

"That would be the *Pegasus,* sir," he remarked laconically even as the spectacle of the approaching spaceship almost took his breath away.

The USSS *Pegasus* (Frigate, Light, Space) was the first spacefaring vessel in the nearly three-hundred-year history of the United States Navy, and she was gorgeous. Silver and sleek, she approached SATSTAR1 slowly, with immense grace. The triple engines arrayed symmetrically around the hull were dark and silent as the pilot used only his small auxiliary maneuver rockets to draw near the station's dock.

Two single-barreled rail gun turrets, the guns retracted and lying flat against the hull, gave her a menacing look. A pair of missile launchers was enclosed in pods along the hull; the hatches were currently closed, but Ruiz knew the power of the lethal rockets waiting there. The big United States flag emblazoned on her side was lit up by the direct rays of the sun, and Ruiz had never seen Old Glory looking so impressive.

Gradually the ship vanished behind the station, and the two SEALS stopped gawking and returned to their training mission. Sanders demonstrated the agility of a monkey in moving around the training module. He released his tether and floated out and back again under the power of his IMS.

The only glitch occurred when Ruiz was about to follow him around the module. As was standard procedure, he checked his IMS before releasing his tether, and he cursed privately when the first twist on the dial sent him cartwheeling away. Quickly he shut the device off and took a firm grip on the line to pull himself under control.

"My damned IMS is malfunctioning again, Enswine," he growled. "I'm gonna have to check you out with my line attached."

There was a pause. It was a moment of truth for the ensign. Technically, standard operating procedure called for Ruiz and Sanders to scrub the training session and take

Ruiz's suit in for repair. If Sanders was an uptight, by-the-book prick, he'd order them back into the station immediately. Of course, real life rarely followed SOP, and Ruiz didn't feel like doing this all over again.

"Gotcha, Chief," Sanders said. "Guess I get to have all the fun today."

Maybe there was hope for Sanders, and he did look like he was having fun. After maneuvering himself for a full circuit around the training module, the ensign embarked on the second task: using the tools on his belt to break into the module's air lock.

Ruiz drifted out, keeping tension on his line so that he could watch the young officer work. The chief was floating on the far side of the module, facing the station, with only the vastness of space behind him. Sanders had reattached his tether (SOP when not floating free) and was holding on to the module with one hand, working his blade into the mechanism of the air lock with the other. All his attention was focused on the problem before his face.

Chief Ruiz felt only the slightest tug but glanced down to the end of the tether that was floating freely in space. One of those unseen objects had spun past and cut right through the line connecting him to the station.

"Damn!" he barked, tumbling helplessly to the side. He flailed his limbs in an unconscious and utterly useless motion. By the time he had completed a single tumble, he was twenty meters from the module, still cartwheeling away. He had no tether and a malfunctioning IMS—he was hip-deep in a shit hole of trouble, and the brown stuff was rising fast.

"Hold on, Chief!" Sanders shouted, his voice strangely calm through the tinny speakers in Ruiz's helmet.

The master chief, drifting backward and moving away from the station—and away from planet Earth!—could only watch helplessly. He saw the ensign unhook his own tether and, with his knees flexed against the module, push off like a diver taking a plunge. Sanders shot through the intervening space, closing rapidly until he bumped into Ruiz, grabbing the master chief's belt as he struck.

Ruiz could feel the ensign's grip at his back but couldn't see him because now he was facing away from the station. The chief did his best to roll when the ensign first grabbed him to absorb his momentum and try to turn it back toward the station as best he could. His efforts resulted in them slowly revolving, but at least they weren't racing away from the station with the ensign's full momentum.

"You know," Ruiz remarked, "if your own IMS goes out, we're going to drift around out here forever."

"Couldn't think of a nicer chief to spend eternity with," Sanders replied, pulling Ruiz around so that he could see the young officer's cheery grin. "Hold on."

With a nimble twist of his control knob, the ensign released a blast of air. Ruiz clung to his belt as he guided them back to the training module, where Sanders reattached his tether.

Two minutes later, the hatch of the air lock was closing behind them.

"Welcome back to the nest, Chief," the young officer said with a grin.

"Welcome to the Team . . . *sir*," Ruiz replied.


For the last week Lieutenant Thomas "Stonewall" Jackson had been aboard the frigate USSS *Pegasus* as she went through her first training mission, a quick run out to the moon and back. He'd gotten to know her commanding officer (CO), Captain Carstairs, and the two men had quickly established a solid working relationship. Two decks of the frigate were compartments that would be devoted to the SEALS—one for the men and their equipment, the other a large compartment holding the two "drop boats," small shuttles that could each carry eight men down to a planetary surface. Both officers were happy with the arrangements.

Having finished decelerating, the frigate pivoted into an orbit parallel to and slightly above that of the ship's destination. SATSTAR1 was an ungainly looking collection of spheres glued haphazardly together. At first glance the large space station looked like a child's toy somehow drifting in space, but Jackson had learned quickly that the globular compartments were crammed with equipment, living space, personnel, supplies, and a lot of high-tech gizmos that the lieutenant hadn't even begun to comprehend.

"I hate to say it, but that place actually looks like home," Jackson said, remembering the barren moonscape that had been the last view they had taken through the frigate's bow-viewing dome.

"At least it makes a good base," Carstairs replied. "We'll have to do a checkdown on the frigate before we load up that rowdy lot of men you command."

"I think we'll be pretty comfortable," Jackson allowed. "And we'll try not to break anything."

"Ah, it could be worse," Carstairs noted. "At least you're not marines."

Jackson chuckled at the old navy joke, but his mind was occupied by the multifarious problems inherent in small unit command—problems magnified exponentially by the deadly environment, the unprecedented nature of the training, and the fact that their nearest support was thousands of miles and a whole atmosphere below them. He would have to bring his new ensign up to speed and find out from Master Chief Ruiz how the external training sessions had gone. There was equipment to load, the drop boats to inspect . . . too many things to think of right now.

"So you're going to check out the FTL drive next?" he asked Carstairs, remembering that he wasn't the only one facing challenges.

"Can't wait to take this thing through deep space!" the captain replied, apparently thrilled at the prospect. "But we'll need authorization. This is the first intrastellar engine installed on a human-built ship. I'm sure that the JCS is going to have inspections from stem to stern and back again before they'll let me activate the drive."

He looked a little crestfallen at the prospect, and Jackson had to sympathize. After all, the SEALS lieutenant was in a similar situation. He was confident of many things: He knew that the sixteen men of his platoon were the best soldiers that the United States of America—and, by extension, the planet Earth—had to offer. They had completed nearly a year of intensive training, including lots of work in zero gravity at the old International Space Station. Until recently, the ISS had been the largest human outpost in space.

All that had changed with the arrival of the Shamani fleet some three years earlier. The aliens had shocked the people on planet Earth when they had first arrived. They looked very human, except for the odd colors of the irises of their eyes, which ranged from indigo to bright crimson. They had come in peace and offered many new technologies. Prominent among them had been the PODS systems of living modules, the "beach balls" that made up the great base of SATSTAR1. They also had provided the inertial dampening technology that protected the passengers of this ship from the crushing effects of acceleration and deceleration, with forces ranging as high as 25 G. Most significantly, they finally had parted with the secret of the interstellar drives that allowed their ships to leap through the vault of space from one star to another. It was the same technology that had been installed in the *Pegasus*, the technology that Captain Carstairs was so eager to employ.

The very origin of the SEALS, in fact, had been prompted by the Shamani's arrival. All the men in Jackson's platoon had come from the famous United States Navy SEAL Teams, the elite commandos who, since the days of the Vietnam War nearly a hundred years earlier, had fought with skill and élan in nautical, airborne, and land-based operations. The SEALS were already used to working in a hostile, almost weightless environment with their continuous underwater operations and use of artificial breathing systems. They were a natural choice for expanding America's combat capabilities into space. With the arrival of the Shamani and knowledge of their galactic empire, the SEAL regimen had been expanded to include space operations for a select few operatives, the best of the best. Jackson and his men were the first to have completed the new training regimen. These, the elite of the elite, were SEALS.

He and Carstairs would work well together, he was certain. The captain had proudly showed him around the space frigate. The ship was sleek and fast and boasted an array of projectile and missile weapons.

Now, as the frigate returned to SATSTAR1, the collection of beach balls actually looked like, if not home, at least a familiar base. Even so, Jackson looked forward to getting his men installed aboard the navy ship. *Pegasus* was too large to enter the station's dock, but she mated to an exterior air lock that would hold her fast and allow for easy passage back and forth as well as the replenishment of fuel and provisions.

Jackson was the first man off the frigate, and he was greeted by one of his NCOs, Chief Bosun's Mate Harris, as soon as he came into the docking back on the station.

"One of the men had an accident, sir. Chief Ruiz went drifting—"

"Dammit! What happened?" Jackson wanted to hurry, but this was where zero G got really annoying—he would have been running if his feet could have found any traction. Instead, he pulled himself along by the handrails, propelling himself as quickly as he could down the passageway while Harris sailed along beside him and continued to explain.

"He'll be okay, sir. That young ensign pulled him back to the station with a dive like an Olympic gymnast. Saved his life, no doubt about it."

"Sanders?" Jackson was pleased but not surprised. He'd seen the quality of the young officer and knew that he just needed some seasoning. Apparently, outside the station, he'd just gotten some. "Well, let's go see—"

"Lieutenant?"

Jackson looked up to see Captain Carstairs coming after him out of the docking bay, gliding smoothly along with an air of unmistakable urgency.

"Yes, sir?"

"We picked up a dispatch from MS1 thirty minutes ago. Seems like an SOS of some kind. We just got follow-up orders from the JCS."

"Orders? Already?"

"Yes, indeed, Lieutenant. Your SEALS are needed—on Mars. Apparently, our first mission together may well turn out to be a live one."

# Two: Mission to Mars

"We're going to be activating the inertial dampener in about five. You two want to ride up top?" asked Captain Carstairs, addressing Lieutenant Jackson and Ensign Sanders as they gathered their notes and stood up around the small, crowded table in the wardroom.

"You'll fly her from A Deck?" Sanders asked. "Not the CIC?"

Carstairs allowed himself a hint of a smile. "Truth is, you can't beat the view from up there. My exec will handle the engine controls, which involves turning a knob very carefully."

Jackson answered for both of them. "Thanks for the invitation, sir. We'd be glad to join you."

Jackson was already familiar with the *Pegasus,* courtesy of the full ten-dollar tour the captain had given him during the shakedown cruise. The ship had a long cigar-shaped hull that was not unlike a submarine's, with one crucial difference. Whereas a sub's three or so decks were arranged in line with the full length of the hull, the space frigate had twelve much smaller decks, each of them perpendicular to the length of the hull. Thus, A Deck was "up top," in the very nose of the ship, while K Deck supported the three massive engines and L Deck was the Aft Con, a bubble similar to A Deck in the stern, or at the very "bottom" of the ship.

Conditions were still weightless, as the ship had just broken free from the SATSTAR1 dock but had yet to begin making way. Gravity would not be restored until the vessel began accelerating. The three officers had been going over orders and plans in the officers' wardroom on B Deck. The orders were simple: The SEALS were to go to Mars, land at Mars Station 1 (MS1), and investigate the call for help that had come from there. Details were sketchy, but apparently there had been some kind of disaster at another research station on the red planet (MS3), and initial reports indicated a suspicion of some kind of attack.

Who or what would attack a peaceful research station on an essentially uninhabited planet? All three officers knew that was the million-dollar question. The Mars installations were multinational projects created and managed under the auspices of the United Nations. It was difficult to imagine that any individual country with hostile designs on those research facilities would have had the resources to manage such an attack. A terrorist group was even more unlikely. But what, then? Space pirates? The idea seemed like something out of a comic book: How would they get to Mars, and what would they be trying to gain there? The Shamani were already on Mars, by invitation from Earth. What could they possibly gain by attacking the research station? After three years of peaceful and productive relations, along with their willingness to share some of their advanced technology, it seemed highly unlikely that they could be involved.

The Shamani had informed the people of Earth that they were one of three great empires, all of them occupying many star systems within the great spiraling wheel long known as the Milky Way. They had been reluctant to discuss much about the other two beyond declaring that they were known as the Eluoi and the Assarn and that the Eluoi were opportunistic and greedy and the Assarn were hostile and warlike nomads. Still, there had never been any evidence that agents of either empire had discovered the existence of Earth, much less reached Earth's star system. With the lack of clues, it seemed pointless to reflect on the presence of an unknown threat. Futhermore, as Carstairs pointed out, if the Assarn or the Eluoi had discovered that system, why would their first appearance have come on Mars instead of Earth?

Frustrated by the mystery, the officers nevertheless prepared to take up positions for the fast journey to Mars. From the wardroom, it was a short jaunt to pull themselves through the hatch to the next deck forward. They were wearing flight uniforms, not the bulky pressurized suits necessary for external work, and Jackson couldn't help feeling a certain Peter Pan elation at the flying sensation as he easily and weightlessly followed the captain into the con.

A Deck was the smallest deck on the ship (except for the comparable L Deck), completely domed over by a thick Plexiglas hemisphere that allowed viewing everywhere except directly astern. Carstairs strapped himself into the pilot's chair while Jackson took a second seat. Sanders headed for the seat for the fire control officer; the helmsman's seat remained vacant. All the chairs reclined fully so that when the G-force was applied, the officers could lie back and look "up" in the direction of the ship's course.

"We only need visual controls for the helm when we're docking," the captain explained. "And my fire control officer is the exec; he's going to sweat this out in the CIC."

The CIC—combat information center—was the fighting "brain" of the ship, and it occupied all of C Deck. It contained the communications links, radar, and other electronic detection systems, as well as fire control systems for the ship's two batteries and a considerable array of rockets and missiles. Damage control ops also were run from the CIC, which was the most heavily armored part of the vessel. As in a submarine, all the compartments of *Pegasus* could be sealed off to prevent a breach from dooming the entire ship, but the CIC, in its titanium-shielded tub, was so solid that it might survive intact even if the rest of the frigate was destroyed around it.

"So let me make sure I understand, sir," Sanders said, only half joking as he belted himself into the sturdy yet cushioned and adjustable seat. "We're going to accelerate at about 20 Gs but the inertial dampening system keeps us alive?"

"Yep," Carstairs replied with a grin. "Once we're moving, we'll be feeling about 1 G, pretty much the same gravitational pull that you feel on Earth. But we'll be accelerating halfway to Mars, then turn around and point our tail toward our destination and decelerate for the second half of the voyage. It'll take us about twelve hours to get there once we leave orbit."

Sanders whistled and shook his head.

"I know what you mean," the captain continued. "Without inertial dampening, we'd all be squashed like bugs by the G-force. The IDS the Shamani sold us makes this kind of travel possible; otherwise, it would take us weeks to get there. Of course, they haven't worked out real artificial gravity, just a way to reduce already existing gravitational forces. Are you strapped in?"

"All set, sir," Sanders replied.

"Roger that," Jackson added.

"Con to bridge. Take us out when you're ready, Pat."

"Aye, aye, sir," came the electrified voice of Lieutenant Commander Seghers, the ship's executive officer.

Seconds later the booming of an alarm whistle, accompanied by a regular pulsing of the ship's lights, flashed through the ship. The warning signals continued for twenty seconds, and Sanders knew this gave the crew on every deck time to report their readiness for acceleration. One didn't want to go from weightlessness to even 1 G of gravity without at least a little warning.

He didn't see any visual change, but he felt it immediately. Whereas at first his straps had been holding him in the chair, he now felt the cushions against his butt and his back. Settling into the seat like he was flopping down to watch a Redskins game back home in Alexandria, he leaned back and watched the world fall away.

"This," Jackson said to Captain Carstairs, "is traveling in style, sir."

"Yes, Lieutenant," the CO said with an easy grin. "It sure is."

Sanders, awestruck, for once had nothing to say.

Six decks below, Chief Ruiz was settled in a more spartan but still comfortable chair in the goat locker—the nearly sacred domain belonging to the chief of the boat. The COB, Master Chief Curt Swanson, had invited Ruiz to join him for the start of the trip. After seeing that his Teammates were securely set up in their quarters just below on H Deck, Ruiz had cheerfully agreed.

The cabin was the most spacious on H Deck, which also contained quarters for the other NCOs as well as large lockers for rocket storage. The best thing about the goat locker was that Swanson got a window—two of them, actually. The small round portholes revealed a view of space just beyond the hull of the frigate. The COB also had enough space for several storage cabinets and a table large enough to seat four for a game of cards.

If the captain embodied the brain of a warship, it was the chief of the boat who most closely personified its heart and soul. Swanson had impressed Ruiz as bringing a very good heart to the *Pegasus*. He'd been in the navy for twenty years, with most of that time spent in subs.

"As soon as they announced the space frigate program, I volunteered," Chief Swanson explained as the two men shared cups of lemonade, the tart liquid slightly enhanced for purely medicinal purposes, albeit in violation of U.S. Navy regulations. "I was sick of living underwater for half the year and figured they could use someone with a good head on his shoulders."

"Better view than you can get out of a sub," Ruiz noted, nodding at the nearest porthole. His eyes were drawn continually to the black void beyond, the dazzling array of stars that looked so much closer, so much brighter, than they did from the surface of Earth.

"Plus, with these Shamani running and flying all over the place, I figured this was where the action would be," Swanson continued.

Ruiz nodded. "So you don't trust them?" he asked.

"What the hell. I don't know. *Who* knows?" the COB observed. "I get the creeps from those red eyes, though, I'll tell you that. And I've just seen 'em in pictures and on the vidscreens."

"I hear you. I haven't met one, either," Ruiz replied, sipping from his cup. He craned his neck and saw that the space station had disappeared behind them almost in a blink and the moon and the Earth were shrinking behind them. He knew they were going faster than any human-built ship had ever traveled, yet the massive gravitational force and powerful engines were not causing so much as a ripple in his cup.

"Splendid libation," he added courteously, hoisting an informal toast.

"Thanks, Chief. I'm from Kentucky, you know, and there are some things we've been doing right down there for quite a few centuries now."

"Hear, hear."

They passed a few companionable hours. A glance through the porthole proved that by now, Earth was only a little bit brighter than some of the other bright lights of the galaxy. Ruiz stopped trying to think about how fast they were going; it made his head hurt. There was no sense of day and night on a spaceship, but when his watch showed 1830 hours, the master chief gave his thanks, said farewell, and went down to check on the Team.

The goat locker and the other cabins and lockers on G Deck all surrounded the central axis, a cylindrical tube of hatches and ladders that gave access to the upper and lower decks all the way from the bow to the stern. Ruiz opened the lower hatch with a push of a button and dropped down the ladder into the middle of H Deck.

This was one of the most crowded spaces on the ship, not only because fourteen SEALS—the entire enlisted complement of the Team—were quartered there but also because the SEALS, as they had been doing for nearly a hundred years, never traveled anywhere without an unbelievable amount of equipment. Most of it was lethal, and some of it was very explosive. Secured in the magazines and racks around them was the firepower equivalent of a World War II destroyer, plus a couple of backpack-sized nuclear bombs, yet the men were sprawled amid their rucksacks and kits with a casual air that was to Ruiz at once reassuring and, even after all those years, disconcerting.

"Hey, Chief," said Gunner's Mate Wilson LaRue. "If Mars has only .1 G, that means I can carry like ten times as much ammo, right?"

Ruiz shook his head in mock exasperation. "First, G-Man, it's more like .33 G. And second, if you're jogging along with six hundred pounds of shit on your back, it might feel like you're only *lifting* two hundred. But when you dig your feet in and try to stop, it will be six hundred pounds of mass that hits you like a truck and makes sure that you keep going."

"Oh, yeah," LaRue replied, apparently crestfallen. "I always forget that part."

"Tell you what," the chief said. "You can carry an extra eight rounds for your rail gun, providing you shoot them or drop them before you try any wind sprints."

"That'll work," G-Man said approvingly.

LaRue was the biggest SEALS on the Team and carried the biggest personal weapon: a recoilless rail gun that fired arrowlike depleted-uranium penetrators wrapped in a copper alloy body. Each projectile packed nearly the punch of a 120-millimeter Abrams tank gun round from forty years earlier. The high-temperature superconductor alloys, high-density energy storage capacitors, and inertial dampening technology Earth had obtained from the aliens made the new weapon possible. But even the inertial dampening coils that surrounded the barrel of the long weapon could be powered by the capacitor-filled backpack only enough to cut down on the incredible recoil. It took the old technology of a recoilless gun, the backblast of an explosive charge, to make firing the rail gun humanly possible. But it still took a big human to handle it, something LaRue did with ease.

"Maybe we'll get to do a little sharpshooting together, eh, G?" Falco suggested. "Knock some cans off a fence post or something?"

Electrician's Mate Derek Falco was an inveterate joker and also the Team's best sniper, carrying the Mark 30 sniper rifle, better known as the Hammer. The long 10.2-millimeter caseless rifle had tremendous range and accuracy with its long, sharp-pointed projectiles and computer-aided laser range-finding sight. Given a stable platform and shooting through a vacuum or near vacuum, he could hit a baseball-sized target from more than ten miles away. He had such range and accuracy that one of his few limiting factors was the curvature of the planet or moon he was shooting on. Falco often operated with LaRue during training, the bigger man acting as the spotter when they worked as a sniper Team. Their two weapons complemented each other, and the rest of the men knew that if either of the pair could see a target, almost out to the horizon, they could hit it. Falco was a chameleon who could hide on a flat plate so that no one would ever see him even after he had fired. LaRue was more of a dragon who could disappear into the brush, but when he fired "Baby," everyone knew where he was from the big backblast.

Ruiz looked over the upturned crate where a couple of Teammates—Chief Bosun's Mate Fred Harris and Hospital Corpsman Harry Teal—were playing blackjack. Murphy and Price were reading. "Smokey" Robinson— the nickname was a joking reference to his Minnesota-blond hair and blue eyes—was inspecting the breather pack on his pressure suit. Dobson, who concealed his intellectual acumen behind an "aw-shucks" Alabama accent, was tinkering with the battery pack of his handheld comlink. Ruiz had been impressed to learn that the tiny radio, as long as it had direct line of sight, could broadcast a signal from a planet's surface to a ship or station in orbit. Marannis and Sanchez, the two best scouts in the unit, were practicing martial arts in the small space of clear deck left to them.

"All right, you sailors," the chief said at 2000. "The LT wants us all bright-eyed and bushy-tailed when we get to Mars. Lights out for eight hours, starting in ten."

The SEALS went to their bunks willingly after first reassembling weapons and equipment that had been taken apart for final inspection. The deck still looked like a scene of chaos, worse than a teenager's bedroom, but Ruiz knew that the disarray was deceiving. His men knew where every piece of equipment was, and if necessary they could grab it all and stow it completely inside of a minute or two.

For six hours, the thin silver pencil that was the *Pegasus* raced toward Mars at steadily increasing speed. There came a brief period, some thirty minutes, of weightlessness as the main engines idled and the ship maneuvered through a serene pirouette, until her stern in effect became her bow, aligned directly with the red planet, which from there appeared even brighter and more strongly hued than it did from Earth. Even so, it seemed to be no more than a bright-looking, somewhat reddish-colored star.

The engines kicked in again, this time to decelerate the speeding ship, and with the inertial dampening system, courtesy of the Shamani, again activated, gravity of 1 G was restored. The Teammates spent the next five hours resting and preparing, checking equipment, and reviewing the schematics of MS3. They got steady updates from the CIC over the intercom, and when they were sixty minutes away from orbit and the drop point, they collected their gear, packed their backpacks and belts and pouches, and made ready to move out. Twelve hours and forty-five minutes after leaving SATSTAR1, the overhead hatch opened and Lieutenant Jackson and Ensign Sanders slid down the ladder to announce that it was time to go.

Now the SEALS were all business. Fully protected by pressure suits, they gathered their equipment and filed through the hatch down to I Deck. This was a long hold that was almost completely filled by the two specialized shuttles—the drop boats—that would carry the men down to the planetary surface. One was the *Norris*, the other the *Thornton*. To the SEALS they were simply *Tommy* and *Mikey*.

Seven SEALS enlisted men and one officer would go in each boat, which was crewed by an additional three sailors: two pilots and a gunner. The pilots guided each boat from the bow, much like the first and second seats in an aircraft's flight deck. The gunner manned a nose turret with two coaxial weapons: a high-powered recoilless cannon that was the boat's main gun, and an electronic cannon that fired an electromagnetic pulse of energy that could have all sorts of nasty impacts on an enemy's electronic, computer, and sensory equipment.

Directed energy beam weapons still didn't work as well as the ordnance people back on Earth would have liked in spite of the power systems supplied by the Shamani. Kinetic energy was a known factor and did work—very well. Thus, even in space, humankind was still throwing rocks—sophisticated ones from exotic launchers, but still pretty much rocks. Jackson and the SEALS were happy to know they were there.

Though the Team had drilled boarding and debarking from the drop boats countless times, this would be their first real drop from an actual ship. Since this mission had come up before the *Pegasus* could be worked into their training regimen, it would be the first time they actually had ridden them down to a planet. Despite the adrenaline rush, every man moved precisely to his assigned place in the column. They embarked smoothly, sliding one at a time through the ventral hatch on each shuttle—a reverse procedure, but in its smooth precision not unlike paratroopers filing out of their C-47s over Normandy 106 years earlier.

Quickly the men settled into the seats in each boat. There was plenty of extra stowage space, or there had been a few minutes before. Every cubic centimeter was now crammed to the gills with satchels, sacks, and backpacks containing weapons and communication and survival gear, as well as ammunition, more ammunition, spare ammunition, and some extra ammunition for good measure.

Lieutenant Jackson sat between the pilots on *Tommy*. Ensign Sanders would drop with the boat crew on *Mikey*. It took less than ten minutes for the Team to get secure in each boat. The keels and hulls of the drop boats were solid carbon-reinforced titanium and were fastened to the axial shaft of the *Pegasus*. The overhead deck was Plexiglas and clear, and so the men had a great view as the massive hold doors slid back.

Mars was there below them, filling the sky from one side to the other in a great rust-red swath. Beautiful and forbidding, the place looked dry and lifeless, scarred by eons of bombardment and erosion. Some of the gaps were small cuts; others were deep wounds that had been torn into the planet's surface with almost palpable violence. Jackson immediately thought of the Roman god of war. The planet, he decided, was aptly named; the bulk of its surface was the color of dusty dried blood.

Jackson was surprised to see another shape in orbit around Mars, larger than *Pegasus* but also a ship. It was silvery metal and long, not like the haphazard attached spheres of a POD station. It had four massive engines near the stern and consisted of many compartments connected by short booms, rather like the segmented body of an ant. He pointed it out to the pilot, Coxswain Grafton.

"That's a Shamani ship, Lieutenant. Called the *Gladiola,* I think." Grafton replied. "Captain Carstairs told me it was up here. It arrived a few weeks ago on a supply run."

Jackson replied, "I knew the Shamani had researchers down on the Martian stations to collect some of their own data. Quite a vessel," he added, impressed by the size and apparent intricacy of the long ship.

"Well, yeah, if you like that sort of thing, sir," Grafton acknowledged. "I'll take *Pegasus* any day. Like a speedboat compared to an oil tanker, if you know what I mean."

"I think I do," Jackson acknowledged.

"Still, that sucker is plenty fast," Grafton allowed. "And that fat section near the engines? That's spare fuel for the reactors. She can travel something like 300 light-years without replenishment—something like six times the range of our frigate. At least, that's what we think."

"I know," Jackson replied. "Your CO is looking forward to shaking her down on a trip to another star system. One of these days."

"You know it, sir. Won't *that* be a ride."

*Pegasus* had settled into an orbit around the planet, and they were rapidly coming up on the dark side. The officer was amazed at how quickly the surface of Mars slipped by. Even though there were no seas, rivers, clouds, or coastlines—the features he'd thought gave Earth its character when viewed from space—he could make out tremendous variation in the dry surface. He spotted some low mountains and numerous channels—the famous "canals"—that scrolled by in a hurry. They passed over the massive canyon known as the Valles Marinaris, a gulf so broad that it was visible by telescope from Earth. Soon they passed the line of sunset, or dawn, and the features were darkened by shadow.

Except for one sparkling diamond of light.

"That's MS1," the coxswain informed him. "The station that sent out the SOS."

Jackson knew about MS1; he and his men had the schematics and relevant information for both MS1 and MS3 uplinked to their wristers. Most of his transit time had been spent reviewing MS3, but still, he already had known that MS1 had begun under the auspices of the United Nations some ten years earlier; it was the first Earth-manned outpost on an alien world. It had been a small workstation, staffed by some two dozen scientists, until the arrival of the Shamani. With the aid of POD technology, MS1 had been expanded to a village-sized base manned by more than a hundred people. Three other research centers, MS2 to MS4, had also been recently established on the red planet, courtesy of the PODs.

Captain Carstairs's voice came through the comlink. "One minute to drop, SEALS. Good luck to you all. We'll be up here just in case you need a little backup."

"That's good to know," Jackson replied. "And thanks for the ride."

With that, the bay doors opened and the residual air in the hold immediately gushed into space. Once the atmosphere was completely gone, the drop boats were released from their docking brackets and expelled from the hold with a lurching blast of air pressure.

The pilots fired the small rocket engines, and the two shuttles began a long, curving descent toward MS1. *Tommy* was in the lead, with *Mikey* a kilometer higher and about five klicks back. Though Mars did have a very thin atmosphere, the boats had no wings for gliding. Instead, the descent would be controlled totally by a series of downward-firing but adjustable rockets arrayed on the underside of the hull. Those boats were designed to get downplanet fast; they weren't designed for air support. Rumor had it the air force was working on some sort of fighter, but it would be years before they would have something operational.

Jackson kept his eyes on the planet's surface as *Tommy* sped forward and down, rumbling slightly as it passed through an atmosphere that didn't really deserve to be called air. In fact, it was so thin that it would be fatal to a man exposed to it almost as quickly as would the hard vacuum of space.

Now they were riding over the dark portion of the planet, and it was harder to sense their speed. Still, it seemed as though the light speck that was MS1 was gradually drawing closer. That spark of illumination was some distance away when *Tommy* was rocked by a sudden hard jolt.

"What the hell?" the coxswain barked, wrestling with his control stick as the bow dropped and the vessel started a long forward tumble. In seconds they were looking through the overhead deck at the planet underneath them.

"I got an energy pulse, sir," came a voice over the intercom. It was the gunner, Jackson realized. "Came from just about below us, still a hundred klicks this side of the station."

The copilot, meanwhile, was flipping switches on a console beside him, consulting a dazzling array of dials and gauges. "Restoring control, skipper," he said. "Our EMP shielding protected us. That blast would have fried all the electronics on a civilian ship."

"Turn up the shields to full."

Jackson knew that like the *Pegasus* herself, the drop boats were fitted with adjustable shielding. Some equipment—especially the communication and detection arrays—was of necessity disabled by the full shielding, but it gave the vessel the best chance of surviving an electromagnetic pulse attack.

"Gunny, you got a bead?" the coxswain asked.

"Still looking, sir. Tracking the ground—wait, yes!"

Even as the gunner announced the affirmative, another jolt knocked into the boat. This time the coxswain was able to right the craft quickly. The starboard rockets punched in, and the vessel kicked into a hard left turn.

"Fire!" the coxswain shouted.

Jackson and everyone else aboard felt the pulsating recoil of the bow cannon as the gunner sprayed the unseen area of the planet's surface. "I'm tracking a power source, sir," he said. "But I'm shooting blind."

The boat was rocked by another jolt, and this time the craft started to yaw with a sickening sense of falling.

"Full power!" Grafton demanded, his voice taut. The rocket engines roared with a power that could be felt and heard through the solid conductivity of the drop boat's hull.

"Still shooting at us, sir," came the gunner's voice. "An unknown attacker with a lot of power. I can get a general fix but not a bead on the target."

"Dammit, this is no time to screw around. I want to lay

an egg on that sucker," the skipper muttered. "Line up a shot with the Mark 90. Hit them with a sledgehammer."

"Aye, aye, sir!"

Jackson knew about the Mark 90. It was a small-yield tactical nuke, a fractional-kiloton weapon similar to what his men had available as major demolition charges. As he thought of his men exposed to the unseen attacker below—and unable to shoot back—he was glad that the drop boat could lay such an egg.

*Tommy* barely shivered as the guided rocket dropped away. Jackson got a brief view of the flare, then lost sight as the coxswain pulled up the bow.

"You don't want to be looking down when that little firecracker goes off," the skipper cautioned.

A minute later the SEALS saw a bright flash of pure white light that blinked through the shadows of the Martian night. There were no further EMP attacks, and in another sixty minutes they were settling gently through the roof hatch of the MS1 shuttle's dock.


"Am I to understand that you detonated a nuclear weapon on this planet before you even touched *ground*?" demanded the florid-faced man who had identified himself as Director David Parker, the station's civilian chief.

"Sir, I was defending my boat," Coxswain Grafton retorted stiffly. "In my view, there was a real threat that both shuttles could be destroyed."

"But a *nuke*?" Parker was an old-family Bostonian, and his voice carried shrill outrage.

"Sir, if I may," Lieutenant Jackson interrupted. "Let's get to work on the real problem: the reason you sent out the SOS in the first place."

Parker turned his attention to the SEALS. Standing at ease, Jackson met his gaze calmly, then tilted his head slightly to nod at the other person in the compartment.

"Ma'am," he said, nodding. She hadn't been introduced, but her white lab coat and surgical cap suggested that she was a doctor. She was short, with olive skin and ink-black hair that just peeked out from under her cap.

"I'm Doctor Sulati," she replied. "Medical director. I see you've already made Doctor Parker's acquaintance." Her eyes twinkled with humor she couldn't quite conceal. She was petite and pretty, and if she seemed rather young to hold a position of serious responsibility, well, Stonewall Jackson could relate. The SEALS lieutenant liked her immediately.

That was the opposite of the reaction he'd had to the MS1 director when Parker had confronted the two officers as soon as they'd debarked from the boat. Even before *Mikey* had settled to the ground in the second docking bay, Parker had pulled Grafton and Jackson into a private office to begin his harangue.

"Irina!" he snapped "Do you know what these—*these cowboys* have done?"

"I know that they're here, and I'm damned glad to see them."

The door opened, and two more people came in, practically floating with each step. One was a small nervous-looking man with white hair and pinched features. His pale eyes watered, and he massaged his hands together while looking back and forth from Jackson to Director Parker. The other was a striking-looking woman, tall and dark, wearing a metallic golden bodysuit that did little to conceal her ample curves. She was tall, maybe an inch over six feet, with vaguely Asian features. She looked curiously at Jackson, and he was startled to see that the pupils of her eyes were bloodred in color.

So this was what the Shamani looked like up close and personal. The lieutenant had never met one of the aliens but, like every other citizen of Earth, had heard them described and seen pictures. They looked just like humans except for those disconcerting eyes.

"You are the warriors?" she asked bluntly.

"Lieutenant Thomas Jackson at your service, ma'am," he said with a bow, ever the southern gentleman. "Of the U.S. Navy SEALS," he added after straightening up and looking the Shamani squarely in the eye.

"This is Shastana fu Char-Kane, consul de campe of the Shamani," Parker said gruffly. "She has been here for half a year as an adviser. Her expertise has come in handy on many occasions." He nodded toward the short man. "Professor Zaro, recently arrived from the University of Caracas. And you have already met Dr. Sulati."

"Are you here to protect us from this—this unknown menace?" the professor said hesitantly. He wiped his watering eyes with the back of his hand. "What do you think it can be?"

"Yes, sir. We really have no idea at this point. But we'd like to find out. Now, about that SOS?" Jackson nudged Parker again.

With a visible effort, Dr Parker forced himself to grow calm. "Yes, well, it's a mystery to us. We heard a garbled message from MS3. Frankly, it sounded a little hysterical. But one of the men said something about an 'attack.' And then their broadcast just stopped."

"An attack? By what, or whom?"

"That, Lieutenant," Parker replied, the frost returning to his voice, "is what you are here to find out. Their signal cut out before we learned anything useful. And we were under strict orders to stay put and wait for your Team. We still have three of the military rovers. I suggest you and your men take them and go have a look."

"There was a message just moments ago," Professor Zaro noted. "It came from your frigate. They passed over the location of MS3 but were unable to discern any useful details from orbit. They tried a direct relay to the station but could raise no response."

Jackson nodded and turned to address the Shamani consul. "We saw a Shamani ship in orbit over the planet while we were dropping. Your people don't know anything about this?"

"None of my people were at MS3 at the time this began. The ship you saw is the *Gladiola*. It is a simple supply ship. It was not over MS3 at the time of the attack and, like your own frigate, cannot make out enough detail from space to give us useful knowledge about the damage to the station. Even so, our offer to send down one of our shuttles to investigate was refused by your government. One might almost think they believe we might have been involved."

"Were you?"

"Lieutenant Jackson, that's just about enough," Parker interrupted. "There's no need to insult the consul de campe. We've been working side by side for months, and I assure you, her concern for our people at MS3 is genuine. In fact, you'll be taking her along as a technical adviser."

"Perfect."

# Three: Down in the Valley

The Valles Marinaris made a garish slash across the face of Mars. The largest canyon in the entire solar system gaped deep and dry, a red the color of old iron rust. Formed by gushes of liquid water eons before and easily visible by telescope from Earth, from a distance it resembled a grinning, leering mouth along the planet's equator. Up close, the Valles Marinaris presented an almost insurmountable obstacle to any land traverse of the Martian surface.

Nevertheless, three little rovers, dwarfed by the vast chasm, scooted soundlessly along the planet's flat surface, rolling right up to the edge of the rim. They came to a stop nearly in unison, a kilometer between each vehicle, all three halting a couple of meters from the canyon's northern edge. The south rim was so far away that it vanished behind the curve of the planet, but the landscape in the immediate foreground tumbled precipitously into the depths.

As the turret gunner in the command rover—the car in the center of the small formation—Chief Harris had the best view. From the raised bubble dome behind the driver's compartment, he could see down into the canyon, across the first of several broad shelves that formed a series of gigantic steps leading to the unseen channel in the very bottom. The ground a couple of klicks below was as flat and featureless as any desert on Earth and nearly as airless as outer space.

Harris's eyes immediately picked out the lone anomaly on that vast dusty plateau. "I got the station complex,

LT," he announced. "At twelve o'clock, maybe five klicks from the base of this cliff in front of us."

"Good eye, Harris—I see it, too," Lieutenant Jackson replied from the driver's seat. The third Team operator in the rover was Gunner's Mate (Missile) Richard Rodale, known as Rocky to one and all. He had his launcher cradled in his lap and watched through the side window without comment.

The fourth passenger in Jackson's rover also was keeping silent, though Harris knew that she, too, was studying their objective with more than passing interest. From his position behind her, he was glad that he couldn't see the woman's eyes. Though she had been attached to their Team for only half a day, every time he caught a glimpse of those bloodred pupils, he felt a shiver of superstitious dread.

Jackson had told Harris that Shastana fu Char-Kane was a consul de campe among the Shamani. Her technical expertise—generations beyond any Earth-born human's—made her presence as an adviser to the SEALS a necessary evil. Even Harris, along with every other guy in the unit, had to admit that she was hot—gorgeous, even—except for those creepy eyes. Her olive skin was smooth, and her shape ideal, with full curves visible even through the puffy overlay of her vacuum suit. Her short hair, midnight black, framed a face featuring full lips and exotically high cheekbones. But she was a cold fish, too, more aloof than any star-encrusted admiral. And now the first field mission for the SEALS Team had plopped him into the seat right behind her.

The fact that the men had only three four-man rovers available to them had forced Lieutenant Jackson to leave one of his fire Teams, a quarter of his platoon, back at MS1 as a reserve. The officer knew that Master Chief Ruiz was a hell of a lot less than happy about staying back with Fire Team Delta and Dobson, who normally acted as Jackson's radio operator. Chief Harris and Rocky Rodale had assured the master chief that they would look after the Shamani woman and the LT, and Ruiz had been forced to settle for that.

Fire Team Charlie of Second Squad with Ensign Sanders was moving along in rover Gamma, and Quartermaster First Class Murphy was acting as the leading petty officer of Fire Team Bravo in rover Foxtrot. They had consoled the master chief by telling him that he could listen to the situation over Dobson's communications rig, though there wasn't much being said.

"Can we get down there in this car?" Char-Kane asked the lieutenant in her clipped, precise diction.

"Yep," Jackson answered. "We won't have enough fuel to rocket out of there, but we'll be able to refuel at the station, or we can get collected by a shuttle after we check the place out." He picked up the communicator and pressed the button. "Foxtrot? Gamma? You guys see the objective?"

The chief could see the other two rovers only a kilometer away to either side. Harris couldn't hear the reply, but it must have been affirmative, since Jackson continued: "Make ready to launch off the edge, here. Hold formation in a powered descent; no advance until all three rovers are down."

With the LT at the controls, the rover backed away from the lip of the canyon, rolling smoothly on its six articulated wheels. When he had about twenty meters of clear space in front of them, Jackson accelerated quickly. The vehicle lurched forward, racing toward the brink, and then it shot off the rim, immediately free-falling through the thin atmosphere of the red planet.

A split second later the rockets, four precise fusion torches underneath the body of the rover, fired simultaneously, rattling the vehicle with their thrust. They pulsed rhythmically, keeping the vehicle steady and dramatically slowing its descent so that it drifted under rocket power toward the plateau within the canyon.

"Better than a parachute jump," Jackson declared laconically, leaning back in his seat. Harris couldn't quite bring himself to relax, but he was impressed as he watched the precipitous cliff scroll past. The LT used a little directional power to ease the rover away from the wall, and in less than a minute they bounced gently to rest on the first shelf of the canyon floor, some two klicks below the rim.

Chief Harris could see that the Foxtrot and Gamma rovers had landed to either side of the command car. The three vehicles rolled silently forward, and as the objective began to take shape before them, Harris swiveled the outside machine gun to the forward position and drew a bead on the central dome of the small complex.

"This is distressing," Consul Char-Kane noted. "Exterior damage is visible even from here. It was administered with serious violence. Projectiles apparently penetrated the outer housing of the dome, probably detonating within."

"No doubt," Jackson observed. Both the *Gladiola* and the *Pegasus* had sent images taken from orbit, but they were inadequate for anything more than a general layout. A small blemish on one of the domes had suggested damage, but the rest of the pods had looked intact. They still hadn't been able to raise anyone on the comm equipment, and nothing had moved since *Pegasus* had taken up a synchronous orbit over MS3.

Harris kept his eyes and his gun barrel trained on the apparently deserted installation. Nothing moved, though his imagination played bouncing tricks with the shadows cast by the setting sun.

The research station consisted of five domed structures, all created from the ubiquitous PODs. In space, the PODs were used as complete spheres to assemble space stations and other orbiting or drifting installations. On a surface such as a planet, they generally were used in a hemisphere configuration, with part of a POD's flexible and durable surface serving as a floor for the dome to maintain atmospheric integrity. The station known as MS3 included two large buildings for storage and Team living quarters, respectively, and three smaller hemispheres housing various research activities. Some thirty-five people had worked there until the sudden attack that had knocked out all communication five days earlier. The Team was there to look for clues to the nature of the attack and to seek survivors. As the Shamani had noted, the first evidence was visible even from a kilometer away: The dome of the living quarters had been punctured and showed several holes. Surrounding each neat black dot, the thin metal of the structure had been scarred and darkened by explosion or flame.

The LT ordered the three rovers to halt. "Mr. Sanders, take the Gamma crew in on foot. Foxtrot, roll up from the left; we'll move around and close in from the right."

The Gamma rover, to the right of the loose formation, came to a halt. The cockpit and gunner domes both popped open, and the four SEALS bounced out. Each carried his weapon at the ready, and they spread out at a fast jog. Despite carrying more than a hundred pounds of equipment, they raced forward in long, graceful strides, aided by the relatively low pull of Martian gravity.

The LT steered the rover toward the far right of the formation while Harris kept his eyes on Ensign Sanders and his men. The fire Team advanced in a leapfrog formation, one pair moving forward while the other covered it with its weapons. The chief kept the outboard multibarreled machine gun, mounted externally but controlled by his hand, ready to support them.

"Flash—got a flash out of the supply building!" Jackson barked.

Harris saw it, too: a bright strobe of light from within one of the darkened buildings. The four SEALS had dropped prone, apparently unhit, but when Harris glanced to the side, he knew they hadn't been the target.

The Foxtrot rover vanished in a silent blast, fire flashing for an instant as fuel and oxygen combusted with searing force. The explosion broke the vehicle in two and left a mist of pulverized material—a vapor with a sickening tint of redness—slowly settling to the surface. One loose rubber wheel rolled a short distance, wobbled, and fell onto its side.

The command rover heeled violently as the LT turned and accelerated, veering unpredictably as he steered a zigzag course toward the station complex. Harris fired at the place where he had seen the flash, the rapid-fire weapon spraying so many tracers that they looked like a fuzzy laser beam licking at the target. He felt the vibration of the weapon in his seat and on his hands. Though the gun was firing in a thin atmosphere, the buzzing sound of the weapon, cycling so quickly that the individual shots blurred together into one long roar, carried through the body of the vehicle.

Another flash brightened the gap in the supply shed's doorway, and the rover lurched hard. The depressurization warning flashed, shocking Harris into an instant of panic until he remembered that he was wearing a suit.

"We're hit!" Jackson snapped. "Shit—I lost power!"

Chief Harris saw the hole in the cockpit dome where the shell had entered; it must have passed out through the body without exploding. Outside, the SEALS were pouring fire out at the supply dome while moving toward the barracks building. He glanced again at Foxtrot. The wreckage was scattered in a wide circle, dust still settling. There was no prospect of finding a survivor. But the SEALS never left one of their own behind, alive or dead.

When they could, the squad would search through the wreckage for their Teammates.

Right now, they were in the fight of their lives on alien soil.

"Dismount—we close in on foot!" barked the LT, pulling the lever to pop the cockpit canopy. Jackson pushed himself up and out, landing in a crouch. Rocky Rodale came right behind him, his rocket launcher cradled in his arms as he looked for a target.

Harris snapped the latch on the turret's Plexiglas, and the dome sprang open.

Only then did he notice Consul Char-Kane slumping limply in her seat. Her suit looked intact. She must have been stunned by the shock of the shell, which had burst through the cabin right beside her head. Biting back a curse, Harris scrambled down the hull and unstrapped the Shamani woman from her seat. Grasping her under her arms, he hoisted her, pulling her with him as he toppled over the side of the rover.

She lay on the ground, and he looked at her face through the clear helmet. Her eyes were half-open, like slits of blood, but he reminded himself that that was the normal color of her pupils. She showed no signs of consciousness. He picked her up in his arms, cradling her against his chest, and sprinted for the nearest dome, about eighty meters away.

His gear weighed more than a hundred pounds, and the consul, even with her lighter suit, added some two hundred more. Though the gravity level was only about a third of Earth's, the mass was the same, and Harris staggered and stumbled, bouncing from one leg to the other as he tried to remain upright, moving as quickly as he could. He was falling forward for the last ten or twelve meters of the sprint. Finally, he and the consul tumbled to a stop against the outer air lock of the research dome.

Sanders's SEALS had taken shelter behind the shattered barracks dome. One by one they slipped through a gap where the wall had been ruptured. The LT scrambled back, looking for Harris and Char-Kane just as the Shamani woman pushed herself into a sitting position. She blinked at Harris, then glanced at the disabled rover before looking back at him.

"Thank you," she said, nodding her head formally.

"Forget it," he said. "Can you walk?"

"I . . . I believe that I can. Help me up, please."

She extended a hand, and he took it, lifting her to her feet. She swayed, and he caught her, holding her for a second until she could stand on her own. "I am all right now. I can walk. Where must we go?"

"Sanders has cleared out a chamber in the barracks. Follow me," Jackson said. "Move fast."

He darted across the space to the barracks dome while their comrades covered them with fire directed at the supply building. Harris and the consul hurried after, hunched low, sprinting for the gap in the wall. In a few seconds they tumbled inside, breathing loudly in the confines of their bubble helmets.

One of the SEALS, Falco, pointed toward the other large dome. "They're shooting from the air lock with some kind of heavy projectile weapon. Might be the same gun that punched all the holes in this dome."

"Any sign of the station crew?" Jackson asked.

"Not out here. The shell is ruptured, but the interior air lock seems intact. Haven't had time to go there, sir," Falco replied.

"I will inspect the living quarters," Consul Char-Kane announced, "while you and your men make war upon this unseen enemy."

The LT nodded in agreement, then pointed to Harris. "Keep an eye on her, Chief," he said. "We'll go after the shooter." He quickly checked his G15 carbine, making sure that a full fifty-round magazine of 6.8-mm caseless ammunition was seated in place with a round locked in the chamber. Then he started out after Ensign Sanders's fire Team.

Consul Char-Kane meanwhile was manipulating the secondary air lock leading to the sleeping quarters while Harris pulled up the schematics for MS3 on his HUD. The door to the tiny vault slid open, and Harris hastened inside after her. A moment later they were closed in the air lock, pressure quickly building around them.

"There is a full atmosphere of pressure inside the living space. Air quality is good," the woman reported, reading the LED display on the interior door. She pushed several miniature buttons on the keypad. "I am attempting communications within, but there is no response. I can detect no sign of life inside."

"Can you get it open?" Harris was barely finished asking the question when the interior door slipped silently to the side. Char-Kane strode forward, and again Harris hurried to keep up. When she placed a hand to the neck latch of her helmet as if to remove it, he touched her wrist. She glared at him, but he shook his head.

"We keep our suits on—standard operating procedure for unknown environments," he declared. With a shrug, she turned and started to look around.

Chief Harris checked out the dining hall and kitchen, finding dishes and rehydrated food on the tables. He was startled to hear a gasp from Char-Kane and quickly found her at the door of one of the barracks rooms.

There were six bunks in the room, and three of them held bodies—gruesomely hacked bodies. Each had been slashed viciously through the torso, separated into two parts.

"This is very, very bad," she said. She looked at Harris, her red eyes cold, almost accusing.

"Hell of a way to die," he admitted, clenching his jaw

against the rise of bile. The bodies were messy, and the one face he saw—an older female's—was contorted by horror.

"That is not the bad part," the consul said dismissively.

"Well, excuse me, but if *that's* not the bad news, what the hell *is*?" Harris snapped.

She flinched away from him as if his anger were a physical presence. Drawing a ragged breath, she struggled for composure. "This is a ritual killing. It means that we Shamani are not the only interstellar empire to find your solar system."

"You know who did this, and it wasn't Terran or Shamani?"

Shastana fu Char-Kane shook her head. "The Assarn are here, on Mars," she stated. "And if they have come to this planet, they most certainly know about your Earth, as well."

"That's all she said, LT," Harris said, completing his abbreviated comlink report on what they had found in the bunker. "That, and she seems to think these Assarn are some kind of super-badasses."

"Roger that, Chief," Lieutenant Jackson said. "Maintain your position."

"Aye, sir," Harris said as he cut out of the net.

Turning to Shastana fu Char-Kane, the young SEALS gave her a confident and, he hoped, reassuring smile. "The lieutenant will deal with whatever is out there," Harris said. "If he can, he'll take a prisoner. That'll let you talk to one of these Assarn you're so worried about."

She didn't seem to notice his attitude. "That is something that will not happen," Char-Kane said coldly. She had regained her composure after seeing what was left of the bodies in the bunks. Now her red gaze focused disdainfully on the SEALS in front of her.

"Your arrogance is only matched by your ignorance of

what you are facing," she continued. "The Assarn are a predatory species; they live for the hunt. To them, you are merely prey, to be hunted and killed. The Assarn do not surrender to prey."

"With Mr. Sanders and the lieutenant out there, your Assarn may find that we're not easy prey," Harris said firmly as he thought about his Teammates assaulting the other dome. "And if they have to call in Master Chief Ruiz, there won't be anything left but a smoking hole in the ground."

Just outside, Jackson moved up to where he could see Ensign Sanders and Falco crouching low behind a stack of tarp-covered containers. Bending low, he ran the last dozen meters to the position in a fast scuttle.

"Sitrep, mister," the lieutenant called out as he asked for a situation report.

"Unknown number of hostiles, sir," Ensign Sanders said without turning his head. "They've built some kind of reinforced position just inside the air lock where they've placed some kind of heavy automatic weapon. No small arms fire—yet. But they're dug in as solid as a tick."

"Then we'll just have to put a hot match on their asses," Jackson said. Peering just past the tarp, Jackson could see that the air lock door had been moved about halfway shut to block any view of what was inside the air lock itself. The thick metal of the hatch would be hard for the SEALS to shoot through with their 6.8-mm carbines, even with armor-piercing ammunition. And charging what was effectively a fortified machine cannon with un-known backup was not the way to keep his men alive.

What Jackson didn't want to do was call in an air strike by the *Pegasus* or try to punch in some 30-mm high-explosive grenades from Falco's underbarrel grenade launcher. In spite of the fact that whoever was in that air

lock had just killed the four SEALS who had been in the
Foxtrot rover, Jackson wanted intel, and one didn't get a
lot of intelligence from dead bodies. He wanted prisoners.

Looking over to where the other shooter pair of SEALS
were crouching behind a stack of heavy building materi-
als, Jackson smiled at the option he had just been given.

Even among the SEALS, Gunner's Mate Wilson
"G-Man" LaRue stood out. In the Teams, where physical
fitness was almost a religion, G-Man was something of a
legend. He had earned his nickname back during the fifth
phase of training, when he had gotten up out of an acceleration couch during an engine burn, dropped down on the
deck, and done push-ups while undergoing 5 Gs of boost.
As a big operator, G-Man liked to carry a big weapon. In
the man's hands, Jackson could see that he had his G15
carbine up and ready to fire. But across G-Man's back
was Baby, the big SEALS' favorite weapon.

The Shamani had not supplied a lot of weapons technology to the Earth forces when they first had arrived.
Weapons were not what they did. But the power supply
technology they did give their human compatriots could
be adapted to power weapons. Not beam weapons—those
were still only in the planning stages. But projectile
weapons—they were something humans had been doing
for a very long time. Every so often, new innovations
were added to the concept of the old slug thrower, and
Baby was just the latest generation in the long and storied
genealogy of lethal firearms.

The Mark IV rail gun G-Man had slung across his back
could punch out a slug of copper and uranium at velocities that couldn't be reached by traditional means other
than with a gun the size of a telephone pole. On Earth, the
hypervelocity slugs could slam through heavy steel armor
plate with the ease of earlier shaped-charge explosive
rockets. In the thin Martian atmosphere, the two-meter-

long weapon was even more efficient. The impact of its projectiles would make steel flow like water.

The drawback with the weapon was that it was big and heavy, and the backpack-sized power cells could fire only eight rounds. A large bulbous cylinder at the back of the weapon carried the eight annular explosive rings that would fire from the rear of the rail gun and help counter the recoil of the copper slugs. Eight shots could be fired as quickly as the operator could recover and pull the trigger again, and G-Man recovered very quickly indeed.

"G-Man," Jackson said over the net, "can you take out that gun?"

"I can hit it, no problem, LT," G-Man said back. "But as soon as I swing Baby here around, they'll open up before I can get off a shot."

"You just get ready," Jackson said. "When we draw their fire, you put a round right into that position and take out their gun."

It was a simple and very dangerous plan. Jackson intended for Ensign Sanders, Falco, and himself to open fire on the air lock hatch. When whoever was inside responded to their fire, G-Man would have a chance to take out their main weapon. Given that the SEALS didn't know the capabilities of the unknown enemy or their weapon, things could get dicey fast. But hesitating in combat will also get a man killed, and Jackson already had lost enough men that day.

"Okay, Dennis," Jackson said. "When G-Man is ready, we all open up on the air lock."

"As good a plan as any," Ensign Sanders said.

"Gun's up," G-Man said. He had the big rail gun cradled in his arms, his G15 carbine leaning against the cover next to him. Derek Falco, G-Man's shooting partner, was crouched next to him, his own G15 up and ready.

"Let's ring their bell," Jackson said.

Leaning out slightly from the cover, Jackson pulled the trigger on his G15, whose selector was set on fully automatic. Next to him, Chief Harris and Falco added their fire to the din. Streams of tungsten-core projectiles smashed into the hatch of the air lock, sparks flying as bits of alloy were knocked off and heated to incandescence by friction.

Instantly, the alien weapon opened fire. Heavy shells impacted on the tarp and detonated against the metal boxes and their contents.

Bellowing a warning shout, "Fire in the hole!" LaRue triggered his weapon as he brought it to bear on the target.

Even over the vibrations of the explosions, the loud pulse of G-Man's Mark IV reverberated, the backblast a bright counterpoint to the green flash of the copper slug.

Whatever the alien weapon was, the ammunition it fired did not react well to being hit by copper metal heated to almost the plasma state from the impact. The cover around the weapon gave no real resistance to the uranium penetrator. The energy from the metal spray was more than enough to detonate the remaining ammunition in the enemy magazines.

A fiery explosion erupted, eerily silent but for the dull thud they all felt through the ground. Flames, metal fragments, and bits of unidentifiable scraps vomited out of the partially open air lock as if fired from a huge cannon. Even in the thin Martian atmosphere, the explosion was enough to knock G-Man to the ground.

Stunned, Jackson got up from where he also had been knocked down by the blast.

"I don't think we're going to find a lot of prisoners after that," Falco said almost to himself, his quiet voice loud over the comlink in the ringing silence after the explosion.

# Four: It's Personal Now

"We have to get back to MS1 immediately!" Consul Char-Kane declared. "This information is crucial! The Assarn are at large on this planet in unknown numbers, and their intentions are clearly hostile. The menace to your people, to your whole world, is too great to ignore!"

"You can make a report by radio. We're not going yet," Jackson replied coldly.

"But the physical proof. We'll need to carry it—"

"Listen, ma'am," the lieutenant said. "Four brave men died out there. They were SEALS, and they were our Teammates. They're coming home with us."

"But—?" The Shamani woman looked genuinely puzzled. "They're dead! Surely you know that?"

The expression on his face as hard as chilled steel, Jackson turned away without allowing himself to speak further. She was still talking when he closed the hatch behind him and met the rest of the men inside the pressurized mess hall. He found the unit's hospital corpsman, Harry Teal.

"Harry. You and Falco take the Gamma rover. See if there's anything you can do for Murphy, Price, Jones, and Kim." As he said the names, Jackson pictured each of his Teammates and understood, as did Corpsman Harry Teal, that the only thing to be done for them was to bring their bodies back with them.

Since that was the only thing to be done, that was what would be done.

"Right, LT," Teal replied.

The two SEALS headed out to one of the two surviving undamaged rovers, and Jackson turned his attention back to the Shamani woman, who had followed him with the tenacity of a bull terrier.

"Go ahead and call in your report. Give them all the data you can. But physical evidence! What, are you planning on dragging half of one of those bodies back with us?"

She flushed. "No." After a moment's thought, she touched her wrist computer, which, like all the Mark III space suit units, was equipped with a high-resolution digital camera. "I will record the images and bring those back."

"Good." Jackson's reply was curt, his mind full of memories of the dead men. "Tell 'em to send a shuttle for us while you're at it. We're going to need transport back to MS1."

Her red eyes narrowed at his commanding tone, but he was too tired to notice, and she apparently was pragmatic enough not to make an issue of it. She went back to the station's communication center with Electrician's Mate Falco, while Jackson found Chief Harris still looking over the wreck of the enemy's automated gun.

"This thing didn't just drop here, LT," Harris remarked. "And I'm wondering where we might find the assholes that set it up."

"I'm thinking along the same lines, Chief. Why don't you set up an OP and keep your eyes open while we secure the rest of this joint?"

"Aye, aye, sir," the chief responded. "I saw a glass lookout tower on top of the biggest dome. I'll get up there and have a look around."

With an observation post established, Jackson spoke to the rest of his men, then determined that Falco had established communications with Master Chief Ruiz back at MS1: "They have a shuttle they'll send for us on an emergency basis, but it didn't sound like they were happy about burning the fuel. I think the master chief had a few choice words with them."

For a moment Jackson's temper flared, the familiar tension tightening his hands into fists. He drew a long slow breath, but the haze of fury didn't go away. Four dead men and they were griping about fuel? "Tell them—" he started.

And just like that it was gone. He could breathe again, and he simply shook his head. "What's their ETA?"

"Ninety minutes, they tell us."

Within a half hour the rover returned with Teal and Falco and four bundled bodies. Jackson watched silently as the two SEALS carefully, even reverently, set the corpses next to the vehicle, neatly laid out on the Martian surface. *They came a long way from home just to die.* The bitter thought arose, and he roughly forced it away.

"Skipper." Chief Harris's voice crackled in Jackson's ear. The officer glanced up to the observation post on top of the large dome and saw the bosun's mate staring through a magnifier toward the horizon of the vast canyon, which was looming as a cliff a dozen kilometers away.

"Yeah, Chief? You see something?"

"I think I got something—a visual. We're expecting a friendly, right?"

"A shuttle from MS1. It should be coming from that direction."

"Here's comes our ride, then."

The SEALS and the consul de campe took shelter in the factory dome—carrying the lifeless bodies of their comrades in with them—and watched the shuttle land, the rocket thrusters throwing up a great cloud of swirling dust. They all hustled aboard and secured seats in the boxy hull. Jackson made his way to the flight deck to find that the ship was flown by a USAF captain wearing an ID

that named him as Joseph Cheever, with a Chinese Air
Force lieutenant in the copilot's chair.

"Any chance we can bring that rover back with us?"
Jackson asked.

"Your master chief said you would want to do that," the
pilot said. "It's the only reason he didn't come along and
bring the rest of your men. I'll drop the hatch. If you can
drive it into the hold, we can carry it." He grimaced for a
moment. "And Lieutenant, sorry about your men. We
heard you had some casualties."

Jackson bit back a sharp retort. Whoever was complaining about fuel usage, it wouldn't be these men who
flew the shuttle. "Yeah . . . thanks," he said.

Twenty minutes later the remaining rover was stored,
and the crew and SEALS strapped in for liftoff. The shuttle blasted upward with explosive force, arcing high above
the planetary surface as its coursed back toward MS1.

On the short flight, Jackson briefed the two pilots on
the unknown threat that had destroyed the station. They
were suitably alarmed, and all the occupants of the shuttle kept their eyes on the ground as they neared MS1.

"Look for any kind of anomaly," Jackson suggested.
"Whatever's out there, we don't know what it looks like,
but it's lethal as hell."

Still, through the viewports the planet looked not so
much lethal as barren. The sandy surface was illuminated
by a setting sun that was casting long shadows from some
of the taller hills, leaving crescents of shadow on the
floors of steep-sided craters. Far to the east a ridge of low
rounded mountains was cast into clear relief by the sun,
and to the west another ridge was shrouded in shadow,
backlit and murky. The flat plain below them showed a
few ripples of terrain: low flat hills and scoured channels
that once had been the beds of flowing streams. The color
that had looked so consistently rusty from a distance now

shifted through a spectrum that included black, yellow, orange, and even patches of dirty white.

"LT, I got something!"

It was Chief Harris, who was peering through one of the hull windows of the shuttle. "Vehicles—two of 'em—tracking toward the station."

Jackson and the pilots leaned over for a look just in time to see a bright light that was unmistakably a muzzle flash.

"Shit!" Cheever cursed, banking hard. "We're sitting ducks up here!"

"Can you put her down there, behind that ridge of hills?" Jackson asked, pointing.

The pilot made no reply but pushed the stick hard around. G-forces sent Jackson straining against the straps on his seat, and the roar of the shuttle's rocket engines pounded through the hull. The officer saw another flash and braced for impact, but the second shot also went wide.

And then the dusty crest was there, a low, flat-topped hill that gave the little ship a solid object between it and the shooters. With a snarl of anger Cheever set the shuttle down hard.

"I don't have to tell you, but we're trapped back here, Lieutenant. I can't fly us out of here without risking fire."

"Leave that to me, sir. Those bastards have just made their last mistake."

Exactly twelve minutes later, the shuttle's hold hatch dropped open and the seven surviving SEALS, fully protected by their pressure suits, dashed down the ramp and back onto the surface of Mars. They had decided that Carstairs would take the *Pegasus* and check on MS2 and MS4 while Jackson and his Team handled this. There was no talking; Jackson used hand signals to direct Sanders,

Teal, and Chief Harris to the left. LaRue and Falco went
to the right, and Jackson and Rocky Rodale took the middle. The consul de campe and the two pilots would stay
with the shuttle for the time being.

The hill between the SEALS and their target was barely
worthy of the name. No more than six or eight meters
above the surrounding plain, it was more than a kilometer
wide at the summit and sloped almost imperceptibly
down to the flat ground on all its other sides.

Staying low, Jackson and Rodale advanced slowly,
heading straight toward the last known position of the target. Each had his G15 up and ready. Rocky had his four-
round M76 70-mm assault weapon secured to his back.
The big black man could drop the G15 into its sling and
bring the guided missile launcher around into firing position in a second. The smart warhead on the self-guiding
missile in the launcher could punch through heavy armor,
rip an aircraft out of the sky, or just blast a big hole for
general use. But if the fight was suddenly up close and
personal, Rocky wanted his quick-handling 6.8-mm caseless in his hands.

The lieutenant kept his eyes on the other two shooter
Teams, knowing that they needed to be in position before
he put his plan into motion. The men were running,
crouching low, but in the light gravity bouncing up off the
ground with each step. Jackson knew they would avoid
showing themselves over the low crest. He spent his wor-
rying effort—there was *always* something to worry
about—wondering about the capabilities of the unseen
foe. If they were Assarn, what did they want? Why were
they here?

At five or six hundred meters away, each group of
shooters slowed down and started to move forward instead of laterally. Jackson and Rodale, too, crouched and
moved toward the summit, keeping their eyes peeled for
any sign of the mysterious vehicles. One man stopped

and leveled his weapon while the other scooted forward; then the pair reversed the process so that the second man could advance.

Again without any spoken command, Jackson and Rodale spread farther apart until they had a good forty meters between them. Slowing to a walk, bent almost double, the officer hoisted his weapon and moved forward like a stalking hunter, which he very much was. Turning to his partner, Jackson played a hunch and signaled for the M76. Rodale dropped the G15 to let it dangle from its sling and pulled the heavy rocket launcher from his back, then slipped up to the top of the rise.

There! A flash of movement crested the horizon of the hill, and Jackson dropped flat. Raising his head very slightly, he made out something like a moving dome. It was probably a turret, he deduced, since he couldn't see the lower portion of the vehicle, and it was easing toward him. He cracked off a shot and saw the flash of a tracer mark a trajectory until the slug bounced off the dome.

Immediately he was moving to the side, away from his firing position. Something flashed, a bright streak even in the sunlight, and he saw several impacts as the high-velocity round skidded along the crest of the ridge without exploding. It passed a dozen meters to Jackson's side, and he crept forward again to get a visual on the shooter.

He saw a rocket flash from Rodale's launcher, eerily soundless in the near vacuum of the Martian atmosphere. The missile flew upward, following the curve of the hill's crest as its guidance system homed in. Something flashed from the moving dome, and the missile exploded a hundred meters short of its target. *Damn.* The enemy had a pretty sophisticated antimissile defense!

The strange vehicle continued to advance, and now Jackson and Rodale, playing their parts in the delicate choreography the lieutenant had laid out in advance, fell back. The second target zoomed closer, moving quickly, the domed turret spinning. From the side he saw a small, short barrel extending from the dome. He couldn't see low enough to tell if it moved on wheels, tracks, or some kind of hover machinery, but it was a hell of a lot zippier than any Terran tank. Jackson kept up the fire from his own gun, and Rodale popped up from cover just long enough to launch another rocket. That streaking missile, too, was intercepted by some kind of energy-weapon defense, detonating before it struck the target.

Remembering the round that had skidded across the ridge, Jackson understood that the enemy had two different weapons, either of which would easily perforate a soft target like a SEALS in a space suit. In another minute both vehicles came into view, zooming over the crest of the low hill. The energy weapon flashed again, a yellow bolt sizzling too damned close for comfort. Against that bizarre silence, it was almost possible to imagine that it was harmless—like the beam of a flashlight—but Jackson knew better and rolled to the side across the rusty ground as another searing bolt of energy puffed into the rocky terrain where he had just been lying.

But the two men had done their job. The enemy vehicles continued to race forward, both turrets swiveling, weapons seeking to train on the elusive shooters. Rolling behind a fortuitously located rock, Jackson raised his head just enough to study the targets. They were small, barely large enough to hold a single adult, he estimated. Now he could see that they moved on tracks, like tanks, and had low, flat silhouettes that would make them difficult to hit.

A difficult target, to be sure, but not an impossible one. The first sign Jackson got that LaRue had drawn a bead came when the round from the rail gun spit into one of the tracked vehicles from the right flank. The molten copper went right through the turret as it followed the uranium penetrator—the alien tank was not very heavily armored, apparently—and the miniature tank immediately stopped rolling. There was a spurt of fire as something incinerated very quickly, but the flames immediately died out in the oxygen-poor environment. The hull remained glowing yellow-hot, sparking and smoking.

The second vehicle scuttled backward, the turret swinging toward G-Man, the lethal energy gun drawing a bead. But that was according to plan, as Ruiz, Teal, and Falco opened up with everything they had, hitting the little tank directly in the back of the turret. The hail of lead and steel perforated the metal dome in a hundred places, casting sparks and fumes and burning bits of metal through the near vaccum of the Martian atmosphere.

The two wrecks were still smoking as the SEALS closed in from three sides. Jackson was the closest, and he got there first. As the others came up, he was already moving toward the second vehicle, having inspected the gaping interior of the first.

"Who are they, LT?" Ruiz asked, his weapon leveled at the smoldering metal target.

"We just ambushed a couple of robots, gentlemen," Jackson said bitterly. "Nothing but a pair of goddamn machines."

"All right. So they had a robot gun and two robot tanks. But *somebody's* got to be setting these things up!" Ensign Sanders declared, as several of the SEALS and the MS1 directors gathered in conference just inside the loading dock.

"I agree," Jackson said. "They have to be controlled from somewhere."

After the little battle, the shuttle had made an uneventful return, but everyone's nerves were on edge. Jackson had radioed *Pegasus* before they had launched, and the frigate had shadowed them from orbit, having found everything A-OK at MS2 and MS4. There had been no further attacks. Captain Carstairs reported also that his sophisticated detection systems showed nothing about any anomalous objects in orbit: There were just the one Terran space station, a number of satellites, and that large Shamani ship, the *Gladiola,* circling the planet. Consul de Campe Char-Kane had traveled to Mars aboard that vessel and testified that the crew and officers were all loyal servants of her empire.

Adding to the tension, the communications and radar center in the station *had* reported other anomalous objects, potentially many more of the robot tanks, closing in on the station from all sides. Master Chief Ruiz was busily deploying the rest of the SEALS in shooter pairs at various locations around the perimeter of the station while Jackson, Sanders, and Chief Harris met with the MS1 command staff. That included Director Parker, Professor Zaro, Dr. Sulati, Captain Cheever, and the Shamani consul.

"These attackers—they could be controlled from space, no?" Professor Zaro asserted. "A remote station in orbit over the planet, perhaps."

Jackson shrugged. "If so, they're doing it from a secret platform, and *Pegasus* has some pretty good spotting equipment. I don't see how they could broadcast a signal and mask it from the frigate. So no, I don't think that's likely."

"It's starting to look like we're under siege," Captain Cheever said. He was the ranking military officer there but served under the command of Director Parker. On the return to MS1 Cheever had let slip that he'd flown A-15 tactical assault bombers back in the early '40s, and Jackson could sense the air force pilot's frustration at being stuck there with only an unarmed shuttle at his command; too bad the drop boats weren't really designed for air support. Sure, they were heavily armed and armored, but they were not much more than ballistic rockets with limited maneuverability. The pilots referred to them as having the atmospheric flight characteristics of cinder blocks.

The Bostonian had grown unusually pale upon hearing the SEALS' reports and now looked toward Jackson imploringly. "What can we do, Lieutenant? What can *you* do?"

"Well, we can fight, sir. And we can keep in touch with the *Pegasus*. She can give us some heavy-duty fire support from orbit. Unfortunately, she doesn't have the precision for antitank work. But she can lay down a nasty barrage if we need one. But dammit, I'm not content to wait here and let these bastards close in in their own sweet time. I lost four good men today, and I intend to find the son of a bitch responsible."

"That's all well and good, Lieutenant," Dr. Sulati interjected. "But we are in a very vulnerable position here. This station was not erected as a military position. One powerful explosion would be enough to kill everyone here."

"Then we're going to make sure that explosion doesn't happen, Doctor," Jackson replied. *Or if it does, it happens somewhere far, far away.*

"You say the killings at MS3 look like the work of the Assarn?" Dr. Parker asked Char-Kane. "What can you tell us about them?"

For just a second the aloof façade that seemed to prevent the consul de campe from showing any emotion slipped slightly, and she visibly shuddered. Quickly recovering her composure, she spoke calmly. "They are like the locusts of the galaxy. They live only for killing and destruction. They are the most barbaric of the three empires—and the most dangerous. The Eluoi, at least, are subject to diplomacy and negotiations. After the Second Spider War we Shamani even worked out a treaty with the Eluoi that has proved effective on a local basis. But the Assarn—they are mad, violent, irrational. If they have discovered your outpost on Mars, then they certainly know about your home planet. And that is a very dangerous thing."

"And you deduced that it was an Assarn attack because of the ritual killings?" Jackson pressed, hoping she would expand on her quickly reached conclusion at MS3.

She blanched and glanced away for a moment before continuing. "Yes. I have never personally witnessed their gruesome violence, but it is not unknown to the Shamani on some of our more remote systems. Every young Assarn warrior, before he is accepted into the ranks of their legions, must commit a ritual killing with a metal blade. The victim must be sliced in two. That is the scene I discovered in the barracks chamber of MS3."

"But what would these . . . these Assarn want with Mars?" Professor Zaro asked. He wrung his hands nervously, blinking eyes that seemed to water incessantly as he looked between the SEALS and his colleagues.

"Information?" Sanders guessed. "Or maybe they plan an attack on Earth and are taking out our remote outposts first."

"I don't think so," Jackson countered. "If they wanted to neutralize the human presence on Mars, they could do it with about four well-placed bombs launched from space. No, they're here doing some kind of recon mission."

"So you are convinced that these robots—and that robot gun—are Assarn weapons?" asked Zaro, looking pointedly at the lieutenant.

"I'm convinced that they're hostile, and that's about it," Jackson said with a shrug. He nodded at the Shamani woman. "It's the consul de campe who seems convinced that they're Assarn." He noticed that she squirmed slightly under his gaze, and he asked directly: "Just how sure *are* you?"

She hesitated just a moment, then shrugged delicately.

"Robotic fighting is not entirely in keeping with what I know of the Assarn, so I must say it is mysterious. But I cannot think of any other plausible explanation."

"Maybe you could check with the *Gladiola* and get us whatever files you might have on the Assarn." Jackson was interrupted by the buzz of a speaker on the bulkhead, and he recognized Dobson's drawling voice.

"Lieutenant?" the radioman inquired. "Can ya come up here fo' a sec?"

"I'll be right there. Ensign, see if you can help the director form an evacuation plan. Find out where the hardest points in the station are in case we need a redoubt."

"Aye, aye, sir," Sanders replied as Jackson trotted through the door.

A minute later, the LT found Dobson in the raised dome of the station's communications and observation center, a transparent hemisphere perched on a slender tower some twenty meters higher than the surrounding plain, which was shrouded in the Martian night. He was seated in the middle of an array of screens and monitors, gauges and dials that controlled radar, electronic sensors, radio, and vidscreen readouts, and he looked right at home.

"What is it?" Jackson asked. "Have you heard from *Pegasus*?"

"That's just it, sir. I can't raise her. We're bein' jammed, and pretty effectively. Seems to be comin' from all sides."

"You can't nail down a source?"

"Well, not precisely." He pointed at a screen, which the lieutenant recognized as a map layout of the station and its surrounding terrain. "But there's a power surge here, to the west, about six, seven klicks away. If I had to take a guess, I'd say that's where it's comin' from. But look at the screen. We got bogeys movin' all over the place."

Jackson could see them: more than a dozen little spots blipping on the green screen, maneuvering slowly on all sides of the station. One by one they would dart closer and then halt.

"It looks like they're advancing on us, covering each other," he guessed.

"Yes, sir, that'd be my guess, too," said the radioman.

The officer considered the screen. He pointed to a blur of lines behind the ring of moving figures. "This is where the power seems to be coming from?" he asked.

"My best estimate is yes," Dobson replied.

"All right," Jackson said, making up his mind. "Let's get the Team geared up. We're going to go for a walk in the dark."

# Five: Counterattack

The sun was cresting the eastern horizon of Mars when the SEALS filed out of the small air lock on the north side of the station. Jackson was not displeased by this. Since the target was to the west, they'd be approaching out of the sunrise, at least for a while. They didn't know what they were going up against, but Jackson was getting used to that.

Over the silent but eloquent objections of Master Chief Ruiz and Ensign Sanders, the lieutenant had told them to keep an eye on the station and all its approaches. He wanted an officer and senior enlisted man he knew he could depend on to be at the base covering his back. One shooter Team also had been ordered to stay behind to help out with any defensive requirements.

That meant there were eight men available to investigate and, he hoped, attack the signal center Falco had detected just over the horizon. They would follow a nearly straight depression, a ravinelike trench that carved a gouge across the Martian surface. It lay just a few hundred meters north of MS1 and conveniently extended almost in a beeline toward the target, passing a few hundred meters to the north of their destination as far as he could tell.

The SEALS burst out of the open air lock and dashed across the intervening distance in single file, each man vanishing into the low gulley as soon as he reached it. Jackson watched them all, and when the seventh—Harry Teal—had ducked over the rim of the ravine, the lieutenant raced after them, tumbling over the steep bank and dropping the three or four meters into the smooth bottom of the natural trench.

Each member of the Team was heavily loaded, carrying the full-G equivalent of some 250 pounds of equipment strapped to his back, shoulders, hips, and buttocks. Of course, in the Martian gravity the actual weight was considerably less, but as the SEALS were rapidly learning through experience, they still had to account for the incredible mass of the loads, which made turning and stopping unusually risky maneuvers. Jackson himself stumbled and lumbered forward, bumping into the far side of the trench before he could break the momentum of his leap. Judging from the grins on the faces of his men, he wasn't the only one who had come in with a rough landing.

They set out in single file, with Chief Harris taking the point and Falco, with his "squirrel gun," coming next. Jackson took the third spot in the line, and the rest of the group trailed out with some twenty meters between every two men. They moved without speaking. Jackson had made it clear that the unknown, unseen enemy might well be capable of discovering them simply by monitoring the electrical signals of their communicators, and so the devices had been turned off since they'd left the station.

Dobson's estimate had been six or seven klicks to the target, and the SEALS were determined to cross that distance in short order. They moved at a trot, grateful for the smooth ground underfoot and the straight routing of the trench. The rays of the sun illuminated the rim of the gully, highlighting the rust-colored terrain, leaving the sky overhead, with its almost nonexistent atmosphere, a black so deep that it was almost indistinguishable from the night.

The Team jogged for half an hour, each man hearing only the mechanical rasp of his own breathing. The pressure suits were tiny galaxies, with the thin, lethal Martian atmosphere separating each man from the others. Without even the radio communicators to keep in touch with one another, the men's thoughts turned inward, to memory and training and determination. Each one held thoughts of the four dead men prominent in his mind, and each vowed, silently and privately and yet utterly in union with the others, that those deaths would be avenged.

After the thirtieth minute Harris held up his hand, fist closed, to order a halt. Every man went down to one knee, drawing deep breaths, taking advantage of the halt to rest, to prepare for the action about to commence.

Jackson moved forward, clapping Falco on the shoulder as he passed, joining Chief Harris in the point position. Several square boulders had broken away from the side of the ravine just before them, and the officer nodded in understanding: Harris had stopped here because there was a good route up and out of the natural trench.

But first they had to see what was up there. Carefully finding solid steps for each foot, Jackson eased himself up until he was crouched just below the rim of the depression. Slowly, almost imperceptibly, he raised his head until just his eyes were above ground level.

The rays of the rising sun slanted almost horizontally across the flat ground, and that was the only thing that allowed him to make out the details. He could see a low, flat dome exactly the color of the Martian surface but too perfect, too symmetrical to be natural. For a long minute he stared at the place and finally was rewarded by a glimpse of movement.

And this was no goddamn robot! He saw one, then a couple more, *men* walking around the perimeter of the huge structure. They wore pressure suits and helmets but were too far away for him to distinguish any other details. They could be Assarn, or Shamani, or humans from Earth for all he knew, but they were mortal targets, and they were involved with whatever was going wrong on Mars.

The lieutenant spent a little more time eyeing the terrain. The dome was a good half klick away from his current position but not as far from the ravine if they were to continue on. Provided that they could find another point of egress from the trench, they could pull to within perhaps 150 or 200 meters before attacking.

There was no doubt in Jackson's mind that the SEALS were going to attack. He dropped back to the ravine floor and used a simple hand signal to get the men to follow him. He noticed several other points of erosion or collapse—there seemed to be one every twenty to fifty meters—so he continued until they reached the closest point of approach to the enemy installation.

Only then did Jackson creep up the side for another look. He could see the place more clearly now and counted a half dozen men, each wearing a suit with a transparent helmet that looked more or less like the SEALS' pressure suits. Each of the men was carrying a long weapon, but they were not familiar to the officer; that was clear enough proof that these men came from somewhere else.

*Somewhere damned far away from Earth.*

This was the kind of close combat the SEALS were known for, trained for. They would strike from the shadows and eliminate the enemy before he ever knew they were there. There was no braggadocio in Jackson's mind when he directed his men against the station and the enemy surrounding it; there couldn't be. He already had lost a quarter of his command, a terrible blow to him and his men. But they had a chance to make the enemy pay for what they had done and to continue the mission and find out who had been attacking the Terran facilities on Mars. The fact that a number of the enemy might be killed—well, that was just a pleasant bonus.

At their lieutenant's unspoken directions, the men prepared to assault the dome. While their Teammates prepped their weapons, Derek Falco and G-Man LaRue moved up to where they could take a concealed position near the rough area of the ravine wall where the rocks had broken away. There, the two men prepared to go into action as a sniper and observer pair. Long hours of training together allowed both men to move without having to say a word to each other.

As Falco adjusted his Mark 30 squirrel rifle, he made the weapon even longer as he slipped a cylindrical tube over the barrel and locked it into place. The big suppressor would cut down on a lot of the noise from the 10.2-millimeter caseless rounds, and the thin Martian air would prevent much of the remaining sound from traveling more than a few dozen meters. As far as the supersonic crack of the long pointed bullets went, any target they were aimed at would be struck down before the sound registered.

While Falco prepped his rifle, G-Man opened both of their packs. From within the containers he pulled rolls of what looked like bulky, shimmering, odd-colored rags. Unrolling the material and shaking it out carefully, G-Man set out one of the ghillie cloaks for Falco while he slipped his arms and hands into the loops made for them on his own cloak. Flipping a tiny switch on a control box the size of a pack of cards activated the electronics of the amazing cloaks. The shimmering suddenly disappeared, replaced by an exact duplication of the color of the ground all around the two men. Not even infrared heat signatures could be seen from a man properly using a ghillie cloak, and the two SEALS were more than expert in its use. Even in the growing daylight, the cloak made the big man disappear. It was only a shadow that slipped up to the edge of the ravine.

Through a miniaturized electronic binocular, G-Man looked at the enemy position. The range to the dome was 527 meters according to his laser range-finder readout, not a challenge to either of the long guns available to the sniper Team. Baby was lying against the side of the ravine, the powerful rail gun having far too noticeable a firing signature for it to be used as a concealed sniping weapon.

As he slowly moved into position next to his Teammate, Falco had no such concerns about his weapon. The Mark 30 would be as quiet as he could make it, silent enough that the enemy he fired at would never hear what killed him. The Hammer, the manufacturer's name for the Mark 30, was about to prove itself in combat for the first time.

The rest of the SEALS were preparing for a silent assault as the sniper Team moved into position. From long pouches among all their other equipment, long suppressors were taken out and slipped over the barrels of the G15 rifles. The back ends of the suppressors were thin enough that they would move into the receivers of the G15 weapons as the actions recoiled during firing. But the thick front ends of the cans would cut the sound of the shots to a loud hiss. Noise suppression was not so important out here in the near vacuum, but if they breached the dome and engaged in a firefight there—which Jackson had every intention of doing—the suppressors could provide a crucial element of stealth to the op.

These were the weapons that Sanchez and Marannis would use as they slipped ahead of the others to open the way. Both individuals were experienced point men. They were used to moving ahead of their fellow SEALS to open the way, uncover any booby traps, and make certain that the direction of approach led to where they wanted to go. At the moment each was a shadow in the base of the trench, moving without sound. They never had to say a word to each other as they operated in the night. Long experience had taught each man how the other thought, what he would do in any situation, how he would move, breathe, and react. If they didn't have their helmets on, each would know the other by his smell in the dark. The two men would have been called ninjas in another time, in a place millions of miles away.

These were the men Jackson had available to him as they readied themselves to attack the dome. As each man finished his preparations, he looked at his partner, then to the LT. After he saw all their faces turned toward him, Jackson gave the signal for each man to turn on his active camouflage system. With a closed fist, he struck his chest twice. At the signal, safety covers were pulled back and switches were closed. The same electronics that were part of the ghillie cloaks used by Falco and G-Man were in the surfaces of the SEALS' combat exposure suits. They did not make the men invisible—the tech people hadn't gotten that to work yet—but the suits now blended in with their surroundings.

The only part of the exposure suits not covered by the electronic camouflage was the soles of each man's boots. The tiny glow strips embedded in the soles made it easier for each SEALS to follow the others out across the Martian landscape when they got down into the prone position. They wouldn't need to uncover the cat's-eye strips of the same faintly glowing material on the backs of their helmets, at least not yet.

Jackson began the movement by squeezing the shoulder of Rocky Rodale, who was standing next to him. The squeeze signal was passed back down the line. When it came back up the line and Jackson felt Rocky's powerful grip at his shoulder, he passed the message up to Sanchez and Marannis. Slipping over the edge of the ravine, the two point men went after the enemy position.

From their position at the ravine, Falco and G-Man could see their Teammates slipping from depression to depression as they moved across the landscape. Even though they knew where to look, the two men had to

strain to catch a glimpse of the ghillie-clad men. Sometimes they could see only the glowing sole strips in the
sand. In spite of all of the modern electronic marvels the
SEALS had at their disposal, they couldn't risk using any
of them to communicate with one another as they stealthily moved across the flat ground. Instead, they depended
on the simplest of items.

In Jackson's hand was the tag end of a coil of string
that Sanchez had attached to his belt. The tiny microfila-
ment line played out and was the means by which Jackson
knew when the point men wanted their Teammates to
move up. At the signaling jerk, Jackson sent another
shooter pair forward to the next spot of cover. Finally, it
was his turn.

It didn't really seem to matter how much training he
did: Jackson could always hear his heartbeat thundering
in his ears when he was supposed to be moving in complete silence. The very breath moving in and out of his
lungs seemed to rasp so loudly that everyone around him
must hear it. But he knew they didn't, and he had to shake
off the feeling. He swore he could feel the sweat trickling
down his back, and if there ever was a technician who
came up with a way for someone to scratch his own back
while wearing this damned suit, he would marry the guy.

All extraneous thoughts fled from the officer's mind as
he suddenly felt the series of jerks come back down the
signal string. Sanchez and Marannis were as close to the
dome as they felt they could go, and the enemy was in
sight. He had to depend on the abilities of his men, men
he had supreme confidence in.

Lying in the dust, Sanchez and his partner, Marannis,
were like spirits in the night, death ghosts who were there
to take the souls of their enemies, if these aliens believed
in such things. Catching a glimpse of movement up
ahead, Marannis suspected the hostiles were about to find
out one way or the other.

The man in the pressure suit who stepped into view was clearly on sentry patrol. He carried his long, thin weapon—like a rifle with a battery pack attached—at the port arms position. His eyes were fixed on the far horizon, and he caught just a glimpse of nearby movement, as if a lumpy portion of the dome wall had suddenly leaned out and flexed. The fellow might have been a trained soldier, but the strange appearance of the dome moving outward gave him a moment's pause, and that was all the shadow needed.

Marannis reached around his back to wrap his hand around the handle of an age-old weapon. His ancestors from many generations back would have recognized the breaching tool he grabbed as a tomahawk. The laminated steel layers surrounding a diamond-hard core, sharpened to a molecular-thin edge, would have astonished those ancestors with the cutting ability of this ultramodern tool.

The SEALS thought of none of these things as his hand automatically grasped the handle of his breaching tool and pulled it down and away from the sheath that held it between two formed sides. Even as the alien turned to face him, the SEALS' point man was silently swinging the sharply pointed piercing end of the tool toward the helmet of the being that threatened him and his Teammates. There was no animosity, no hatred of the alien that might very well have tripped the controls that had killed his Teammates back at the station. There was only the sure knowledge that if he didn't kill the being in front of him, his fellow SEALS in the sands surrounding them right now would be discovered before they could assault the dome behind him.

The hardened point of the axlike breaching tool struck at the base of the sentry's helmet. The hard alien plastic at first resisted, then gave in to the onslaught. Air whooshed out before the alien could even scream, if such was an instinctual response of his kind. Nearly decapitated, the guard died almost before he knew he was under attack.

Another hostile had been trailing a dozen paces behind the first guard, but he didn't survive his patrol partner by much longer. His dark green eyes widened as he watched a shadow rise up and strike down his comrade, and then his chest exploded outward as Falco's big 10.2-millimeter bullet smashed into him. The guard fell, killed instantly, but the crackle of static and a strange language in their earpieces told the SEALS that the proverbial feces had struck the atmospheric oscillator.

More sentries came into sight, running around both sides of the broad, relatively flat dome. One of the long guns spit, and a round zinged off the ground near Sanchez, but that shooter, too, was slammed to the ground by a well-placed round from Falco's squirrel gun. The other guards dropped flat, weapons tracking the two point men, who also fell prone, their cloaks helping them essentially vanish from sight.

But their enemies were trained soldiers, as evidenced by their quick reactions and coordinated deployment. As he realized that his men had been discovered, Jackson ordered the rest of his unit into action. Hitting the switch with his chin, he keyed his mike open to the broadcast command frequency.

"Bingo, bingo, bingo!" he said clearly and rapidly. The SEALS officer had released the dogs of war, and they had been straining at the leash.

As aliens came running from around the two sides of the dome, the SEALS got up from where they lay on the ground and started to send short, vicious bursts of fire from their suppressed G15 weapons. The short bullpup guns fired three-round mechanically controlled bursts at a cyclic rate of more than 2,000 rounds per second. They functioned so quickly that no human could have released the trigger before nearly a dozen rounds had been fired. But with the mechanically limited three-round burst, the last shot had left the barrel before the recoil from the first round had even been felt, let alone reacted to.

Under a barrage of dozens of tungsten-core 6.8-millimeter bullets, the approaching soldiers withered under the SEALS' fire. Those who were farther away had time to raise their exotic-looking weapons, only to notice the odd feeling of the Martian air as their helmets and then their heads exploded from the impact of 10.2-millimeter projectiles fired from more than half a kilometer away.

While alien projectiles screamed away into the Martian sky, fired by unfeeling fingers that pulled triggers by reflex, Falco methodically searched for more targets. Even as the sentries came around the dome and dived for cover, the SEALS sniper struck down the alien forces, helping them down into the dry Martian soil, which greedily absorbed their life's blood. They had come light-years only to die on this barren land without knowing what had killed them. But those aliens who were still inside the dome had been warned, and they had the tools at hand to fight the SEALS assaulting their fortress.

As he saw the first of the robot tanks come from wherever it had been patrolling off in the distance, G-Man knew that this was a target worthy of Baby's attention. As the tank started to come around the curve of the dome to a point where it could bring its weapon to bear on his Teammates, G-Man braced himself and laid the heavy weapon down across the edge of the ravine. The electronic reticle in his sight picture automatically adjusted after he lased the range to the target. The computer read the velocity the controls had been set to—maximum—and adjusted the aiming point accordingly. Even as another tank appeared, G-Man shouted, "Fire in the hole!" and pulled the trigger.

A huge gout of flame and gas belched out the rear of the rail gun as the recoil-canceling counterblast charge fired. There was a brilliant splash of green-colored plasma as the copper and uranium slug struck the robot tank and penetrated to the interior. But G-Man had no time to admire his handiwork as his first armored target exploded. It had a partner that needed to be destroyed, which Baby did with a quick follow-up shot.

While the echoes of the roaring shots from the rail gun quickly dissipated in the almost airless Martian atmosphere, the nearly dozen enemy forces that had been outside the dome were falling to the sudden violence of the SEALS' onslaught. The men knew how to creep up on a target stealthily, and they prided themselves on being able to complete a mission without having to fire a shot. But when it came time to start shooting, the Navy SEALS took a backseat to no one, and they had just proved it.

With rapid hand signals, Jackson had part of his forces establish a security perimeter around the single air lock they had spotted during their examination of the exterior of the alien dome. Now Chief Harris and Harry Teal went into action as breachers while the rest of the unit maintained security.

With practiced motions, the two SEALS placed long, thin explosive charges along the outer edges of the single air lock door. There wasn't time to try to persuade the enemy inside to come out and surrender, and the SEALS wouldn't have known how to communicate with the aliens even if they could have spoken to them. With Falco and G-Man once again providing overwatch security, the rest of the SEALS lined up in what they called a train as the two breachers completed their work.

Once more, the squeeze signal went up and down the line. When he pressed down on the shoulder of Chief Harris kneeling down in front of him, Jackson knew what would be coming a moment later. Compressing the firing device in his hands, Harris detonated the linear explosive charges with which he and Teal had lined the hatch.

In traditional SEAL fashion that dated back to the frogmen of World War II, because the two breachers hadn't known the strength of the hatchway that blocked their entry, they had overloaded the entryway with explosives. The blast cut away the frame and the hatch. Then the internal pressure inside the dome blew the free chunk of alien alloy out into the Martian desert.

For three seconds the gush of air spewed across the nearly airless landscape, a visible mist of whitish vapor carrying small objects, followed by chairs and a table and a couple of empty pressure suits, all blasted out by the explosive decompression. Three of the alien men, none of them wearing pressure suits, came tumbling out, carried by the blast of air. They rolled across the sand, thrashing and flailing helplessly, dying very quickly. They wore startlingly white uniforms, like jumpsuits, but the cloth was torn and tattered by the explosive force of the air escaping into near vacuum.

*Not a pleasant way to go,* Jackson thought before turning his attention back to the breach.

While the dome was decompressing, Sanchez and Marannis pulled the serrated fragmentation sleeves from two grenades and discarded them. When the blast of air had slowed to the equivalent of a stiff breeze, the two SEALS turned the inset levers at the bottom of the grenade fuses to their lowest setting. After squeezing the safety lever and turning the arming caps, they quickly pitched their grenades into the darkness beyond the hatchway. The two hand-thrown weapons, set for blast and flash only, detonated only 1.5 seconds after their safety lever were released when they left the operators' hands.

The blast was more seen than heard, and the SEALS already were moving even as the dust and smoke blew out of the open hatchway. This was a maneuver they had practiced for years while in the operational SEAL Teams on Earth. Shooter pairs went in the doors and split to either side. Not putting their backs against the walls in case a ricochet followed the curves and plowed into them, the SEALS swept the interior compartments with the muzzles of their weapons. One pair leapfrogged over the other, and their Teammates maintained security. Again and again, the thunderous blast of concussion grenades roared out, often followed by the stuttering thuds of a quick burst of suppressed 6.8-millimeter projectiles.

The aliens seemed to be stunned by the suddenness, the shock, and the violence of the attack, not to mention the catastrophic decompression of their dome. In the initial entryway they found half a dozen dead soldiers, unsuited, with tongues protruding and eyes bulging and bloodshot. Several of the men in the garrison, in pressure suits, snapped off hasty shots and quickly were cut down by the lethal and vengeful SEALS.

There was no way to tell any of the alien enemy forces inside the dome to surrender. Any of the human-looking aliens who survived the sudden decompression of the dome to the Martian atmosphere who tried to face the SEALS immediately were cut down by sudden gunfire. There was no way to tell what was a weapon and what could have been the alien version of a coffee cup, and the SEALS didn't feel like taking chances.

The fire Teams worked quickly, clearing the outer ring of compartments, then meeting on the far side of the dome's interior.

"They've got a secondary air lock and a pressurized compartment in the middle of this place," Marannis reported to Jackson. The point man was holding his bloody ax when the lieutenant found him standing between two corpses.

"Right, you know the drill," the officer said, once again gathering his Team outside a sealed lock.

The heavy door caved inward under the force of the charge, revealing a large, very dark chamber. This time when they blew the lock there was no release of pressure. The surviving enemy soldiers apparently had bled off their air in anticipation of the attack.

Not that it did them any good. Once again, grenades preceded the charging SEALS, and their small arms fire cut down the four men, all of them in pressure suits, who had tried to fort up in what was obviously the station's control room. Suited, Marannis and Sanchez went around, making sure that none of the hostiles was feigning death. And they were really, really dead when the two point men got done with them. Unfortunately, this was the case with every hostile. The SEALS simply didn't have the luxury to make capturing a live one a priority.

Jackson took a look at his watch. It was only nine minutes since Marannis had swung his breaching ax, and the interior of the dome was secure, cleared of all obvious alien life. There were some ten dead aliens outside and maybe a dozen of them within the dome. Not a single SEALS had so much as had his suit breached.

"Target secured," Jackson said into his microphone. "Stand down but maintain security."

Falco and G-Man would know to watch the area around the dome. The lieutenant went to the command console at the center of the room. It was a large control bank with many sets of identical controls. In the middle was a large vidscreen displaying a number of glowing spots. It took the LT about two seconds to realize that this screen indicated the position of the robot tanks arrayed around MS1.

Tentatively, he reached out and flicked a toggle switch beside one of the controls. Immediately one of the lights indicating a tank turned from green to red and began blinking. The tank was one that had been moving; when Jackson had flipped the switch, it had stopped in its tracks.

One by one, he turned the other toggle switches, stopping each tank, making the steady green lights into blinking red dots.

"I think," he said with a tight grin, "we've just knocked out about a company of tanks with the turn of a few switches. Good work, SEALS."

It hadn't been enough, but the payback for their lost Teammates had started in a satisfactory manner.

# Six: Treachery

Master Chief Ruiz paced around the confines of MS1 like a caged tiger. In a rational sense, he understood why he, Ensign Sanders, and two other SEALS had been left behind while the LT led the attack mission. But *damn*! It just didn't feel right to be here with all these civilians, useless as tits on a bull, while his Teammates were out there risking everything and maybe taking apart the bastards responsible for their lost comrades.

Ensign Sanders was with Director Parker and Professor Zaro in the station headquarters, and so Ruiz avoided that stuffy office. Instead, he made the rounds of the perimeter. He was wearing his pressure suit but didn't have his helmet closed and latched because the atmosphere inside MS1 was fully pressurized. Still, he was ready at a moment's notice if he needed to go outside.

He checked on the shooter Team, Dobson and Robinson, who were positioned just inside the main air lock. They were alert, with weapons loaded, and had planned out zones of fire that would enfilade anyone who burst through the station's main entrance. Even so, such was Ruiz's mood that he gruffly ordered them to move back a few meters, to double-check their magazines, and to make sure they had smoke and fragmentation grenades handy—which, of course, they did.

They followed his instructions to the letter, no complaints, but when Ruiz stomped away, he only felt worse for taking out his frustration on two good men. Still, he didn't go back and apologize. He was a master chief, goddammit, and by definition didn't make any mistakes that would be acknowledged in the presence of his men. Still, he was dour and worried as he continued to stalk the corridors of the research station.

Once again he gave the HQ offices a wide berth, instead checking on the two pressurized docking bays, one of which held the *Tommy,* and other the *Mikey.* The station's shuttle, the ship that had brought them back from the Valles Marinaris, was too large for either bay. Instead, it rested on its four legs about 200 meters away from the station. He studied it through the viewport and couldn't see anything amiss out there.

Next he made his way through the laboratory area, conscious of the eyes of the scientists and researchers as he carefully made his way between crowded tables. The work was proceeding only in a desultory fashion, he sensed; these people were freaked out by the unknown danger visiting the planet. Ruiz felt acutely the hopes they placed in him and his Team. The SEALS were up to the challenge, but he still felt like a bull in a china shop in the middle of all this crowded academic activity. With a few desultory greetings followed by a terse farewell, he fled from the lab.

He breathed easier as he made his way past the barracks and through the mess hall, where a half dozen staffers were eating reconstituted freeze-dried food. The chief politely declined an offer to join them.

"Gotta finish the rounds," he said.

Following a corridor between several storage compartments, he looked in the window of each door, again observing nothing amiss. He saw several large chambers in storage that looked like spare air locks and made a mental note that if they needed to fall back to a hardened redoubt, these storage compartments would be the place to do that.

One more stop with Dobson and Robinson gave him

the chance to offer "Good job, keep your eyes open" encouragement.

"You got it, Master Chief," Smokey Robinson said, grinning. He knew an apology when he heard one.

Finally, he made his way up the ladder to the MS1 observation dome. It would give him the best position to act as a spotter for his men and, if necessary, the *Pegasus*. The floor hatch was open, and he pulled himself up to find Consul Char-Kane and Dr. Sulati already there.

"Hi, Rafe," said the doctor, flashing a warm smile. "Come on up."

"Uh, sorry. I don't want to interrupt—"

"Don't worry about it. We're just killing time, waiting for your men to come back."

"Yes, please do not depart on our account," said the Shamani ambassador, nodding coolly. "You may wish to take a seat and observe, yourself."

"Sure. Um, thanks."

In fact, he was glad they'd invited him to stay. He settled into a chair and looked across the barren landscape. With the harsh sun still low in the east, the shadows of the station's domes stood out in clear relief. He remained acutely conscious that the LT and the rest of the Team were out there somewhere.

The doctor's face clouded. "I heard about the loss of your men at MS3. I didn't have the chance to tell you. I'm so sorry. I wish there was something I could have done."

Ruiz felt a constriction in his throat. "They knew the risks," he said, immediately regretting the harshness and recognizing his own bullshit. *How could anyone know these risks?* "I mean, I appreciate your thoughts," he amended awkwardly.

"Your men are very fierce warriors," the consul de campe said approvingly. "I think the Assarn will come to fear you very much."

"If they live that long," he growled.

Wanting to change the subject, he stood up and went to the viewing panel that looked west. The sun, smaller and cooler than it seemed on Earth, was still low in the east behind him. He could clearly see the ravine that the Team was using for its approach. "Have you seen anything out that way?" he asked.

"Not yet. But I saw something move over there, to the south," Dr. Sulati said.

"What did it look like?"

Immediately the chief was focused, unconsciously touching his sidearm while he pivoted and looked in the direction indicated by the doctor.

"Well, it was a flash of silver. It might have been my imagination."

Ruiz knew it had not been her imagination. He remembered the robot tanks and knew that Falco had reported the potential for many more of them out there. Staring at the bright ground, he could see no anomaly on that dry red surface, but that didn't mean there was nothing out there. His glare was so intense that if it had been tangible, it might have melted the Plexiglas. The sun continued to rise with the morning, but the rays were still more horizontal than vertical. He should be able to see a shadow, to see *something,* dammit!

Then he did: a flash of reflection, sunlight on metal. It was moving, and once he saw the first spark of light, he could follow the object that had caused it. There were two, no, three, of the robot tanks in view, creeping very slowly in line abreast toward MS1. They were still a couple of klicks away, but they were coming in his direction. Picking up a pair of binoculars, he studied the vehicles. One halted, barrel trained forward, while the other two continued to creep forward, toward the station.

"Look—over there!" Consul Char-Kane called with more urgency than Ruiz had ever heard in her voice. She was pointing to the east, shading her eyes against the rising sun.

Following her gaze, the chief saw it, too: another group of the robot tanks, a line of six or more, gradually approaching the station. They moved with tactical precision, half of them sitting still, barrels trained forward, while the others darted quickly, 100 or 200 meters at a time, before halting and covering the advance of their comrades. If Ruiz hadn't seen the electronic guts of two of those things, he would have sworn they were tanks manned by actual, thinking crewmen.

That didn't change the fact that they were very deadly opponents.

"We've got company," Ruiz announced curtly. "Time to get everyone out of the perimeter compartments and into their suits, just like we planned. If those tanks open fire, they could puncture the domes like so much Swiss cheese. We need to take shelter in some hardened rooms, like those air locks in the storage chambers."

"Tanks?" Dr. Sulati said in alarm, coming to his side and squinting into the distance. "I see them out there. Do you think they're what attacked MS3?"

"Can't be sure," Ruiz said. "The Team mixed it up with a few of them on the way back here. They're robots but must be controlled from somewhere. They have guns that could punch a hole right through one of these domes, and that's probably how the attack on MS3 started."

"Maybe that control center, the place where these robot tanks are operated, is the installation that your lieutenant found and is attacking," the consul suggested.

Ruiz nodded; the idea made sense. "Get below—and spread the alarm."

The two women went to the hatch, Dr. Sulati starting down the ladder with the grace and speed of a gymnast. Char-Kane followed more deliberately, and Ruiz took another look around while he waited for his turn on the ladder.

The flash of light came from the west, and he almost missed it. Stepping closer to the window, he watched and saw more of them: explosions, fiery sparks lighting up the ground, spewing into the dark sky, where, momentarily, they were visible against the background of space. A column of fire shot straight up, brilliant and blazing for a moment before vanishing. Even the smoke that would have remained in a normal Terran atmosphere vanished almost immediately in the low pressure of Mars.

The SEALS were attacking, he knew instinctively. He was still watching as Char-Kane came back up the ladder.

Spying him, she came to his side. "Is that your warrior Team?" she asked.

"I'm pretty sure it is," he said. They watched for another few minutes, but there were no more fireworks. Shaking his head, Ruiz glanced around at the distant tanks, wondering how much closer they'd gotten. He saw the three to the south and six to the east, just where he'd last seen them.

"They're not moving anymore!" he exclaimed.

"You're right," the Shamani woman agreed. "Do you know why?"

"My Team took out the command center; at least that's going to be my guess until I'm proved wrong!"

"That is indeed good news," the consul said approvingly. "Perhaps, then, we do not have to flee to this—what you called it?—hardened place."

"Well, we need to keep an eye out. But it looks like the threat might be put on hold, at least."

This time he followed the two women down the ladder. They found Director Parker, Ensign Sanders, and Professor Zaro in the command center. Quickly Ruiz described his observations.

"You think the attack neutralized the tanks, then?" Professor Zaro queried. His tone was oddly casual, but Ruiz didn't think anything of it. As usual, the academician's eyes were watering, and he pulled out a bulky handkerchief.

"That's my best guess, yes, sir," he replied.

"Then we shall need another plan," the professor noted.

"What?" the chief asked.

Too late, he saw that the man was concealing something small and round in that bulky handkerchief. The alarm popped in the chief's mind: grenade! Zaro tossed the device past him, and Ruiz lunged too late.

Something loud popped behind the chief. He felt a blow to the back of his head, and then, for some reason, the floor was coming up to smash him in the nose.

He didn't feel anything after that.

Lieutenant Jackson led the file of SEALS across the surface of Mars. He had inspected one of the robot tanks after they had destroyed the alien installation and was relieved to find it out of operation. The power source was a heavy but compact battery, and when Falco did a quick check with his electronics array, they learned that the power was shut off, the whole vehicle resting in the alien equivalent of standby.

He wanted to get back to the station quickly to confirm his initial estimate, and so they were making a beeline for the MS1. Jackson didn't want to waste time detouring through the trench. He was not a hundred percent certain that the threat had been removed, but he felt pretty confident that they had taken out the controller for the remote-controlled tanks that had been menacing the station.

Considerably lighter for the ammunition they had expended, the Teammates moved at an easy lope. The domes of the station were clearly visible before them, still three or four klicks away, when Jackson heard a voice—Chief Harris—crackle in his earpiece.

"Eyes on the sky, Team."

Jackson looked up, and his first thought was that a me-

teor was blazing down toward them. Yellow fire seared
and flared against the backdrop of the dark sky. The blaze
was descending, but slowly. When he squinted, the fiery
brilliance quickly focused into four individual blazes—
rocket engines. A vehicle, similar to the station's shuttle
but larger, was descending toward MS1.

"Who the hell is dropping in at this hour?" he demanded crossly. "Let's pick up the pace, men."

The easy jog became a run, the file of eight SEALS
closing in on the station as fast as they could. Even with
the load and the bulk of their pressure suits, they made
good time. But they were still two kilometers away when
the strange shuttle came to rest just outside the main air
lock. It was a bulbous, almost spherical craft that was
resting now on four legs: one support beneath each of the
rocket engines. There were windows atop the craft, as if
to indicate a flight deck or small bridge.

They saw a ramp descend from the belly of the craft,
and a number of figures, all wearing pressure suits,
emerged from the ship and hurried to the air lock. The
suits were white instead of camouflaged for the Martian
surface, but in every other respect they looked identical to
the pressure suits worn by the garrison of the station they
had just wiped out.

The air lock to the station stood open, and that indicated
that at least one person in MS1 was welcoming the new
arrivals. Even so, Jackson felt a frisson of alarm; something wasn't right here.

"You two"—he indicated Sanchez and Maraniss—"go
in through the back way. The rest of you, follow me."

A quick check of their meters showed that they had
nearly two hours of air left, and so Jackson decided on a
roundabout approach. Still moving quickly, they pulled
close to the large dome of one of the docking bays, using
the building to block them from the view of the newly arrived shuttle.

Pressed against the base of the dome, the SEALS skirted the perimeter of MS1 until they could peer around the edge and get a view of the craft. There were markings on the hull, but they were not in any language Jackson had seen before. He wondered if this was the scrawling, ornate script of the Shamani, with which he was relatively unfamiliar.

"Harry?" he asked Teal, the platoon's intellectual. "Would you know Shamani writing if you saw it?"

"I would, LT," replied the corpsman. "That looks like it. Couldn't read it to save my life, though."

"Still, I don't like the looks of it. I wonder if it's a trick by those goddamn Assarn," the lieutenant told him.

There were two figures, apparently guards, holding weapons at port arms and standing to either side of the sloping entry ramp beneath the shuttle.

The intruders that had entered the station through the open air lock emerged again. They were carrying limp bundles, one bundle per carrier. The first four were long sacks that looked disturbingly like body bags; Jackson couldn't see what they contained, but the contents were the right size and shape to be humans. He could discern no movement of the bags. If they held people, the people were either dead or unconscious.

"Dammit—sir! Look!" Chief Harris spit.

Jackson saw a fifth figure being carried out of the station. This one was not in a bag, probably because he wore a pressure suit. At this range, less than a hundred meters, Jackson recognized the SEALS trident on the arm of the suit. The buzz of black hair visible inside the helmet meant that it could only be Master Chief Ruiz. He was not moving.

"LT!" hissed Falco. "They've got the master chief!"

"Not for long," Jackson declared. Already the four sacks had been carried into the shuttle. The last man was carrying Ruiz, and he started up the ramp while the two guards remained at their posts, their attention directed toward the air lock.

"Falco. Take out those two." The sniper was all but guaranteed a kill at that range. "The rest of you, follow me!"

Jackson burst around the curve of the dome, sprinting in long, leaping strides through the low-G environment. One of the guards spun and went down. Eerily, there was no sound from Falco's shot, but the spray of blood and escaping air from the man's suit indicated a hit to the heart. The second guard saw his comrade fall and raised his gun, spinning toward the approaching SEALS.

The officer was already halfway to the shuttle—each stride seemed to cover five or six meters—when the second guard went down, fatally hit.

"Watch the air lock!" Jackson warned, not sure if some of the intruders were still in the station.

Chief Harris had been doing just that and sprayed a burst into the hatch as two more figures emerged into view. They both went down, gas and fluids escaping from numerous holes in their perforated pressure suits. Another came after them; his crystal helmet shattered when Harris loosed another burst, and the man thrashed horribly as he tried to suck a breath from the virtually airless atmosphere.

That target was still twitching as Jackson reached the base of the ramp. He held his weapon at the ready and sprinted aboard the shuttle, looking for targets, mindful that an unconscious Ruiz was somewhere ahead of him. Nothing moved, and so he charged up the ramp, confident that the other SEALS were following him.

He found himself in an air lock, with a sealed hatch before him leading, obviously, to the interior of the ship.

"Breaching charge!" he called, and Harry Teal tossed him a small pack of C-6 explosive.

Catching it, Jackson saw Falco charging up the ramp behind the others—logically enough, since the lieutenant had not ordered him to stay put. He was moderately surprised to see Sanchez, Marannis, Dobson, and Robinson also emerge from the station, the two fire Teams sprinting toward their fellow SEALS in the shuttle bay.

"Watch the station air lock—there might be more of them!" Jackson barked, and Falco and Harris immediately knelt on the ramp and leveled their guns at the station's entrance.

Jackson slapped the explosive against the hatch; the magnetic coupling held it fast. Only then did he hesitate for a second. There were ten SEALS in the relatively spacious air lock, but even in the large chamber, there was too much risk to set the charge off while they were there.

Yet the only way to put some distance between themselves and the blast would be to head back down the ramp and out of the shuttle.

Jackson had the soldier's view of a hard-won position: Don't give it up unless you have to. He held off on setting the charge. "Chief! Got any idea how to work this hatch without blowing it to hell?"

Harris came up and studied the mechanism. "Looks to be a mechanical latch, LT. But this box here—that's some kind of electronic override. Nothing like I've ever seen before, and pretty tough to—"

His words were blocked out by a piercing shriek so loud it was like a pair of daggers stabbing into Jackson's ears. The others bolted upright. Clearly, the electronic attack was affecting all of them. Immediately Jackson snapped off his communicator, and the squeal stopped.

"They're jamming us!" he shouted, pointing to his ears; the others quickly disabled the comlinks.

But that was the least of their problems. One glance at the ramp confirmed that the platform was moving. It snapped upward quickly, nesting into a tight gasket around the base of the air lock.

The SEALS were trapped.

# Seven: Tezlac Catal

"Drop and flatten!" Jackson shouted as the shuttle lurched abruptly.

He forgot that the Team's communicators were shut off, but the men clearly didn't need any prompting: All ten SEALS dropped flat on the deck as the rockets kicked in. They felt the acceleration surge, quickly passing 1 G—no inertial dampening on this shuttle!—and the pressure continued to build. Noise pounded through the hull as the rockets roared and the spacecraft blasted away from Mars; the gravitational force continued to increase until Jackson couldn't lift his head off the deck.

He felt as though his lungs were being crushed, as if a massive weight—a boulder or even an entire house—were resting on him, flattening his body, pummeling his organs, clutching at his heart. Straining hard, he drew in a breath; when he exhaled, the air seemed to drain right out of him. He tried to draw another breath and felt like he was suffocating, felt that his lungs lacked the power to fight against the crushing force.

Then, gradually, it eased. The SEALS were still flat on the floor, but the shuttle was already high over Mars, and the G-force had eased back to perhaps four times Earth's gravity. With an effort, the lieutenant turned his head and saw his Teammates similarly prone, all of them gasping in the confines of their bubble helmets.

G-Man was the closest, and with a grimace LaRue pushed himself up to his hands and knees. It was an awesome display of strength, since he weighed the equivalent of some 800 pounds. With a thud and a grunt, LaRue flopped down on his side. He flipped on his communicator, and when he didn't wince, Jackson did the same. The jamming noise had ceased.

"I guess I need to work out a little more," LaRue gasped.

In spite of everything, Jackson laughed, albeit weakly. He rolled onto his back and stared at the overhead bulkhead, his mind whirling, seeking ideas, making plans, discarding them. They were in a tough spot, of that there could be be no doubt. But one thing was sure: They still had their weapons and enough explosives to blow this shuttle right out of the Martian sky, including all the SEALS and the other captives with it, of course. That seemed a little drastic right now, though Jackson didn't rule it out as an eventual possibility.

With shocking abruptness, the pounding of the engines ceased, and in the sudden silence, the SEALS were immediately weightless. Jackson drew deep breaths with immense relief, feeling the pressure of the deck simply vanish. He could see that he was drifting slowly upward and reached out to take hold of one of the many handles recessed into the deck.

"Don't float too high," he cautioned the men of his Team. "If those rockets kick in again, you don't want to slam down on the deck with 6 Gs of weight."

Staying prone, the men crawled through the compartment, looking for anything that might prove useful to know about. With each refreshing breath he took, Jackson was considering another problem. He checked the HUD on his helmet visor and saw that he had less than an hour of air left in his breather; he knew the rest of the men would be in the same predicament.

Each pressure suit was equipped with an outside atmosphere sensor, and he activated the device, watching the data as it, too, was projected onto the inside of his visor. The air was good quality, just a little less than 1 atmosphere of pressure: about the equivalent of 12,000 feet of altitude on Earth. Warily, he unsnapped the seal holding his helmet to the collar of his suit and lifted the Plexiglas bubble off his head.

The air was cool, and dry and smelled vaguely of metal. "Seems safe to breathe. Let's conserve our breathing mix for now, but be ready to snap the helmet back on," he suggested.

The other SEALS followed suit.

"What now, LT?" Chief Harris asked.

Jackson patted his VP90 sidearm, then picked up and checked the chamber of his assault rifle. "Well, these bastards won't get us without a fight. And I want us to set some charges in case it comes to that."

If any of the SEALS were dismayed to realize what "that" meant, they didn't let it show.

"Aye, aye, sir," Harry Teal said. He was probably the best man in the platoon when it came to using the C-6 explosives, and he quickly started digging around in his pack for a few of the deadly packages. Pulling them out one at a time, he clipped them to his suit to keep them from floating away.

The shuttle seemed to be drifting weightless, but they felt something clunk through the hull, a solid pressure that pulled the vehicle and the air lock around them to the side. The SEALS bumped into the bulkhead, though it wasn't a violent maneuver, and then felt a buzzing vibration that seemed to hold the little spacecraft steady.

"I have a feeling we just docked onto something," Jackson observed. "Get your helmets back—"

The air lock hatch suddenly buzzed, and the men snatched their weapons, watching as the metal ring spun and the aperture abruptly opened. Six fingers backed slightly off their triggers when they recognized Consul Char-Kane. The Shamani woman looked a little disheveled, her normally smooth black hair scattered in disarray, but her gaze was steady as she came through the hatch, holding on to the handrails to keep herself from drifting. She was followed by Director Parker, whose ruddy complexion had paled. One of his eyes was surrounded by a purple bruise.

"Are you men unharmed?" asked the Shamani woman.

"Close enough," Jackson retorted. He glared at her, then at the director. "But what the hell is going on? What ship is this? And what about Master Chief Ruiz? We saw him carried aboard!"

"Please," Char-Kane said, holding up her hand as if to ward off the onslaught of questions. "Your master chief is bruised but not badly wounded. He, the ensign, and Dr. Sulati already have been taken from the shuttle onto the ship."

"So Ensign Sanders was in one of those body bags? I suppose you were, too."

"I do not know how they brought us out of the station and onto the shuttle, as I was unconscious. But you are probably right."

"And now we've docked with a ship. What ship is it?"

The consul de campe drew a deep breath. "I was mistaken about the Assarn. The attackers on Mars were agents of the Eluoi. The shuttle has brought us into the hold of the Shamani ship *Gladiola*, which was in orbit about your planet. But the ship has been captured by the Eluoi. We are all their prisoners."

"Wait. These attackers, they weren't Assarn? The robot tanks, too?"

"No. I am sorry that I was wrong, but apparently it was the Eluoi who struck your installation on Mars. They disguised their tactics to resemble the Assarn."

"Why would they do that?" Jackson demanded.

"I do not know. But I fear we will find out soon enough."

"What do *they* want with us?" Jackson asked. All he

knew about the Eluoi was that they were one of the three galactic empires. This was the first he or anyone else had heard about them being present in the solar system.

"I am afraid I do not know. We will have to wait to find that out."

"W-wait . . . ?" Jackson tried to spit out the question, but his tongue stumbled clumsily in his mouth. He shook his head, but his neck was having trouble moving. And why did Chief Harris just fall to the deck?

The red light on his air-quality indicator was blinking. Too late he understood: gas!

And then all the lights went out.

Jackson was lying in a reasonably comfortable bed when he awakened. The first thing he realized was that he was between silk sheets. The second was that he was naked.

"Shit!" Memories came flooding back, and he pushed himself upright, moderately surprised to find that he wasn't restrained. He looked around. He was in one bed in a compartment that looked like a small medical ward-room. There were sixteen single beds, eight along each facing wall, and most of them were occupied. Chief Harris was on one side of him, Master Chief Ruiz on the other. There was no sign of his uniform or any of the SEALS' equipment.

The gravity had been restored; that suggested that they were accelerating away from Mars. The pressure seemed to be about 1 G.

From his sitting position he saw Dr. Sulati perched on the end of one bed across the compartment. Director Parker lay slumbering in the farthest bed on the opposite wall; the roster of prisoners looked like twelve SEALS and two civilians. The doctor was wearing what appeared to be a pair of white silk pajamas, and Jackson flushed at the helplessness of his own nakedness.

As if reading his mind, Sulati pointed to the foot of his bed and spoke. "They have a suit like this for each of you. Each of us, I should say." She politely turned her back while he scrambled out of the bed and slipped on the trousers and shirt. There were no buttons, just drawstrings, but the garment fit well and was comfortable, not unlike a lightweight martial arts uniform. Still, he felt only a little less naked than he had before. There was nothing to put on his feet, but the temperature in the room was comfortable, and the smooth metal floor was rather warm.

Some of the other SEALS were stirring. One by one they awakened, groggy and pissed off. As they dressed themselves, the officer went over to Ruiz, who was sitting up. The master chief had a pair of black eyes and looked as though his nose might be broken.

"Fucking Zaro!" Ruiz snarled. "He got the drop on me, on all of us, in the station. Tossed some kind of knockout grenade that took me out before I even knew he was a hostile!"

"Dobson, Smokey? What did you guys see at the air lock?"

"We were tipped off by some of the station staff, LT," Robinson replied. "We were closed in the station's main air lock, watching the front, and these bastards came in the side door. We went to check on the master chief, but they were already bundling him and the doc—and that Char-Kane woman—out to the shuttle."

"When Sanchez and Marannis came in, they said you were going after them, LT. *Damn*!" Dobson's Alabama accent stretched the word into two syllables. "We didn't want to miss the party."

"Of course not," Jackson said, proud of his men even though their courage had brought two more of them into this untenable situation. He turned back to Ruiz. "So it was Zaro, huh? What the hell was he after?"

"I don't know, sir. But I'd like to wring his skinny little neck, I'll tell you that."

Ensign Sanders, also dressed in white pajamas, came stumbling over, rubbing a bruise on his cheek. "I never liked that son of a bitch," he grunted. "Kept prattling on about Caracas; asked if I'd like to visit it someday. Damn! I bet he's never even seen the place. I saw him on the shuttle, and his eyes were different—green as emeralds, sir."

"So he's one of them. An Eluoi," Jackson deduced.

The hatch opened, and a man stepped through. He was wearing a white suit not unlike the pajamas except for some gold braid on the arms. A shiny black belt encircled his waist, with a few mysterious-looking tools, including what looked like a pocket computer and an obvious utility knife, attached. He also had a red hat that was wrapped like a turban around his skull. The pupils of his eyes were a piercing green.

There were two others behind him bearing small weapons that could have been machine pistols, except that they were attached by cords to compact packs that the men wore on their backs. They, too, wore turbans but had no gold braid decorating their sleeves. The two were green-eyed like their leader and clearly ready to defend themselves. They kept their guns trained casually on the prisoners.

After a critical look at the ugly short-barreled weapons, Jackson didn't much like the SEALS' chances if they tried to rush them. But he knew his men were already measuring distances with their eyes and calculating the odds of taking the aliens down. He stretched elaborately and lowered his hands, palms down, to his sides, knowing that the SEALS would see and obey the sign language version of an order to stand down. Instead of attacking, they would watch and wait.

The man who had entered the compartment said something that was utterly unintelligible. It didn't even sound like a language but was more of a series of clicks and sibilant whistles.

"What?" Jackson asked. "I can't understand you."

The man reached into one of his belt pouches and pulled out a very small device. He pantomimed placing it in his ear, then handed it to the lieutenant, turning his head sideways so that Jackson could see that the fellow wore an identical device in his own ear.

Suspicious but intrigued, the LT pushed the plug into the canal of his right ear. The gold-braided visitor spoke again.

"Are you Lieutenant Jackson?" he asked. The sounds emerging from his mouth were smoothly and immediately translated by the device in the officer's ear so that he could understand perfectly.

"That would be me," Jackson replied. "Who wants to know?"

"Please come with me." The man turned and quickly stepped back through the hatchway.

There seemed to be no point being stubborn at that juncture, and so the lieutenant followed him, nodding as Chief Harris whispered, "Be careful, LT."

The SEALS all looked at their platoon leader as he moved toward the door. They saw the lieutenant's right hand open flat and then close into a fist twice, as if he were flexing his fingers. The men remained sharply alert but would not move for now. They all had read the signal for them to stop and wait on the lieutenant. They would follow his orders until they knew it was time to move.

The two guards stepped back, providing no opportunity for the SEALS officer to grab for one of the guns, even if he could have used it. But Jackson had no intention of doing anything rash, at least not yet. He needed intel desperately, and this little excursion seemed like the first, and maybe best, chance to get it. The pair of soldiers fell in and followed a half dozen steps behind as Jackson trailed his guide down a long corridor. All four of them entered a small room, which the lieutenant guessed was an elevator; his guess was confirmed as the doors snapped shut, and he sensed the momentum as they whooshed upward at a surprisingly high velocity.

Given the speed, it seemed that they rose for a long distance before the elevator stopped and the doors opened. They emerged at a confluence of six corridors radiating out like spokes from a hub. Each of the passages was a good fifty meters long, and so Jackson knew he was in an immense ship.

That impression was confirmed as his guide led him through an electronic hatch past another pair of guards, onto what he guessed was the bridge. There were dozens of people in view, many of them manning consoles, consulting screens, or operating keyboards and other equipment.

But a few of them apparently were waiting for him. He immediately recognized Professor Zaro and Consul Char-Kane. Zaro was wearing one of the white tunics that seemed ubiquitous on this ship; Jackson noticed with a start that the professor's eyes were that shocking green that seemed to characterize their captors. He remembered the way the man's eyes watered and realized that he must have been disguised with contact lenses.

*So that son of a bitch is one of them. You will get yours, Professor—I promise you that.*

The consul wore her metallic golden bodysuit, a shocking drop of bright color amid all the white clothing. She did not seem to be a prisoner, but she was watching him with an expression that looked sympathetic, not threatening.

Between her and the professor stood a tall hawk-faced man who studied Jackson with disconcerting intensity as the lieutenant was led into the room.

*He's in charge here.* There was no question in Jackson's mind even before he took in the rings of pure gold extending up and down the man's sleeves. He continued to stare with eyes so dark yet so fiercely penetrating that Jackson almost felt as though his mind, his very thoughts, were being scrutinized. He tried looking back, realizing that those almost-black eyes were actually a very dark green, but he couldn't meet the man's gaze for more than a few seconds.

The lieutenant advanced with all the dignity he could muster, and when his eyes shifted from the face of the enemy commander, he stared at the treacherous Professor Zaro. He noticed a slight smirk on Zaro's face and made a silent vow that the spy would pay for his betrayal somehow, someday.

The hawk-faced man lifted his head with a haughty expression of disdain. Jackson thought the fellow was about to say something, but instead it was Zaro who spoke in his slightly accented English. "This is Tezlac Catal. He is a very prominent lord among the Eluoi. You are a prisoner on his vessel."

"For what purpose?" Jackson demanded, addressing Catal. "Why did you take us off Mars?" He cast a contemptuous glance at Zaro. "Why did you have this weasel infiltrate our colony?"

Tezlac Catal shrugged and smiled slightly, and again it was Zaro who answered. "Because we are curious."

Catal stared at Jackson with a peculiar intensity that made the officer feel as if his skin were being peeled back; it seemed that the enemy commander was getting a look directly at his insides. He grimaced, fighting the distressing sensation, trying to assure himself that his thoughts remained private. With an effort, he forced his expression to blank.

"You are all Eluoi?" he asked, still suppressing a shudder of disquiet.

"We are the one true race of destiny in the galaxy," Zaro

said calmly. Jackson noticed Char-Kane grimacing, but the Shamani woman made no objection to the statement.

"True race? We've had some people on Earth make that claim over the years. It didn't work out too well for them."

Tezlac Catal merely smiled coolly, and Jackson got the idea that Zaro was hearing the other man's thoughts and speaking for him. The professor explained with unself-conscious arrogance. "Let me put it this way. We are the supreme race. The Shamani aspire to be our equals, but they are not. The Assarn are mere dogs compared to us. And you humans of Earth . . ."

"What about us humans?" demanded Jackson.

Catal shrugged again, a maddeningly condescending gesture. He looked almost bored as Zaro noted helpfully: "You are the fleas on the dog."

"Your point?"

"It may become clear to you eventually; whether or not it does is not our concern." Zaro stood up, and the Eluoi commander gestured to a large screen high up on the bridge wall. A picture glimmered there, a very high-res image of the galaxy. Jackson recognized the constellation Cassiopeia before he turned to Char-Kane.

"Are you in alliance with these Eluoi?" he asked coldly.

"No," she replied. "I am a prisoner, too. They captured this ship from the Shamani crew while I was on Mars. My crew—those who survived the attack—are being held in a cargo hold. But I have been given private quarters not far from your own."

Zaro smiled thinly. "There is a certain amount of status associated with an elite member of the Shamani. I would not treat a consul de campe the same as any routine prisoner. She is more important than most."

Jackson regarded his captors again, not sure if he believed the professor but wanting to learn as much as he could while he was there. He tried to shake Catal up by addressing him directly.

"Why do you let this sneaking weasel do your talking for you?" he asked bluntly.

Tezlac Catal opened his mouth and spoke. "Thisss issss why," he said quietly.

The words assaulted Jackson's brain like a spike being driven through his skull. He staggered backward, clapping his hands to his ears, exerting every bit of his willpower to keep from collapsing to his knees or passing out. His head felt like it was exploding, and the pain brought tears to his eyes.

He wasn't the only one affected. He saw Char-Kane groan and go down as if she had been coldcocked. Even the Eluoi of Catal's crew winced and started at the powerful sound. Professor Zaro gasped and quickly produced a handkerchief to mop his suddenly perspiring brow. He looked queasy but gritted his teeth and forced himself to swallow, then took a couple of deep breaths.

By that time Jackson had regained his equilibrium, shaking his head to clear away the lingering echoes of pain. He looked at Tezlac Catal's dark eyes again, saw modest amusement there, and grimaced at the memory of that agonizing spike in his ears.

"I take your point," he said dryly.

"Tezlac Catal is more than a lord," Zaro said, his voice shaking. "He is a true savant, one of the masters of the Eluoi. His powers are great, and not to be wasted in conversation with mere mortals."

"He is immortal, then?"

The professor shrugged. "He is already some six hundred years old by your star system's reckoning. And he is at the prime of his power now. He will outlive all of us by centuries."

*Maybe. Maybe not.* Jackson articulated the thought

bluntly, watching the savant for a reaction. But those almost-black eyes remained cold and expressionless.

"You said you took us prisoners because you're curious. Why are you curious about mere fleas?"

Tezlac Catal regarded Jackson coolly. Once again, the officer had the sense that his whole being had been laid open before this strange and admittedly frightening captor.

It was, as usual, Zaro who did the talking. "You humans have demonstrated a certain . . . vigor. When your system was abandoned ten thousand years ago, you were naked savages, beating each other with clubs and stones. And yet here you are now, sending out ships—pathetic little craft, it is true—of exploration to another planet in your system. There are those among my people who believe that you are worthy of study."

"You say we are vigorous? Do you want us to remain that way when you bring us to your planet? Or would it please you if we all perished, wasted away?"

"It is not an important concern to me, really. Why do you ask?"

"Because if you want us to survive—and I am guessing that you do—we'll need some more space. We need to keep physically active or we will atrophy and eventually die." Jackson lied boldly, keeping in mind that it was really more of an exaggeration. It was a strange and unsettling thing to wonder if the person he was talking to could actually perceive his inner thoughts, but he was becoming more and more confident that that wasn't the case.

"You wish us to give you a compartment simply for activity?" Professor Zaro asked in some surprise.

"Yes. It's important to us—and to you, if you intend to deliver us in our natural state."

"Tezlac Catal will consider your request. For now, you will return to your fellow humans."

"How long will we be traveling? Where are you taking us?" the lieutenant pressed.

"It is enough for you to know that we are moving quickly," Zaro said dismissively.

Tezlac Catal gestured to the viewing screen, which showed an image of space dominated by a single bright speck of light in the center of the image.

Zaro asked the question: "You see that bright star there?"

"Yes," the officer answered guardedly.

"That is your sun. It looks faint because we are already passing the orbit of the planet you call Jupiter. Soon we will be far enough from your system's sun to engage our interstellar drive. And then we will be gone, farther from your world than you have ever imagined. Look well, human, and watch it blink to nothingness. In another hour, it will simply be one more star in the galaxy of the sky."

# Eight: Through the Void

The captives from MS1—twelve SEALS, Director Parker, and Dr. Sulati—had started referring to themselves, inevitably, as the Earthlings. They had been left alone for the twenty-four hours or so since Jackson had been interviewed by Tezlac Catal. True to Catal's word, Jackson had watched the sun vanish, the whole vista of space turning dark as the ship accelerated far beyond the speed of light. Even so, the travel through the vastness of interstellar space had little effect on the sensations aboard the ship. They still felt as though they were under a pressure of about 1 G and had no sensation of either great movement or standing still.

Familiarizing themselves with their small prison, they had discovered a kitchen and galley attached to their wardroom and a head with toilet facilities and a shower in a small alcove at the other end of the room. The kitchen was furnished with a variety of dehydrated food that, while not gourmet quality, looked like it might possess the basic nutrients needed to keep them alive.

Now all fourteen Earthlings were conversing quietly in a corner of the barracks room that was their prison on this interstellar flight. They had gone over the walls, floor, and ceiling with careful scrutiny. Though they had not found any indications of surveillance equipment such as concealed cameras or microphones, they assumed that their captors were watching them. Nevertheless, they did have to talk, to discuss plans and options, and they settled for doing it in a tight huddle, speaking in whispers.

"If we can get the drop on a couple of these bastards

the next time they come down here for a parley, maybe we can take over the ship," Master Chief Ruiz suggested in a hoarse whisper.

Jackson shook his head. "I got a look at this place when they hauled me up to the bridge. It's the size of an aircraft carrier—think *Nimitz* class." He referred to a class of ship from the late twentieth century that had been replaced in recent decades by smaller aircraft carriers, but every one of the SEALS knew what he meant.

Ruiz shook his head in frustration. "Then what *are* we going to do, LT?"

"We're going to keep our eyes open and our wits sharp. For now, we're going to learn as much as we can."

"That outer door is sealed but good," LaRue said grimly. "Rocky and I worked on it for an hour and couldn't get the sucker to budge."

"There's not much to see in this room," Chief Harris said bitterly. "The ventilation ducts are all too narrow for anything bigger than a house cat even if we could pry off the grates. There's nothing useful in that little kitchenette they call a mess: plastic bowls and those flat paddles they use for spoons. And the only exit from the head is the water drain, and that has a valve in it."

Jackson nodded, not surprised. "I've requested another space, somewhere where we can exercise, from Catal. I stressed that we will atrophy quickly and that if he wants his people to study us, he needs to allow us to keep in shape."

The door to the barracks room whooshed open at that moment. Consul Char-Kane of the Shamani, flanked by a pair of Eluoi guards, entered. The guards remained outside, and the door closed behind her.

"So, you're up and about, I see," Jackson said sarcastically. He wasn't entirely sure he trusted her, especially since she seemed to have the run of the ship where she was supposedly a prisoner.

"I am up, yes. But what am I about?' she asked, puzzled.

"Never mind," the lieutenant replied. "What brings you down to our little corner of the ship?"

"The savant has agreed to your request for an exercise space," she announced. "He requested that I come here to inform you of that fact."

"Savant?" Dr. Sulati asked.

"That's the Tezlac Catal fellow I was telling you about," Jackson explained.

Char-Kane nodded. "It's a title of very high esteem among the Eluoi. They are a mystical people, given to superstition, much of it based on the legacy of their great prophet, who lived some five thousand years ago. The savants are his direct descendants, and they wield absolute power in Eluoi society."

"You seem quite friendly with him," Director Parker declared pointedly. The Bostonian had been growing increasingly restless and vocal as the hours had passed with no overt action taken against them. "We have been betrayed. Why should we accept anything you tell us?"

"My people have been betrayed, too," Char-Kane said with no outward sign of offense. "There were many Eluoi agents planted among the crew of this ship. A number of my people were killed when the ship was taken over. The rest are in captivity in another hold."

The MS1 director huffed. "I still don't see—"

"So Catal is willing to let us stretch out a bit?" Jackson interrupted.

"Yes. There is a large space down the corridor from this room. He has agreed that those three compartments can be opened to you, since he can easily seal off the transport shaft connecting this area to the rest of the ship. But it will give you room to move around, to, as you called it, 'stretch out.' "

"How long are we going to be traveling, and where are we going?" the LT wondered.

"I do not know our destination, though it will be one of the Eluoi worlds near this rim of the galaxy. We are in the void between the stars now, traveling far faster than light. At these speeds, intervals of travel can be minimized but not eliminated. A trip across the galaxy, for example, would still take something like one of your years. But Tezlac Catal is not taking us anywhere near that far, I am confident. In fact, I expect the voyage to last only perhaps three or four of your Terran days."

"Well, thanks for your efforts on our behalf," Jackson said. He still didn't entirely trust her, but neither did he have a choice. And the expansion of their prison, even by one compartment, was a tangible benefit.

"I will do what I can for you," she said. "Your people have treated me and mine with honor." Her red eyes flicked, just once, to Harris. "And, too, Chief saved my life in warfare."

Harris shrugged and looked down sheepishly, a reaction not unnoticed by the other SEALS.

"Can we see this workout room?" asked Master Chief Ruiz.

Char-Kane nodded and turned toward the door.

"Wait, one more thing," Jackson interrupted quietly. The consul turned back to him, her eyebrows raised in mute curiosity. "Are they listening to us in here? Watching us?"

She shrugged. "I cannot be certain, but I don't believe these compartments are equipped for that kind of spying."

"You said this is a Shamani ship, taken from you by the Eluoi?"

"That is the truth, yes."

"Then . . . what are the chances you could get us some deck plans, a schematic, or something that will show us how this thing is put together?"

Her eyes widened in surprise, a disconcerting effect as it emphasized their crimson redness. "That would be—"

She started to voice an objection but then halted and thought expressionlessly for a moment.

"I'll see what I can do," she said in a soft whisper.

The new compartment more than doubled the size of the space available to the Earthlings. It was a large, square chamber with white metallic bulkheads. Most of the floor space was open, though there were two benches mounted against the walls and a large metal table squarely fixed against the bulkhead opposite the electronically controlled sliding entry door. There were bulkheads around the skirt of the table so that it stood as a solid white cube.

Still, the extra space was useful, and the men wasted no time resuming a regimen of calisthenics and martial arts. Without exercise equipment, wrestling quickly became popular as the men developed a healthy sheen of sweat pitting their muscles against one another. By the second day Falco had invented a game, sort of a cross between soccer and dodgeball, that utilized two of the plastic bowls from the mess hall, weighted and fused together around the rim. The activity provided some escape from the depressing truth that they were being carried far from the star system where humans had been living throughout eternity and that they had no indication of whether, or how, they would ever see home again.

After an especially vigorous workout, the SEALS returned to the barracks compartment, except for Chief Harris and Falco, who announced that they were going to do some checking out in the exercise space.

It was after about fifty hours in space that Char-Kane returned. After making some small talk—no easy task for the formal, ritual-loving Shamani—she pressed a rolled object the size of a large cigar case into Jackson's hand and made her farewells. Together with Ensign Sanders and Master Chief Ruiz, the lieutenant took the mysterious gift into the exercise room, assigning Chief Harris to stay outside and watch the door.

He discovered that Char-Kane had given him a foil wrapper containing several very fine pages, each of which contained schematic drawings of the great starship in which they were being held.

They unrolled the pages, which were quite large, onto the table and began to study them. After a few minutes Jackson felt safe making a few assumptions.

"We're here," he said, indicating a small quadrant of compartments deep in the belly of the ship. "The transport shaft must run all the way to the bow, through these narrow booms that connect the large hull sections. Yep, that's the shaft where they took me to the bridge"—he traced the shaft to the nose end of the ship—"up here. And here are the shuttle bays, not far from us in the stern. Looks like they can carry four shuttles."

The SEALS looked up suddenly as a man cleared his throat in the door of the room. Director Parker stood there rather awkwardly. Master Chief Ruiz was beside him, looking sheepish.

"What is it?" Jackson asked, irritated at the interruption and the fact that if one of the Eluoi had come along, their possession of the schematics would have been discovered.

Ruiz nodded cheerfully. "I think you should hear what the man has to say, LT."

"Go on," Jackson declared coldly.

"It's just that—perhaps I can help," the director said with unusual diffidence. He nodded at the sheets on the table. "I guessed that was what the consul brought you. My background is aeronautical engineering; I did design work for the ISS and was a consultant as we adapted Shamani technology."

Jackson was surprised but immediately recognized the potential usefulness of his skills. "Have a look," he said, moving to the side to make room at the table.

"Hmmm . . . yes. Remarkable, really. You were right about the size. This ship is comparable to the great nuclear aircraft carriers of fifty years ago."

Jackson bit back a sarcastic reply and waited with mounting impatience.

"Yes, well, this would be the communications center," Parker said, indicating a hivelike nest of compartments in the very middle of the ship. "These are the external batteries. Looking at the connections, I would guess that they would be controlled from this deck, not far from the hangar bay."

"What kind of guns?" the officer asked.

"I would suspect a mixture of energy pulse and missile launchers. That has been typical of Shamani tech, though as you know, they have been reluctant to share ordnance technology with us."

"It's interesting, but what good is this going to do us?" Sanders asked.

"Perhaps you should call your master chief in here," Parker said. "He has made a potentially useful discovery."

Moments later Ruiz entered at Jackson's command. The chief was carrying one of the metallic paddles that served as eating utensils.

"Chief?" the lieutenant asked, letting the word hang in the air.

"Have a look at this, LT," Ruiz replied, unabashed. He crossed the compartment to the large table and knelt beside it. With a quick twist of his makeshift tool, he pulled out a white enamel screw. "I left two in place, you know, to anchor it. But Falco and I pulled them all out less than an hour ago. Derek, can you give me a hand?"

Falco went over to Ruiz, and the two men pulled on a corner of the solid-looking block. Amazingly, it pivoted away from the bulkhead on the one corner that was still screwed to the deck. Immediately the Earthlings felt a blast of fresh air and found themselves looking into a wide, dark passageway.

"When were you going to share this news, Chief?" Jackson asked, surprised and a little miffed.

"Right away, sir. That is, we were just fixing to tell you when Harris's girlfriend showed up with them plans."

While the chief shot him a dirty look, Ruiz grinned impishly, and Jackson couldn't help but chuckle. "Well," he said, pleased. "First we get a road map, and now it looks like you might have found us an on-ramp."

"Girlfriend, huh?" Harris whispered hoarsely. He and Ruiz were wedged into a tiny crawl space that seemed to connect all the compartments of the shuttle, prisoner, and storage decks. Sweat-streaked and exhausted, they paused to catch their breath, having being conducting their recon for about an hour now.

"Hey, we all saw the way she looked at you," Ruiz said with a chuckle. He mimicked her precise diction: " 'Chief saved my life in warfare.' "

"Well, I was just in the right place at the right time. She's got some nice curves, though," Harris admitted. "Anyway, she sure came through in the clutch."

"That," Ruiz couldn't help but agree, "she did."

They had memorized as much of the schematic as possible before starting out, since Jackson had deemed it too risky for the two chiefs to take the plans with them. Besides, they'd be able to explore only a small portion of the ship before they'd have to return. The LT had given them a two-hour window.

Although they hadn't found a way to get out of the ventilation systems—most of the grates were only about a hand span across—they had been able to look into many compartments. The shuttle bay was huge and currently occupied by two ships, including, presumably, the one that had lifted them off the surface of Mars. Two other docking berths were empty.

They located the control center for the ship's massive external batteries as well. A dozen Eluoi worked in that large compartment, watching screens and fiddling with massive and intricate controls. The humans studied the gunners silently but were unable to deduce how to control the weapons. But at least they knew where they were controlled from.

They also located the large barracks where some fifty prisoners were contained in more crowded conditions than those of the Earthlings. These were obviously the original Shamani crew of the ship, judging by their hair and eye color. They were a mix of males and females, and most seemed to sit about lethargically. Some of them appeared to be meditating, others sleeping. Conversation was minimal, and the males and females apparently had segregated themselves on either side of the large compartment, though there was no physical barrier between them.

The two snooping SEALS received a nasty start when a horn blared while they were observing the Shamani prisoners, but it proved to be just some sort of summons. They watched while half the captives filed slowly out the door. There was a smell of strong spices wafting through the compartment, and they eventually concluded that the horn simply might have been an announcement of mess time.

Nearby was another, more luxurious compartment just beyond the prisoners. Feeling a little bit like Peeping Toms, they watched Consul Char-Kane enter that room and deduced that those were her quarters. She began to peel off her tunic as the SEALS hastily moved on to the next observation.

Now they were making their way slowly back to their own compartment. After catching their breath and wiping off the sweat, they continued on. Master Chief Ruiz noticed with some surprise that their white clothes were staying very clean; the vast network of ducts seemed to hold very little dust.

Harris stopped at another grate and looked down into a dimly lit storage locker while Ruiz waited behind him.

"Psst!" the bosun's mate said urgently. "Master Chief, have a look!"

The master chief crawled forward and looked down with eyes already used to almost zero illumination. As a result, the satchels and uniforms, backpacks, guns, harnesses, and pressure suits secured in the racks of the storage locker were instantly recognizable as very welcome old friends.

And in that recognition he found renewed hope.

"We found our equipment, LT," Ruiz explained in a hoarse whisper. "It's on the same deck as this compartment!"

"Good work, Chief," Jackson replied. He listened intently as the two men, pointing out the details on the schematic of the ship, described their reconnaissance. They showed him where the control room for the ship's external batteries was, as well as the shuttle bays, the dormitory quarters where the Shamani prisoners were contained, and the other features they had discovered during their excursion.

The conference was interrupted, however, when Parker came in and announced, "Consul Char-Kane is outside. She said she needs to see you right away."

"Bring her in," the lieutenant said, and the director stood back to let the Shamani woman enter.

"What's up?" Jackson asked.

"Several things. We're nearing our destination, which is an Eluoi city on a world called Batuun. The savant intends to take you to the anthropology lab there for study."

"Not without a fight!" the lieutenant growled.

"Actually, there will be no fight if Tezlac Catal has his way. In about one hour he intends to have your compartments filled with disabling gas, the same gas that he used to knock you and your men out in the shuttle when you first arrived here. You will be trundled up like so many sacks of flour and borne down to the planet's surface."

Jackson felt a cold stab of fear. Gas! He hated the very thought. Momentarily he wondered if they could conceal all the Earthlings in the ventilation duct. But that seemed like an option with little chance of helping them in the long run.

"But you think there's something we can do about that, don't you?" It was Chief Harris, looking carefully at the woman.

She flushed, an unusual display of emotion for the aloof Shamani. "Yes." She extended her hand, and Jackson saw that she was clutching a number of tiny gauze pads. "These are emergency air filters. Put one in each of your nostrils and be careful to breathe only through your noses. There is a good chance that they will filter out enough of the gas to leave you conscious."

"A good chance?" Ruiz demanded. "And if they don't work?"

Char-Kane drew herself up, her demeanor again haughty. "This is all I can do for you. I have already risked much on your behalf."

"Yes, and thank you," Jackson said gratefully, flashing Ruiz a warning look.

"I must go," she said. "The danger will begin when the ship enters orbit around Batuun. You will know when that is because when deceleration is completed, our condition will once again be weightless. I wish you luck." She turned toward the door.

"Wait. Thanks," Jackson said, studying her. She merely nodded and departed quickly.

Jackson wasted no time handing out the filters. His mind was churning, coming up with and discarding plans by the dozen. What could they hope to do? He wasn't sure, but finally he *had* some hope. If their captors came to collect them, assuming that all the SEALS were disabled or unconscious, they could at least give the Eluoi a very nasty surprise.

He whispered terse instructions to each of the SEALS, who nodded in grim understanding. Each would do his part, Jackson knew. He suggested to Parker and Dr. Sulati that they try to stay out of the way, assigning them the two bunks farthest from the door.

The Earthlings made their preparations and lay in their bunks. Within another thirty minutes they felt the powerful engines shut down, and immediately a condition of weightlessness pervaded the ship. Each of the humans collapsed on his or her mattress, held down by the weight of a top sheet, feigning unconsciousness. Breathing slowly through his nostrils, his mouth tightly closed, Jackson couldn't tell if there was any gas in the room. But he wasn't about to take any chances.

The minutes ticked by interminably, but none of the Earthlings moved. Jackson had to suppress a start of surprise when the door to the room whisked open. Through narrowed eyelids, he saw four burly Eluoi enter the room, pulling themselves along the wall handles in their weightless state. Two others remained outside the door. All six of the visitors were wearing breathing filters over their mouths and noses. Only the two outside the door were armed with the machine pistol and backpack combinations they had observed earlier. The weapons were slung casually as the guards stood back from the door. Clearly, they were not expecting any resistance.

Jackson and LaRue were in the bunks closest to the door, with the two chiefs just beyond. The four orderlies approached, hoisting each of the first four SEALS by an arm. Jackson allowed himself to drift along, still apparently unconscious. Floating weightlessly, he felt himself being tugged through the door. Timing the moment precisely, he opened his eyes just as he was pulled past one of the armed escorts.

He kicked his feet hard into the solar plexus of the orderly who was moving him, driving the air from the fellow's lungs with the powerful blow and using the momentum of the kick to drive him directly into the face of the startled guard. Before the Eluoi could raise his gun, the apparently helpless patient ripped the mask from the guard's face and then grappled with the man, preventing him from raising his weapon until the gas had done its work.

Immensely grateful for all those hours of hand-to-hand weightless combat training in the ISS and SATSTAR1, Jackson saw immediately and without surprise that LaRue had remembered that training as well: The second armed guard floated unconscious like the first.

The four unarmed orderlies were being overcome by the rest of the Team. The men pulled the masks off their captives and watched as the four Eluoi almost immediately collapsed.

Jackson and Ruiz first donned the guards' masks, then armed themselves with their mysterious guns. Each included a heavy backpack—presumably a battery—connected by thick wires to the "firearm" device. Harris went to check, reporting that the hatch to their compartment was open. The orderlies presumably had intended to pull them right on through and into the shuttle bay.

"What's the plan, LT?" Ruiz asked.

"First, take us to our gear!"

Soon they were outside the storage locker where the two chiefs had spotted the equipment. When the door proved to be locked, Jackson had the others get back and unleashed a burst from his weapon. The fire turned out to be some kind of energy ray with zero recoil and the cutting power of a plasma torch. In seconds, he had burned away the lock, and the SEALS rushed inside, gathering their gear.

"Ruiz, Teal," Jackson said. "Take a block of C-6 and find that control center for the ship's gun batteries. You said it was around here, right?"

Master Chief Ruiz nodded. "Timing on the charge, LT?"

"Give it fifteen minutes. And then meet us at the shuttle bay. Harris, you come with me, show me where those Shamani were locked up."

In few more minutes, Jackson had burned through another door. He entered Consul Char-Kane's chambers to her wide-eyed surprise. "We're getting out of here. Come with us?"

For a moment she hesitated, then nodded.

"And what about the rest of the Shamani?" Jackson asked. "Will they make a run for it?"

"No, they will wait for orders from a commandant."

"I need at least one of them—one who can fly a shuttle."

Char-Kane blinked. "I can fly a shuttle," she declared.

"All right. Let's go."

The Shamani woman moved with remarkable speed, joining the Earthlings as they hastened to the transport shaft and quickly took it two decks down to the hangar bay. They passed many busy Eluoi crewmen, but though Jackson had his finger ready on the trigger, none of them seemed to take any notice of the unusual party.

"Why are they ignoring us?" he whispered to Char-Kane when the last of the alien crew members had passed. "Not that I'm complaining," he hastened to add.

"Theirs is a rigid society, and these men come from the lowest levels of that culture. The deference for others—their betters and those they do not recognize as their equals or inferiors—is ingrained. It would be as if you were to stop and ask an admiral or your president why he is walking in a particular place."

He nodded, amazed but relieved. Entering the hangar, they found themselves in a glass-enclosed booth with several air locks leading to long passages, not unlike airport jetways, that led to the four shuttle bays. Two of the bays were empty, but the other two were connected by the flexible tubes to the booth where the SEALS had entered.

The SEALS could observe teeming activity in the great compartment. The outer hangar doors were slowly opening on the first bay, indicating that the air already had been expelled from the hangar itself.

The air lock leading to the first shuttle opened, and an Eluoi officer emerged. "What are you doing here?" he demand in that bizarre, hissing language, automatically translated by the device Jackson still had in his ear. The lieutenant replied with his heat gun, a single burst that instantly silenced the fellow.

"Go, go!" he barked, and the Earthlings and the Shamani woman floated through the air lock.

"Disable the other shuttle," Jackson ordered, and LaRue and Falco went to plant charges on the air locks. It was not enough to blow up the ship, but breaching the hatches certainly would render the shuttle unusable for a while.

Jackson followed through the first air lock onto the flight deck of the shuttle to find that Consul de Campe Char-Kane already had settled herself in the pilot's seat.

Finally Ruiz and Harry Teal came floating down the causeway, pulling themselves along at high speed. As soon as they were in the shuttle, Jackson closed the hatch, and Char-Kane pulled the release lever. Immediately the ship broke free, propelled by compressed air right out through the hangar doors. They tumbled into orbit, suspended very close to the utterly massive ship just above them.

Char-Kane flipped some switches, and the shuttle's rocket engines fired immediately.

"We're away!" she called. "Are you sure you disabled those batteries?"

Ruiz looked at his watch. "Give it another twenty seconds," he said tersely.

"We don't have twenty seconds!" she cried as the little rocket ship tumbled farther from the belly of the great ship. Char-Kane applied a surge of power to the rockets, and the shuttle raced away from the massive vessel.

Jackson was at the copilot's porthole. He could see the massive barrels of the EMP cannon start to swivel, moving to track the shuttle as it tumbled toward a very green-looking world. An electromagnetic blast would disable all the shuttle's controls, he knew: They would tumble to the planet as violently as a meteor and probably burn up on the way down just as thoroughly.

"Four, three, two, one," Ruiz was counting down as the barrel almost drew even with the shuttle.

There was neither sight nor sound of the blast occurring somewhere in the guts of the great spaceship. But something must have happened, because the gun stopped tracking. The shuttle sped freely into the unknown and alien atmosphere of Batuun.

# Nine: A World of Trees

"What about ground defenses?" Ensign Sanders asked, perhaps a little belatedly, as the shuttle bumped and rocked through the Batuunian atmosphere, descending steadily and blasting along at thousands of kilometers per hour. "Will they try to shoot us out of the sky?"

"In a word, yes," Consul Char-Kane said tersely. "That is why I am trying to lose altitude as quickly as possible. The horizon is our best line of defense from their batteries."

She was guiding the shuttle with both hands on a control stick, with the ensign and Lieutenant Jackson occupying the two other seats in the cockpit. There was a bewildering array of dials, levers, switches, and controls before them, and the two humans had been instructed to "touch nothing." It was advice they willingly accepted.

The world below them seemed to be a place of vast green lands surrounding small serpentine seas, and those seas had an emerald cast that was clearly alien in contrast to Earth's blue oceans. Wisps of cloud stretched over both land and water, but they were thin and vaporous in appearance; none suggested even a modest low-pressure front, much less a cyclone or another great storm.

True to Char-Kane's intention, the ground was coming up fast. The shuttle shook violently, and though the four rockets were thrusting steadily, they seemed to be falling fast. There were no wings to provide lift in the atmosphere, and Jackson wondered if they would, in fact, burn themselves up to avoid getting shot.

"Hey, LT, have a look at this." Sanders indicated a viewscreen to starboard, just below the cockpit window.

The picture showed an image that matched the green horizon, only in much greater detail. With a sidelong glance at the pilot, who was totally focused on the controls, the ensign worked a small knob just below the screen, and the image zoomed into an even more detailed picture.

"That's some kind of city," Jackson guessed as he studied the gleaming metallic whiteness that showed on the screen. Domes and spires and walls came into view, and when he looked out the window, he saw in the distance the same alabaster locale that was being magnified on the screen.

"Yeah, it's huge," Sanders agreed. "Maybe the size of New England."

Jackson could only nod. The sprawling center covered a stunningly wide swath of the planetary surface. Everywhere else, there was just that wide, vast green.

And it was still coming up fast.

Finally, Char-Kane reached out and twisted a knob. Immediately the rumbling of the rocket engines exploded into a thunderous roar. The passengers were pressed hard into their seats as their plummeting descent slowed dramatically, just about the time the white city slipped past the horizon and out of sight.

"Your charge must have neutralized the ship's batteries," the consul said approvingly. "Or else we would all be dead by now."

"What about that city? Do you think they'd be shooting at us if they could?" Jackson asked.

"No doubt. The Eluoi worlds typically have at least one PDB."

"What's a PDB?"

"I'm sorry: planetary defense battery. It is an installation in a single tower, several kilometers high typically, and can fire an EMP weapon or a plasma ray that can strike a target in space. They are lethal even to large ships, not to mention a small shuttle like this."

"Good thing you got us below the horizon, then," Jackson acknowledged.

Char-Kane nodded, though her eyes never left the viewscreen in front of her. "Yes. We are safe for the time being."

"Okay, what now, then?"

"We need to find a place to land." Char-Kane flipped some switches, and more view screens flashed pictures. Magnification of the view underneath the shuttle seemed to indicate trees and more trees. They were still dropping fast, but the woman seemed to be in control of the shuttle; they were making some lateral movement, easing along far above the forest, still under control.

"Do you see a clearing, anything that looks like it could be a landing zone?" asked Jackson, growing tenser by the second.

"No. And we are running out of fuel quickly. They were apparently planning a direct descent toward the city that we saw; the Eluoi did not load a lot of fuel onto this shuttle."

"Keep looking," Jackson encouraged, but she shook her head.

"We are going to have to land at once," she said. "In minutes we will be out of fuel, and that would be fatal."

"Take her down, then," the lieutenant said. "And hold on!"

The canopy of greenery became more detailed so that they could see individual trees, some of them very tall, most of them merging together in a leafy blanket. The shuttle descended slowly, right into the tops of the trees. Branches splintered around them, and the little vehicle lurched sideways. There followed a loud crash.

And then silence.

"No fires!" Jackson barked. "We're getting away from the crash site—pronto!"

Director Parker, who had removed his cigar lighter and was about to touch it to a pile of tinder he had gathered painstakingly, looked ready to object. Something in the lieutenant's eye changed his mind, and he shrugged and put the silver rectangle back into his pocket.

Already the SEALS had removed their gear and as much other equipment as they could salvage from the shuttle. The little rocket craft had come to rest between two massive trees, and though it was canted at an angle, the hatch had been able to descend to the ground. They had all gotten out quickly.

"Do you think they'll come looking for us?" Dr. Sulati asked.

"*Someone* will; you can count on that," Jackson replied.

"What do we take with us, LT?" asked G-Man. He was inspecting his rail gun and already had slung two pouches of the heavy copper shells and counterblast charges from his shoulders. On his back was a double-up set of capacitors to fire the ammunition he was carrying for the big weapon. The load was huge, but it was ammunition, the one thing the SEALS would never leave behind.

Jackson had been thinking about that. He already had consulted a meter and confirmed that the Batuunian air was breathable, very comparable to Earth's. "We leave the pressure suits, the air bottles. Bury them nearby. Bring all the weapons and ammo we can lift. Give the civilians all the rations and water they can carry. But do it fast."

Doctor Sulati's scream shot through the crash site. The lieutenant spun around to see her stumbling back from a black vine and caught her just before she fell. At the same time, he realized that the vine was moving, whipping itself around into an S shape at the end of which was a very ugly reptilian head.

Ruiz reacted instantly, his combat knife out and driving down in a single smooth motion, pinning the head of the snake to the tree behind it. The serpentine reptile thrashed for a moment, whipping around a body that was at least four meters long. Pulling back his knife, the master chief slashed again, and the head flopped free of the still-thrashing body. The mouth gaped, and a pair of ugly curved fangs gleamed menacingly from the widespread jaws.

"And, uh, let's watch our step, people," Jackson said calmly. His hands were on Sulati's shoulders, and he could feel her trembling, but he was impressed when she drew a deep breath and stood on her own.

"Thank you," she said to Ruiz.

"No problem, ma'am," the chief replied with an easy grin. He wiped the blade on some leafy ferns before sliding it back into the sheath on his thigh.

"Where are we headed, sir?" asked Ensign Sanders, settling a heavy pack on his shoulders. He carried his assault rifle in one hand while he checked a compass with the other.

"Only one place makes sense," Jackson said, stopping to think about it. "This whole planet looked like a wilderness from up there except for that huge installation we spotted. It's somewhere over the northeast horizon. I guess we'd better head in that direction and see what we can make of it."

"How far do you think it is?" Dr. Sulati asked hesitantly.

No point in sugarcoating it, Jackson decided. He spoke bluntly.

"If that city was New England, then I'd guess we came down somewhere in Ohio. That means that we've got a long walk in front of us."

The unrelenting jungle covered them with an upper canopy of foliage, blocking any view of the sky except for an occasional gap where a beam of hot sunlight spilled all the way down to the sTeaming, fern-shrouded floor. Fortunately, the underbrush was not terribly thick.

The SEALS moved in standard file, Chief Harris starting out at the point, followed by Falco and then Jackson. Parker, Consul Char-Kane, and Dr. Sulati walked as a group in the middle of the column; G-Man and Chief Ruiz brought up the rear.

Jackson noticed suddenly that the forest in front of them was growing much brighter. Harris crouched down at a screen of daylight and peered through a dense frond as Jackson silently moved up to join him. A quick glance at his watch showed that they'd left the crash site about ninety minutes earlier.

"That's the biggest goddamn marsh I ever saw," the chief said in disgust.

Jackson had to agree. There were wide swaths of open water surrounded by reedy plants. The whole place had a fetid air, and he saw some insects that looked to be the size of small birds buzzing low over the muck.

"I guess we'd better try to go around it, Chief," he said. Jackson squinted into the distance. To the right, the flat swamp seemed to extend all the way to the horizon, with no promise of any resumption of the trees. To the left, the fringe of forest seemed to extend outward and onward; that pretty much made the decision for him.

"Harry, can you make like a monkey and climb one of these trees for a look-see?" Jackson asked the nimble corpsman.

"I thought you'd never ask, LT," Teal replied with a grin. Shucking off his pack, he handed his weapon to Chief Harris and selected one of the tallest trees. The trunk was bigger around than a man's waist, and though the bark was rough, there were no branches for the first fifteen meters straight up from the ground. The corpsman wrapped his belt around the bole and leaned back for leverage, bracing his feet against the rough surface. In a matter of moments he had scrambled up to the first of the limbs, and from there he pulled himself easily upward.

The foliage was so thick that he vanished from sight on the ground, leaving the rest of the SEALS to wait around uneasily for several minutes.

Finally he dropped back into sight, retrieving his belt from where he had left it on the lowest branch. He dropped down to the ground in a swift plummet, bouncing easily. But the grim shake of his head belied the apparent ease of his climb.

"We got grass and patches of water as far as I could see," he reported. "It looks like the edge might curve around to the left. To the right, it might just go on forever."

"To the left it is, people," Jackson said immediately. "Let's move out."

Harris continued to lead, with the file of castaways staying just within the shade of the overhanging trees, close enough so that they could get frequent looks at the open water and the flats of reedy muck. For another hour they kept moving. It was hard to tell if they were actually following a curve of shoreline or if the marsh was just a vast blob of impassable terrain. Remembering his Ohio-- to–New England comparison, Jackson shuddered at the thought that this barrier might be the size of Lake Erie.

Nor did it seem that the sunset was going to come along any time soon to help them figure out which way was west. After three hours on Batuun, the sun seemed as high in the sky as it had been when they had landed. Jackson was forced to accept the realization that the days on this planet could be much, much longer than the neat twenty-four-hour intervals they had grown up with on Earth.

He was lost in those gloomy thoughts when he heard a loud splash like something very large moving through the water. The sound was followed by an even louder "Holy shit!" in Falco's voice.

Jackson spun to see a whole slew of green water rising into the air, flowing away from a platform of some kind, about 100 meters from shore. It looked like a submarine was rising out of the muck, flat and broad and long, lacking only a sail to resemble a sleek undersea craft.

Until it opened its mouth.

Jackson's mind seemed to trip over itself as he saw a gaping maw filled with rows of massive fangs, teeth that looked to be nearly a meter long in the front of the mouth. The monster shook itself, and stinking water sprayed, some of it splashing into the fringe of forest where the castaways were trudging.

Then the beast roared, and it was a volume of sound that struck them like a physical attack. The lieutenant actually felt himself stagger backward under the onslaught of noise.

"Give me a break!" Falco cursed. "Not a fucking *dinosaur*?"

If not, it certainly would have been at home in the Triassic. With a furious shiver, it threw off more of the muck, and the SEALS could make out a studded back with jutting ridges of bony plate. A great tail, ten meters long, thrashed through the brackish water while the monster held itself on four massive legs. A stench of rot and musk filled the air, almost gagging them as gases were released from the bed of the marsh, and vile breath spewed from the monster's lungs.

And it was coming for them! Those horrible jaws gaped as it moved forward, not fast but with implacable determination, churning up a wave of brown water two meters high. Shots ripped out from the line of SEALS, but the rounds seemed to have no effect as the monster charged from the marsh, shouldering between a pair of massive trees and knocking both of them down as if they were matchsticks.

"Run!" Jackson shouted to the three civilians, unnecessarily, it turned out, as Parker and Char-Kane were stumbling away. Doctor Sulati had started to flee also, but she tripped on a vine and sprawled headlong as the looming horror approached.

Ruiz and Harry Teal were blasting away, aiming for the creature's head, with no apparent effect. G-Man launched a round from his rail gun, the hypervelocity slug tearing through the great maw and passing out the other side without giving it any pause. Rocky Rodale could see that the mountain of angry flesh was already too close for him to use his M76 Wasp on it. The warhead wouldn't have time to arm itself before it struck, and the creature was getting closer every moment. How could something so big move so fast?

The beast came closer as if drawn by the curtain of fire. Falco helped Dr. Sulati up and pulled her deeper into the forest. Someone threw a grenade that went off like a firecracker against the monster's skin but only made it snap to the side in annoyance.

"Fall back!" the lieutenant shouted, wondering what in the world—what in the whole goddamn universe!—they were going to be able to do to stop this thing.

G-Man could see that his first round hadn't hit anything vital, but it had penetrated deeply into the creature before punching out the far side. All he had to do was find a vital area. But how the hell could he find a vital area in something the size of a space shuttle? Still, he knew his weapon could be effective in more ways than one.

Running to the side, G-Man hoped that whatever the damned thing used for eyes wasn't able to see him or was concentrating on the running figures in front of it. The lumbering body started to pass only meters away from G-Man as he quickly unscrewed the cylindrical hollow muzzle cap that protected the rails that made up Baby's barrel. The big rail gun was powered by the capacitor bank that G-Man carried like a backpack. A heavy quick-release cable connected the weapon to the capacitors. Unlocking the firing handle with his thumb, G-Man twisted the grip to push the velocity of the weapon to its maximum, a velocity normally reserved for times when the gun was being used in a mounted position, not handheld. The rail gun used electric power to create the magnetic field that drove the projectiles out of the barrel at such an incredible velocity. Now he was going to use that power for something in addition to pushing out a copper and uranium slug.

All his actions took less than a few seconds to complete once he had made the decision to act. While the front third of the massive body slithered past him, G-Man ran up to the monster and shoved the muzzle of the rail gun hard against the glistening wet flesh. It was smooth and shiny, more like a salamander than a scaly lizard or snake. Knowing that the inertia dampeners surrounding the barrel wouldn't help with the tremendous recoil of the gun when it was pushed up against a target, G-Man gritted his teeth and pulled the trigger, hoping Baby's barrel wouldn't burst from the obstruction he was pushing it against.

The backblast charge went off with a roar, but that sound was almost drowned out by the whistling scream that came from the throat of the great beast as the rail gun fired. The copper and uranium slug left the muzzle of the weapon at more than 2,500 meters a second, punching through the flesh of the beast as easily as if it were passing through the air. The shock wave from the hypervelocity projectile blew into the giant creature, almost liquefying the flesh as it passed through. And the heavy pulse of electric current that drove the projectile to such high velocities, speeds that couldn't be reached with any other type of gun, cut into the damaged tissue, shocking the internal organs of the beast as it fried and burned the flesh.

As the copper and uranium projectile burst out the other side of the great mountain of muscle and bad attitude, it was followed by a huge gout of flesh, blood, and streaming tissue from internal organs. The power of the shot actually flipped the monster over on its side as it twitched and thrashed. It would take some time with something that big before every part of its body got the message that it was dead.

The SEALS and the others stood and stared for a moment as they saw the rippling movement of what looked like wide vanes or scales along the bottom of the great creature. The rippling slowed and stopped over the next few minutes as the rest of the cells in the huge body found out that they weren't working anymore.

Nearly ten feet back from where he had pulled the trigger, G-Man lay on his back where the recoil had tossed him. His arms ached from the strain and beating they had taken, but he had had the presence of mind to cradle his weapon and protect it from the impact even as he had flown through the air. Baby looked to be unharmed but was covered in goo where the long weapon lay across the big SEALS' chest.

Harry Teal, the corpsman of the group, got to G-Man before the big man had recovered enough to sit up.

"Hold still, you idiot," Teal growled as he quickly started checking the other man over. "You're lucky to be alive. Jesus Christ! What the hell were you thinking, anyway?"

"I'm fine," G-Man growled. "Just get me to my feet." He grasped weakly for the corpsman's shoulder, but Teal batted his hand away and continued probing LaRue's chest and shoulders, looking for broken bones.

"You stay down, sailor, until the corpsman says you can get up," Master Chief Ruiz said in a tone that allowed for no argument. "How does it look, Harry?"

"He's intact, I guess. Maybe the doc can look him over, too."

After a brief examination, Dr. Saluti looked up in disbelief. "Being airborne and blasted away from contact with that beast must've spared you the worst of the electrical discharge. You're lucky to be alive, Mr. LaRue."

"So, G-Man, are you done showing off for a while?" Falco said as he joined the huddle around the flattened SEALS.

"Yeah," LaRue admitted, grimacing, still lying on his back. "At least until the next one of those sons of bitches comes along. Anybody seen Baby's muzzle cap?"

# Ten: Ambush Applied

"Looks like meat to me," Chief Harris said as he appraised the corpse of the giant creature.

Doctor Sulati and Harry Teal had dragged LaRue to his feet and were helping the big man move away from the swamp. Jackson had suggested that they find some sort of small clearing to make camp, but he wanted it well removed from there in case the huge mound of flesh drew unpleasant scavengers.

"Well, let's cut a few prime steaks out of there and haul them over to camp, then," Jackson decided. Ruiz, Harris, Robinson, and Sanchez set to work as butchers, and the LT found Ensign Sanders and sent him to supervise the setting up of camp.

In a half hour, the castaways assembled on a small grassy patch of ground surrounded by giant trees. Since they had moved well away from the body of the giant creature that G-Man had killed, Jackson finally relented about lighting a fire. They had only limited rations with them, and survival training had taught all the SEALS not to waste a potential food source when they didn't know where the next one might be.

Sanders kindled a carefully prepared fire, and soon the aroma of sizzling steaks—filet of dinosaur, Falco described them—wafted through the campsite in the small opening among the tall trees. The sun still had shown no sign of moving toward any horizon, but the castaways needed rest, and they couldn't pass up this chance to take advantage of some fresh food.

The lieutenant had made it clear that they'd be moving

out again very soon, but for now all of them were enjoying the remarkably savory and tender cuts of meat.

"You can almost forget it came from a giant lizard," Dr. Sulati said, wrinkling her nose. *"Almost."*

*"Garcon!* I'd like mine medium rare next time," LaRue said. "I think my salad was a little warm. And what vintage did you say this swamp water was?"

"At least it doesn't taste anything like chicken," Rocky piped up as he chewed a big mouthful of meat.

"Actually, I hate to say it, but it tastes a lot like lobster," Dr. Sulati said reluctantly.

"Pass the drawn butter," LaRue quipped. The big man was in pain, but he refused to show anything but a bit of stiffness in his movements.

The doctor had worked with the SEALS corpsman, and both had been pleased to pronounce that nothing was broken in the G-Man; he was just beat up a lot and a little singed around the edges. For now, LaRue was basking in the glory of his kill. "The largest damn big-game trophy in the whole history of the human race, and that includes woolly mammoths!" he'd boasted.

For a few minutes at least, the castaways were simply comfortable, well fed for the first time since leaving Mars. Still, there was an undercurrent of tension and fear of the unknown lurking in everyone's mind: an unknown journey, an unknown destination, and an almost completely unknown world that would be their home, or their prison, for the foreseeable future.

"What's that?" Ensign Sanders said suddenly, holding up his hand. "Listen!"

They heard it clearly and growing louder: the sound of jet- or rocket-powered aircraft approaching.

"Douse the fire!" Jackson snapped. Master Chief Ruiz was already on it, carefully pouring a pot of swamp water on the smoldering blaze. The coals immediately vanished, sTeaming momentarily as they went out.

Meanwhile, each SEALS reached for his weapon, and they trained their barrels on the sky. They were a hundred meters from the edge of the swamp, in an area completely covered by trees, but every man was ready to shoot as the roaring of the aircraft drew closer, finally thundering almost directly overhead. Rocky had dropped his steak into the dirt and was holding his M76 Wasp missile launcher up and ready to fire.

Only gradually did Jackson relax as the sounds roared past and faded quickly.

"They're going to check out the crash site," the lieutenant concluded immediately, calculating the direction of the flight. "Three, maybe four machines," he speculated.

"Permission to climb another one of these trees, LT?" Harry Teal asked. "Maybe I can get a look at them."

"Good idea," Jackson agreed with a nod.

The corpsman found a sturdy trunk, one of the thickest, which seemed to suggest a crown that might be higher than the surrounding forest, and started up. In a few minutes he disappeared from the view of those on the ground. Jackson paced around, looking up worriedly, listening for any sounds. He heard the roaring of the jet aircraft in the distance and guessed that they were circling the crash site. With a grimace of concern, he heard the noise increasing in volume, as if the planes were coming back their way.

The roar approached to within a few kilometers, then swelled in volume but not in proximity. It was as if the pilot were powering his engines to extreme velocity but staying in one place.

The *whoomp* of sound penetrated to the forest floor as a powerful, crumping explosion. More than noise, it was a shudder in the planet that carried through the ground, causing it to shake tangibly underfoot. The sounds of the aircraft engine came loudly again, reaching a punishing crescendo before winding down. With a slowing whine, the machinery came to a stop, leaving the forest in silence again.

"What the hell kind of bomb was that?" Falco asked.

"I don't think it was a bomb," Jackson said. "Maybe some kind of sonic weapon. I'm guessing they used it to smash a flat place in the jungle so they could land the aircraft—VTOL."

Vertical takeoff and landing aircraft had been common on Earth for a hundred years, beginning with the helicopters that had performed such valuable service in the Korean War. But the thought of a jet that could fly at the speeds these aircraft had attained and then flatten a landing zone for itself was a little shocking.

They all looked up as Harry Teal came sliding down the tree, dropping the last few meters to the ground.

"Seems like we got visitors, LT," he reported grimly. "Those things looked more like flying buses than airplanes—big engines, stubby little wings. There were two of them that stopped not too far away. One of 'em blasted something into the trees—I'm sure you heard the noise—and then they all settled down."

"Damn. They might have put some troops on our trail. How big did you say they were—like buses? What did they look like?"

"Well . . ." Teal shrugged. "Best guess is that each one could have ten or twelve men aboard. They had lots of windows along the body and a flight deck up front. One of 'em banked as it went past, and I got a glimpse of a dorsal turret, low, with a single-barreled weapon sticking out. They're basically white with some marks on the side. They had a big green spot, kind of like a bull's-eye, painted on the fuselage."

"All right," Jackson said, thinking, planning, considering options. "We could keep running, but I don't like our chances. Best guess is that they're on to our trail and that they'll come looking for us."

The LT spoke to Char-Kane. "Are you familiar with these vehicles—I don't know if you'd call them jetcars or what—that Harry is talking about?"

"I believe so," she said. "They are not an uncommon transport craft for both military and civilian purposes. Of course, they require more fuel and entail more risk than ground transport, but they are fast and can carry a remarkably heavy load."

"You did a pretty nifty job bringing that shuttle in. Any chance you could fly one of these aircraft?"

"It's quite likely," she replied with no trace of arrogance. "The Eluoi and Shamani have a great deal of technology in common. Chances are it would be like a human driving a motor vehicle on your own world. Even if you had never operated that model of vehicle, you could still discern how to control it."

"Yeah, okay," Jackson said. "We have to consider that possibility if we don't want to walk through a thousand miles of monster-infested jungle."

"Makes sense," Ensign Sanders agreed. "What do you suggest?"

"I think we arrange a little reception for them, somewhere they won't be expecting to find us. If it works out well, we might even be able to steal one of those buses and make up a little travel time."

Consul Char-Kane, Director Parker, and Dr. Sulati would wait for the SEALS a few hundred meters away from the place where they had been cooking. Jackson told them that this would be the rally point, and if his men had to break contact with the enemy, they would all meet there. Intelligence was what the SEALS officer wanted right now: information about the enemy, how many of them there were, how they were armed, what their communications were, just where exactly their transport was, and how it was secured.

His best chance to find out anything before taking action involved breaking up his forces, something any leader is always reluctant to do. But there wasn't any other choice. He would send a small detachment to gather information and deploy the bulk of his men to react to developing events.

The best point men also made the best scouts. Any information Jackson could get on the enemy right now would be more valuable to him than any weapon could be. His men knew this, and Sanchez and Marannis were prepared to move out along the Team's back trail. After a quick briefing with the LT, the two men disappeared into the jungle. While they were gone, Jackson wasn't going to waste one minute.

"All right," he said quietly, addressing the rest of the SEALS as they huddled around him. "No comlinks—no electronics of any kind—because we don't know what kind of scanners they have. Hand signals, no unnecessary talking. Let's move out."

The rest of the Team headed onto the back trail on the double, ready to give the Eluoi searchers a very hot reception. The SEALS clearly relished the prospect of action; they moved in utter silence but with a grim sense of purpose that boded much danger for any enemy they encountered. They moved with almost complete silence; even when jogging, each man placed his feet carefully. In what was second nature to them, the clips and grenades, packs, and canteens that they wore were suspended so carefully that nothing jingled or bounced.

For more than eighty years in the SEAL Teams, these men of action had studied the art and science of the ambush. It was one of the first combat tactics their forefathers had used in the jungles and swamps of Southeast Asia. Every man in the Teams learned how to prepare an ambush, lay it out, and conduct it, along with how to break one. Jackson's men were no less skilled than any of those SEALS of the last century. Their jungle might be on another planet, but the rules of the ambush hadn't changed across the light-years.

Jackson's last orders to Sanchez and Marannis were that if they were being pursued, they should bring the enemy forces up along the pathway the men had already followed through the jungle. There was a slight rise that looked back along what must have been some kind of animal trail, and that was the point where the SEALS would set up an L-shaped ambush.

At the top of the rise, Jackson and Chief Harris would establish the short leg of the L. Along the left side of the path the rest of the SEALS would be strung out. While the rest of the men got into position and established their fields of fire across the path, Jackson spoke quietly to Ensign Sanders.

"Dennis," Jackson said," I want you to be prepared to take the master chief, Dobson, and Robinson back along the trail to follow any of these aliens if they decide to pull back. The rest of the platoon will engage and pursue if necessary, but you and your men hold your fire."

"What's your plan?" Sanders asked. There wasn't any question in his mind that he would follow orders, but it was obvious to him that Jackson had something in mind.

"I want you and your men to be prepared to seize one of those landing craft we saw," Jackson said quietly. "If we can, we're going to conduct a suppressed ambush, take out as many as we can without resorting to the mines. It's going to be hard as hell for us to get through the jungle on our own. We're never going to make it if we have to drag all these civilians along with us. They are getting beat to hell right now. One or both of those transports we saw could be our ticket out of here, maybe even to a ship that will get us the hell off this planet and back to Earth. Char-Kane feels she could operate one of those craft. But we have to take control of it first."

It was a desperate gamble to try to take over an enemy craft from an unknown number of hostiles, but Sanders could see how it could be their best shot at surviving. He could see now why Jackson was setting up for an ambush and why he had sent the scouts back to learn about the enemy deployment. If the ambush worked, it could take down a large number of the enemy before they could react.

"Aye, aye, sir," Sanders said simply.

While the officers talked, the two demolition experts, Chief Harris and Harry Teal, were laying out a serious surprise for any aliens who were unlucky enough to move into the killing zone of the ambush.

Although there were a few giant hardwoods such as the one Teal had climbed for his look-see, most of the tall, thin plants that passed for trees in this jungle were about fifty centimeters thick at their spongy bases. While Chief Harris walked along the side of the trail, being very careful not to leave any marks to show his passage, he uncoiled behind him a thin, dark line. Teal was kneeling at the base of some of the trees Harris had already passed and was working with a C-6 explosive block he had removed from his pack.

Tearing open the package of explosive, Teal separated the block into six long, wide wafers. Pulling open another package, he laid out what looked to be dull cloth strips the same size as the blocks of explosive and nearly as thick. Stripping off a protective film on one side of the cloth strip, he used the exposed adhesive to stick the strip to the wafer of explosive. Another adhesive strip on the back of the assembly allowed him to stick the whole thing against one of the "tree" trunks. He carefully adjusted the location of the strip, making sure it faced exactly where he wanted it to, then connected it to the line Chief Harris had laid out.

With one tree prepped, Teal moved on to the next one

after carefully concealing his work behind mulch and junk he scraped off the jungle floor. When the two SEALS were done, there was a string of nearly a dozen of the odd assemblies facing along the trail that had become the killing zone of the ambush.

The rest of the men had laid out their weapons and concealed their positions in less time than it took Chief Harris and Teal to complete their work. At the far end of the ambush, Falco lay concealed with his G15 in his hands. Propped on the ground next to him, facing back along the trail, was his long rifle. Next to him was his partner, LaRue. G-Man had put aside Baby, long since cleaned of any dinosaur residue, in exchange for his G15 and underbarrel grenade launcher. Every one of the SEALS had laid out a spare magazine next to his position for a quick reload. The men with the 30-millimeter grenade launchers also had a spare round for that weapon laid out. And each of the G15 weapons had the long shape of a suppressor slipped in place over the muzzle.

While everyone waited in position, Jackson looked back along the trail. He had the best view of the killing zone, and he needed it because it would be his decision to initiate the ambush. The jungle noises continued to increase all around the men as the critters that lived there, the local equivalent of bugs and birds, grew used to the SEALS' presence and went about their business. Several winged creatures that were as large as eagles glided just above the upper branches of the trees, but they simply soared past and took no note of the men taking position below them. Despite the noisy din—or perhaps because of it—there was a peaceful calm settling over their situation, making it easy to forget that the men were lined up to unleash violence on the next group of beings to pass in front of them. The sudden sound of two clicks over his earpiece told Jackson that the time for the ambush might be approaching rapidly.

Tugging the nearly invisible line that had been laid out along the ambush site, Jackson signaled all his men that the scouts were approaching. As each man felt the single jerk on the line, he passed it on. It was a simple, silent, and nearly foolproof way of communication among the SEALS. It was primitive, but there wasn't any way an enemy force could detect it; that was why the whole force had been maintaining radio silence as much as they possibly could.

Suddenly, Sanchez and Marannis were in the clearing, moving up through the killing zone as had been arranged. That single action told Jackson that his men were being pursued. Now it was time for the SEALS to get down to the business of warfare.

Sanchez passed over the small rise and then dropped to the ground at the sound of a quiet hiss from Jackson. Marannis did the same thing, only he moved over to the opposite side of the trail, where Chief Harris lay in concealment. Crawling up to where he had heard Jackson, Sanchez saw the officer concealed in the undergrowth. He moved to where his lips were only inches from the lieutenant's ear.

"Eighteen hostiles about thirty meters behind us," Sanchez whispered. "Two of those flying buses back at a clearing blown in the jungle about five hundred meters back along the trail. There's only one or two guards back watching the ships; everyone else is on our trail."

At his lieutenant's nod, Sanchez moved off to the left slightly and took up his position behind the officer, looking across him and back down the trail. Pulling on the signal line, Jackson sent two jerks down along it. His men had been warned that the enemy was approaching and that things would be moving very fast, very soon.

Even as he snugged the plastic stock of the G15 against his shoulder, Jackson saw movement back along the trail. He could see the entire killing zone and about fifty meters

beyond that before the jungle swallowed the trail. He
thumbed off the safety of the G15, moving the selector to
the full automatic position. The weapon was prepared to
send fifty 6.8-millimeter slugs the length of the trail, with
the suppressor probably keeping the enemy from ever
hearing where the shooting was coming from. Now there
was distinct movement as he saw several heads bobbing
along the trail.

Two Eluoi soldiers led the party, staying off the direct
trail and moving through the brush, walking just to the
right and left of the path followed by the castaways when
they first had come this way. They wore off-white uniforms that stood out with remarkable clarity against the
green of the forest. Each man had a white helmet on his
head that ran from the nape of the neck over the cap and
included a pair of cheek protectors that looked oddly like
something a gladiator in Roman times might have worn.
But the weapons in their hands were all too modern; they
looked like the same plasma-ray battery-powered guns
carried by the soldiers aboard the starship. The scouts
were trailed by more of their men, already in view as the
first pair approached. The Eluoi advanced with a swagger
that bespoke real confidence, and they made a lot of
noise, at least by SEALS standards.

In the lieutenant's free hand was a green plastic box. He
already had pushed the safety cover back and locked it
open against the tension of its spring. All he had to do
was squeeze the exposed handle and a firing charge
would move through the line Chief Harris had laid out so
carefully. Moving at more than 30,000 meters a second,
the flash along the line would detonate the explosive
charges on the trunks of the trees at effectively the same
instant.

He hadn't wanted to use the mines unless he had to, but
the chances were that he could take out a large percentage
of the enemy force in the first blast. As the aliens moved

into the killing zone, he held back on pressing the detonator, continuing to watch the Eluoi patrol.

The aliens moved well through the jungle, operating on both sides of the trail. The two scouts were followed by the main mass of the enemy, with the soldiers organized in two files, one on either side of the trail. The aliens looked competent, but it was obvious that they had never faced explosive weapons. They were too bunched up, with only a few meters between them. If they were under his training, Jackson knew that Master Chief Ruiz would have kicked their tails up between their ears for making such a mistake; at least it was a mistake to the SEALS. Maybe for these troops it was just an easy way for them to support one another with the odd weapons in their hands.

The two scouts were moving closer and closer. Then they passed the spot where Jackson and Chief Harris lay in concealment. The officer ignored the enemy passing only a few meters from where he lay. He trusted Sanchez and his partner, Marannis, to deal with them.

The soft thud of a suppressed G15 on single shot, instantly followed by another, told Jackson that the threat behind him had been dealt with. Now he watched as the killing zone in front of him started to fill up. There wasn't any choice for him now. There were just too many of the enemy, and this would be his best chance. As he saw what looked to be the trailing man enter the far end of the killing zone with no one behind him, Jackson crushed down on the handle of the firing device in his left hand.

A thundering roar filled the jungle as the explosive charges all detonated as one. The cloth strips had held hundreds of dense metal fragments, each tiny cube capable of killing a man. And there were thousands of the fragments sleeting across the killing zone as all the SEALS in concealment opened fire.

With the initiation of the ambush being the detonation

of the mines, the men knew that silence had taken a back
seat to expediency. Chief Harris and G-Man closed off
both ends of the killing zone with high-explosive grenades
fired from their underbarrel launchers. Every one of the
rest of the SEALS followed standard operating procedure and covered his field of fire with a swath of automatic fire from his G15.

Jackson and Chief Harris were joined by Sanchez and
Marannis as their fire swept the length of the enemy column. Once one magazine was emptied, it was yanked out
from the front of the weapon and the reload was slipped
into place. The action of the G15 automatically fed a new
round from the magazine into the firing chamber, and the
controlled firing of the SEALS continued without respite
for nearly a half minute, though it seemed a lot longer to
the men doing the shooting.

Except for the crump of the grenades, the shooting that
followed the exploding of the fragmentation mines was
almost soundless. Each man went though his planned ex-
penditure of two magazines, except for the grenadiers,
who went through one magazine and then fired a last
grenade. The crump of the grenades going off was the
last sound of the firefight.

As the echoes of those explosions faded quickly into
the surrounding brush, the SEALS lay still, listening. For
a moment there was no noise—even the animals had
fallen silent—and then there came a sudden crashing
through the brush at the far end of the killing zone.

One alien had escaped. It always seemed that no matter
how well an ambush was planned, there was someone
who escaped. But the SEALS had a backup plan in place
to cover that contingency.

Even as they got up from their positions, the men recognized the soft noise of Falco's sniping rifle. The fact
that there wasn't a follow-up shot told them that the
sniper hadn't felt a need for it. But the enemy forces scat-

tered in the newly created clearing in front of the ambush could still be a threat. Moving quickly, the SEALS went forward to check out the dead and dying.

As alien hands scrabbled for a dropped weapon, a quick thump of a suppressed shot ended the threat. Bodies were checked, and undamaged equipment and weapons were quickly stripped away. Everything was checked, and while the rest of the Team was looking over the killing zone, Ensign Sanders moved quickly up the trail, led by Marannis. Sanchez remained back with Lieutenant Jackson.

The killing was complete; none of the enemy had escaped. It had been a nearly perfect ambush, but the mission for that day was far from over.

Ensign Sanders and his men were in position at the clearing barely ten minutes after leaving the ambush site. Following Marannis through the jungle had been like trying to play keep-away with a ghost. But he had kept them on line to the clearing, and in spite of their speed of movement, they made almost no sound as they approached the clearing blasted into the jungle canopy.

Now they could see what they had been rushing for. Two alien ships, boxy affairs, were resting in the clearing, placed almost nose to tail with each other but separated by a few meters of distance. They rested on tripod landing gear that resembled skis or skids, allowing the ships to perch with a fair degree of stability on the flattened swath of timber and brush. Sanders saw wheels retracted above those skids and deduced that the ships could land more like traditional aircrafts if they had a proper tarmac underneath them.

What interested the young SEALS officer the most were the open ramps at the rear of the craft and the single alien figure standing at the back of the left-side craft, the ship that was behind the other one. The alien was looking off

into the distance and holding some kind of optical device
up to his eyes. It was obvious that he was looking for
something, but what it was, the ensign had no way to tell.

Pulling back to where the rest of the men were, Sanders
whispered very quietly and gave them a very simple plan.

"Master Chief," Sanders whispered. "You and Dobson
take up positions on this side of the clearing and cover
both craft. Marannis, Robinson, and I are going to move
over to the left and try to come up from behind these
things and take out the crew. We can only see one man,
but there may be others. Remember, above all else, don't
let one of these things lift off. They don't look like
they're alerted, but they probably heard the ambush and
are going to be wondering why no one from that patrol is
contacting them."

The men all nodded silently; there wasn't much of anything to say. In moments, Sanders and his two Teammates
had eased around the makeshift clearing to get a look at
the ships from the other side. They caught a glimpse of a
man in the window of one transport's flight deck and had
to assume that both ships had pilots aboard.

"Permission to move in closer, sir?" Marannis asked in
an almost inaudible whisper into the ensign's ear.

Sanders nodded, wondering what the point man had in
mind. He watched in awe as the scout dropped to the
ground and began to move through the tangled greenery,
squirming forward like a snake. In two minutes Marannis
had moved up to within a few meters of the rear end of
the trailing craft. The plant life that had been knocked
down by whatever the aliens had used to make the clearing looked to be totally flattened, but the SEALS point
man was finding cover where no one else could see it. He
was only meters from where the alien stood when whatever luck he was using finally ran out.

The alien put down whatever it was he had been looking through and turned to the rear of his craft, where the

open ramp was. He shouted something unintelligible and grabbed at a pouch at his waist as he suddenly saw Marannis on the ground close by. The suppressed three-round burst from Sanders's weapon blended in with the single shot fired by Marannis. The head of the alien seemed to explode as all four rounds struck it almost simultaneously.

Even as the body was falling, Marannis darted up the ramp and into the hull of the nearest transport. At the same time, the engines of the other craft turned over, quickly winding up to full power. Breaking away from the cover at the side of the clearing, Ensign Sanders ran to where he could see the rear ramp on the other craft starting to rise. The downward-firing jets kicked up dirt and debris, sending a blinding cloud into the young officer's face.

He thumbed his weapon to full automatic as he pulled the trigger back and held it. One long thudding burst hissed out of the suppressor, heating it so much that the rising waves almost burned the ensign's face. Behind him, he could feel more than hear Robinson's weapon adding its firepower to his. The ramp kept closing, but now there was smoke starting to come out of the inside of the craft, and dozens of tungsten-core projectiles tore into the electronics, machinery, and fuel containers inside the hull.

The ship started to lift off, canting away from them as the adjustable nozzles of the jet engines began to swivel backward. Tongues of flame shot along the ground, igniting even the damp brush, and Sanders shifted his aim, pouring rounds right into the whirling turbine of the jet engine. Smoke spewed thick and heavy as the whining engine abruptly lurched and sputtered. It shrieked to a halt, and the transport toppled sideways, landing near the edge of the clearing and bursting into flames.

Whoever was inside that craft was facing an inferno, and they certainly wouldn't be going anywhere. The sound of the engine died away, and the smoke continued to pour out from the interior. No flames were showing, but the acrid stink told all the men around the clearing that there couldn't be much of anything alive inside that craft unless it was wearing a full exposure suit, something that was possible but not very likely.

Marannis, meanwhile, came back down the ramp of the second ship. That transport had escaped damage, and as the scout knelt to wipe his bloody knife on some large leaves, Sanders knew that they wouldn't find any living Eluoi inside.

Instead, it looked like the SEALS were now the owners of at least one working enemy transport ship.

# Eleven: A Trip to Town

"How do I look?" Ensign Sanders asked. He was wearing a captured Eluoi uniform garnished with gold braid on the sleeves. They had found the undamaged garment in a storage locker aboard the captured transport aircraft. It fit the young ensign perfectly, though he had been spending a few minutes trying to adjust the white silken turban on his head.

"Like a desert sheik ready for his wedding night," Master Chief Ruiz opined solemnly to a general chorus of agreement.

"Or maybe the valet parking supervisor at the Beverly Hills Holiday Inn," Jackson suggested.

"I think you look like a surgeon, ready to operate," Dr. Sulati noted, not unkindly.

"He's an unmarried member of the Teams, ma'am," Jackson pointed out. "He's *always* ready to operate."

The light mood did not alleviate the tension wracking the castaways. Jackson found himself looking at the sky, listening for some sign of the jet engine that would signal the return of Falco and Consul Char-Kane—and the captured transport craft that had launched, ten minutes earlier, on a high-risk test flight.

The ambush and the aftermath, he had to admit, could not have worked much better. These Eluoi may have been hell on wheels as far as deep space and extraplanetary combat went, but for close-quarters combat on their own ground, they seemed never to have suspected that it could really happen. They needed an education in unconventional warfare, something the SEALS would teach them at the graduate level.

Marannis had taken out the two pilots in a quick rush of the cockpit, capturing the aircraft intact and undamaged. The Teammates had inspected the jet curiously, discovering that the rear compartment was a large hold with spartan benches along each wall. It was spacious enough to carry a dozen passengers or a fairly good-sized load of cargo. The flight deck included two chairs for pilots and two additional seats directly behind them. The gun turret was above that deck.

The capture did an awful lot to enhance their options, Jackson and all of them realized. With an aircraft, they could cover vast distances of the planet's surface. The control panel was pretty basic—certainly compared to a shuttle or even a comparable aircraft on Earth—and Consul Char-Kane had felt comfortable at the controls. Many of the actual details of flight, she explained, were handled by automated and computerized controls. Falco, probably the most technically proficient member of the unit, had been enthusiastic about the prospect of learning to pilot it, and so the Shamani woman and the SEALS had embarked on a shakedown flight.

In the meantime, the lieutenant and Chief Harris also donned uniforms claimed from some of the slain Eluoi. They felt pretty lucky, at least a lot more so than the previous owners of the uniforms, when they found out that the material they were made of didn't stain easily. A quick rinse in one of the small streams nearby and the uniforms were clean and mostly looked like new, except for the odd small hole.

The rest of the SEALS would go in their standard fatigues, since there were not enough intact uniforms to outfit the rest of the Team. When he stopped to think about it, Jackson wondered if they were crazy to try to infiltrate an alien city, a place of a size suggesting a population of teeming millions. But his objective remained to get off this planet, and since the alternative seemed to be to try to survive in that trackless jungle for the rest of their lives, his options were reduced to this one desperate tactic.

Finally, he heard the welcome roar. Swelling from the distance, the noise exploded into a thunderous wave of sound as the transport aircraft skidded to a halt, then slowly settled into the middle of the clearing. Bits of smashed trees and leaves swirled through the air, propelled by the power of the rushing jets, but the craft landed with surprising quickness in the exact middle of the open space.

"She's still got a good reserve of fuel, LT," Falco reported, grinning like a teenager who just had been handed the keys to a sports car as he emerged from the tail ramp. "Those turbines just seem to sip away at it. And so much of the flight is automated that a kid could probably fly it."

"Well, we don't have a kid, so you'll have to do," Jackson said. He turned to the Shamani woman. "Our best bet is to get a message back to Earth, see if they can send *Pegasus* for us. What are our chances of finding a communications center? Where are we likely to find a broadcaster powerful enough to send a signal beyond the star system? I know you Shamani supposedly cannot create an FTL broadcast, but maybe the Eluoi?"

"That will not be possible," Char-Kane answered with a shrug. "There have been attempts to create such pulse transmitters, but all have failed. We Shamani lack the technology to send a faster-than-light broadcast, and we are the most advanced culture in the galaxy."

"So it's not possible to send a message back to Earth?" Jackson summarized, his heart sinking at the prospect.

"That is correct," she replied.

"Okay," Jackson said, conceding the point for the time being. "It looks like we'll just have to steal us a spaceship and get home on our own. Let's go, Team."

The ramp descending from the rear compartment was the main means of access to and egress from the craft, though there also were emergency escape hatches to the port and starboard of the flight deck. The SEALS filed up that ramp into the passenger compartment. Rodale, LaRue, Ruiz, Harry Teal, Harris, Robinson, Marannis, and Sanchez would take up positions on the benches in there. They could see out through a series of viewports, but the windows were too small to allow an outside observer to get a look at the uniformed men within the aircraft. Director Parker and Doctor Sulati also would ride in the back.

Ruiz found a storage locker with a simple latch and was going through it when the lieutenant passed him. They noticed some coils of thin, flexible rope and a box of mundane-looking tools that included adjustable wrenches, a crowbar, and some screwdrivers with exotic heads. The master chief picked up a small plastic pouch and opened it.

"Look here, LT," he announced. "It's a couple of them earpiece things like they gave you."

"Excellent," the officer said, seeing three of the tiny translators in the chief's hand. "Why don't you put one in and give another to Harris? I'll take one for Ensign Sanders."

"Sure thing," Ruiz said, giving one tiny device—they were no bigger than small earplugs—to the officer and placing one in one of his own ears.

Jackson made his way forward and handed Sanders the device as they took seats on the flight deck, behind Falco and Char-Kane. The gun turret was a small Plexiglas affair with a single automatic gun mounted squarely behind the cockpit atop the machine, and Gunner's Mate Dobson, who was a master at any kind of automatic weapon, would do the honors up there. He settled in easily and found that the turret swiveled smoothly with nothing more than the pressure of a knee to the right or left. The gun tracked cleanly and had a ready ammunition supply of metal slugs in a large canister feeding directly up into the breach.

"She has a couple of forward-firing guns, too," Falco reported. "They're operated from the flight deck. And this"—he pointed to a red button prominently marked on the port side of the cockpit—"seems to be the sonic weapon, the blaster they used to level the trees so they could land in the jungle."

"I suggest you not touch that button," Jackson said seriously.

"My sentiments exactly, sir," Falco agreed. He donned a headset with earphones and a small microphone. When he next spoke, his words were broadcast through the flight deck and passenger cabin.

"Please make sure your seats and serving trays are locked in the upright position," he announced solemnly. "Flight zero-zero-one of Alien SEALS Airways is about to depart. Fasten your seat belts and hold on for dear life."

The engines roared, and the aircraft began to vibrate. Jackson looked out the cabin windows, watching hopefully as the flattened circle in the jungle slowly fell away below them.

"We're cruising at almost a thousand kph if I'm translating this indicator correctly," Falco said with a low whistle. "Even if I got the units wrong, from what the consul told me, we are pretty much hauling ass no matter how you measure it."

"And you can hardly feel it," Jackson acknowledged.

Indeed, the jet transport sliced through the air so cleanly that it was only the sight of the ground flashing past that confirmed to the SEALS their incredible speed. The few tremendously tall trees provided a good benchmark as they jutted a hundred meters or more above the general forest canopy. They came into sight, whipped past, and vanished very quickly as the aircraft roared along at 500 to 1,000 meters of altitude. They flashed above some stretches of boggy marsh and crossed over one of the narrow serpentine seas they had observed from space.

Jackson gawked at the sight of a massive, coiling creature—a genuine sea serpent—sinuously working its way through those waters. He was very glad they weren't traveling by small boat. They saw great flocks of birds rising from the marsh, some of which looked to be the size of small airplanes. The avian creatures were clearly spooked by the sound of the aircraft's approach and had the good sense to stay out of their way.

"We are coming up on Batuu City," Consul Char-Kane noted, looking forward.

The sprawling swath of the planet's metropolis—the only civilized area on this world if the Shamani woman's estimate was accurate—was so white, so purely reflective, that Jackson found himself squinting as they approached the great city. Though still a hundred kilometers away, it dominated the horizon like a small continent, stark and clean against the pure green that outlined the rest of the verdant planet.

"What about security?" the officer asked. "Will there likely be some kind of radio signal we have to countersign?"

"I think it is most likely we will be pulled in on an automated flight path. These craft move too quickly for manned posts to control the dense flight patterns over populated areas. If we relinquish the controls, the aircraft will be taken to one of the military landing sites around the city. These will typically be small posts, with landing zones on top of the tall buildings. Once there, of course, we will have to see what develops."

"I'd like to see if there is some kind of communications center—someplace where we can try to broadcast a message to the *Pegasus*—even if the consul thinks it's a long shot," Jackson declared, thinking aloud. His eyes swept the landscape below, where the tall trees of the jungle at last had been left behind. "If we strike out, we'll have to scout the spaceport and make a plan to steal a ship." If the first option was a long shot, he didn't even want to think about their chances of implementing the backup plan.

The outer band around the city, he now saw, was a swath of fields, ponds, and orchards at least a hundred kilometers across. There were roads crossing the farmland, and many types of ground transportation were moving along those roads. These resembled Earth-type trucks and cars, though they seemed to be moving very quickly. Smaller roads and tracks fed into wide, multilane highways, channeling the road traffic along at speeds that would have been utterly reckless on Earth.

As they approached Batuu City, he could see that the whole place was surrounded by a lofty wall and that all the roads converged to pass through a relatively small number of gates in that high barrier. Lakes and streams meandered across the ground, and some of them were spanned by graceful bridges.

Many other aircraft, including fixed-wing and VTOL, moved from the city out and over the surrounding farmland. The flying machines, like those on the ground, seemed to follow defined flight paths that were like highways in the sky. A few of the other vehicles were sleek, armed military aircraft like the one the SEALS had captured, but the vast majority seemed to be civilian machines. Some were large, lumbering cargo haulers with broad wings and massive turbofan engines that blasted mostly downward; others moved more quickly, with thin fuselages and multiple windows suggesting that they were transporting passengers. They tended to have swept, graceful-looking wings, and darted here and there, sometimes at nearly supersonic speeds.

Falco kept his hands lightly on the controls, and they

fell into line, following a stream of aircraft moving between two lofty towers. The spires bracketed one of the large gates at ground level, where the highways converged to pass through the city wall. A glance down suggested that the roadway consisted of ten or twelve lanes going in each direction. There was no sign of a gate or even a tollbooth at the boundary of the city, a fact that Jackson took as encouraging.

Nevertheless, he hunkered down in his seat and watched out of the corner of his eye as they approached the nearest of the great towers. Somebody somewhere down below them eventually was going to notice that two aircraft and a military unit were missing. The SEALS had buried the bodies of the slain enemy and cleaned up the area. But scavengers could dig up the corpses, and the camouflage they had piled on the other burned-out aircraft wouldn't last forever. Still, it was better not to think about the things he couldn't control and to pay attention to the layout of the city section they were approaching.

The two towers were about a kilometer apart, and all Jackson could see was a vast bank of tinted, almost black windows. A number of domes were visible across the top and on balconies and parapets on the sides of the tower, and it didn't take a lot of imagination to picture those domes quickly opening up to reveal defensive batteries or elaborate detection systems.

But none of them displayed any sinister attributes as the jetcar glided past. Now they were over the city, and Falco still had full use of the controls.

"Man, look at the size of this place," he declared. They slowed somewhat to maintain position in the stream of traffic, but even so, the vast buildings scrolled by at an incredible rate.

Most of the structures seemed to be unadorned, with white being the color not just of choice but of almost universal employment. A number of the buildings were boxy and cubic, but many others were narrow and tall, thrusting so far up in the air that they seemed to be a good 800 or 1,000 meters above the ground. In many places broad, flat roofs capped those spires, providing landing pads for VTOL aircraft. Some of those expanses stretched far and wide, like umbrellas over the lesser buildings. In most places only the narrowest of gaps yielded views downward. The structures were so close together that whatever ground there was between them was utterly lost in the shadows.

A few domes lent some curvature to the views. Several great citadels stood out from the common planes of the flat roofs. Breaking up the alabaster whiteness were a couple of spectacular structures that seemed to be made of crystal or glass. They reflected the sunlight in dazzling prisms of color, shifting in appearance as the aircraft moved past. One, a great pyramid structure that looked to be made of white marble, loomed like a mountain in the distance. It was easily two or three kilometers tall and dwarfed every other building in sight.

"That is the seat of government—and religion," Char-Kane explained. "Every Eluoi world is ruled by a savant, and they each have a grand temple where his court is gathered."

"Are they all male, the savants?" asked Jackson.

Char-Kane's red eyes narrowed slightly, and she nodded. "The Eluoi are bound in many respects by some rather primitive constraints in their religion. It has caused them to relegate half of their population—the female half—to a subservient status."

The officer filed that information away even as he continued to take in details of the alien landscape. There were a few glimpses of green and some canals or channels of dark-looking water. A couple of the parks were very large, on the order of ten or twenty klicks across, and frequently the greenery was broken by bright fountains or elaborate gardens of exotic, brightly colored blossoms. Aside from those parks, nearly every acre of the ground was covered, buried beneath the ubiquitous white cubes, domes, and spires.

The aircraft continued past the great pyramid, moving toward the far end of the huge city, still traveling at dazzling speed.

"What's that thing?" Jackson pointed to another massive building that came into sight as they neared the far edge of the city. This was a spire climbing even higher into the sky than the grand temple. It was much narrower, and several tubes of dark metal bristled from the top and the upper surfaces of the walls. It seemed to be positioned just outside the city wall.

"That is their planetary defense battery. It is capable of destroying a ship even beyond the outer reaches of the planet's atmosphere. It is the weapon I was so anxious to avoid when we rode the shuttle down to Batuun."

The lieutenant nodded. He saw other facilities, buildings with tops as broad as an aircraft carrier, and noticed many of the military-style jetcars circling about. "Those would be the garrisons, I'm guessing."

"Correct. The largest will no doubt have wings for a hundred or more aircraft. But there will be smaller outposts throughout the city. I suggest we choose one of those to land."

"Good idea," he said wryly. "Since you don't think we'll be able to call for help, I'm guessing we'll have to make our own way off this place. For now, let's find a place where we can fuel up and maybe get our bearings."

Giving the grand temple a wide berth, they circled over the city, again moving toward the PDB. It extended more than a hundred square klicks or more, and they began to make out a vast array of runways, launch pads, towers, and massive hangars.

"Is that a military installation?" the lieutenant wondered.

Char-Kane followed his pointing finger. "I doubt it. I suspect that is the spaceport, where shuttles land and launch and receive service. Of course, it will have a military component, but I suspect it serves the whole planet."

They watched as rockets flared on one blunt-nosed shuttle and the craft rocketed into the sky, trailing smoke, accelerating on a course that suggested it was heading for orbit. Moments later, another shuttle came into view, this one a circular vehicle that was descending, braced against gravity by the thrusting of four rockets.

"That looks just like the one that came down to Mars," Jackson noted, observing the different shape of the round ship compared to the sleeker and more pointed shuttles that were standing here and there on the spaceport.

"It is!" Char-Kane said, an unusual degree of excitement in her voice. "That is a Shamani shuttle. It must be the other one from the *Gladiola*."

"Can you hold this pattern?" Jackson asked. "I'd like to keep an eye on that shuttle."

"You got it, LT," Falco replied. With a gentle touch on the controls, he guided the aircraft into a gently banked turn, allowing them to circle some distance away from the spaceport.

The lieutenant was looking over the controls, seeing several vidscreens that currently were displaying views before, behind, and to either side of their transport. "Is there any way to zoom these things in?" he asked Char-Kane.

Before she could reply, Sanders had figured out the controls and managed to bring one camera into position to get a fairly good look at the descending shuttle just as it was touching down in the middle of a great cloud of billowing smoke. Backing out a bit to widen the view, the ensign whistled.

"Looks like they're pulling out all the stops with the honor guard," he said, pointing to the screen. Jackson saw large formations of troops, all drawn up with parade-ground precision, marking off a large square, with the shuttle landing in the middle. Each formation looked to be the size of a full battalion and was centered on a flag bearer who held up a white banner on which that green bull's-eye was prominently displayed.

"One'll get you ten the savant is aboard that shuttle," the lieutenant suggested.

They watched for a few more minutes as the smoke cleared and the debarkation ramp lowered from the belly of the shuttle. The resolution was not clear enough to recognize faces, but from the glimmering gold around the sleeves of the first passenger to debark, they were pretty certain Jackson was right. Several other people trailed behind him, and the newly landed travelers broke into two parties.

One, led by the savant, entered a large transport craft that took off immediately, escorted by several fighter-type jetcars. The other passengers got into a transport similar to the one the SEALS had captured, and that one, too, quickly took to the air.

"Follow that ship, the smaller one," Jackson ordered.

Keeping about ten klicks back but watching their target through the vidscreen, the SEALS trailed along. A visual inspection showed that the larger transport, the one presumably carrying the savant, was heading directly for the pyramid. The small aircraft traveled in the same direction but finally slowed and settled into a landing approach on one of the flat-topped buildings right next to the government center.

They held back, still watching, until Falco looked at the officer and indicated one of the dials.

"This thing has been flying all day, LT," he declared. "And it looks like we're getting near the end of the reserve tanks. We'll have to set her down pretty soon."

"All right, Derek. Hold on just a sec—move in a little closer and let's see what happens."

They maximized the magnification of the viewer and watched as the jetcar landed on a circular pad between several large hangars. Falco eased them as close as he dared, and they watched the screen as the ramp descended and two passengers emerged into the sunlight.

"It's Zaro, that son of a bitch!" snapped Sanders. "Damn, LT. Look at that!"

It was indeed the treacherous agent who had betrayed the Martian outpost. He stretched casually, spoke to several white-clad Eluoi of the ground crew, and then entered one of the hangar-type buildings.

"Let's drop in and see if we can catch him at the office," Jackson declared.

Falco nodded and tried to mimic the smooth landing approach made by the Eluoi pilot. They watched as a small tractor pulled Zaro's aircraft off of the landing circle. Char-Kane took over the controls, slowly settling them toward the same place.

The lieutenant touched his mike and addressed the rest of the Team. "We're going to be touching down in a few minutes. I want everyone standing by, ready to move, but wait for my orders. Except you, Dobson—keep a finger on the trigger up there and be ready to cover us. Acknowledge."

"Aye, aye, sir," he heard, repeated multiple times from the passenger bay. Dobson, up in the turret, leaned down into the cockpit and gave him a thumbs-up.

The approach went smoothly, the engine rising to a high pitch as the jetcar came to a stop in the sky and slowly settled straight down. The landing zone Char-Kane had suggested was currently empty of aircraft, though there was a hangar to one side that was closed. A few Eluoi in the unadorned white suits stood back to watch as the aircraft gently touched down with barely a bump.

One of the ground crew advanced toward the aircraft as

the jet engine slowed to a whine and then settled into silence as Falco cut off the fuel. Another Eluoi emerged from the hangar hauling a long hose, obviously a fuel line.

The first person to approach the machine looked up at Falco in the pilot's seat and touched his throat mike, obviously asking something that wasn't coming through the machine's comm system. Falco shrugged and pointed to his earphones, then indicated the fueling port on the side of the jetcar.

The ground crewman nodded and gestured to his comrade, who brought over the hose and inserted it into the port.

"Now we've got to move fast. I want to get inside and take out their alarms before they know what hit 'em," Jackson said. Peering into the shadowy hangar, he didn't see any other people moving around, a sign that he took as very encouraging. "Everyone ready?" he asked.

"Aye, aye, LT," came Master Chief Ruiz's reply from the passenger bay. "Just drop the ramp and we'll roll."

"Dobson, stay up in that turret in case we need some cover," Jackson said to the SEALS gunner. "Those of us in Eluoi uniforms will go out first. The rest of you get ready to come charging out if we need you." He nodded at Falco, who pushed the lever to open the hatch.

The shot took them all by surprise. It came from a small building to the side, a structure he barely had noticed. A wall had fallen away to reveal a small gun with a crew of three Eluoi. A projectile struck the front of the aircraft with a heavy punch, rocking the nose to the side and dropping it heavily to the ground.

"Shit, they knocked out the landing strut!" Falco shouted. "We're grounded, sir!"

The two ground crewmen were racing back to the hangar. Dobson let them go and directed the fire of his weapon against the Eluoi gun. A stream of slugs spewed from the turret gun, knocking out the gun crew and perforating the small shed that had concealed the weapon.

"Drop the hatch! Move out! *Go!*" Jackson bellowed.

Falco already was lowering the exit ramp. The lieutenant, Sanders, and Falco ducked into the passenger compartment. "You two stay here," he told Sulati and Parker. "At least until the coast is clear. You SEALS— move out!"

The SEALS automatically split up by shooter pairs and went on the attack. Falco and LaRue darted toward the doors on the east end of the pad. Chief Harris and Harry Teal ran to the west. The other two pairs closed in on the disabled battery, spraying it with their G15s as more white-uniformed Eluoi tried to advance out of the shed.

Ruiz and Rodale took up stations at the stern of the jetcar, just below the still-shimmering-hot jet exhausts.

"Stay with the civilians," Jackson ordered the ensign, who bit back his protest and nodded. "Get up to the flight deck; use those vidscreens for intel."

Ensign Sanders scrambled back to the flight deck with Dr. Sulati and Director Parker. Dobson sprayed another burst from the turret gun while the lieutenant popped open a storage locker in the cargo hold. He saw a large coil of light, supple line, grabbed it, and ran out onto the landing circle. They were taking fire from the hangar now, but Ruiz sprayed the open doors with well-placed bursts, keeping the shooters from drawing a bead.

But Eluoi commandos were attacking from every direction, some of them even dropping out of the sky, as four other jetcars swooped down toward the landing circle. This was more than a quick response, Jackson suspected. Somehow, the SEALS had been lured into a trap.

Still, the Team had not exactly been defanged. Rodale brought down one of the Eluoi aircraft with a well-placed rocket, and LaRue fired a round from the rail gun, the backblast billowing across the landing pad as he punched a slug through the whirling turbine of a second aircraft. That machine disintegrated in a cloud of smoke and fire, raining debris directly onto a platoon of Eluoi that was charging from another hangar. The two surviving aircraft quickly zoomed up and away.

Where the hell was Zaro? Jackson caught a glimpse of him in the open hangar, ordering a dozen soldiers to charge. They did so reluctantly and instantly were cut down by a scythe of slugs from the turret gun and the SEALS' G15s. Zaro darted away, vanishing through a door into the building.

It was too risky to pursue him for now. They needed to get out of there and regroup. Jackson raced to the edge of the landing circle and looked over the edge of the building. The platform proved to be something like 400 meters above the ground. Taking a look over the rim was like staring into a canyon. A neighboring building, maybe 100 meters lower in height, was only twenty meters away. The space between the two structures was lost in shadows so that the bottom was invisible in the darkness.

"Over the wall!" Jackson shouted, unrolling the long spool of line. He could only hope it ran all the way to the ground. The SEALS raced toward him and one by one seized the rope and flipped over the edge. He fired a burst from his G15 when he saw an Eluoi soldier dare to show his face, and the man quickly dived into the cover of his hangar.

The Eluoi swarmed toward the aircraft, surrounding the machine with Sanders, Dobson, Parker, Sulati, and Char-Kane still inside. He saw the two females pushed roughly out of the ramp by gun-toting captors. The turret was empty, and he hoped Dobson and Sanders would have the good sense to surrender, at least for now. Biting back a curse of frustration, Jackson made a silent promise: They'd come back for their companions before this was over.

Then he went over the side and almost blacked out as something powerful, violent, and searingly painful slammed into his left shoulder. Clinging to the rope with one hand, the lieutenant slid downward, plunging toward the black, shadowy alley in the very bottom of Batuu City.

# Twelve: Turning the Tables

The SEALS descended the line at a frantic speed, knowing their vulnerability if the Eluoi recovered quickly enough to cut it or dislodge the anchor at the top. Jackson was the last one down, almost landing on top of Harris. The chief tumbled out of the way at the last second, and the lieutenant hit hard, gritting his teeth against the cry of pain that almost forced itself out of his mouth. His left arm dangled uselessly, and his shoulder felt like it was on fire.

Only vaguely did he realize that he was standing in muck up to his ankles. They were in some kind of narrow alley that was almost fully dark because of the height of the two buildings flanking the passageway. The sky was a strand of pale blue that looked impossibly far away overhead. There seemed to be some tracks—really just a pair of ruts—down the middle of the muddy, smelly trench, but there were no vehicles or people in sight. It was, Jackson thought, more like dropping into a sewer than falling onto a city street.

That fact was all right with him.

The other SEALS were already organized and had set up a moving security perimeter, traveling quickly along the alley to put distance between themselves and the shooters above. At least, they moved until the lieutenant grunted quietly and brought them up short.

"You okay, LT?" asked Harry Teal.

"My shoulder—I think I busted it," Jackson said. "They hit me with some kind of cannon as I was going over the wall."

Another wave of pain shot through him, and he bent at the waist, retching, bracing himself against the building with his good hand. Teal gave him a shoulder to lean on and helped him slump down heavily onto the wet ground.

"Let me have a look, sir," the corpsman said.

"Dammit, we have to move! You can look at it when we're clear."

"Sir!" Teal insisted, startling the officer with the intensity of his challenge. "I need to examine you now! *Then* we can move."

"Shit," Jackson said wearily, giving up. He looked around at the concerned faces of his Teammates, which were pale and grimy in the shadowy confines. "Anybody else hurt?" he asked gruffly.

"I got a nick in the leg. Flesh wound," Sanchez said with a shrug.

"Check him out first. That's an order!" the officer said as Teal started to probe his shoulder.

"I already put a Band-Aid on Sanchez's boo-boo," Teal said. "So, Lieutenant, I guess it's your turn."

Wincing and gritting his teeth, Jackson grunted acknowledgment and leaned his head back against the cold stone of the wall. He felt the mud soaking his trousers, but he was too groggy and too wracked with pain to care. It was a relief to sit down, to take the load off his feet, and to let the wet ground and the solid stone at his back support him.

The corpsman probed the joint, apologizing at Jackson's hiss of pain. Trying to ignore his ministrations, Jackson took a look around. He saw Sanchez leaning on Marannis's shoulder with a bloody bandage wrapped around his thigh. "Christ, did you get it in the artery?" he demanded.

"No, sir. Just a little nick, like I said," the SEALS scout replied. "Bled like a son of a bitch for a few seconds till

Harry wrapped it up nice and tight. Hell, sir, I could do wind sprints right now. Want to see?"

Jackson couldn't help but laugh, heartened by the man's—by *all* the men's—fighting spirit. "Nah, save the energy," he said. "I'll send you on a beer run as soon as Harry finishes with me."

After a few seconds, Teal squatted back on his haunches. "Looks like it's dislocated," he said. "I'm going to pop it back in, sir. But it's gonna hurt like hell."

"Do it," the lieutenant grunted, closing his eyes.

He was vaguely aware of a couple of other men gathering around. Someone's big hands took a grip around his chest in response to whispered instructions from the corpsman. A stab of pain shot through him as he felt Teal manipulate his dangling arm, then take a grip on his bicep.

"Ready, sir," the corpsman said. "On three. One—"

Before saying "two" and allowing his patient to tense up, the young SEALS pulled on the arm, twisting it up and out, forcing the joint back into place. Jackson croaked out a cry of pain and blacked out.

When he came to, he was walking, being helped along by the strapping LaRue. Somehow, even unconscious, Jackson had been moving his feet, and now he shook his head, groggily looking around. Daylight was that strip of blue sky far overhead, with looming stone walls to the right and left, flanking an alley that was only some six or eight meters across.

*Doesn't the sun ever set in this fucking place?* He wanted to snarl the question at everyone, at anyone, in earshot. But he wouldn't give in to that frustration. Instead, he grunted a more practical question: "Any sign of pursuit?"

"Not yet, sir," LaRue replied. "They didn't follow us over the wall. But they have to know we're down here."

"Then let's keep moving." Jackson's eyes were slowly becoming used to the gloom. He looked for signs of an entrance or even an irregularity in the smooth stone walls to either side, but they seemed to plummet straight down to the ground and sink into the gummy mud.

"Sir?" It was Harry Teal. "I put a patch on your shoulder that should help cut down on the swelling and some of the pain. I can give you a shot of endorphin for the pain if it's bad. Would that help?"

"It sure as hell would if I was gonna lie down and take a nap," Jackson replied. "Thanks, but no. We've gotta keep moving, and I don't want anything that might slow me down."

"Just give the word if you change your mind, sir."

"Thanks, Harry," the lieutenant said seriously.

It was damned tempting, but he wouldn't allow it. These were his men, his platoon, and he was responsible for them. Christ! What a clusterfuck this mission had turned into! Four men lost in the first action. The rest of the Team captured, stranded, lost somewhere in the galaxy, with two good men—not to mention the civilians who were also Jackson's responsibility—still in the enemy's hands.

Roughly he forced the wave of self-pity away, recognizing the emotion for the destructive force that it was. He tried to lift his arm and failed, but the resulting jolt of pain was like a shot of common sense. They still had their weapons, their wits, their skills. They were SEALS, dammit!

And they were far from finished.

The reduced Team made its way through the murk. Chief Harris was on point, followed by Falco and Rodale. LaRue and Teal accompanied the lieutenant—despite his bravado, Jackson was grateful to have the strong man's shoulder for support—while Sanchez, Marannis, and Robinson came directly behind and Ruiz brought up the rear.

They finally came to a four-way intersection where a

crossing alley led to the right and left. From there they couldn't discern the nature of the buildings rising up on each quarter of the crossing, but Harris turned right, leading them away from the base of the structure where they had landed the jetcar.

"Got something back here!" Ruiz declared curtly.

A sliding door on the side of that structure, some ten meters above ground level, slid to the side, and one of the Eluoi soldiers leaned out. He was carrying one of the battery-powered firearms they first had encountered on the ship, and he immediately spotted the master chief.

Ruiz dropped him with a quick suppressed burst, and the fellow toppled out of the doorway to fall all the way down to the muddy ground. A pair of soldiers stuck their heads out, squeezing off a flash of electrical energy that went high, scouring the wall overhead and leaving the stink of ozone lingering in the air.

LaRue was being even more miserly with the ammo for his big weapon than Falco was with his sniper rifle. The big SEALS was husbanding the remaining copper slugs and the power cells on his back until he encountered another target that really called for them. For this situation, he kept Baby strapped to his back and pulled up his G15. He still had plenty of 30-millimeter grenades and the launcher to send them flying after the enemy.

Falco snapped off a single shot from his underbarrel grenade launcher. Pressing a control on the launcher switched the fuse in the grenade over to impact. When it smacked into the ceiling of the corridor revealed by the open door, the explosion of his round was more than enough to drive the remaining Eluoi back into shelter.

The SEALS moved quickly away. Ruiz held his weapon ready, snapping off another burst at the first glimpse of one of the white turbans. Something rolled out of the open doorway, clattering down the walls, and they saw that the pursuers had dumped a decidedly low-tech ladder down the wall.

"Wait!" Jackson barked as the coiling ropes dropped all the way to ground level. "They just opened the door for us. Master Chief, close in."

Ruiz was already charging toward the dangling ladder. Pulling a grenade from its bandolier, the rangy Puerto Rican grabbed one of the rungs with his free hand and started clambering up the ladder faster and more easily than if he was going up a caving ladder back in training. While the master chief began his climb, Harris and Falco chimed in with their assault rifles, spraying the entrance with quick, controlled bursts as Ruiz scrambled up the swaying ladder.

LaRue anchored the bottom of the ladder as the master chief reached the area just below the door. He armed his grenade and pitched it hard into the doorway. The blast belched out smoke and debris from the opening as the SEALS' NCO ducked down below the edge of the floor. Even before the dust had begun settling, Ruiz pulled himself up and over the entryway. Then G-Man started up the ladder, his rail gun and power pack dumped and left in the trusted hands of his Teammates. The big man's long arms lifted him up the ladder with startling agility. Next came Robinson and Marannis, with Sanchez following a little more slowly but only slightly favoring his gimpy leg.

"Can you climb, LT?" Harry Teal asked as LaRue vanished above them. They heard the explosion of another grenade, muffled this time, as the two SEALS moved farther into the building, putting the little bombs out in front of them.

The suppressed fire of the G15s was eerily quiet, mere puffs of sound; the Eluoi defenders replied with chattering automatic weapons and the occasional sizzling burst from those deadly plasma guns. They had yet to take a hit from the battery-powered weapons, but the officer remembered the way he had used it like a welding torch to cut open doors on the starship. He suspected and fervently hoped that the range would be limited, especially in a smoky environment such as the corridor was certain to be, but he didn't want one of his men finding out the hard way that the LT was wrong.

"Yeah," Jackson declared. "You go first. I'll anchor and then follow you up."

Tracers came zinging out of the doorway as, within the building, more Eluoi soldiers recovered enough to return fire. Once more Ruiz's gun snapped off a short burst, whisper quiet but very deadly, and as Teal scrambled upward, taking G-Man's heavy load with him, Jackson could only wonder how his men were faring.

The answer came with another dull explosion from G-Man's grenade launcher, echoed by Ruiz's sustained firing. The two SEALS were clearly still full of fight. Rodale came running up to Jackson, and the lieutenant sent him up next.

By that time Harris and Falco were there, and Jackson had them hold the base of the ladder while he pulled himself up. His left hand was usable, but the arm couldn't bear any weight, nor could he lift it over his head. Using just his right and his feet, the officer clawed his way up the ladder and gratefully offered a hand to Rodale, who pulled him over the ledge and into the shrapnel-pocked hallway.

He couldn't see Ruiz or LaRue, but he could hear them firing not far away. The smell of cordite filled his nostrils, and the swirling dust and smoke stung his eyes. Leaving the last two SEALS to come up on their own, the lieutenant and Rodale charged down the smooth stone floor into the depths of the Eluoi garrison house.

Even as he ran, Jackson was thinking about the objec-

tive. Two of his Teammates, plus their civilian companions, were prisoners up at the top of this building. The
SEALS needed to get there to effect a rescue before the
Eluoi had the chance to move them out. It was as simple
as that.

It was and it wasn't. In the back of the officer's mind
was another reality: Zaro, the spy, was up there, too.
That wasn't the reason he had ordered this headlong,
aggressive—some would say rash and foolhardy—attack.
He would never risk his men on a mission of personal re-
venge. But Zaro was also a link to home, one of the very
few Eluoi who had ever been to Earth's solar system and
who might know how to get back there. It was a simple
truth that the spy, right now, represented their best chance
of ever getting back home.

Jackson immediately noticed a number of doors, metal
portals that apparently slid to the side, to either side of the
corridor. There were at least six dead Eluoi soldiers
sprawled near the entry, and smoke prevented him from
seeing very far into the building. A gust of air came
through, clearing the murk just enough for him to make
out Ruiz and LaRue, each sheltering in an alcove on either side of the corridor, some twenty meters into the
building. Their barrels were trained down the hall, but for
the moment, they didn't seem to have any targets. Three
other SEALS were nearby, catching their breath with
weapons at the ready and waiting for orders. Good men
all—they knew better than to let the Team get separated
in this huge installation.

Sprinting forward, Jackson and Rodale joined the two
men of the advance guard.

"I'm taking one of those plasma guns," the lieutenant
said. "Harris and Falco and I will check out these
rooms—I don't want any nasty surprises coming up behind us. You men keep pushing forward. If you find a side
passage, look for a place to set some C-6. I want to give

these bastards the impression that they're getting attacked by a whole battalion."

"You got it, LT," Ruiz said, and then turned to LaRue. "Cover me."

The big man merely nodded as the master chief dashed down the corridor that led deeper into the Eluoi building.

Jackson pulled one of the plasma guns off a dead Eluoi soldier—the fellow had taken the burst of one of Ruiz's grenades full in the face from the look of him—and strapped the heavy battery pack to his back. The controls were the same as those on the weapon he'd used on the starship, and he wasted no time setting the power dial to the Eluoi hieroglyphic he had deduced meant "maximum."

With Harris and Falco covering him, he quickly seared through the heavy metal doors that were near the doorway through which the SEALS had entered the building. The first two rooms he discovered looked to be simply garrison quarters, with two double bunks, some chairs, and a small table, as if four men lived there. The next room was a weapons locker, with several cases lined up against the wall and standing open, as if the Eluoi had grabbed their guns out of there and hastened to the attack without waiting to secure the room behind them.

But none of them showed any indication of an ambush party lurking in the rear. By this time, the sounds of the firefight were moving deeper into the massive structure, and so the three SEALS hastened after their comrades.

Jackson heard another explosion and found Ruiz and LaRue crouching, moving through a large room where six corridors converged in this single circular chamber. Rodale came jogging in from one of the side passages. Sanchez snapped off careful suppressing shots down the other side corridor, the rounds making little noise as he shot but sparking and skipping off the stone floors and walls.

"Looks like a big storage locker down there, LT," Rodale reported. "Might be a good place to set off a charge."

"Make it happen," Jackson replied. "The rest of you, let's find a place to move upward. Sanders and the others are probably still up there, unless they've been taken away by aircraft." He remembered the shot that had knocked out their gear when they had landed and imagined a silver lining. "With a disabled transport on the landing pad, it might be a little while before their flight ops are open for business."

A moment later Ruiz reported back. "Elevator shaft over here, LT. Do we risk it?"

Jackson considered it for just a moment. The risk was not trivial: If they entered an elevator and their progress was being tracked by the defenders, it might be easy to shut off the car and isolate them. Or even, as he remembered the savant's tactic on the spaceship, to pipe in immobilizing or poison gas.

But they had to keep moving. Right now they had the initiative, and the defenders were clearly taken aback by the humans' aggression in charging into a fortified structure with such a small group. The SEALS had taken the pursuit by the garrison force and shoved it right down the enemy's throat. The only thing to do now was to keep up the pressure.

"We'll take the chance. Hold the car and we'll take it as soon as Rodale gets the charges set."

Thirty seconds later the gunner's mate came charging out of the side passage. "We got about two minutes," he reported breathlessly, joining the others in the large stainless-steel cubicle of the elevator cage.

Falco worked a control, and the elevator shot upward very quickly. A series of symbols, unreadable to the humans but obviously numbers, scrolled past as they ascended steadily. When he guessed that they were a couple of floors from the top, Jackson stopped the elevator. As soon as the doors opened, the SEALS tumbled out, weapons ready, but they were in an empty corridor.

"Any second now," Rodale said, checking his watch.

When it came—only two seconds later—the first explosion was relatively small; the secondary blast that immediately followed it was so powerful that it shook the stone floor underfoot. Several long cracks appeared in the walls, and pieces of slate broke free from the ceiling to shower down on the floor in a hail of small stones and stinging dust.

"Guess I must have set off one of their magazines," Rodale said just a little sheepishly.

"Nice work, Rock," Jackson said, clapping him on the shoulder with his good hand. "That should give them a little something to think about."

"Hey, LT. Here's an old-fashioned stairway," Ruiz reported. "Goes up and down."

"Well, then, men. We're still going up," Jackson said, pleased. "Let's see if we can't give these bastards a real shock."

"Hey, G-Man," Teal shouted. "You want this big-ass gun back now?"

# Thirteen: Out of the Frying Pan

"The hangar is right through that door, LT," Ruiz reported. "I cracked it open enough to get a look. Counted three hostiles working in there; technicians or mechanics, they look like. They have another jetcar set up just inside the door; looks like it's ready to go."

The master chief had just rejoined the Team at the top of the stairwell. They had advanced this far without raising an alarm, and the lieutenant had sent Ruiz ahead to recon.

"What about the one we rode in?" asked Jackson.

"One of the technicians—I counted him in the three—was out on the landing circle on a tractor, pulling it toward the hangar. I couldn't see any sign of Ensign Sanders or the others—or Zaro, either."

"Then we're going to have to get us a prisoner and ask him some questions," Jackson decided. "Let's take 'em in a rush."

Ruiz led them to the door he had just peeked through. "You'll find two on the right, just a couple dozen steps away," he whispered. "The one on the tractor is the problem: He's too far away to take by surprise."

Jackson nodded to Falco. "You'll have to take him out right away, then."

"Sure thing, LT," the sniper replied, cradling his rifle.

In a few seconds the Team was in position. At a nod from Jackson, Ruiz pushed open the door. LaRue and Rodale rushed through and charged the two startled technicians, who were consulting an electronic meter beside the idle aircraft.

A powerful engine rumbled from the direction of the landing zone, and they could see a squat, heavy tractor moving toward them. The disabled jetcar, with its mangled front landing gear, loomed behind it as it was towed toward the hangar, the skid scraping over the tarmac. Falco immediately knelt down and leaned, bracing himself against the doorjamb, and took aim, squeezing off a single round. The powerful projectile made only a little noise coming out of the big sniper rifle, and the men actually heard the impact as it knocked the tractor driver off his seat.

The compact tractor kept chugging onward, towing the disabled jetcar toward the hangar. Harry Teal sprinted out the door and hopped up onto the seat, bringing the tractor to a halt a few seconds before it ran into the frame of the hangar door. By that time, LaRue and Rodale had secured the hands of their prisoners and dragged the sullen men up to the rest of the Team. Once again slinging his sniper rifle, Falco stood with his G15 in his hands.

"Take a look around; make sure that's all of them," Jackson ordered Chief Harris. Together with Falco, the chief sprinted across the hangar, then climbed into the jetcar that was parked there. They looked into the engine shop on the far side and came jogging back, shaking their heads, as Teal dragged the body of the slain driver off the landing circle and into the shelter of the hangar.

"Master Chief," Jackson said. "Let me borrow your translator earpiece for a minute. I want these guys to know what I'm saying to them."

Ruiz popped it out and handed it to the officer. Jackson looked at the two prisoners, who were staring wide-eyed at the dead man. They wore white uniforms like coveralls and were equipped with tool belts but no weapons. Both had the unsettling green eyes that characterized the Eluoi; otherwise, their features were similar to those of a human of Italian or Greek ancestry. Jackson was pretty sure they were workers and not soldiers. One was just a kid, not even ready to shave, but the other was older, with a weathered, lined face and thinning gray hair. The officer held out the earpiece to the second prisoner, gesturing toward his own ear. The man took it with visible reluctance but placed it in his ear canal with an ease that suggested that the translating device was not unknown to him.

Jackson indicated the dead Eluoi and fixed the two prisoners with his most formidable glare. "I need information. If you don't want to end up like him, you'll give it to me. Do you understand?"

The older Eluoi nodded. "What do you want to know?" he asked, his voice quivering slightly. The words emerged from the fellow's mouth in that spitting bizarre language of the Eluoi, but the translator in Jackson's ear still functioned perfectly. The lieutenant could see that the prisoner was afraid, and he intended to capitalize on that emotion.

He indicated the disabled aircraft. "The other passengers on that jet—what happened to them?"

The man's eyes flashed quickly to a door on the other side of the hangar, but immediately his gaze reverted to Jackson. "I didn't see any other passengers," he said. Then he nodded his head, an overt gesture, in the direction of the closed door. "Nobody else was on that ship, not when I came out here."

His eyes were wide, and he was trembling with fear. Clearly, he was afraid of someone who might be watching or, more likely, listening.

"How long have you been here?" Jackson demanded loudly and sternly. At the same time, he gestured to Ruiz, Harris, and Falco, pointing silently at the door.

"Um. Only a few minutes. I just got here," the worker said, watching nervously as the three SEALS moved smoothly and silently over to the door.

"What about that aircraft?" the lieutenant demanded, indicating the jetcar that remained parked in the hangar. "Is it ready to fly?"

"Yes. Yes, sir, it is," said the technician, nodding eagerly.

At the same time, Ruiz smashed open the door and Harris and Falco plunged through. Not knowing what to expect, LaRue and Rodale threw the prisoners to the floor and held them down while Jackson followed his Teammates into the adjacent room.

Suppressed shots thudded out, the short bursts of gunfire quickly followed by a very female scream and two SEALS simultaneously shouting, "Clear."

When the lieutenant charged in, he found Consul Char-Kane standing, her hands over her mouth, between two dead Eluoi soldiers. Each had been shot in the chest, and the Shamani woman, though unscathed, had been spattered with blood from at least one of them; her golden jumpsuit was spotted with crimson drops. On either side of the doorway, Ruiz and Falco kept sweeping the room, maintaining security as they "cut the pie" with the muzzles of their weapons. They had both shot the Eluoi soldiers as they stood within a half meter of the shocked consul.

Harris caught Char-Kane as she swayed and helped her sit on a bench. A glance around suggested that they were in some kind of wardroom, perhaps a place for an air crew to prepare to fly. A bank of metal lockers lined one wall, and a hallway led toward additional doorways.

"Check it out," Jackson said, motioning with his head. Ruiz and Falco immediately darted down the short corridor as Char-Kane drew a ragged breath and wiped at the blood on her jumpsuit. Chief Harris came over with a towel he found in one of the lockers, and she took it gratefully.

Falco and Ruiz returned a few seconds later.

"Looks like a shower room and a lavatory, LT," the master chief reported. "There's an office, too, nobody in it, and a door connecting to another stairwell. I looked in, just to be sure."

"Are you all right?" Jackson asked Char-Kane, kneeling to look into her disturbingly crimson eyes. Her face was pallid, and she was shaking and leaning into Harris, who didn't seem to mind the contact at all.

"Yes. I—I think so."

"Where are the others?" the lieutenant asked, sitting next to the Shamani woman on the bench. "Are they still alive?"

"Yes, they were taken off the jet and brought in here with me. The two of your SEALS and the doctor and Mr. Parker. Then Zaro came in. He was very angry, and he cuffed your ensign in the face. And he kicked the man, Mate Dobson, I think you called him, who used the turret gun to kill so many Eluoi."

Jackson's jaw tightened in cold anger, but he pressed on with the questions. "Where did they go then?"

"Zaro took them through the door in the back of this room. They were starting to go down into the building when there was a large explosion. They came back up here in a hurry."

"Sounds like you flushed the game, Master Chief," Jackson said approvingly before returning his attention to Char-Kane. "But they didn't take you with them? Why not?"

She shrugged. "I do not know. Perhaps they do not need to study the Shamani as much as they wish to examine you humans. After all, they have known about us for many millennia, and your people are brand-new to them."

The idea made sense, but Jackson was still suspicious. Ignoring Harris's look of reproach, he queried her harshly. "Where did they go after they came up here?"

The consul de campe met his glare coldly. "They proceeded back into the hangar, but the door was closed, so I could not see where they went after that."

"But no aircraft landed or took off since we arrived, did they?" Jackson was pretty sure that the disabled transport in the middle of the landing circle would have prevented flight ops, but he still watched the Shamani woman carefully as she answered.

"None," she replied.

"All right." The options were few, the LT realized. Either the captives had been taken down a different route into the building, or they were still up in one of the buildings surrounding the landing zone. He trotted back into the hangar, where LaRue was still watching the prisoners with his G15 held casually in his lap. The large doors were open, and he could see two more structures atop the building. One was the shed where the gun that had ambushed them had been hidden, and it was perforated like Swiss cheese, the two metal doors hanging loosely from their hinges. The other was another hangar similar to the one the SEALS now occupied. The large door to that one was closed, as were the two smaller doors to either side of the main entry.

"We're going to take that building in a hurry," he said to his Teammates. Char-Kane, her tunic cleaned of blood finally, had joined them, and he looked at her seriously. "Do you want to come with us? We're getting out of here."

"Yes, I'll come," she said. "I do not want to be a prisoner of the Eluoi."

"Okay." Jackson gestured to the transport aircraft in the hangar. "Take a seat in the pilot's chair and get the engines warmed up."

Jackson cradled the plasma gun in his hands but decided he wanted to make an even faster entrance than the cutting tool would allow. "Harry, Derek, each of you get a C-6 charge ready. I want each of you to blow open those small doors. The rest of you, spread out, and let's go."

The Team emerged from the hangar at a run, splitting into shooter pairs and sprinting across the LZ toward the opposite hangar. The two men with explosives ran ahead, each choosing one of the doors. They were only halfway across the circle when the large hangar door before them slid upward with remarkable speed.

"Down!" cried Ruiz, the first to glimpse the interior of the darkened building.

"Watch for our people!" Jackson shouted, slamming to the deck, painfully jarring his shoulder.

A bolt of plasma energy sliced out of the shadows, searing across the pavement. One of the SEALS shouted, "Shit!" and Jackson knew one of his men was hit.

Now he could see a rank of a dozen or more Eluoi soldiers standing or kneeling in front of another transport. Even as the aircraft's turbines started to whine, the enemy troops opened up, sending slugs and beams across the tarmac where the Team lay prone.

The SEALS returned fire with precision. The suppressed G15s spit quietly, and one by one the Eluoi toppled. After half of them had been shot in the first seconds, the others started to scramble back toward the rear of the transport.

"Kill them! You can see them, right there! Kill them!"

It was Zaro, exhorting his men from the base of the aircraft's ramp. Jackson sighted along the short barrel of the plasma gun and shot a beam, cursing as the energy weapon seemed to diffuse over the fifty meters of distance. Zaro spit a curse, clutching his arm where he had been burned, and then sprinted up into the aircraft.

The turret gun started to stutter, and the SEALS fell back, taking shelter behind the tractor and in the ruined shed. The aircraft moved forward, jets roaring, until it was out in the sunlight. Jackson saw a man's face at one of the side windows and recognized Ensign Sanders.

Rocky, meanwhile, hoisted his rocket launcher as the transport started to rise into the air. One missile would bring it down in flames, but Jackson shook his head and shouted, "No!"

The word was lost in the roar of the engines, but the gunner's mate understood and lowered his launcher. In another second the aircraft was veering away from the pad, the jets rocketing it on a beeline course toward the massive pyramid rising like a majestic mountain just a few klicks away.

"All right, regroup!" the lieutenant shouted as the roaring faded quickly into the distance. "Mount up. We're bugging out in that!" Jackson pointed toward the freshly refueled jetcar that was still parked in the hangar.

"What should we do with these two?" La Rue asked. He was sitting in a chair, Baby resting on the floor and the G15 held casually across his lap, the suppressor muzzle facing in the general direction of the two Eluoi technicians. The prisoners were handcuffed and bound at the ankles, sitting against the interior wall of the hangar.

The lieutenant looked around and saw the metal grids of a heavy shelf unit nearby. "Leave 'em," he ordered. "They'll keep until someone comes along to turn 'em loose—after we're long gone."

Ruiz gestured to the older prisoner, pointing to his ear, and the man removed the translator and returned it to the master chief, who put it back in his own ear. Meanwhile, Falco climbed up to join Char-Kane in the cockpit while his Teammates removed the wheel chocks from the jetcar's landing gear. The Shamani already had the turbines spinning as the the SEALS scrambled aboard. Harris climbed into the dorsal turret to check out the gun, and Jackson joined Falco and Char-Kane on the flight deck.

"This one look the same as the one you flew?" the lieutenant asked.

Falco nodded. "Same make and model, sir." From his seat in the pilot's chair he threw a couple of switches. Immediately dials and lights came to life across the instrument panel. "Fuel tanks are topped off," he noted approvingly.

Char-Kane advanced the throttles from the copilot's

seat while Jackson strapped himself into a spare chair just behind the two pilots. There he had a good view out the starboard windows and, by craning his neck a little, could also see out the other side of the cabin. He noticed with a small sense of surprise that the sun at last seemed to be dipping below the zenith. He guessed it was now the equivalent of middle to late afternoon on the world of Batuun.

There were wireless headsets at each seat, and the lieutenant slipped one on and flicked the speak switch. "Everyone strapped in back there?" he asked, receiving a chorus of "aye, ayes" in response.

With another couple of switches flicked, Falco started the powerful engines. The turbines kicked over slowly at first but quickly swelled to a thundering roar. Even with the high RPMs, Jackson was interested to note, there was very little vibration in the tightly constructed machine.

With a little pressure on the stick, Falco eased the jetcar out of the hangar and then quickly bounced it up into the air. Jackson watched only a little nervously as the landing circle dropped away below them. He glanced at the hangar but saw no sign of anyone moving there. The shock of the SEALS' audacious attack, coupled with the explosive diversion in the base of the big garrison building, had done its work well, he concluded. The enemy soldiers were still concentrating their search on the bottom levels of the massive structure.

The aircraft lurched slightly as Falco moved it into forward flight, and then they were flying away, climbing easily. The massive bulk of the city's great pyramid—where Zaro's aircraft with the prisoners aboard had flown—was visible some four klicks away, and the pilot started off on an oblique approach, keeping the huge structure off the port bow. From this close they could see that it bristled with domes and gun batteries; it did not look like an inviting place to fly.

Jackson thumbed his mike. "Anybody hurt back there?" he asked.

"I took a burn down the side from one of those ray guns, LT," Robinson replied. "But I'll be okay. Harry's having a look at me now."

"Okay, hang tight," the officer replied.

More of the large white cubes that made up the city rolled past below them. Jackson saw smaller aircars scooting about below and larger aircraft streaming above, mostly following those invisible highways in the sky. He was restless and tense and kept glancing out one window and then the other, certain that things were going too smoothly. It couldn't last.

And it didn't. Harris shouted the first warning, his words crackling through the earphones.

"LT! We got bogeys, swarming from twelve o'clock, six o'clock—hell, just about every direction you can fucking imagine!"

The usually unflappable Chief Harris sounded a little tense through the intercom as he spoke from the jetcar's dome turret.

Jackson could see them through the cockpit windows even as the aircraft lurched to the side. Several aircraft similar to their own vehicle were closing in from above and below. The lieutenant saw the muzzle flashes coming from the forward-trained chain guns as well as the single-barreled cannons on the dorsal turrets.

Their own transport vibrated, and for a moment Jackson thought they'd been hit. Then he realized it was Harris, returning fire with his own turret-mounted gun. Falco put the jetcar into a steep dive, and the gunner's shots went wide. But the dramatic evasion seemed to take the pursuers by surprise as the other aircraft flew past and then came around only slowly.

The ground was coming up in a rush, and Falco worked the stick like a veteran, pulling them out about fifty me-

ters above the roofs of the massive buildings. He jerked
the stick back and forth, violently rocking the flying vehicle, banking hard to go around a tall tower that loomed
above the flat tops of the other buildings.

Harris continued to shoot at the targets overhead, and
Jackson saw an Eluoi jet dive away, trailing smoke. The
enemy wasn't shooting at them from above, and he
guessed it was because they didn't want to spray their city
with explosive rounds. He thanked his stars for that small
mercy and held on tightly as Falco dived even lower so
that he was almost skimming the tops of a vast bank of
buildings.

"Shit, LT, I'm not sure I can hold it!" the pilot snapped,
jerking back on the stick. The machine responded instantly, bouncing higher, clearing the buildings by a more
comfortable margin. But now there were pursuing aircraft to both sides, all with their turret guns trained on the
SEALS. Jackson had to resist the urge to duck as he saw
those barrels flashing and knew that a hail of slugs was
converging on their jetcar.

Something caused the aircraft to lurch violently, and
this time it wasn't the pilot's frantic maneuvering. The
lieutenant could see a line of holes appear in the starboard
wing, and then the whining turbine banged loudly. Bits of
metal spewed from the exhaust vent, and the jetcar
slowed abruptly, like a bus when the driver slams on the
brakes.

"We're hit!" Falco shouted. "I can't hold altitude."

"Make for that greensward, there." Consul Char-Kane
indicated a gap between two square buildings, still man-
aging to sound calm and reasonable even as flames spit
along the base of the starboard wing.

The aircraft was banking heavily, but Falco somehow
managed to shoot the gap. The two white walls flashed
past like the sides of a canyon, and then they were over
one of the natural areas that had been allowed to survive

in the midst of Batuu City. Jackson saw ponds, some meadows that were bright with wildflowers, and several groves of lofty trees.

Falco picked out a flat field and struggled to level the jetcar's flight. They were still descending, the starboard wing lower than the port. He pulled back on the stick, and the sole remaining engine pivoted into VTOL mode, slowing the aircraft even more but emphasizing the list to starboard with a sickening lurch.

The ground was coming up fast, and then it was right there. The impact came as the starboard wing crumpled like tinfoil, and then the fuselage slammed into the ground with a jolt that snapped Jackson's neck forward.

Harris, in the turret, continued to fire at the pursuing aircraft. There were nearly a dozen of them, buzzing like bees, swarming and circling around the stricken jetcar. Falco pushed a switch, and fresh air flooded the cabin as the emergency hatch on the port side popped open.

Jackson unstrapped himself and stood up, surprised to find that nothing was broken. Shells impacted the wrecked machine, and he saw flame and smoke erupting from port wing.

"Bail out!" he shouted, reaching up to slap Harris's foot.

The chief slid down from the turret, joining the lieutenant, Falco, and Char-Kane in tumbling out of the cockpit. Jackson saw that the rear ramp also had dropped, and the four SEALS in the passenger compartment were falling to the ground. Each carried his weapon and as much gear and ammunition as he could manage.

They raced away from the aircraft, making it maybe ten or a dozen steps before the remaining fuel exploded in a fireball and a cloud that blotted out the sky.

# Fourteen: Custer Had It Easy

The force of the blast sent Jackson sprawling, slamming him flat on his face with stunning force. His nose was bleeding when he pushed himself off the ground, and his injured shoulder collapsed without warning, planting his face into the ground a second time with even more painful results. For a moment he fought a wave of darkness and nausea, but he refused to yield to the comforting blackness. Instead, he pushed himself to his knees, braced by his good arm, shaking his head while he tried to ignore the pain shooting through his nose and arm.

Consul de Campe Char-Kane lay beside him, and he roughly pulled the moaning woman up as he stood. Together they swayed; a glance backward showed him that the jetcar was engulfed by flames, spewing a cloud of smoke high in the sky. It was that plume, he realized, that was keeping them alive for the moment, since the Eluoi in the swarming aircraft couldn't get a good look at the ground.

"Head for the trees—move, goddammit!" Jackson shouted, more for his own benefit than for that of his men, who had anticipated his order. The SEALS already were sprinting toward the looming cover as each man regained his feet. The sturdy trunks were only a couple of dozen meters away, their leafy branches rising high, with obscuring shadows darkening the grove beyond the fringe of woods.

Harry Teal, Master Chief Ruiz, and Rocky Rodale were the first to reach the tree line. Each man threw himself down behind a log or knelt at the side of a thick, sturdy trunk, using the wood for cover as the Team snapped off individual rounds carefully. Most of the Teammates were between the three men and their targets, and the swirling smoke critically impaired their visibility, and so they took only the safest, surest shots that the rapidly deploying Eluoi allowed them.

Engines roared on all sides, and through the swirling smoke Jackson saw a number of the pursuing jetcars settling onto the grassy field. LaRue raised his rail gun and, after checking behind him for friendlies, sent one of his slugs shooting through the turbofan of the nearest aircraft. The stricken vehicle dipped nose down and plunged into the ground with a satisfying explosion while Baby's backblast trimmed the grass in a wide, fan-shaped swath.

Another transport craft roared almost directly overhead, and Jackson held up his hand to shield his face from the searing heat of the jet exhaust. Char-Kane leaned against him, almost falling, and he supported the Shamani, half carrying her as he stumbled toward the welcome cover of the dense grove of trees. Bullets and plasma rays from the pursuing Eluoi shot past him, and he veered instinctively, dodging back and forth while lumbering as fast as he could. In another second he and the consul de campe passed between two large trees, and he released her. She collapsed against the trunk, safe for the moment, as the lieutenant raised his G15 and took a look at the flame- and smoke-swept field.

He saw that Rodale, like LaRue, had his weapon up and was standing boldly just outside the fringe of woods. Rocky sent a missile set to heat-seeking mode sizzling toward another one of the Eluoi aircraft. The round went right up the tailpipe to blast the jetcar out of the sky, scattering shrapnel almost as far as the retreating SEALS. The three wrecks burned furiously, spilling smoke everywhere, but there were still more aircraft settling to the ground, jet engines roaring. Rodale retreated into the woods as a hailstorm of bullets chewed up the turf around his feet.

Ramps dropped from the descending transports, and soldiers spilled out of many of the aircraft, moving with skill and discipline. Some dropped to the ground and opened up with firearms or launched searing bolts from the plasma guns. One of those bolts crackled past close enough to set Jackson's hair bristling on the nape of his neck, but the smoke still was giving them some cover. The Eluoi advanced in a rough skirmish line, keeping space between the men, some providing covering fire while the others rushed forward.

Jackson dropped one of the charging Eluoi with a well-placed single round from his G15, then looked for the positions of his men. Robinson limped past, his trouser almost torn off his left leg by the energy bolt he'd taken back at the landing pad. Teal had patched him up with gauze and a bandage wrap, but the officer could see blood seeping through the dressing; the wound looked worse than the man had let on.

Then all the SEALS were in the trees, the cool darkness shading and sheltering them. A quick glance showed Jackson that his men were lined up at the fringe of the grove. Each man had found good cover and was using it to snipe at the enemy troops, who were still out in the open, protected only by the smoke and the wrecks of the burning aircraft. The SEALS understood the situation well enough that each man was conserving his ammunition without any orders from his leader.

From the air Jackson had seen that this grove was a small clump of tall trees, and he knew that the enemy aircraft were landing on all sides, disgorging dozens of soldiers. The way the lieutenant reckoned it, they had about sixty seconds to catch their breath and set up a perimeter before they would be in the fight of their lives. Their lethal controlled fire from the fringe of the woods had given the enemy pause, and now it looked like the Eluoi soldiers mostly had gone to ground and were creeping forward very carefully, in many cases worming their way around the bodies of comrades who had attacked more impetuously.

There wasn't any time to set up a hasty ambush and no place to do it, anyway. At least a half dozen aircraft had disgorged their troops in the arc right in front of the SEALS' position, and many more of them had flown over the woods or circled to the right and left; presumably, they would be sending more soldiers in from wherever they came down. The officer had to assume that the enemy would be approaching from all sides.

Jackson knew that their ammunition count was starting to get low. Rocky was probably down to his last two rounds, and G-Man couldn't have much more than half his load for the rail gun left. The best move they could make would be to withdraw under cover, peel back, and run. Maybe if they made things expensive enough for the Eluoi, they could hold them off until dark, whenever the hell *that* might be. Then he would order the men to break up and follow their escape-and-evasion training as individuals. E&E training hadn't covered trying to hide on an alien planet, but it was worth a chance, considering that the other two options seemed to be to get the detachment wiped out here or to surrender.

Even as he considered the situation, his men were adjusting the odds against them. Pulling up Baby, G-Man shouted, "Fire in the hole!" and pulled the trigger. The backblast tore the trees and shrubs behind him but did far worse damage to one of the jetcars as the copper and uranium slug punched through the nose plate and ripped into the interior of the craft. A massive gout of flaming debris shot out the rear of the aircraft, and the transport dropped like a stone. Nobody made it out.

Even as the first target was impacting the ground,

G-Man wrenched the big gun around and fired off another round. This one hit an aircraft in the flank, punching through one engine, sending searing bits of metal tearing through the hull like it was tinfoil. The second Eluoi jet-car was destroyed in the green flash of the copper plasma, and it crashed right on top of a half dozen infantrymen who had been advancing across the grassy field. The approaching enemy forces were stunned for a moment and in disarray. It was time to go. One man, an officer to judge from the gold braid on his sleeves, stood up and tried to order his men forward until Falco blew his head apart with a well-aimed slug from his squirrel gun.

But there were too many Eluoi. A glance to either side showed that they were closing in on the fringe of the grove to both flanks. If the SEALS stayed there at the edge of the grove, they could pin down the men in front of them, but they'd be caught like rats in a trap once the flanking forces moved in.

"Leapfrog rear," Jackson shouted. "Master Chief, Rocky, on me, base. Harris, Falco, G-Man, back! Teal, find us a back door!"

Grabbing the consul, Jackson pulled her down next to him. He slung the plasma gun from his back and picked up his G15 again. Conserving ammunition, he switched the weapon to semiautomatic and started punching out single shots to hold the Eluoi at bay. While Ruiz and Rocky also put out fire, the other SEALS withdrew, peeling back to the left so that they wouldn't cross in front of their Teammates' line of fire. They all moved back about thirty meters, turned, and took cover. The only one who didn't stop was Teal, who continued to move back to find an avenue of escape.

The Eluoi infantry before them dashed up to the edge of the grove, spraying the trees with fire. The plasma guns didn't seem to be very useful in the foliage: The beams could burn the shit out of a leafy limb, but the resulting smoke and sTeam seemed to dissipate the energy burst, robbing it of most of its power to hit anything beyond ten or fifteen meters. But their slugs went whistling and chipping through the trees, thwacking into trunks, snapping small branches, buzzing like bees past the heads of the cautious, ducking SEALS.

The volley of return fire from the Team was, of necessity, much lighter than what their attackers were pouring onto them. Still, their marksmanship and steadiness under fire and the strength of their defensive position allowed them to make their shots count. Jackson saw three Eluoi, clearly visible in their off-white uniforms, fall one right after the other as Ruiz fired his G15 in single shots. Several of the enemy rushed between a couple of large trunks, and a grenade boomed through the woods, dropping the attackers, sending shards of shrapnel tearing through the leaves overhead. Once again the advancing Eluoi went to ground, taking up positions behind trees, fallen logs, and other cover.

But Jackson remained keenly aware of the unseen enemy soldiers who certainly were closing in from the right and left. He dispatched Sanchez and Marannis to watch the left flank while Rodale and the limping but furious Robinson moved out to guard the right.

By the time the two fire Teams had moved into position, the Eluoi in the front were advancing again. Chief Harris, Falco, and G-Man started to put out fire, conserving rounds but making sure the enemy knew they were there. As the 6.8-mm projectiles snapped past them, Jackson and Master Chief Ruiz, who had been the base of fire, peeled back, turning to the right so that they wouldn't step into the line of fire. With a rough jerk, Jackson pulled the consul along with him with his left hand. This wasn't the time to worry about the niceties of polite society. It was far more important to move fast and not get shot by friendly fire than to worry about manhandling somebody.

The pursuing Eluoi were slowed by another grenade, the concussion blasting explosively through the woods. The men in the white uniforms kept their heads down, returning fire blindly, creeping very carefully from one protected position to the next. Even that tactic wasn't very effective as G-Man launched a grenade that burst in the air right over a pair of crouching infantrymen. Neither of them got up. Still moving back, the SEALS pulled away from their pursuers.

"No one in sight on the left, LT," Rocky called out from behind a nearby tree. "I think we put some distance between us."

*Good.* It was only a delay in the ultimate confrontation, not a victory, but it gave the SEALS a chance to keep fighting.

Rodale, in a hoarse whisper, added another bit of information that was far less encouraging. "Smokey's hurt bad, sir. He's biting the bullet and shooting the hell out of those white shirts, but damn, that burn—"

"Okay, thanks for the heads-up, Rock." *Nothing we can do about it now, dammit!*

Passing the others once more with Char-Kane in tow, Jackson and his men continued into the woods, turned, and set up a field of fire. Within only a few moments, all the SEALS were a hundred meters back into the woods without any of the enemy in sight. Robinson was leaning on Rodale's shoulder, his face pale, and when the lieutenant got a look at his leg—where the plasma beam had scorched him and Teal had placed a hasty bandage— Jackson knew that Rodale had been speaking the truth. Blood was seeping through the gauze, and the wound stretched from his chest to his ankle.

As the officer looked ahead of him, he saw a small flower garden where Teal was kneeling. The enemy wasn't in sight, and his man might have found a way out for all of them.

"Consolidate!" Jackson said loudly as they set up a final perimeter around the flower garden. This time his men held their fire as there weren't any targets visible in front of them. Only the trees and their oncoming Team-mates met their eyes.

"Tell me you have good news, Teal," Jackson said as he let the master chief see to the men.

"I really wish I could, boss," Teal said. "Right now, we're in the middle of these damned woods. There isn't anything around us but flat grasslands and hostiles. There must be a dozen of those ships out there, each with a load of troops. We've got nowhere to go but right here."

"We can make it damned expensive for them, sir," G-Man said from where he knelt in the flowers. The big man and his huge weapon were incongruous among all the colors and perfumed smells.

"Roger that, sir," Chief Harris put in.

All Rocky did was unship his M76 Wasp and hold it in his hands. On their blast setting, the missiles he had left would take out a lot of the enemy. Char-Kane looked on stunned as she realized that all the men expected to die in the next few minutes but seemed to care only about mak-ing their deaths as expensive as possible in terms of casu-alties among the Eluoi. These humans were terrifying to any civilized being, but in their determination and loyalty to one another they were fascinating.

"All right, we use this garden as our perimeter, but stay in the trees: Don't let them spot you from above. Harris, can you see to the consul? Get her somewhere as safe as you can find." He glared at the Shamani woman, who still seemed strangely impassive in the middle of the chaos. "For God's sake, keep your head down!" he ordered.

"I shall do that," she replied, allowing Harris to take her arm and lead her laterally through the woods.

The SEALS found firing positions, with Teal, Maran-nis, and Sanchez on the far side of the garden, which was a mere twenty meters across. Jackson settled himself behind the stump of a large tree that apparently had been felled by a saw fairly recently, since the base was still solid and had begun to rot only where the cut had been made.

Would the Eluoi reconsider? They had to have taken scores of casualties already, and the fight had cost them a half dozen aircraft. Maybe they would decide that the SEALS were not worth rooting out of this redoubt. Maybe the sun would set soon, and they could separate and slip away in the darkness. Maybe—

Jackson's train of maybes was interrupted by the flash of an off-white helmet some twenty meters away. He squeezed off a shot, sending the Eluoi diving for cover, and reconsidered.

Maybe his Team was just screwed.

"I would like a weapon," the consul de campe said to Chief Harris, sounding very decisive.

The chief had overturned a stone park bench that he had found just under the canopy of trees. At one time a park visitor might have sat upon it and admired the flowers in the garden. Now, tipped over, the seat provided a bulletproof barrier facing the enemy, and the sturdy wide marble legs to either side gave the chief and the Shamani woman a little bit of flank protection.

"Really?" he said, completely surprised by the request.

"Would you allow me to use that?" Char-Kane added, pointing to the chief's sidearm, the VP90 10-millimeter caseless pistol in the holster strapped to his leg.

He shrugged. With several clips left for his G15, he didn't need the pistol for the time being. "Sure," he said. Unsnapping the holster cover, he pulled out the handgun, checked that there was a round chambered, and set the weapon to semiautomatic.

"This is the safety," he explained, showing her the little

switch. "I'm flipping it off, so don't point it at anything you don't want to shoot."

"I understand," she replied solemnly, taking the pistol that he handed to her butt first.

"I'd hold it in two hands," he counseled. "It's gonna kick back when you pull the trigger. It'll fire one bullet every time you pull."

She nodded and leaned over to peer around the leg of the park bench, impressing the chief, who was going to warn her not to raise her head over the top of their protective barrier. He leaned out on the far side and spotted a pair of white-clad soldiers worming forward, not ten meters away.

He sighted down the barrel of the G15 and planted a slug right through the helmet of the nearest Eluoi, killing the man instantly. The fellow's comrade crawled next to the corpse, using the body for cover, but when he raised his head for a look, Harris sent a round whistling right past his ear. The soldier dropped back, pressing his face into the ground.

Harris was stunned by a loud report right next to him and whirled around to see Char-Kane, her red eyes wide, holding the smoking pistol in both hands. She glanced around the bench leg, then turned to the chief.

"You are right. It has much kick," she reported. "But I seem to have killed the"—she paused, groping for a word, then concluded proudly—"son of a bitch."

He glanced past her, saw the body only a couple of meters away, and whistled. "Nice shooting," he said, wrestling with guilt. He popped off a few more rounds, making sure the Eluoi kept their heads low, and then turned back to the Shamani.

"Listen," he said awkwardly. "We don't have much of a chance here. But there's no sense you going down with us. Maybe you could go to them and, you know, surrender. I don't think they'd hurt you. It's us they're after."

"That is a kind thought," she said, looking at him very seriously, her face about twenty centimeters from his. "But I think I belong with the SEALS now."

The impulse was too strong to ignore, and he leaned in and kissed her very lightly on her full red lips.

She blinked. "That was a surprise," she noted.

"Uh, yeah. It was for me, too," Harris allowed. "I'm sorry—I shouldn't have—I don't know what the hell—"

"Do not be sorry," she said, leaning close and kissing him back. "I liked it."

It was all Harris could do to spin around and shoot, but he knew the Eluoi were too close to ignore. "Of all the rotten timing," he muttered to himself as he saw at least six or seven of the enemy infantry closing in on the little park bench redoubt.

Jackson was saving the last magazine for his G15. Using the plasma gun as the enemy closed in, he held them at bay, cutting smoky swaths through the sagging undergrowth. But every time he hit one of the enemy, there seemed to be two or even three more to take his place.

And he knew this was the condition of his Team all around the little perimeter. The SEALS were shooting only sporadically as the cross fire continued to get more intense.

Looking up, Jackson saw the calm eyes of Master Chief Ruiz. The SEALS would die at their officer's command, but he was considering an order that was even harder for him to issue. As if sensing his agonizing quandary, Ruiz simply nodded, his dark eyes sympathetic and understanding.

"Dammit, this isn't Horatio at the bridge," Jackson said as he let his G15 drop down and hang in his hands. "We aren't holding the pass while anyone makes their escape. And it sure as hell isn't Fort Apache. There isn't going to be any cavalry coming to the rescue."

He stood up straight and turned to face the oncoming Eluoi. "Put up your weapons, SEALS," he ordered. "This is not exactly an order I ever expected to give," he added quietly, almost to himself.

A shadow flashed across the blossoms, and Jackson looked up to see three Eluoi jetcars roaring in a tight circle over the flower-dotted clearing. Landing gear lowered, they came to a halt in the air and started to drop vertically into the garden.

The envelopment was complete.

# Fifteen: Fight in the Skies

Before Jackson could say another word, a streak of fire slashed across the sky and the nearest Eluoi jetcar exploded while it was a hundred meters off the ground. Fire and debris rained down from the air, bits of flaming oil spattering across the grass and trees. Jackson wrenched his shoulder as he threw himself flat. Ignoring the pain, he covered his head with his arms, looking sideways to see the other SEALS protecting themselves with the same crude tactic. The ground shook underneath him as the smoldering body of the jetcar, one engine still whining, crashed to the ground in the middle of the garden.

Fuel spilled out, a shimmering sprawl of burning liquid gushing closer to them. Blistering heat seared the lieutenant's hands, growing quickly to a dangerous onslaught as the fire continued to spread.

"Move!" he cried, pushing himself to his feet. The others were already in action. Harry Teal took a moment to grab the lieutenant by his good hand and pull him along. They all scrambled across the flat ground and tumbled into the cover of the trees as the burning fuel quickly consumed itself. The Eluoi soldiers in the woods took a few shots but backed off quickly as the SEALS replied in force. The enemy troops seemed shaken, perhaps by the new developments in the air battle; they showed little fight as they retreated from the aggressive Team.

"What the hell is going on?" LaRue demanded, looking skyward. His rail gun once again was cradled in his arms, but he wasn't shooting at the moment.

Another aircraft shot past their window of sky as they

looked up from the circle in the trees. This one staggered visibly in the air as it opened up with some kind of heavy automatic cannon. Another plane exploded a short distance away. Their view of it was blocked by the trees, but Jackson felt certain another of the Eluoi craft had been destroyed.

Ruiz moved into the smoking clearing to confirm. "Looks like these bastards have a few other enemies besides us," the master chief reported. "We got us a box seat for the dogfight."

Indeed, there were dozens of newly arrived aircraft wheeling through the skies overhead. The sleek twin-engined jetcars of the Eluoi had been bounced from above by a motley collection of clearly lethal machines. Firing rockets and the tracers of automatic weapons, the newcomers had plunged from the heights in a very loose formation, scattering the Eluoi craft. Already Jackson counted five or six fresh pyres of black smoke, with clouds billowing up over the tops of the trees, marking places where the jetcars had crashed.

There were at least a dozen of the newcomers. Some of them were much larger than the jetcars and bristled with guns and other armament. Volleys of rockets hissed through the sky, curling around nimbly as guidance systems steered them into Eluoi engines and hulls. Roaring jets whirled past, and more aircraft—the white fighters of the Eluoi—came diving toward the fray.

"Harris, Rodale, Sanchez!" Jackson barked, seeing the three men nearby. "Move into the woods—give me a sitrep!"

The air was full of screaming aircraft, crackling rockets, stuttering automatic guns, and blasting explosions. On the ground, however, Jackson couldn't see any of the Eluoi soldiers in the woods. Just a couple of minutes later his men reported back.

"The bastards are pulling out, sir," Rocky Rodale shouted

breathlessly from a dozen meters away. "They must be pretty shaken up."

"Then let's keep shaking!" Jackson shouted. "SEALS, advance—these woods belong to us, dammit!"

Grenades crumped through the trees, and the silenced G15s fired away as the Team surged through the woods, the men retracing the route of their retreat less than an hour earlier. Their targets were few: Most of the Eluoi ground troops had simply run, and the few who stood and fought were quickly cut down. In a couple of minutes the Team had fought its way back to the edge of the woods, where they had a view of a whole swath of sky over Batuu City.

One of the attackers soared overhead, banking sharply, spitting shells from a nose-mounted cannon. The stream of shots caught a jetcar in the side, and the nimble little craft came apart with a searing explosion. Bits of metal and fire rained down while the two engines broke free from the disintegrating body and tumbled forward, rolling along the field until they splashed into a nearby pond.

The surviving Eluoi soldiers were fleeing headlong across the field. Jackson watched dozens of them scrambling into four of the transports that had brought them to the fight. Jets whining, the transports lifted off one after the other.

But the same strafing fighter that had just flashed past was coming around again. With an impressive display of marksmanship, the newcomer poured fire into the first of the four transports, exploding it in a dramatic fireball; in quick succession, the pilot shot the second, third, and fourth transports out of the sky. They crashed in a row, almost exactly where they had been resting. Searing flames swirled around all of them, and no one got out.

"Nice shooting," the lieutenant remarked, impressed.

Jackson and Ruiz knelt behind a tree trunk at the edge of the grove, where they had a clear view of the dramatic aerial battle. The lieutenant looked up to see Consul Char-Kane and Chief Harris behind a neighboring tree, and he quickly scrambled over to her.

"Do you know what's going on?" he asked. "Who are these new guys?"

"They are the Assarn," Char-Kane said in disgust. "Pirates, as I told you before. Brutal, violent savages!"

"Sorry, ma'am," Ruiz replied. "But they look like the cavalry to me. They sure pulled our asses out of a sling back there."

"That was purely accidental, I assure you. They are making an attack in force on Batuun, probably for the purpose of thievery, perhaps even to take captives as slaves."

Jackson considered her assessment. He could see dozens of the attackers in their motley ships. A few were engaged in the freewheeling dogfight, and many more were swarming around the pyramid, directing fire against the massive structure and taking some nasty shots in return. In the space of a few seconds, the lieutenant saw three or four of the Assarn ships blasted out of the sky. Whatever kind of people they were, they had courage.

And they had numbers. Flying in pairs and larger groups, they continued to flash across the skies above Batuu City. The Eluoi were mounting a more concerted defense now, sending in wings of a dozen or more jetcars and larger aircraft. Contrails twisted and spiraled through the air in ornate patterns, and the roar of engines was frequently, if temporarily, overwhelmed by the blasts of explosions.

Clearly, the center of government was the primary target. Rockets rained down on the pyramid, and one by one the batteries on the sides of the massive structure were knocked out. Smoke billowed from many of the impacts until the mountainous building was obscured like a peak buried in a storm cloud. Massive blasts tore great chunks of stone and steel out of the thick sides of the massive structure.

"We going to move out on foot, LT?" Ruiz asked.

"I'm thinking about that," Jackson replied. "Doesn't look like we could salvage any of these wrecks, does it?"

Indeed, there were more than a dozen Eluoi jetcars scattered around the huge field, but every one of them was a complete wreck. Some were still burning, and the ones that weren't actively aflame were already charred, blackened hulks.

"No, sir. But I don't like the thought of crossing three kilometers of open ground just to get to that line of buildings."

"I hear you, Chief. At the very least, I think we should stay put here until nightfall. The men could use a break." He saw that the sun, with agonizing slowness, was still creeping gradually down to the west. In disgust, he estimated that they had been in daylight for some thirty hours.

For another hour they continued to watch the air battle from the shelter of the grove. The Eluoi were clearly gaining the upper hand as they massed their ships in larger and larger formations, a dozen or more of them swarming around each pair of Assarn attackers.

Still, the "brutal, violent savages" continued to give a good account of themselves. The SEALS saw two Assarn ships weaving back and forth, each covering his wingman, as the Eluoi jets tried to line up a killing shot. Finally, one of the intruders was hit by a volley of missiles and disappeared in an explosion. The second Assarn dived away, with the Eluoi in pursuit. Flying low, the target of all that attention skimmed over the rims of the buildings flanking the large park and then dived almost to ground level.

Rockets flew toward it, but the pilot maneuvered frantically and the shots all missed, many of them plunging

into the ground to erupt in geysers of dirt and grass. The
Assarn flew toward the grove, then banked sharply, using
the pyres of smoke from the wrecked jetcars as cover.
Wheeling through a tight semicircle, he came out shooting, picking off one of his pursuers with a blast that shattered the cockpit windows and dropped the jetcar like a
pigeon hit by a blast of birdshot.

Amid the unique and varied shapes and colors of the
Assarn ships, this one looked strangely familiar. Jackson
noted the twin forward-firing barrels and the now-empty
rocket launchers under the short wings. Shaped like an
old X-15 test rocket he'd seen only in pictures, the fighter
seemed to have incredible maneuvering powers; they all
stared as it almost came to a halt in the air, then pivoted to
pursue a trio of jetcars they dived past it. With one snap
shot from the coaxial guns, the Assarn blew the port engine off one of the Eluoi aircraft, sending the vehicle
tumbling out of control to crash explosively on the increasingly torn grass of the vast field.

"Isn't that the same guy who took out our attackers?"
Ruiz asked.

Jackson remembered the impressive shooting that had
knocked down the four transports, one after the other, and
nodded. "I think so. I don't remember seeing another ship
like that one."

"Ah, shit. It looks like he isn't going to make it," the
chief growled.

Jackson saw the same thing: A murderous Eluoi cross
fire had ripped through the slender black fuselage. The
roaring engine hiccupped, and the aircraft started to
smoke. Leveling out, wobbling awkwardly, it began to
lose altitude.

The attacking jetcars didn't give the Assarn a chance
to escape. Instead, they pressed in from above and on
both flanks, continuing to rake it with fire. Abruptly, the
black fighter's engines quit completely. The stubby

wings couldn't provide much lift, but somehow the pilot kept his nose up. The fighter smacked into the ground, bounced once, then skidded through the field, churning up dirt and grass in a long trench before coming to rest some 500 meters away from the grove where the SEALS were concealed.

Jackson saw the canopy pop open and a lone figure emerge, tumbling down the side of the fuselage and landing on his feet. He started to run, but two of the Eluoi jetcars swooped down, engines roaring. They landed to either side of him, ramps spilling open to disgorge armed soldiers. Surrounded by eight men with upraised plasma guns, the pilot stopped running and raised his hands.

"Jesus, look at them pound that poor son of a bitch," Ruiz muttered as the Eluoi soldiers kicked their prisoner again, then hoisted him roughly to his feet. They had been beating the fellow for several minutes but still hadn't subdued him. His uniform, a black coverall, was half torn away and his face was a bloody mess, but he still thrashed and struggled in the grip of his captors.

Jackson wondered if they would just shoot the fellow and be done with him, but instead the Eluoi threw the pilot to the ground again and pinned him there. A line was lashed around his outstretched wrists, and his captors roughly pulled him onto his feet again, then started dragging him toward the waiting jetcar.

"Poor bastard. He's even more unpopular around here than *we* are," Ruiz remarked.

"Where some men see a poor bastard, I see only opportunity," Jackson said. When the master chief raised his eyebrow, the officer simply clapped him on the shoulder and said, "Follow me. I think it's our turn to ride to the rescue."

"Righto, LT," the master chief replied, brightening. "You wanna just rush 'em from here?"

"I don't think we have any time for subtlety," the offi-

cer agreed. "At least they have their backs to us." Quickly
Jackson issued his orders to the waiting SEALS. "We go
in a rush. No shooting until they spot us, then give 'em
hell. Falco, LaRue, covering fire as necessary. But we
want to keep that pilot alive."

The Eluoi on the ground were focused on their prisoner
as they prodded him toward one of the waiting jetcars.
There were eight armed soldiers on the ground and, presumably, a couple of pilots in each of the jetcars. The
Teammates could see through the clear canopies that the
gun turrets were empty.

The SEALS sprinted from the grove, charging abreast
in a line. They had nearly 500 meters to cover, but they
moved quickly. For the first half of the distance the Eluoi
didn't notice the danger. It was one of the pilots, looking
toward the captors and their captive, who finally saw the
attackers. The Eluoi raced down the ramp onto the field,
shouting something, and the captors spun around.

Immediately the SEALS opened fire. The range was
long for the G15s, but they were all expert shots, and four
of the eight Eluoi went down in the first volley. The first
to die was the Eluoi with a gun pointed at the back of the
Assarn pilot. Then Falco drew a bead and took out the
Eluoi pilot who had shouted the warning. To him, the distance didn't mean much.

The Assarn prisoner reacted immediately. Jerking on the
line binding his wrists, he pulled the captor immediately in
front of him down onto his back. Next he launched a vicious kick to his right, breaking the leg of another of his
captors. After the kick, he dropped flat on the ground.

The two standing Eluoi started shooting, but it was too
late. Ruiz and Teal snapped off a couple of short bursts,
and both men fell. The engines on the jetcar to the right
roared, and the aircraft started upward even before the
stern ramp snapped shut. Clawing for altitude, it banked
away as the pilot tried to flee the sudden, shocking at-

tack. LaRue's Baby thundered from across the park, but his round only grazed the aircraft and passed through it without igniting anything vital. Rodale had his launcher on his shoulder, and the tube spit a sizzling rocket. The deadly projectile chased the aircraft up into the sky, striking the tail and exploding immediately. The jetcar spiraled into the ground a kilometer away and quickly began to burn.

By the time the SEALS reached the prisoner, the Assarn pilot had used the rope attached to his wrist to strangle the Eluoi he had pulled over. Drawing a knife from the dead man's belt, he quickly dispatched the final one of his captors, the soldier who had been writhing with a broken leg.

He watched warily as the SEALS approached. Despite the bloody nose and the cuts on his cheeks and face, he stood tall and proud. Better than six feet in height, he had long blond hair bound into a tail hanging halfway down his back. He held the knife in his hand and offered a sheepish smile as he studied the guns of the SEALS and looked at the carnage they had wrought among his captors. With a shrug, he dropped the knife and planted his hands on his hips.

"I guess I owe you some thanks," he said. "But who are you?"

His language was different from that of the Eluoi, more guttural, with long "u" and "o" sounds pronounced clearly. But the translator in Jackson's ear functioned perfectly, and the electronic speaker clearly transformed his words into English.

"It's a very long story," Jackson said. "Can you understand me?"

The pilot nodded and pointed to his own ear. "I have a translator implant. Comes in handy in my ... business."

"Then maybe we can help each other out." The lieutenant gestured to the remaining jetcar, which still was idling on the ground nearby. "But first, can you fly this thing?"

The man smiled broadly, a very reassuring expression.

"In my sleep," he said cheerfully.

"Then let's go for a ride," Jackson suggested. "We can talk and get away at the same time."

"Let's move, Team," Master Chief Ruiz growled. "We've got another ship to steal."

# Sixteen: Olin Parvik

The rescued pilot made his way through the small cabin to the flight deck with Falco trailing after him. Jackson moved to follow but was restrained by a hand on his wrist. He looked back in surprise to see Consul Char-Kane holding him. She glanced meaningfully past him, where the stranger had just gone through the forward hatch.

"Are you sure you can trust him?" she asked. "He is of the Assarn!"

"So he's one of the Assarn," the officer replied. "The way I see it is we've done him one helluva favor. I'd like to think he knows he owes us. And don't forget, we were burned toast back there in that garden, as good as dead— or captured—until he and his pals showed up to pull our fat out of the fire."

"I told you, they are savages, uncivilized, untrustworthy!" she insisted, her red eyes wide with alarm.

Jackson's tone turned cold. "He's done nothing savage so far," he retorted. "And he seems like our best chance to get out of here alive and maybe even get our people back. Do you want to come along for the ride or not?"

She pursed her lips, and those eyes seemed to flare with a little more intensity than usual. Saying nothing, she stalked past the lieutenant to take the number three seat in the cockpit. Jackson took the fourth chair, and Chief Harris scrambled up the few steps into the low dorsal turret.

"Strap in, everybody," the pilot declared cheerfully. "We go!"

Jackson repeated the announcement through the intercom for the benefit of those of his men who were not wearing the translator earpieces.

Immediately the big turbofans roared, the force of their blast directed straight down, burning what remained of the grass into the ground. Quickly the vehicle rose into the air, with the pilot, as well as Jackson, Harris, and Falco, scanning the surrounding skies. Thankfully, there were no other aircraft in their immediate vicinity. Even as he looked around, the lieutenant couldn't help noticing that the craft moved much more smoothly than it had with Falco at the controls.

For now, the air battle seemed finally to have ended. There were many columns of smoke in the sky, a number of them rising from the park where the SEALS had fought the oncoming Eluoi. The mountainous bulk of the Batuu City pyramid continued to smoke and burn in a number of locations. The huge structure seemed to have been the focus of the attacks. The turrets and emplacements of its defensive batteries had been pretty well demolished, in many cases leaving gaping craters in the thick concrete walls. From the depth of some of those holes, it was clear that the walls must have been dozens of meters thick.

Two massive airships hovered above the wrecked pyramid, directing streams of water down onto some of the raging fires. To Jackson, those firefighting machines seemed more like dirigibles than winged aircraft—they had long swollen fuselages with numerous hover fans mounted on the sides—but to judge from the impressive volume of liquid they dispensed, they must have had some seriously powerful engines simply to get themselves off the ground with all that weight.

The only other aircraft they could see were white Eluoi jetcars similar to their own flying circular patrol patterns over the perimeter of the city or buzzing back and forth over the heavily damaged pyramid. There was no sign of the Assarn attackers who had survived the frenzied battle.

The flying machine banked away from the park, gliding smoothly under the control of the blond long-haired pilot. He took them up at an easy angle, flying toward the east and the city's outer wall. Approaching that lofty barrier, which by then was far below them, he banked to port and assumed an easy cruising altitude, as if they were simply another Eluoi jet on perimeter air patrol.

Holding the control stick casually with his left hand, the pilot leaned back and twisted in his seat so that he could see Falco and Jackson. His breezy confidence was infectious, and he seemed to have a natural feel for controlling the aircraft.

"So you are strangers here," he remarked. "I think not Eluoi or Shamani and certainly not Assarn." He twisted farther and flashed a wink at Char-Kane, who was seated directly behind him. "Except you, a consul of the Shamani, I am assuming."

"You are most observant," she said coldly. "I am a consul de campe."

The pilot whistled. "You're keeping rather casual company for one of your exalted status, are you not? No offense, but these men seem a little rough around the edges compared to the serene Shamani and the ritualistic Eluoi."

"We're from a planet called Earth, in the star system known as Sol," Jackson explained. "Only recently have we ventured into the stars. Our world was first visited by the Shamani some three years ago."

"Ah, I see. We have been preparing to contact you, but here you are on an Eluoi world." He cocked an eyebrow, making the statement an unspoken question.

"They took us against our will," the officer said. "The Eluoi infiltrated one of our outposts. They brought us back here when their presence was discovered."

He glanced over at the third chair, where Char-Kane was watching the exchange, her expression aloof and haughty. Jackson continued. "In fact, we had initially been informed that the Eluoi presence in our system was in fact your own Assarn."

"Of course. The Shamani and the Eluoi each consider us to be the scourge of the universe. Did you hear that we eat our children? Worship beasts as gods? Or perhaps that we ritually slaughter our women when they are done with their breeding years?" asked the pilot cheerfully.

"Actually, we heard that you practice ritual killing, that your young warriors must find an innocent civilian of some other race and cut them in two with a steel blade."

"I am Olin Parvik, of the Assarn," the pilot announced. "And that is not true. We are indeed a warrior society. We have to be with enemies such as the Eluoi and Shamani. But there is no honor in the killing of innocents."

"Why did your ships attack Batuun?" Jackson asked, adding: "Not that I'm complaining! We were in a pretty fix there until you came along. But you were fighting against some damned long odds."

Parvik made a spitting gesture toward the window and the great white city. "The Eluoi are little more than slavers—kidnappers, in fact. They have been raiding our worlds on this rim of the galaxy for many years. It was only recently we learned that this planet, this place called Batuun, is where they collect those slaves and prepare them for transport to the far side of the galaxy. They have thousands of our people held captive in that great pyramid. We were attempting to rescue them, but sadly, our numbers were too few. The air defenses, especially in the pyramid, were too many, and more than half our ships were destroyed. The rest were forced to withdraw—for the time being, at least."

"Do the Eluoi control many worlds in this area of the galaxy?" Jackson asked.

"Not terribly many. But where they have outposts, they are like this, teeming with millions of population and defended against attack by our starships." He nodded toward the massive square tower that loomed just beyond the northeast wall of the city. "The PDB—that is, planetary defense battery—would destroy any spaceship in orbit over this hemisphere of Batuun. So instead we launched our shuttles from the far side of the world and came around to make the attack at low altitude after we took out their satellite detection and defensive systems."

"You came down to the surface in your little fighters? Brave move, but isn't it foolhardy, too?" the lieutenant probed.

Parvik shrugged, his blond ponytail bouncing on his back. "Rash, perhaps. But they will remember us for a long time, you can be sure. You can see we damaged their local defenses and sowed a great deal of confusion. And I have hopes that we still might meet with some success."

"I notice you attacked the pyramid but not the PDB. Wouldn't it make sense to try and take that out so that your starships could close in?"

The pilot shook his head, grimacing in frustration. "We lack the weaponry even to put a dent in that tower. It is shielded with steel as well as forty meters of concrete. Our missiles would barely dent it."

"What kind of weapon is it? Or are there more than one?" Jackson probed, studying the square structure. It was even taller than the pyramid and must have been very well armored if the weapons that had chewed up the central structure were impotent against it.

"A plasma beam cannon. It cuts through the atmosphere with enough force to simply boil the air out of its path. When it reaches space—which it does at nearly the speed of light—it can slice through anything in its path. In the vacuum, its range is nearly unlimited—say, at least a half million kilometers."

"So any ship that even goes into a high orbit is a potential target," the officer realized. Olin Parvik nodded.

"What's your plan now?" Jackson asked. "Do you intend to try and get back to your ships in orbit?"

Parvik shrugged. "To do that I would need a shuttle; this jetcar will not take us out of the atmosphere." He looked at the officer frankly. "And what are your intentions . . . your plan?"

Jackson was forced to shrug. "I haven't got one. We have four comrades who are prisoners of the Eluoi—we have reason to believe that they, too, are being held within that pyramid—and I hope to rescue them. But our people back home don't even know where we are, and I have no way to get word to them."

"Did you know there is a broadcaster in the top of the pyramid, a device that can transpond between star systems, using a phased signal?" the pilot asked.

"No, I didn't think that was possible," Jackson admitted. He glanced at Char-Kane. "The consul told me that such devices were still in the planning stages."

"Maybe for the Shamani. Do you see that mast emerging from the summit?" Parvik indicated a tall shaft extending straight up into the air from the very top of the pyramid. As they flew closer, they could see coils of tubing enclosing the lower half of the spire.

"I was wondering why that wasn't destroyed when you were blasting holes in the sides of the place," the lieutenant admitted.

"The truth is, we hoped to capture the device. The Eluoi have developed the technology; it allows signals to be pushed through distances of many light-years, almost instantaneously. Once they arrive, they can be set to convert back to any waveform of communication, fit any of your radio frequencies for example. So . . ."

"So if we could reach that transponder, we could send

a message back to our own system," the officer concluded, finishing the thought.

"Precisely."

"This is rumor, nothing more!" snapped Char-Kane, finally breaking her silence. "Such a transponder is merely
theoretical. Our best scientists have determined that it is
not even possible to make such a device! And I warned
you not to trust this—this Assarn!" She all but hissed the
last word.

"There are some things you Shamani told us that have
turned out not to be true," Jackson replied. "And a few
other key details that you seem to have withheld."

"You humans are like children!" she retorted. "You are
not ready for all the secrets of the universe."

"I think we're ready for this one," he replied pointedly.
"It sounds like we need to go to the pyramid and see about
getting inside."

"And that might be easier now than it would have been
just a few hours ago," Olin Parvik declared. He pointed
toward the great pyramid, which was only a few klicks
away now. For the first time Jackson could get a good
look at the battle damage, which appeared to be significant. Gaping craters yawned in the sides of the massive
structure, and several of the holes were spewing dense
columns of smoke. Most of the battery emplacements
had been blasted into rubble, and in many places they
could see directly into the interior of the massive building
through gaps ranging from small cracks to, in a couple of
places, yawning breaches where they could see Eluoi soldiers and gun crews setting up mobile field pieces, presumably to defend against a subsequent attack.

The two big firefighting ships were focusing their attention on the far side of the huge building. Ground
equipment was arriving from all directions, mostly truck-
sized transports clustering around the base of the pyramid,

which Jackson guessed was at least three klicks wide on
each of its four sides. There were workers and repair
crews swarming around the lower slopes of the structure,
but the upper half, where much of the damage had been
inflicted, was mostly devoid of activity. A few jetcars
similar to their own were landing here and there on the
few surviving docks or on some of the few large flat
spaces within the gaping craters on the steeply sloping
sides.

"Can you get us a closer look?" Jackson asked.

"Sure." The pilot swooped the vehicle over one face of
the blasted structure. They saw a particularly large crater,
no longer smoking, that was surrounded by blasted concrete and reinforcing bars but offered a bed of rubble at
the bottom that looked flat and larger than the aircraft.
With a few deft touches of the controls, Parvik brought
the jetcar to a smooth landing within the smoldering ruin,
high up on the side of the pyramid.

Jackson unstrapped himself and stood, turning to the
rear in time to see Ruiz sticking his head through the
hatch to the flight deck.

"Hey, LT," the master chief said. "Take a look at what
we found in a locker back here."

He was carrying two garments of slick white cloth: uniforms of Eluoi officers, Jackson guessed immediately.
The smaller of the two tunics had an impressive array of
gold braid running up and down the arms. He held it up so
that the flight crew could see it in all its gilded glory.

Parvik let out a whistle of astonishment. "That's a
mijar's braid. They're the aides to the savants, the ones
who do the talking for them. This aircraft must have been
his personal transport. It might be a perfect disguise for
someone who wanted to have a look around the pyramid."
He looked more closely at the uniform, then turned to grin
at Char-Kane.

"Looks like it's cut for a female," he said with a grin,

eyeing her up and down while she glared back at him, flushing.

"I think you'd fill it out rather nicely," Olin Parvik said in a tone of approval.

They decided to make the little crater in the upper wall of the pyramid their base of operations as they worked out a plan. With a little vigorous scooping, they piled enough shards of concrete in front of the jetcar to block it from view except for directly overhead, leaving enough space that it could fly out of there in a hurry. Ruiz took charge of selecting firing positions to defend against anyone approaching from outside, and Jackson and Olin Parvik started looking at the great cracks extending through the wall at the back of the crater.

"This one is wide enough for a person to fit through," the pilot concluded after crawling forward into one gap. "It drops right into a corridor. I saw lots of dust and rubble but no smoke. More important, no guards, either."

"Let's have a little look-see," Jackson said. He found a piece of wire and draped it down through the crack, which seemed to be in the ceiling of the corridor. After tugging hard to make sure it was secure, he shinnied down the cable. Olin Parvik, nothing loath, came right behind.

Dim lights glowed from panels high on the walls, and they guessed they were emergency lights. They stepped over chunks of concrete and made their way along the eerily silent passageway. Several doors stood open to one side, and they entered what proved to be living quarters. With a definite purpose in mind, Jackson hunted through several bedrooms—sleeping chambers much like those a person would find in an elegant hotel in New York or Paris—looking into the wardrobe closets. He found and ignored a number of ornate robes and shimmering gowns, but in the fourth apartment they inspected he struck the jackpot.

White uniforms—Eluoi officer's garb—lined the racks in the closet. They were a close enough fit for him, so he took one. Olin Parvik watched in mute curiosity as the lieutenant then proceeded to rip the gold braid off several more uniform tunics. In short order they made their way back to the breach, climbed up the cable, and crawled back into the crater where the aircraft was parked and the SEALS—and the Shamani woman—awaited them.

"You're mad if you think you're going in there!" Char-Kane snapped when the officer proudly displayed his trophies. "What do you hope to accomplish?"

Jackson smiled with more confidence than he actually felt. "I'd like to get to that transponder and send a message back home, specifically to the *Pegasus*. While I'm at it, I'd like to get some intel on the interior of this place, find out where the prisoners are kept, at the very least."

"Your translation program in the earpiece only allows you to understand the language," the Shamani woman said sharply. "How do you expect to pass yourself off as an Eluoi officer when you can't talk to them?"

"That," Jackson said, smiling even more broadly, "is where you come in." He turned to Parvik. "That uniform we found in the ship gave me the idea. You said it was a 'mijar,' right? The aides who do the talking for the savants?"

"Yes," the pilot replied, intrigued.

"Well," Jackson declared, holding up the uniform he had claimed from the apartment wardrobe. "I figure I have enough gold braid here to make those rings around the sleeves. I intend to promote myself to an Eluoi savant."

The Shamani woman looked startled, but then she frowned. "It is an intriguing idea," she admitted. "And your eyes are dark enough that you could pass for an Eluoi. But what about me? As soon as they see the color of my eyes, they will see through the charade."

"Damn. I hadn't thought of that," Jackson replied, grimacing.

"I might be able to help," Olin Parvik said. He reached into a pocket on his coveralls, which he had patched up so that they at least covered most of his body, and pulled out a small packet. He tossed it to Char-Kane, who, despite her surprise, caught it with agility.

"Dark green contact lenses," the pilot explained. "Part of our standard escape-and-evasion kit when we're venturing into Eluoi lands. I also have a packet of black hair dye, but you won't need that."

"So now we know you can do it. The question is, will you?" Harris urged Char-Kane, who studied the chief with a strange expression. If Jackson hadn't known better, he would have guessed that the aloof Shamani was looking at Harris with affection.

"Very well, I will try," she said. "But I still believe it is a mad scheme."

A short while later Char-Kane and Jackson entered the pyramid through the crack in the corridor ceiling, taking as much care as possible to keep their white uniforms clean. The gold braid on the LT's sleeves glittered appropriately, a reasonable approximation of the badges of rank worn by Tezlac Catal.

There had been a fire there, but the blaze had been extinguished, and they didn't encounter any Eluoi in the immediate vicinity of the crater. They walked through a doorway, past a shattered blast door, and found themselves in a corridor with dozens of Eluoi workers, soldiers, and technicians. Bustling here and there, the workers and technicians quickly stepped aside to allow the pair in their command uniforms to pass. The soldiers offered salutes, palms pressed to the forehead, and Char-Kane casually returned them while Jackson ignored them, as he had been coached to do by Olin Parvik and the Shamani woman.

They quickly came to a transport station where Eluoi were lined up, filing into cars that rode on monorail tracks and glided smoothly to a stop. It looked like a cross between a metropolitan subway station and a tourist ride at an amusement park, and it served as a vivid reminder of exactly how huge the building was.

Despite the uniform, which clearly awed nearly everyone he encountered, Jackson was keenly aware of the risks they were taking. The translator allowed him to understand the Eluoi language without difficulty, and so he could at least react like an arrogant commander if someone addressed him. However, he could not speak that language, and any attempt to talk would immediately reveal him as an impostor.

Consul Char-Kane did speak the language, which certainly was an asset for their mission. But the officer felt keenly vulnerable as he and the Shamani woman made their way up to the transport station.

As soon as one of the workers caught sight of him, he whispered something to his neighbors, and like magic, the line parted so that the "savant and his mijar" could go right up to the next car. The vehicle was easily large enough to carry twenty people, but the rest of the Eluoi held back. Trying his best to look as haughty and aloof as a five-star admiral, Jackson took a seat near the front, and Char-Kane looked at a schematic and then punched in a destination.

Immediately they glided away from the station, riding on the single rail without vibration or noise. Char-Kane sat beside him as they entered a well-lit tunnel, quickly accelerating to the speed of a fast automobile.

"I found a label for the communications center," she explained to him quietly. "We should start to climb pretty soon."

In fact, the car quickly shot through a sharp curve, moving upward. The seats smoothly shifted orientation so that instead of resting on the floor, they now seemed to be attached to the side wall of what was essentially an elevator. They continued up for a long way, and again Jackson pictured the truly mountainous size of the building. Finally, the car curled onto a horizontal rail again, the chairs smoothly pivoting, and then glided up to another station.

Here there were far fewer Eluoi waiting than there had been below, and most of them seemed to be in uniform. However, the savant's braid continued to be the lucky charm, and the soldiers saluted smartly as Char-Kane emerged, then stood aside to give Jackson plenty of room to pass. It helped that they kept their eyes downcast. He had remembered that on the bridge of the *Gladiola*, the Eluoi crew generally had avoided looking directly at their master, and he had been hoping that the same thing would hold true here.

On foot, they made their way down a long, wide hallway brightly illuminated by glowing tubes on the ceiling. Char-Kane glanced quickly at a sign covered with hieroglyphics that were utterly unintelligible to Jackson. She led him into a side passageway and finally up to a large door made of stainless steel. A pair of guards snapped to attention as they approached.

"The savant wishes to inspect the transponder room," Char-Kane said curtly.

"Of course, madam. Do you wish for us to summon the director?" asked one of the guards. Another guard pushed a button, whooshing the door open.

"That will not be necessary," the woman said dismissively.

Jackson concentrated on walking in as if he owned the place. He saw many banks of equipment with technicians poring over screens, keyboards, and other pieces of equipment. At the sight of him, they all stopped what they were doing and stood to attention.

"At ease," Char-Kane said, coming up behind him. "This

is a surprise inspection. The commandant wishes everyone to cease their work and assemble in the entry hall. We will be looking at each workstation for any irregularities."

Casting nervous glances among themselves and furtive looks at the gold-ring sleeves of Jackson's tunic, the workers hastened to obey.

Fifteen seconds later, the two had the communications center to themselves.

# Seventeen: A Phone Call

"Can we give them coordinates?" Jackson asked the consul de campe. He was poring over the interstellar communications transmitter, a vast bank of switches, slides, and dials. The hum of electrical power, suggesting the output of a good-sized turbine, suffused the room, and the pole of the antenna, surrounded by a coil of cooling tubes, extended through the ceiling.

"I don't have the navigation skills to be that precise," Char-Kane said. "But we can set the target for your star system here." She indicated a computer screen where she was scrolling down through a long list of names. "Found it: Sol. All the empires have assigned it the name you yourselves use; this is the naming convention throughout the galaxy."

"So they can hear from us and know we're alive, at least," the lieutenant said with some relief. "But we can't tell them how to get here."

"It is not hopeless. We can include the name of this planet, which they will be able to find if they can consult a Shamani navigator. Furthermore, there is a chance that the men of your navy ship will be able to follow the transmission back to its source. Batuun is one of the closest star systems to your own, after all. They will not need to look terribly far."

"All right," Jackson agreed. He glanced at the door, which remained closed. But he wasn't certain they'd have much more time before somebody—an officer who was looking for a chance to do some serious ass-kissing, perhaps, or even another savant—would come in to discover them on their unauthorized mission. He shuddered at the thought of another encounter with Tezlac Catal, who would merely have to speak a sentence or two to knock the intruders silly. Jackson wished he could have brought along his G15.

"I am ready to broadcast," Char-Kane said, poised over a switch beside the computer screen. "Do you want to craft your message?"

"All right." Jackson took a seat at the keyboard and immediately encountered the next problem: Every key was a strange hieroglyphic, utterly unintelligible to him. Even if Char-Kane helped him pick out the right symbols, there was no one on *Pegasus*, probably no one on the whole planet Earth, who would have any idea what he was trying to say.

"I suggest you make a verbal recording of the message," Char-Kane said, pointing to a small device he took to be a microphone. "We will send that."

"Right, sure." Why hadn't he thought of that? He was irritated by the fact that sometimes the Shamani woman seemed to be one or two jumps ahead of him.

He tried to imagine a proper protocol, but in the unprecedented circumstances he just ended up sending a straightforward message:

> **To JCS USA, United Nations Command, USSS *Pegasus;* all Terran stations.**
> **Broadcasting from Planet Batuun, Eluoi Empire.**
> **Human captives taken on Mars by hostile Eluoi force. Transported here against our will. Roster: Twelve SEALS, Detachment Alfa, ID code zulu-zulu-tango. Civilians David Parker and Doctor Irina Sulati. Engaged with enemy forces; seeking transport home. Send the cavalry!**

He signed off with "Lt. Thomas Jackson, USN—SEALS."

Char-Kane pushed a lever forward, and the hum of power rose to a bass thrum that they could feel through the floor. The coil around the transmitting shaft pulsed with color, blue fading to white. There followed a single crack of sound, almost like a gunshot, and immediately the background noise settled back to the earlier hum.

"There. It is sent," the Shamani woman said. "Now we should leave here."

"Wait," Jackson said. "Can we access their main databases from here?"

"If you mean the main computer, records, and so forth, yes," she replied, glancing nervously at the outer door to the command center.

"Then I want to look in the database and find the prisoners, my ensign and Dobson, as well as Parker and Dr. Sulati. Will that information be in the machine?"

Char-Kane grimaced but then shrugged. "It is possible," she agreed.

"You said that you guessed they would be brought here to this pyramid, and we all watched them fly here. If they're in this very building, I'm not leaving until we make every effort to bring them out."

"Very well." The consul de campe sat down at the console and began to type rapidly. Leaning over her shoulder, Jackson watched as a bewildering array of information scrolled past on the screen.

"Here!" Char-Kane declared suddenly. "They are in an isolation cell in a workers' containment facility, set for transport away from here along with other prisoners—the same Assarn, I fear, that Olin Parvik came here to try to rescue. There are some five thousand of them ready for departure, most classed for slave labor on distant planets in the Eluoi home systems. Your people are not to be slaves but instead will be studied by Eluoi scientists."

The very idea made Jackson sick to his stomach.

"Can you find them? Locate where they are in this place?"

The woman looked toward the door, and Jackson shared her nervousness, expecting an interruption at any time.

"I will look," she said.

She looked. She found.

To Jackson's immense satisfaction, she was even able to print out a map.

Several dozen gold-braided Eluoi officers stood at attention as the gleaming steel doors to the communications center silently whooshed open. Char-Kane's reminder—"Look straight ahead; acknowledge no one!"—still echoed in Jackson's ears. He took it to heart, stalking out of the large compartment like an old Roman emperor.

The officers lined both sides of the corridor and snapped palm-out salutes as, trailed by the Shamani consul, the SEALS lieutenant marched between them. The Eluoi didn't venture to speak; apparently, they just wanted to make themselves available in case they were needed.

They very much were *not* needed, Jackson thought to himself. He proceeded to the transport station, relieved to see a car waiting for them. The doors slipped to either side as the pair approached. The two of them stepped inside the car, and Jackson didn't exhale until those doors again slid shut. Only then did they take seats, feeling small in the large car.

Char-Kane pushed a button, and the transport moved laterally, then swiftly turned down a tunnel that descended straight down. The chairs switched orientation as the floor dropped away, but the sudden motion created a momentary weightlessness, and sent a shot of adrenaline through Jackson's body as he instinctively reached for the nearby railing. Quickly he settled back into the seat as the level of descent settled in at about half a G.

"Christ!" he exclaimed. "This thing is fast!"

"It is a large structure," the consul replied. "The top is three kilometers from the ground."

He nodded, impressed. The Shamani woman was looking straight ahead, the green lenses masking her eyes to an even higher level of inscrutability than usual. The officer cleared his throat.

"Thanks," he said. "That wouldn't have been possible without you."

"No," she said, "it would not have." Char-Kane turned suddenly and appeared to look the SEALS lieutenant up and down with a curious sense of appraisal. "But I could not have created the aura of command. You made them fear you, just as they would fear a true savant. My heart was pounding in my throat, and you looked like you would have struck one of them dead if he so much as dared to look you in the eye."

He was suddenly embarrassed. Touching the blueprints, which were thin enough for him to fold multiple layers into a tiny bundle concealed in his tunic, he reflected on her skill at manipulating the communications machine.

"You're a remarkable woman—person," he said. "You can land a shuttle, operate a complicated processor, and infiltrate an enemy installation."

Her eyes turned down to the floor for just a moment until she raised them to look at him frankly. "I spent much of my childhood among the Eluoi," she offered. "The language and the symbology are very familiar to me."

"Were you some sort of exchange student?" wondered Jackson.

She snorted dismissively. "Hardly," she replied. "I was a slave. I was rescued during the Second Spider War, when the Shamani armies expelled the Eluoi from an entire star cluster. But I used my time with the enemy well."

She held out her arms and hands, flexing her fingers as

she gestured to Jackson's. "And besides, we all share the same basic physiology and anatomy. The tools of the Eluoi, or the Assarn, or the Shamani, all fit the hands of the three races."

"*Four* races, don't you mean?" Jackson suggested. "Or are you forgetting us Earthlings?"

For the first time ever in the lieutenant's experience, the consul de campe of the Shamani actually smiled, a thin, wry expression that indisputably conveyed humor. "I think you will find—eventually—that you humans are not so different from the rest of us as you think." She stopped, pensive for a second, and Jackson saw that look again. He was sure it was an expression of affection, and it was strangely disconcerting, as well as appealing, on the vaguely Asian features of the haughty Shamani.

"Perhaps," she said softly, "it is we who are more like you than our people would have suspected."

"What do you mean by that?" the SEALS challenged as the gravity increased abruptly and dramatically. The two passengers in the car flexed their knees against the sudden heaviness and felt the ride come to a smooth halt.

"We can talk about it later," Char-Kane said, still amused. "This is our floor."

As soon as they were back at the jetcar concealed in the crater, the lieutenant gathered his men, as well as the Assarn pilot and Consul de Campe Char-Kane, for a council of war. He was moderately surprised to see that the world of Batuun—this side of it, anyway—was shrouded in twilight. A lush mixture of purples and violets shaded the west, the setting sun still visible but low between the towering clouds.

Harry Teal spoke to him privately: Robinson's condition had continued to deteriorate even though the corpsman had used the most powerful antibiotics in his medkit. The wounded man needed a hospital soon if they were to have any chance of saving his life. With a muffled curse, Jackson accepted the report, knowing there was nothing he could do about it at the moment.

The Team, together with Parvik and Char-Kane, assembled quickly, squatting on the rough stone under one of the aircraft's stubby wings, and considered the myriad problems arrayed before them. Jackson and Char-Kane produced the printed schematic the woman had printed out, and the lieutenant laid out his intentions to his Teammates and Olin Parvik.

"Let us say that we can save your comrades. Nevertheless, if your ship comes into orbit around Batuun, the planet's main battery will simply blast it out of space as soon as it appears over this hemisphere," Olin Parvik explained grimly.

Jackson was not about to be deterred by details. "I know. That's why we have two missions: rescue the prisoners and take out the PDB."

"So far we've survived several crashes," Teal said with irrepressible humor. "Stolen and flown away in a number of alien aircraft. Rescued a prisoner—the very capable pilot here. Fought a small army to a standstill, and G-Man got to kill a dinosaur—ate him, too. So what's the problem?"

Quiet laughter went though the SEALS as they thought about what the corpsman had said.

"Two difficult missions even if you had two armies. How will you do it with ten men?"

"We're SEALS, Parvik. The best warriors in the galaxy," Jackson replied.

Olin Parvik shrugged. "I may not argue that point right now. At the very least, I have to admire your courage. I will do what I can to help you."

"That counts us ten SEALS and an Assarn pilot," Master Chief Ruiz noted drolly. "I would guess that makes it a slam dunk."

Jackson was pleased with the spirit even though he and Ruiz and everyone else knew this mission was about as far from a slam dunk as one could get. He turned to the chief bosun's mate.

"Harris, do we still have a Mark 92 available in the demolitions kit?"

"Yep, LT. I grabbed it up when we dumped ship, and it's not like I was going to drop it along the way; the paperwork for the loss would be incredible. One compact tactical nuclear weapon, personally carried by yours truly and set up for delayed-action deployment. Switching it over to command detonation is the act of a moment. It's set for minimum yield right now, but I can dial it up to half a kiloton on your say-so. Sounds like you might have a target for us."

"Yep. We're going to have to take out that PDB before we ship out of here—or let *Pegasus* come shipping in. I think our little firecracker is just the ordnance for that job."

"I like your audacity," the Assarn pilot said, listening to the exchange. "You speak of a fission weapon, do you not?"

"Yes. It's technology that we on Earth have possessed for about a century," Jackson explained. "This one is compact, small enough to be carried by a man, but packs enough punch to take out just about any installation." He thought for a moment. "Are nuclear weapons a part of your arsenal? Or the Eluoi, or the Shamani?"

"Yes. We can all make such devices. Generally they are avoided because in the past their use escalated to the point where whole worlds were destroyed. It is one of the few ironclad treaty points that have been established among the three empires."

"Maybe we'll sign that treaty someday. But we haven't yet," Jackson allowed.

Parvik nodded approvingly. "And the yield of this weapon you classed as a half kiloton. That will rouse fear and distress on Batuun, but with luck, it won't be large enough to attract the vengeance of the entire empire."

"Good." Jackson had more immediate concerns than the long-term repercussions, but it was reassuring to think that his tactical escape plan wouldn't result in an Eluoi attempt to obliterate planet Earth.

"You'll need to sneak past a thorough defensive perimeter," Parvik noted.

"Then we'll do it," Jackson replied. "How much do you know about this planetary defense battery, or about the PDBs in general?"

"Very much, actually. All of us were briefed on the one outside Batuu City. It was to be a secondary target of our recent attack—if the initial attack met with success," he noted bitterly.

"Now, what would be the most vulnerable point in the system that we could reasonably expect to reach?"

"The outer fence, perhaps," Parvik said. "That is, if you wanted to be reasonable. They will shoot our jetcar out of the sky if we try to fly within the perimeter: All air operations are forbidden within about five kilometers of the tower. But if you can penetrate the fence on the ground, I would think the power supply ventilation system would be your most effective target. That device of yours could crack the containment field of the power system if you could place it closely enough, say, within a dozen meters or so of the core. The secondary blast would just about level the facility. The power generation building is that heavy squat structure about fifty meters inside the fence. There are heavy batteries of defensive firepower all around it. If you get inside the building, you will recognize the power core by the blue secondary radiation around it."

"Radiation?" Falco said.

"Why, you want to have kids or something?" Chief Harris snapped back.

Ignoring the banter, Parvik continued: "One more point, however: Even if your ship reaches orbit around Batuun, we're going to need a shuttle to get up into space. In effect, we will have three missions, because we're going to have to steal that shuttle after you destroy the PDB and we rescue the prisoners. Once we have a shuttle, we can try to rendezvous with my destroyer or wait for your frigate."

"Any ideas where we could find the right transport?" Jackson asked.

"The spaceport. It is a large space to the north side of the city, and there will be many ships there."

"Right, I remember. We observed it from the air. That's where we saw Tezlac Catal and our old buddy Professor Zaro land on the planet."

"You have a buddy, Zaro? Who is he?"

"Well, it's a figure of speech and a very long story," Jackson said. "Let's just say I wouldn't mind running into him here if I have the chance."

Olin Parvik gave a shrug that seemed to communicate "You humans are an odd lot." But he let the question go and continued on task for the upcoming missions. "Of course, if we do make it to the spaceport, the shuttles will likely be guarded."

"Naturally," Jackson said sarcastically. "Why would they make it easy?"

Ruiz simply shook his head. "That would take away all the fun," he remarked laconically.

# Eighteen: Nuclear Diversion

Four hours later the plans were made, the troops were rested, and it was at long last fully dark on Batuun. Master Chief Ruiz would lead Harry Teal, Marannis, Sanchez, and the two gunner's mates on the rescue mission. They had the benefit of the maps and schematics Char-Kane had printed out in the pyramid's command center. They also had most of the Team.

Olin Parvik would fly the jetcar and carry Jackson, Chief Harris, and Falco on the mission to sabotage the planetary defense battery. The officer had deemed the smaller force better for the infiltration nature of the mission. They made the badly burned Robinson, who was feverish and very ill, as comfortable as possible on makeshift mattresses in the crater. The Shamani woman would stay with him, and if all went well, the Teammates and their rescued captives would gather there when both missions were concluded.

The rescue would be timed to begin a few minutes after the nuke destroyed the space battery. Both Parvik and Char-Kane assured the humans that the attack would shock and disrupt the activities in the great city, and they were counting on the benefit of the diversion. The long-awaited darkness was a welcome asset for both missions.

At the same time that Ruiz led the rescue attempt, the sabotage Team would fly back to the pyramid and collect the rest of the SEALS and, they hoped, the freed prisoners. Then the whole group would head for the spaceport. Still relying on the diversion caused by the battery's destruction, they would attempt to steal a shuttle, take off, and, if all went well, rendezvous with Parvik's starship in space. He classified the ship as the rough equivalent of the destroyer class—slightly larger and more heavily armed than a frigate. There they would await the arrival of *Pegasus* from the star system known as Sol.

To the SEALS, of course, it was home.

The planetary defense battery was in a massive tower just outside the city wall. Well aware that no flying vehicles were allowed in the area, the Team had based its plan on the idea that they would have to go in on foot. Parvik flew the jetcar over the city wall and then settled down in a field just past one of the twelve-lane highways where ground transport entered and departed from the metropolis.

"It will draw suspicion if I wait here for you," Parvik said, "so I will take to the air and circle a safe distance away. When the bomb detonates, I will immediately come back in this direction. Use your communicators to guide me to your exact position."

"Right," Jackson said. "And thanks for the lift."

"Good luck," replied the Assarn. "If you destroy that target, you will provide great assistance to our next attempt to strike Batuun."

The three SEALS had concealed their skin under green and black camouflage paint. Stealth was at a premium—more important than firepower on this mission—but they still carried their suppressed G15s with a spare magazine of ammunition for each man. Falco, of course, had his squirrel gun strapped to his back. Wearing standard jungle camouflage fatigues, with Chief Harris carrying the Mark 92 nuclear bomb in a backpack, they spilled out of the opened ramp of the aircraft and immediately melted into the shrubbery beside the field. Parvik wasted no time firing up the downward-oriented turbines, lifting off, and quickly soaring away.

The target loomed some seven or eight klicks away, a structure similar in shape to the old vehicle assembly building on Cape Canaveral, though it was about ten times as large. Groves of fruit trees filled the ground between the SEALS and their target. The massive space cannon perched atop the structure, but at least, Jackson reminded himself, they would only have to get the bomb into the smaller building they could see next to the main structure.

The men moved carefully though the groves, keeping as much cover as possible between themselves and their target. The two point men, Sanchez and Marannis, were particularly missed right now, but as a sniper, Falco was more than competent at stealthy movement. Harris, with the bomb, followed behind him, and Jackson brought up the rear. The electrician's mate led the group to within several hundred meters of their target. It was just past a small curve in the road that wove around several of the groves.

The SEALS took cover in a pile of brush and tree trimmings, with the road leading up to what looked like the main gate just a short distance from where they were hiding. This was the best chance to examine the compound and determine the optimum way to penetrate it.

"There's cover to within a few dozen meters of the fence," Chief Harris commented as he lowered his electronic binoculars from his eyes.

As the men watched the compound, a quiet noise came up from the road behind them. Without a word being spoken, they all ducked and silently watched a vehicle of some kind that was moving along the road. It was an odd-looking rectangular thing with six wheels evenly spaced along each side. The front of the vehicle was transparent, with a row of lights across the top. As they watched it pass, they could see that there was a single driver and a passenger in the front. It looked like the driver was the individual looking straight ahead on the left side of the front compartment; the person next to him was leaning back and looking out to the right side.

The vehicle passed by without noticing the SEALS or the suppressed G15 rifles that tracked the two people sitting in the front every moment they were in sight. Slipping up quickly, Lieutenant Jackson and Chief Harris watched what had to be a truck of some kind go up to the front gate and stop. The gate was a series of heavy bars that extended the width of the road and terminated in thick pillars at both ends. The whole fence was a series of horizontal bars stretched out between posts. There was maybe a ten or twelve centimeter gap between the bars, an open space that gave the SEALS a more or less clear view inside the compound.

As the truck stopped, two heavy gun emplacements on top of the pillars tracked its every motion. Spaced out along the pillars of the fence were smaller versions of the same gun mounts. The tree grove indicated to the SEALS that there probably weren't any sensors in the immediate area of the fence. If the guns were automatic, it would be very hard on the workers who tended the trees. Any critters coming in to feed on the fruit would set off a lot of false alarms. The gate, for all its impregnable look, might have been the weakest point in the security system.

To the side of the truck was a tall post with a box on the top. It was at just the right height for the passenger to be able to reach out and pull some kind of coiled cable away from the box and into the front compartment of the truck. None of the SEALS could see what was happening, but suddenly the guns moved back to pointing up the road and the heavy bars of the gate began to retract to alternate sides. The gap opened, and the truck rolled into the compound.

As they watched the gate bars slide shut, the SEALS could still make out the truck from their vantage point. Moving quickly to one of the trees, Jackson clambered up as quietly as he could. Now at a higher point but still covered by the three-pointed leaves of the tree and the aromatic fruit that dangled from the branches, he could see the crew of the truck as they stopped by one of the gun emplacements. They moved to the back of the truck, lowered a ramp, and disappeared inside. A moment later, they were back out, carrying what appeared to be a heavy box. They moved into the gun emplacement, and that was all the officer could see for a few minutes. Then the men appeared again and repeated their actions twice more. Finally, they climbed into the vehicle and moved on to the next emplacement in the line.

Climbing down, Jackson headed back to where the other SEALS were waiting in concealment. He quickly informed them of what he had seen.

"Looks like an ordnance resupply to me," Chief Harris commented. "It could be that they expended a load of ammunition during that fracas earlier today."

"There's a lot of gun emplacements in there, Chief," Jackson said. "That truck didn't look big enough to carry three of those boxes for each gun in there."

"Maybe this is another one coming up right now, boss," Falco said as he pointed back along the road. Now that they were looking for it, they could all see the wavering lights of what could have been another vehicle coming up the road.

"Quick, Chief," Jackson said, making a fast decision. "Help me move some of these bigger chunks of brush into the roadway. Falco, if that vehicle doesn't stop, you stop it."

Without a word, the sniper pulled his big rifle from his back and got down into a firing position. He would be able to see the oncoming vehicle easily through his electronic and optical sight. The big 10.2-millimeter projectiles of the rifle had the best chance of penetrating any obstacle if he had to fire at the truck.

Moving fast, Jackson and Harris dumped enough brush

into the roadway to block any kind of easy passage. Then they both took up hasty ambush positions on either side of the road. Each SEALS was careful to make a mental note about just where his Teammates were placed so that he wouldn't fire accidentally in their direction. It was far from a safe way to set up a hasty ambush, but it would have to do.

The truck appeared and started to slow as the beams of its lights illuminated the brush piles. If the SEALS were lucky, they could take the vehicle without firing a shot. If they weren't, they would have to find another way into the compound.

The truck slowed and stopped just a few meters from the brush pile. Both doors opened, and the men inside got out. Knowing that the front two men were his Teammates' concern, Falco kept watch in the direction the truck had come from while also paying attention to the back of the truck.

The two men walked up to the brush and started to talk in the hissing, clicking language that still gave Chief Harris the willies. Still, he was wearing one of the translator earpieces they had recovered earlier, and through that device the chief could tell that the men were complaining that the other vehicle must have knocked the brush over and dragged it into the road. Cursing didn't translate well at all, but Harris got the impression that the two men were definitely pissed.

As the men bent and lifted some of the brush, the SEALS struck. In a sudden rush, Harris and Jackson moved in and seized the two men. With their faces covered in green and black camouflage, the SEALS' appearance froze the two aliens in midmotion. Jabbing with the muzzles of their weapons, the two humans knocked both of the prisoners down and quickly searched them. Flipping them over, Jackson got down into the faces of the two men as Chief Harris covered them from a few steps away.

The two prisoners started to yammer in their native language until Jackson stopped them with a curt gesture. "Chief?" he said. "You still got that earpiece? Let's loan it to one of our new friends, here. But do it on the QT."

"Sure thing, sir." Harris turned his head and stepped behind the truck. Out of sight of the two prisoners, he removed the translator and came back, slipping it into the officer's outstretched hand.

Jackson indicated the passenger, who was a fairly stout fellow. "You take Hardy here around to the other side of the truck. I want to have a little talk with Laurel."

Harris prodded the chubby Eluoi to his feet with the suppressor on the barrel of his G15. Looking between the two men with a defiant glare, the prisoner reluctantly let himself be pushed to the far side of the truck.

The officer handed the earpiece to the driver, who had watched the whole exchange in wide-eyed fear. With simple sign language Jackson instructed him to put the device in his ear, which the Eluoi did as quickly as his trembling hands would allow him to.

"It would be really good if you would talk to me," Jackson said as he pressed the muzzle of his suppressor against the driver. "Otherwise, you're of no use to me and I'll just kill you where you lay."

"I will talk," the man said in a shaky voice.

"Good," Jackson said. He called out in a louder voice, "Chief, bring Ollie back over here."

The chief complied. The heavier prisoner glared defiantly and looked down almost in contempt at his companion, who still lay on the ground.

"Now tell me," Jackson said to the driver harshly in English, "are you making another ammunition delivery to the guns inside?"

The alien under the muzzle of Harris's weapon must have been braver than average. He babbled a string of alien words to his companion. Of course, he had no way of knowing that the SEALS officer had the translation device in his ear.

"Tell them anything," the prisoner said rapidly. "Once they're inside the perimeter, they won't know which way to turn, and the guns will cut them down."

"That was the wrong answer," Jackson said as he straightened up. He raised his G15 and pulled the trigger. A single suppressed round smashed into the overweight alien's head, and the Eluoi toppled hard to the ground. The body twitched once and lay still.

Jackson's Team was at risk, and the officer had no reluctance to be as ruthless as the situation required.

"Don't tell me just 'anything.' Tell me the truth," Jackson said to the surviving captive.

The other prisoner couldn't talk fast enough. After Jackson indicated that Chief Harris and Falco should move the body and dump it in the brush pile, the alien driver explained how they had been delayed en route and were delivering another load of ammunition for the automatic defenses of the facility. There should have been another truck that delivered its load along with them, but it had gone on ahead.

While the SEALS made fast work of pulling the brush out of the way, Jackson had the germ of a plan hatching in his head.

"Get in the back of this thing," he said quietly. "Bring all of the gear. Fast now. That other truck will be coming back soon, according to our prisoner."

There was an external control that lowered the ramp, and the other two SEALS clambered inside. While Chief Harris covered the prisoner, Jackson quickly wiped off as much of his face camouflage as he could with a cleaning rag he habitually carried in his pocket. Then he pulled Ollie's shirt over his own.

"Get in and get ready to move," Jackson said as the

ramp was closed behind his men. "We're going to pass that other truck when it comes out, and you had better act as normally as you can."

The eyes of the driver automatically went to where the other Eluoi had been dumped in the brush. He wanted nothing more in the world than to please this deadly apparition that was standing in front of him. They both climbed into the front of the truck through the passenger side door, Jackson never letting the prisoner out from under the threat of his weapon. As soon as they saw the lights of the other truck move along the road, they knew it was back out of the gate.

"Move," Jackson said as he held his weapon down below the view of anyone outside the vehicle.

As the driver started the truck forward, the lights of the oncoming vehicle grew brighter. Jackson looked around in the compartment for something with which to shield his face and picked up what looked to be a very thick tablet, an electronic clipboard. As the other vehicle approached, he lifted the tablet and tilted his head down as if he were studying something on its blank screen. His left hand never released its grip on the suppressed G15, something the driver noticed very clearly.

"They're waving at me," the driver said nervously.

"Then wave back if that's what you would normally do," Jackson growled.

The other truck passed them without any hesitation. Turning in his seat, Jackson watched it continue down the road away from the facility until it disappeared around the curve in the road. Then they were pulling up to the gate and stopping.

"Oh—by the will of the savant," the driver prayed, "the guns are tracking us. Plug in the pass. You have to plug in the pass or they will annihilate us!"

"Pass?" Jackson said.

"The plug on the pole outside," the driver said desperately. "We only have a few moments. Plug the wire on the pole into the pass you're holding."

Moving a control on the door lowered the window, and Jackson was able to reach the control box the driver seemed so terrified of. The robot guns on top of the two posts had turned and lowered to cover the truck. Whatever they fired, Jackson didn't want to find out. He pulled in the coiled wire and stuck the unfamiliar plug into a socket in the tablet he had been holding to cover his face. The tablet chirped, and the guns turned away. That was all there was to it.

The driver moved the truck forward according to Jackson's directions and turned to follow his normal routine. They pulled up closely to the squat power structure without incident, and Jackson ordered the driver to lower the ramp. Then he turned to the alien.

The driver looked into Jackson's eyes, and all he saw there was death. Before the SEALS officer could say or do anything, the alien's eyes rolled up into his head until only the whites showed, and then he slumped down into the seat.

Prepared to kill the man, Jackson looked down at the inert form as he lifted his weapon. Touching his neck, he felt a pulse, but it was pretty clear the fellow hadn't been faking his swoon. Shrugging, and with his conscience a little relieved, the officer looked behind, through the viewing window, into the cargo space.

In the back of the vehicle, Falco and Chief Harris were moving forward. Between them, they had one of the big boxes, the top of which they had covered with a cloth they had found in the cargo compartment. The lumps under the cloth were the two SEALS' weapons set so that they could grab them as they dropped the empty box. They had removed the contents and set the big rounds of clipped ammunition to the side in the back of the truck.

Inside the case was the demolition pack holding the Mark 92 and a coil of line.

As they came up to the front of the truck, the door opened and both men expected to see a dead body and their lieutenant. What met their eyes was the sight of a bundled prisoner, his arms and legs secured with plastic ties and his mouth covered with the sleeves of his shirt, which had been torn off his arms. Jackson looked down at the other two men.

"Okay, Chief," Jackson said. "We've got this truck pulled up tight to the building. You use it to climb to the roof, and Falco and I will make the deliveries."

"You'll want this, sir," Chief Harris said rather formally. He handed the detonator box to his lieutenant. Jackson knew what the chief meant. He could see that the telltale indicator on the box was glowing with a faint red light, indicating that the nuclear device had been armed. In case something happened to the chief, he had given Lieutenant Jackson the means to detonate the bomb remotely.

"Get up topside, Chief," Jackson said as he took the lethal little box and slipped it into his front pocket. "We'll wait for you here or at one of the other emplacements up the line."

"Roger that, sir," Chief Harris said as he and Falco set the box down close to the front of the truck.

Quickly opening the case, he pulled the backpack holding the Mark 92 out and slung it from his shoulders. He quickly went up the side of the truck where it was close to the power building and clambered onto the flat roof. No shots rang out, and there wasn't anything else Falco or Jackson could do. The lieutenant came down from the cab and helped Falco move the box into the enclosure surrounding the gun right in front of them. It had blocked most of the movement at the front of the truck, and there didn't seem to be any personnel in the area.

"Damn," Jackson said as they moved into the weapon enclosure. "There's no one here at all. These people depend entirely on machines for their defense. All the troops around here are doing is feeding the weapons. They're servicing the machines, that's all."

"So what does that mean, LT?" Falco said.

"It means that we may have a chance to pull this off," Jackson said as he looked around the enclosure at the tools of war inside. "You follow procedure and you can fool a machine. It's meant to notice something out of the ordinary and will ignore anything that's supposed to be there. Now let's go back and bring up another crate."

While the two SEALS continued moving the boxes around, up on the roof Chief Harris could see that there were several more gun emplacements that he had to be concerned about. But the guns were each in one corner of the roof. They didn't swivel back to face him, and they certainly didn't depress their barrels; otherwise, they could have shot at the building they were meant to protect. Up on the rooftop were several ventlike structures, shaped like inverted J's. He went up to the center one and heard a fan running somewhere inside the building.

Ducking his head, the chief moved under the open mouth of the ventilator and peered inside. Darkness met his eyes. When he shone a dim blue light down into the darkness, the only thing he could see was what looked like a rotating fan blade. There was no way to get into the building from there.

As he moved from vent to vent, Chief Harris noticed the same thing at each opening. There was nothing below him but a fan blade. If he tried to enter the building through the ventilation system, he would be cut to ribbons. Then, at the third vent he examined, he turned off the light before pulling his head back. Far below, he could see a faint light glowing. It was a blue light, the kind of light the alien pilot had said showed the position of the power core. It made as much sense as anything else, and the chief was running out of options. He pulled the pack off his back and flipped it open. Reaching inside, he armed the electronic timer on the Mark 92, quickly spinning the combination dial through the timing sequence. As a backup, he also released the locks and pulled the old-fashioned safety pin that released the mechanical timer.

Finally, he took a breath and entered another sequence of numbers on the covered keypad. A bright green light started flashing. He watched the light flash for thirty seconds, and then it settled into a bright red glow. The anti-handling system had been fully armed. Now there was no way to move any of the controls without detonating the bomb. There was a thirty-minute interval on the clock, and both systems were running. The last glowing light told him that the remote command detonator circuit also was armed. This bomb was going bang.

Using the line, he lowered the demolition charge into the building, looking over the edge of the ventilator shaft to put the bomb as close to the fan blades as he could without touching them. At least the bomb would detonate inside the walls of the power building.

Securing the line and checking everything twice, Chief Harris made note of the time on his wrist chronometer. It was time to get the hell out of Dodge before a small sun was born just a few meters from where he was standing. Moving back to the wall, the chief peeked over to see where the truck was. It was just one gun emplacement over from where he had left it, and he could see Jackson and Falco moving another box. Going over to a spot where he was right above the truck, the chief slipped over the side of the building and dropped softly to the roof of the truck.

"Checkout time, gentlemen," the chief said quietly.

Not acting as if they had heard anything at all, Jackson and Falco returned to the truck. As Falco moved to the rear hatch, Chief Harris rolled off the roof of the truck and down onto the open ramp. The two men went back inside the cargo compartment, and Falco hit the interior ramp control. The control had been easy to locate; it was a duplicate of the one on the outside wall of the cargo compartment.

"Wake up, mister," Jackson said inside the truck cab. He roughly shook the prisoner and slapped him twice. He was not trying to hurt the man, only to shock him awake.

As soon as the prisoner stopped struggling, Jackson held him tightly and looked straight into his wild eyes above the gag.

"We're leaving now," Jackson said quietly. "Play along and you'll get to live through this."

Calming only slightly, the man nodded. That gesture was the same on Earth as it was on this planet, Jackson thought. At least he hoped so as he cut the prisoner's bonds.

There was a tight moment at the front gate when the machine seemed to resist letting the truck out. Jackson fingered the detonator in his pocket, and the driver spoke into a grid next to his door. He simply said that they had to go back for additional supplies, that the requisition had been short.

A mechanical voice from the grid stated that the discrepancy would be noted and reported. Then the gate bars slid open. None of the men started to breathe until they were well down the road and had stopped beyond the groves, more than ten kilometers from the facility. The SEALS officer had forced the alien driver to push the vehicle as fast as it would go, risking everything to put some distance between themselves and the hell that was about to be released behind them. They finally stopped when the truck had passed over a small rise and was next to a deep, wide irrigation canal with sloping sides. It was the best cover that could be seen anywhere close by, and they were running very short of time.

"I would take cover if I were you," Jackson said as he left the stopped truck.

"One minute, LT," Chief Harris said urgently from where he lay in the canal. Falco already was lying prone on the side of the canal, his feet crossed at the ankles and pointing back toward the facility; his hands were crossed over his head, and his arms were covering his ears. Chief Harris was looking up at Jackson with some concern in his eyes.

"Thirty seconds, sir," Harris almost shouted.

"Don't look at the facility," Jackson warned as he trotted over and jumped in next to his men. They all took up the same strange prone position.

As the driver wondered about the odd behavior of the puzzling aliens, he felt heat on his back as the night suddenly grew as bright as the day. The small hill behind them would give them some cover from the blast, but it wouldn't be much. Without turning, he dived into the shadow of the truck with the name of the savant on his lips. It wasn't enough.

The pilot had been right. The secondary explosion when the power core was breached was even brighter and more powerful than the half-kiloton explosion of the nuke.

# Nineteen: Prison Break

"Shit, there it goes," Ruiz said, almost to himself. The announcement wasn't strictly necessary: He and his Teammates all saw the flash of brilliant light like a powerful strobe piercing the night at the far rim of the city. The sudden spark of nuclear fission brightened the landscape only for a moment, but it was such an extreme brightness that it left an impression on Ruiz's retinas even though he hadn't been looking directly at it. The secondary reaction, thermonuclear in strength, followed almost immediately with an even brighter pulse.

Now the four men stared as a churning fireball blasted into the air, billowing upward like a living, hungry creature. It was easy to imagine the fires of hell or the churning essence inside a star as the furious, raging inferno exploded skyward. Dust and smoke and ash mingled with the flames, in some places masking it completely, in others allowing the fire to blaze through the murk like the eyes of an angry god.

The cloud of dust and debris and the fireball rose straight up into the air over the place where the planetary defense battery had been. The kilometers between them and the blast had cut the pressure wave down to almost nothing, but they still heard the sound. When it arrived, the sound was a sharp crack followed by a long, steady roll of thunder. The rising cloud began to billow outward, assuming the ominous mushroom shape that had represented a specter of doom to humankind for more than a hundred years.

"Jesus, I sure hope the LT got damned far away from there," Ruiz breathed, awestruck.

"I believe Chief Harris may have just set a record for the biggest secondary explosion of all time," Harry Teal said with awe in his voice.

The master chief, together with Harry Teal and Gunner's Mates LaRue and Rodale, was still hiding in the crater that had been blasted in the side of the central pyramid at the time of the Assarn attack. The SEALS had not been molested by guards or repair crews for the twenty or so hours they had been concealed in shallow niches in the blasted concrete. Robinson, now heavily sedated, lay on his mattress in a sheltered corner of the crater; Char-Kane was staying with him, safely out of sight.

Sanchez and Marranis had taken up a hidden position in the tunnel where Char-Kane and Jackson had entered the pyramid. They had a good view of the shattered compartments just inside the great structure and maintained an open comlink to the SEALS outside the wall. Thankfully, they had had nothing to report during the long period of waiting.

On the exterior of the pyramid, each man had prepared a firing position with at least some cover as well as a good view of the approaches. They had camouflaged themselves and their redoubts with dust and rubble. Despite their firepower, they understood that their only real chance rested on avoiding discovery until it was time to begin the mission.

Now, it seemed, that time had come.

The master chief crawled over the rubble leading to Robinson and Char-Kane's hiding place. The Shamani woman looked up in surprise as he wormed through the hole, her expression warming slightly in relief as she recognized him.

"I heard the explosions," she said. "Was that the PDB?"

Ruiz nodded. "It's time for us to move out. How is he?"

She touched the unconscious man's forehead. "The fever is still very bad, but it's not getting worse."

"Wait here. We'll be back as soon as we can."

She nodded, then asked hesitantly, "The chief . . . Harris. He set off the bomb?"

"That was the plan," Ruiz replied.

"I hope he got away from there very quickly," she said with surprising fervor.

"You and me both, sister," the master chief said. "The bomb should keep them busy for a while. They'll be trying to get a damage assessment and figure out who hit them. Now's the time for us to go in after the rest of our Teammates, as well as Doctor Sulati and Director Parker."

Char-Kane nodded. Those red eyes studied Ruiz seriously, and he wondered if he actually detected a trace of concern there. She surprised him by reaching out and giving his hand a squeeze. "Please be careful," she said.

"We will," he said gruffly. "You'll probably want to move back to the outside so that you can see the LT and the others when they come back."

After a final check on Robinson, she followed him through the narrow tunnel, carefully avoiding the jagged ends of the metal bars as the chief emerged to find his Teammates ready to go. Sanchez and Marannis, dusty with the chalky debris, emerged to join them.

"Was there any reaction from anyone inside the building when the bomb went off?" Ruiz asked.

"There were some alarms: a siren and a horn sounding. I heard some soldiers running past, but they didn't come in this direction," Sanchez replied.

"Okay. We'll have to hope that keeps 'em busy for a while. Let's move, SEALS," Ruiz said. He and Teal checked the actions of their assault rifles while LaRue gave his rail gun a careful inspection and Rodale readied his rocket launcher. The two gunners arranged their remaining ammunition until each one could move easily even though he was loaded with nearly a hundred pounds of gear. LaRue had abandoned one of his power packs for the rail gun, its charge fully exhausted. All the men had consolidated their remaining ammunition for the G15 rifles, grenade launchers, and hand grenades and divided them evenly. Ruiz had studied the blueprints until he had the entire approach and escape routes, as well as several alternatives, fully memorized.

The prison pens were near the bottom of the massive structure. After studying the plans Char-Kane had printed out, Ruiz had decided that the SEALS would descend the outside of the building to the dock where captives were brought in and shipped out. The master chief had conducted a recon a few hours earlier, and found that the Eluoi had only a few guards on duty. And although the heavy-duty autoguns in place over the vehicle entrance were a couple of very nasty pieces of work, they were designed for use against ground and air transport, not someone slipping down the building slope directly behind them. As with so much of their security and military apparatus, they relied on machinery and technology to take the place of eyes on the ground.

Ruiz had resolved to make them pay for that mistake.

They slid down the steeply sloping side of the pyramid, the six SEALS rappelling on three long lines that were secured to exposed beams near their hiding place. The exterior surface of the pyramid was smooth, and without the support of the ropes, the men would have tumbled and skidded uncontrollably downward. As it was, they were able to make an easy controlled descent.

They avoided the few windows and skirted a large ventilation grid that was expelling a steady gush of warm, moist air. Darkness masked them, and there was no moon in sight; Ruiz didn't know if this planet even had one. In

their camouflage paint and dark uniforms, they were as
hard to see as shadows and made just about as much
noise. There was a little bit of starlight, but that only en-
abled them to keep track of one another and their
progress along the sloping side of the massive building.

The Team came to a prearranged halt about fifty meters
above the lip of the wall poised directly over the landing
deck for incoming and departing prisoner transports.
Ruiz and Teal carefully eased up under the autoguns and
went to work. Within a few moments, both were rendered
inoperative. The Team moved to the edge of the lip. Ruiz,
Teal, and Rodale dropped simultaneously, gliding down
their dangling lines to plunge the thirty meters from their
ledge to the flat, open circle of the deck. As soon as they
had their boots on the floor, the other three followed.

There were two guards at the heavy steel door, standing
exactly where Ruiz had spotted them during his recon.
They stared in astonishment at the trio of SEALS who
suddenly had appeared out of the dark sky. One fumbled
for his communicator, and the second was just raising his
weapon when a quick, silent burst from the chief's assault
rifle dropped him. Teal took out the right sentry with an
equally accurate and precise three rounds, killing him before he could activate an alarm.

Already the gunners were rushing up to the door.
Marannis and Sanchez covered them, leaving Ruiz and
Teal to make sure there were no guards lurking in the cor-
ners. Within thirty seconds all six SEALS converged on
the large door. The other three men leveled their weapons
while Ruiz pushed the button that sent the barrier sliding
quickly upward.

The opening portal revealed a large, well-illuminated
corridor extending inward so far that it appeared to shrink
to a tiny dot before they could make out the other end.
The floor was smooth and well polished, and each wall
had a series of stairs and catwalks leading up to four lev-

els of barred enclosures. Ruiz knew at once that those enclosures were cages holding the vast numbers of Assarn captives Parvik had talked about—and, he hoped, Dobson, Sanders, Parker, and Doctor Sulati. According to the schematic printout, they were secured in a special cell several hundred meters in from the outer door.

Surprisingly, their arrival seemed to have attracted no attention. There were no interior guards in the vicinity of the door. Ruiz could see a pair of glass-lined cubicles up on the fourth level—one to either side of the wide, long corridor—that were apparently security posts. However, the guards he could see there, wearing the traditional Eluoi white, all seemed to be paying attention to unseen instruments or watching the prisoners who were lined up against the bars of their cages in numbers that could only be described as teeming.

"Let's take those security posts," the master chief ordered quickly. "With luck, we can open the cages from there—five thousand escaped prisoners oughta create a bit of a distraction." He quickly gestured to Teal and G-Man, sending them to the right. Rodale followed him up the frame steel ladder toward the left-side guard post. Marannis and Sanchez stayed on the ground just inside the open doors, covering the advance and watching for any unpleasant surprises that might develop outside the building.

A high-pitched scream echoed through the huge space before Ruiz was halfway up the ladder. He looked across the central space and saw Teal holding his assault rifle in a firing position, aiming upward. An Eluoi guard dropped his gun, balanced on the waist-high railing for a moment, then toppled over to fall the four stories down to the hard, shiny floor. The body seemed to take a long time to fall, and the prisoners, guards, and SEALS all watched in utter silence until, with a sickening thwack, the corpse impacted.

Then all hell broke loose. A horn of some kind, pierc-

ing and high-pitched, began to shriek. The prisoners
erupted into cheers and wild howls that sounded almost
animalistic. The Eluoi guards shouted to one another in
their sibilant tongue.

Breaking into a sprint, the master chief scrambled up
the steep steel steps, pulling himself with his left hand
while keeping his weapon trained upward in his right.
Guards emerged from the glass-enclosed room above him,
guns trained on Teal and LaRue across the hall. Harry Teal
snapped off several quick three-round bursts with enough
accuracy to drive the Eluoi back toward their hardened
compartment, the shells ricocheting off the glass.

After checking that the backblast area was clear—he
was standing in front of one of the few empty cells—
G-Man let loose a slug from his rail gun. The superheated
copper and uranium slug punctured the armored glass and
spattered around the interior of the cubicle, slicing and
dicing the bodies of the guards who had sought shelter
there.

Ruiz opened up with his own short bursts, coming up
the last flight of steps and dropping three guards who
were outside of the cubicle but fatally focused on the two
SEALS across the hall from them. Rodale put his shoulder to the weakened door into the command cubicle and
smashed it open while the master chief knelt and snapped
off another burst across the way, distracting the guards
who were starting to shoot at the still-climbing Teal and
LaRue. Sanchez and Marannis added covering fire from
below while the prisoners mostly dropped flat on the
floors of their cages, withdrawing from the exposed en-
trances.

Ruiz's shots from enfilade swept the platform on the far
side of the corridor, dropping several guards and sending
the rest into full-fledged flight. Apparently, they gave no
thought to sheltering in the control booth, having ob-

served the lethal effects of G-Man's first shot across the way. With his rocket launcher slung over his back, Rodale emerged from the gory booth and added assault rifle support to Ruiz and Teal, ensuring that only a couple of the Eluoi soldiers made it to the next supporting position, a half-walled cubicle a hundred meters down the fourth-story catwalk.

The master chief stepped into the booth, ignoring the gory mess on the floor as he tried to make sense of the ruined control panel. Dials and gauges had been wrecked by the spatter of molten copper. Sparks flashed, and the smell of ozone was heavy in the air.

He stuck his head out the door and shouted to the pair of SEALS on the opposite catwalk. "This one's useless. See if you can work any of the controls over there." He turned to Rodale. "Let's keep the pressure on."

The people in the cages were dirty and emaciated, a mixture of males and females with the fair complexion and long yellow hair of Olin Parvik. They were climbing to their feet as the SEALS charged past, shouting derisively at the retreating Eluoi. Ruiz saw one of the guards turn and spray a cage with his machine pistol, cutting down the defenseless prisoners, until a couple of rounds from the master chief's gun blasted the top of his head off.

Rodale, meanwhile, advanced at a crouch, still using his rifle, the rocket launcher being almost useless inside a building. Ruiz followed, squeezing off shots at the Eluoi on the far side of the wide corridor as Rocky suppressed any return fire from ahead of them. Sanchez kept even with his Teammates on the catwalks, advancing along the floor of the wide corridor, leaving his partner to keep an eye on the outside of the pyramid.

And then, just like that, the cage doors began to pop open. Stunned Assarn prisoners looked out as the two

SEALS ran past, then emerged to scramble along the catwalks, sliding down the metal ladders, fleeing toward the still-open doors at the loading dock.

"I got it, Chief!" Teal crowed, operating the latches from the control booth.

"Keep it up!" Ruiz shouted. He raised his rifle, ready to squeeze off another burst, but now escaping prisoners were spilling out of cages on the far side of the passageway. He held his fire to avoid hitting the Assarn, then watched in grim satisfaction as the guards on the fourth catwalk were picked up by escaping prisoners and summarily pitched down to the hard floor below.

More escapees swarmed down there, and the guards were literally torn to pieces by the vengeful Assarn. The floor between the two banks of cells rapidly filled with fleeing prisoners, a throng quickly expanding from hundreds to thousands as cell doors continued to snap open farther and farther into the deep passageway. Ruiz found himself bumped and jostled by the people spilling out of the cages, though they made no attempt to interfere with him. He saw another group of Eluoi guards, surrounded by the mob, go down shooting and gave a silent prayer of thanks that he and his men had not tried to charge in there disguised in those distinctive white uniforms.

"Chief, there's Dr. Sulati! And the ensign!" Rodale shouted, pointing toward a cell on the ground floor on the opposite side of the corridor.

The two humans were peering cautiously through the open door of a cell but, unlike the Assarn, had not joined the stampede for freedom. Director Parker and Dobson appeared behind them, and Ruiz allowed himself another prayer of thanks: All four were alive and had been located.

"Ensign!" he shouted down, the familiar word penetrating the rising clamor as only a master chief's voice could.

Sanders looked up at once and raised his fist with a whoop of triumph.

"Stay put!" Ruiz cried, emphasizing the request by extending his palm. "We'll be right there!"

Rodale already had flagged down the other SEALS. Sanchez fell back to rejoin his partner at the outer door, and the other four men descended the nearest stairways, joining the stream of fleeing Assarn until they reached the floor. They had to fight through the crowd to make their way to the four Earthlings. They approached the cell, which was cleaner and better lit than those of the Assarn prisoners, and Ruiz ordered his three Teammates to watch the approaches while he stepped inside.

"Damn, Chief, am I glad to see you!" declared Ensign Sanders, wrapping his arms around Ruiz in a hug that broke about five regulations.

"You, too, sir!" the master chief replied, disengaging only to be hugged by Dr. Sulati while the normally aloof director pounded him on the back and Dobson, in a momentary flight back to his native Alabama, shrieked a rebel yell.

"We've got to get out of here pronto," the chief urged, delighted at the reunion. "We've stirred up a hornet's nest on this planet, but if all goes well, we'll be able to hop the next bus out of town."

"Lead the way, Chief," Sanders said. He was still clad in his olive cammo uniform, though he looked rather naked without his equipment harness or weapon.

"Here, sir," Rodale said, extending his assault rifle butt first toward the young officer. He passed over a pouch on a shoulder strap containing the last of his half dozen spare magazines.

"I can always crack off a shot or two with this," the gunner's mate noted with a grin, pointing to the rocket launcher on his shoulder as he pulled out the VP90 10-millimeter caseless pistol from the holster strapped to his thigh.

"Let's move," Ruiz said, glancing out to see that the mob of Assarn had thinned considerably.

"We got company, Chief," G-Man reported grimly, looking deeper into the pyramid. Men in white uniforms, dozens of them, were advancing at a trot along each side of the fourth-story causeways.

The Eluoi aimed downward, and shots zipped out, ripping streams of slugs into the fleeing prisoners. A young woman, her blond hair suddenly streaked in crimson from a head shot, fell to the floor a dozen paces away. More of the Assarn tumbled, shouting and screaming in pain, as the two columns of Eluoi soldiers moved forward along the catwalk, raking the defenseless crowd with lethal fire.

"Bastards!" Ruiz spit. Pointing to the approaching reinforcements, he shouted, "Take out that far catwalk, Rocky."

As Rodale shrugged the rocket launcher off his shoulder and brought it to bear, Ruiz screamed "Down" at the Assarn behind Rocky and then hit the deck, hoping they'd have the sense to get the idea. Many of them did.

In a searing burst the missile exploded from the tube, climbing on a straight trajectory toward the first of the Eluoi on the left catwalk. The projectile hit the metal grid and exploded in a burst of fire and shrapnel, killing a half dozen of the enemy in the blast. The heat was so intense that the catwalk buckled, dropping twenty more soldiers precipitously onto the lower catwalks or, for the less lucky, all the way to the floor.

As Ruiz got back to his feet, he noticed that at least a handful of Assarn didn't get back up. But the building worry about how the Assarn would react to the unfortunate collateral casualties was quickly washed away as the Assarn gave out a ragged cheer

The SEALS kept returning fire with their small arms as well. In one smooth motion, Rodale released the grip on his M76 Wasp and brought out his pistol again. Thumbing the safety over to full automatic, he held the weapon steady with his strong right arm as it blasted out a stream of slugs. All the SEALS were putting out a storm of high-velocity slugs from their weapons. In the odd hissing noise from the suppressed G15 rifles, Rodale's pistol sounded out in one long roar.

There was something familiar about the Eluoi officer who was directing the columns of reinforcements forward, though he stayed well behind the front rank. Still, when the soldiers charged ahead, Ruiz got a good look.

"It's that fucking Zaro!" he shouted to his Teammates. "Right there!"

"Let me take this one, Chief—please?" LaRue asked. He had his grenade launcher cradled in his hands.

"Fire away!" Ruiz replied.

There was a thump as LaRue fired his 30-millimeter underbarrel grenade launcher. The high-explosive grenade passed up and over the railing, exploding against the ceiling above the enemy troops who were firing down. The blast rained fragmentation down among the Eluoi, slashing through them like a steel rain. Zaro, his body pierced by shrapnel, staggered against the railing, then toppled over to take his last fall.

More of the reinforcing soldiers went down, some killed on the catwalk and others falling, like Zaro, all the way to the floor. Liberated Assarn quickly snatched up the weapons of the fallen Eluoi, and a spirited firefight erupted between the escapees on the floor and the rest of the company up on the high, shakily swaying catwalk.

The rest of the SEALS continued firing with their weapons set on full automatic, spraying both exposed columns of guards as they backed toward the still-open doors to the loading dock. As a magazine was emptied, they reloaded without conscious thought and continued mowing down the enemy. Enough of the Assarn were armed now that the pursuing Eluoi were fully engaged in a fight for survival. They no doubt were calling for more reinforcements, but Ruiz intended for the Teammates and their rescued comrades to be out of there before they could arrive.

They reached the loading dock at a full sprint to find the Assarn spilling down the two broad ramps that led to the street below. Other freed prisoners went right off the edge of the dock, skidding down the sloping side of the pyramid, sometimes losing their balance to tumble among their comrades, knocking them down until an avalanche of liberated Assarn rolled and bounced down the sloping side. Fortunately, the ground was only a hundred meters down from there. Ruiz could only hope that most of them would make it alive, with limbs intact.

"Do we go down there?" Sanders asked dubiously, watching the throngs of Assarn that now jammed each of the wide ramps.

Ruiz shook his head and pointed toward the sky. "We're going up," he announced.

Sanchez and Marannis already had collected the three lines, which still were attached from when the SEALS had rappelled down.

"Do we have to climb straight up there?" Dr. Sulati asked hesitantly, looking at the lip of the landing deck some thirty meters overhead, with the rope freely hanging like a trailing jungle vine.

"Only if you want to," Ruiz said genially as his men pulled the lines, a pair at each, to either side of the deck. They easily reached the sloping side of the pyramid. "I think it'll be easier to walk up the side of the building, though."

"You and me both," the doctor agreed.

Teal, Sanchez, and Marannis started up first, their guns slung across their backs as each man held his line in both hands. The pyramid was steep, but with the aid of the rope it wasn't difficult to walk upward, using a hand-over-hand grip. The two civilians and then the rest of the SEALS followed, quickly skirting the alcove of the landing deck, making their way higher and higher on the long, sloping side of the pyramid.

They saw the trails of Eluoi aircraft swarming closer, and Ruiz was grateful for the concealment of the full darkness. The escaped Assarn prisoners would put up a fight, he knew, but for the most part they were unarmed and disorganized. He didn't much care for their chances as the stunned Eluoi recovered from the twin shocks of the nuclear attack and the mass escape. Their vengeance, he expected, would be terrible, but from what he had seen of the Assarn, they wouldn't exactly go meekly back into captivity.

For now, he would use them as a diversion. There was nothing else to do.

It was more than fifteen minutes later when they drew near the crater where they had concealed themselves on the side of the pyramid. The former prisoners' hands were raw and blistered from holding the ropes, and sweat sheened every forehead. Even through their exhaustion, though, they were elated at their success. Even Char-Kane, as she greeted them at the crater's edge, allowed herself a rare smile of pleasure.

As Ruiz came by, she reached out and gave his hand a squeeze. Touched and moved, he almost hugged her, but some memory of that frosty aloofness held him back, and he merely squeezed her hand in return.

"Someone's coming, Master Chief," Sanders noted. They watched an Eluoi jetcar bank past, engines almost whispering at low idle as the machine wobbled back and forth in the prearranged signal.

"Check your boarding passes and carry-on bags, people," the master chief said in delight. "This looks like our ride. If everything's gone all right, he should have the LT, Chief Harris, and Falco on board."

# Twenty: Unfriendly Skies

"Those are the refueling docks," Olin Parvik explained, guiding the jet transport in a careful descent toward Batuu City's spaceport. "We'll want to take a shuttle that has a full load on board, I assume, so I suggest we keep an eye on where the fuel is delivered."

"Of course," Jackson said. He was busy gawking like a tourist out the window as they approached the massive installation. He had never seen the like for the simple reason that there was nothing like it on Earth. During their telephoto scrutiny earlier, when Zaro and Tezlac Catal had debarked from the shuttle, they hadn't flown directly over the port. Now he found himself overwhelmed by the sheer size of the place.

The shuttle port was a rough square some twenty or thirty kilometers on each side. Much of the space was overgrown with brushy wetlands and thickets, though there were no tall trees within the compound. Roads crisscrossed the whole place in a network of pavement that looked from the air like a great spiderweb.

Huge enclosures contained rows of massive silver tanks, and he guessed that they were the fuel stores. An array of equipment resembled a chemical plant or a refinery, and he assumed that that was where the volatile propellant mixtures were prepared. The nerve center of the installation was an array of huge white buildings, many of them with monstrous doors suggesting that they were used as hangars or warehouses. Several shuttles rested, nose up, on pads around the massive central complex. One of them was a winged craft attached to the stem of a tall, slender rocket, not unlike the original space shuttles on Earth. But most of the ships had self-contained, sharp-nosed shapes with stubby bodies resting on struts, with two or three downward-tracking engines.

The bristling array of the central complex was only a small part of the huge spaceport. At a single glance Jackson could see at least two dozen landing zones in the distance, each connected to the central hub by a surface road. Massive tractor-trucks crawled along some of the roads, and at least two of them were pulling shuttles into position on the launching pads. The shuttles were pointed upward, in launch orientation, ready to streak toward the stars or, more likely, toward starships and space stations in orbit around Batuun.

He was relieved to see no evidence of an overt military presence: There were only a few jetcars, similar to their own, on aerial patrol. He couldn't see any indication of land-based batteries, but neither could he rule out the possibility that guns might be concealed in one or more of the massive buildings. The SEALS and their civilian comrades were crowded into the captured transport. Doctor Sulati had set up an emergency IV for Robinson and had declared herself guardedly optimistic that the man would recover, mostly as a result of Harry Teal's skilled treatment.

"Any preference where you want to set down?" Parvik asked, banking gently and easing them away from the huge central complex.

Jackson had been thinking about that very issue, his eyes darting around the landscape. He spotted one remote launch pad where a shuttle rested, oriented toward the sky, while one of the massive tractor haulers was slowly rumbling away. The shuttle appeared to be standing alone for now; at least, he couldn't spot any signs of activity around it as they approached. He reasoned that it was a fueled shuttle that had just been hauled into launching position. It was no more than three or four kilometers beyond the far end of the vast tank farm where the rocket fuel was stored.

"How about that one?" he said, leaning past the pilot and pointing. "Do you think you can fly it?"

"Does a pig have wings?" Parvik replied with a grin. "Of *course* I can fly it."

"Good. But—um—pigs don't actually have wings where we come from," the lieutenant pointed out.

The Assarn looked at him, eyes wide in mock astonishment, and Jackson couldn't help laughing. The fellow's swashbuckling good humor was infectious and actually made him think that they might just possibly get away with this harebrained off-the-cuff operation.

"SEALS, get ready," the officer ordered through the intercom. "I want you to hit the ground running."

"Roger, LT," crackled Ruiz's reply from the passenger cabin. "We'll drop the door as soon as we stop moving."

"Take her down," Jackson said to Parvik.

The pilot pushed the control stick, and immediately the jetcar swept into a dive. The launching pad, which was a flat circle of concrete some hundred meters in diameter, appeared to grow rapidly as the pilot brought them in a little faster than regulations specified. Even so, he pulled up smoothly and dropped them vertically onto the pad just a couple of dozen meters from the fueled shuttle.

An Eluoi officer, his sleeves gleaming from a heavy load of gold braid, came jogging toward them, waving his arms over his head. A dozen soldiers trotted behind him, spreading into a skirmish line, holding their weapons at port arms.

"Looks like the reception is going to be a warm one," Jackson announced. "Chief, how fast can you swing that turret around?"

"Give the word, LT."

Parvik signaled that the back ramp was ready to drop.

"Here we go," Jackson declared. "No slowing down until we're off this goddamn planet. Chief, start the party!"

Harris had been holding the barrel of the turret gun trained to the rear to avoid alarming the welcoming committee. Now, with the slight pressure of his knee on the control, he wheeled it around quickly, dropping the muzzle of the weapon to shoot almost parallel to the side of the fuselage. His first burst cut the Eluoi officer in two and scattered the man's escort, dropping two or three of them at the same time.

The ramp dropped sharply, and the SEALS came tumbling out. Falco dropped prone and started cracking off shots with his rifle, taking the time to aim carefully before squeezing the trigger with cool precision. Three quick shots dropped two more hostiles onto the tarmac. One lucky Eluoi soldier tripped and fell with such fortuitous timing that the 10.26-mm slug merely grazed his scalp instead of splattering his brain. The terrified man crawled away, and Falco let him go, knowing he'd have one hell of a headache to remember the SEALS by.

Ruiz and Teal sprayed suppressing fire with their assault rifles, charging from the jetcar in a crouch while LaRue and Rodale, firing with more careful aim, covered them from the open hatch. Marannis, Sanchez, and Sanders tumbled out of the hatch and sprinted toward the nearby shuttle, which had an inviting ladder dangling from the low open hatch.

Chief Harris kept up a devastating barrage from the turret gun, and in seconds none of the Eluoi soldiers was moving. Jackson and the three civilians came down the ramp with Olin Parvik and looked at the shuttle, which had been untouched by so much as a ricochet, thanks the precise shooting of the Team.

"Teal and Chief Harris, get Robinson over to the shuttle as soon as Ensign Sanders secures the ship," Jackson ordered, seeing that the situation on the landing pad had been clearly resolved in the SEALS' favor. "Olin, Parker, Doctor Sulati—follow them over there, on the double."

The group immediately raced across the bloody tarmac, Chief Harris and Teal bringing Robinson on his stretcher behind. Sanders had vanished into the narrow hatch near one of the shuttle's three engines.

"Gunners," Jackson said, addressing Rodale and La-Rue. "You got a few rounds left for a farewell volley?"

"Two rockets, LT," Rocky Rodale replied, and LaRue held up one finger.

"See those tanks over there?" asked the lieutenant, gesturing to the silver cylinders looming over the low-cut brush. "They're even bigger than barns. See if you can hit them in the broadside, would you?"

"You got it, sir," G-Man replied with an anticipatory grin. The two men scrambled up the ladder onto the wing of the jetcar to gain the best line of fire toward the huge, motionless targets. LaRue raised his rail gun, and Rodale punched the target coordinates into the rocket launcher. Without a word of communication between them, they shouted, "Fire in the hole!" in unison as they let fly at the same time.

The copper and uranium slug from G-Man's gun covered the one-plus klick of distance in the blink of an eye. Rodale's rocket spit from the launcher and trailed after it. The plasmalike slug punched through the thin steel skin of one fuel tank as if it were tissue paper, and immediately the superheated metal ignited the combustible liquid within. The fuel tank erupted in a spectacular explosion, a fireball billowing skyward, spewing bits of flaming debris as the liquid inferno roared upward.

By then Rodale's rocket had struck the neighboring tank, exploding against the exterior surface. The shaped charge was potent enough that much of the energy of the hit was directed inward; burning metal seared through the metal skin, plunging into the mixture of fuels within. A second later the second fuel tank erupted, a matching explosion sending a churning, smoking fireball to rise beside G-Man's kill.

At the same time, Jackson heard another sound, a burst of fire spitting from the bottom of one of the shuttle's engines. A second engine came online a moment later, and only the third—the one closest to the entry hatch—remained silent.

"All aboard!" Ruiz was shouting from that hatchway.

The three SEALS still on the surface of Batuun sprinted across the tarmac in record time, scrambling up the short ladder, assisted through the hatch by the willing—though none-too-gentle—hands of their Teammates. Robinson had been strapped to a cot, and the others were grabbing seats in a well-equipped passenger compartment. Looking up, Jackson could see right into the flight deck, where Olin Parvik was activating the engines.

"Parvik says we'll want to be strapped in for this," Ruiz said, indicating the padded seats on the lower deck. "He also says we have about ten seconds before liftoff."

Jackson was just snapping the clasp of his harness into place when he felt the powerful crush of multiple G-forces pushing him into the seat. The rockets surged, and the small portholes immediately were obscured by a billowing cloud of white smoke. The shuttle blasted upward with crushing force, the roar of the engines loud enough to drown out any attempt at conversation.

But they all knew that they were leaving Batuun behind.

"Look at that SOB burn," LaRue said admiringly as the shuttle coursed away from Batuun. The G-forces were lapsing, and the Teammates were able to sit up and look out the portholes that ringed the round, stubby hull.

No one had to ask what particular SOB he referred to:

The gaping crater where the planetary defense battery once had stood was outlined in red, and a deep orange glow permeated through the thick smoke that wafted through the depths of the big hole in the ground. The flaming fuel tanks at the spaceport, though spectacular in their own right, were now tiny, sputtering plumes of smoke compared to the horrific devastation left by the explosion of the tactical nuke and the resulting meltdown of the battery core.

Already Parvik was easing back on the boosters, and Jackson felt himself drifting against the straps holding him in place. Black space yawned outside the viewport, and he felt an overwhelming sense of relief as they left the atmosphere of Batuun behind.

"I've got her in a low orbit," the pilot said as he twisted some dials on the communications array. "I'm trying to raise my destroyer, the *Starguard*. No luck so far, but we'll have a better chance as we come around the far side of the world. Like I said, she had to keep out of range of the PDB, so she might still be staying below the horizon."

Despite Parvik's confident words, Jackson detected an undercurrent of worry that was alarming to observe in the previously unflappable Assarn. The lieutenant got the impression that even if the *Starguard* was on the other side of the planet, Parvik had expected to be able to make contact. The SEALS officer hoped he was right. Without a sanctuary on the Assarn vessel, they would have precious little chance of surviving in orbit until, and if, *Pegasus* arrived for them.

For a long fifteen minutes the pilot worked at various channels, sending out a coded summons and listening for a response. The great splotch of Batuu City slowly crept away from them, finally vanishing over the horizon as the shuttle, engines silent now, completed a half orbit around the green jungled world.

"I'm getting a beacon—a homing signal," Parvik said through clenched teeth. "It's *Starguard*. But there's no response to my call."

Jackson noticed that the pilot's knuckles were white as he worked the controls, making adjustments to the shuttle's orbit as he brought the little spacecraft closer to his ship. His face was creased with lines of worry, and the lieutenant sensed that he was afraid of what he would find when they got closer to the warship. They followed its position on the vidscreen as the shuttle closed in, and it was clear that the destroyer was drifting, not moving under its own power. They closed in farther, and some of the men started staring out the portholes, looking for a visual sighting.

"There she is!" cried the keen-eyed Falco. "In orbit there, maybe ten klicks away."

The SEALS and their companions were silent as the shuttle moved closer to a drifting object that slowly resolved itself into a cigar-shaped spacecraft. But even from a distance, it was clear that something was terribly wrong.

"*That* is our destination?" Director Parker said in dismay.

The shuttle moved into orbit less than a kilometer from the Assarn destroyer, and it was obvious that the ship was a derelict. The hull was perforated in a dozen places, and one of the two engines was dangling limply, attached only by a few strands of torn metal. There were no lights, no signs of power anywhere on the ship.

"The Eluoi must have caught her napping," Parvik said grimly. "By the tombs of my ancestors, they won't get away with this!"

"I'm sorry," Jackson said, touching the pilot on the shoulder, feeling the grief—and fury—coursing through the man's taut, wiry frame.

"So am I," the Assarn growled. They drifted in space,

very close to the derelict, and the officer keenly felt the helplessness of their situation. Without pressure suits, they couldn't even cross over to *Starguard* to look for the remote chance of any survivors or clues to what had caused its destruction.

"What's our survival time frame?" Jackson asked the pilot bluntly. "How long can we stay up here and wait for *Pegasus*?" He was acutely aware that he had no way of knowing if the light frigate had even received their SOS call, much less been able to find the Batuun star system.

"Air and water for a hundred hours, give or take," the pilot said. "No food to speak of, but we'll suffocate before we starve, for what that's worth."

"We could always land on the planet so LaRue could kill another dinosaur," Falco whispered, drawing a dirty look from the master chief.

"More to the point," Parvik said, "the Eluoi have some armed shuttles in orbit around the planet. When they track us down, we're pretty much sitting ducks. Unfortunately, I've been watching a few anomalies on the screen. I think we might be in trouble."

"Any external weapons on this tub?" Jackson asked.

The pilot, still studying the vidscreen, shook his head. Then he cursed, a sound so guttural and explosive that the translator chip in the lieutenant's ear didn't even try to render the word into English.

"We've got company—hostiles!" Olin Parvik barked suddenly, pointing to the screen with the blip designating the derelict warship. That image was suddenly lighting with multiple contacts, all of them closing in on the shuttle.

Jackson counted them on the screen: four blips of red color approaching rapidly from two directions. They flew in pairs, just like fighter pilots and their wingmen in standard air-to-air combat tactics. It seemed likely that they were closing in for what they expected to be an easy kill.

"Dammit! They were waiting up here in orbit for us," the officer guessed.

"Everybody, hold on!" the pilot shouted. By the time Jackson repeated the command in English, Parvik had flipped a switch and the shuttle was heeling violently, tumbling through a sharp change of course. G-forces slammed the passengers into the sides of their seats.

"We got nothing to shoot at them, but I can try to make us a tough target. I don't like our chances much, though," the Assarn declared grimly.

A rocket flashed past the shuttle, close enough for Jackson to make out the hieroglyphics on the tube. The Assarn pilot veered to the side—only the straps held the lieutenant in his seat against the violent maneuver—and the weapon exploded in eerie silence a short distance away.

"That was too close," Jackson grunted.

"And we're burning up most of our maneuvering fuel," the pilot noted. "Not only that, but there is another ship coming from space. We look to be trapped here."

Jackson looked at the display, which showed the array of ships in three dimensions. The two Eluoi vessels before them and the second pair astern were holding position. A fifth bogey was zooming toward them from a higher orbit. A glance out the viewport showed the latter ship as a spot of brightness that was growing more brilliant with each passing second as it sped closer.

There was no place to go, no direction that offered even the slightest hope of escape. Jackson grabbed the arms of his chair and held on, hating above all else the thought that he and his men were going to die without even having a chance to shoot back.

# Twenty-One: Alliance

A sudden brightness sparked through the interior of the shuttle's cabin, light strobing through the windows in a stuttering series of flashes. Jackson winced, waiting for the explosion, the rush of expelled air that would, likely as not, carry him and his men into cold, deadly space. But there was no impact, no sound. When he looked out the porthole, he saw that the flashes had come from the flaming exhaust of rockets, a veritable stream of them, that shot through the dark vacuum but completely bypassed the vulnerable shuttle.

Through the porthole Jackson saw one of the Eluoi ships tumbling away, spewing flames from a massive rupture in its hull. Tiny figures were expelled through the breach, and he knew without a doubt that they were Eluoi sailors carried into the vacuum by the violent decompression of their dying ship. The newcomer, the ship from far above the five orbiting shuttles, had blasted the Eluoi ship with the volley of missiles, some eight or ten bolts spewing toward it with lethal force. Now the firing ship veered enough for the SEALS to get a good look at it.

More sparks flashed from the approaching starship, and a second barrage of missiles streaked one after the other from a hull-mounted battery. The deadly darts curved past the SEALS' spacecraft and impacted in lethal succession on the hull of the second Eluoi shuttle. That ship exploded with such force that it left nothing but a cloud of debris.

"That's *Pegasus*!" Ruiz whooped in pure elation. "The cavalry is coming over the hill!"

The navy ship was visible to the naked eye now, its powerful engines decelerating the sleek silver hull as its auxiliary rockets maneuvered it gracefully into an orbital pattern. Slashing past the drifting shuttle some ten kilometers away, it opened up with its twin batteries of rail guns—giant versions of Baby, two barrels that launched uranium-cored projectiles at incredible velocity—to bombard the two remaining Eluoi ships.

The copper and uranium slugs punctured the hull of the first enemy ship without losing velocity; Jackson saw them spark and burn like meteorites as they struck the atmosphere below. Gas, vapor, and debris spewed from a dozen holes in the stubby shuttle. Its interior lit up with flames as debris, bodies, and fiery wreckage scattered down toward Batuun's atmosphere. The fire was snuffed out almost immediately by the vacuum, leaving the hulk drifting and dark.

The remaining Eluoi craft simply turned and fled. The last they saw of it was the fiery tail of its rocket engines propelling it along the outer reaches of Batuun's atmosphere toward the safety of the far side of the world.

The SEALS' shuttle, having expended the last of its fuel in desperate evasion, was dead in space, drifting in orbit around that planet. The hemisphere below them was dark, but they knew that dawn—and the bustling Eluoi city—lay not far beyond the horizon. Even with the planetary defense battery destroyed, Jackson wasn't eager to attract the attention of the numerous shuttles, some of them outfitted with weaponry, still on the ground at the spaceport.

Thus, the SEALS and their companions watched intently as Pegasus maneuvered closer, its helmsman expertly using the auxiliary rockets to match the frigate to the shuttle's orbit, only a few dozen meters away. It was a simple matter for a bosun's mate in the I Deck of Pegasus to extend a robot arm and secure a grip to the shuttle's tail, temporarily locking the two vessels into one object.

The air locks of the two ships, each alien to the other, didn't match up, and so two sailors in pressure suits emerged from the frigate's air lock and floated into the shuttle's pressurized entry hatch, towing a string of sixteen spare suits behind them. The twelve SEALS and their four companions—Parvik, Char-Kane, Dr. Sulati, and Director Parker—all suited up and easily made the short journey over to the frigate. Almost immediately the shuttle was released, and the warship powered up, making sure that it stayed over the portion of the planet where it could not be tracked from Batuu City. Luckily, the Assarn had taken out most of the satellite defense grid.

Jackson and Dr. Sulati wasted no time in finding the frigate's medical officer, who, accompanied by the doctor and Harry Teal, quickly saw that the injured Robinson was taken to the infirmary, a high-tech compartment with a surgical center in the space between the batteries on D Deck.

Captain Carstairs greeted the rest of the Team warmly and was especially interested in meeting the Assarn pilot when Jackson introduced him.

"Ignore the fact that he looks like a pirate, sir. He saved our lives," the SEALS officer said sincerely.

"No more than returning the favor," the pilot replied graciously. "I would be bound for an Eluoi slave ship right about now if these men hadn't come along when they did."

With that endorsement, the captain was pleased to show the pilot some of the features of his frigate and led Olin Parvik and Stonewall Jackson up through the battery deck, to the CIC and the officers' wardroom, and finally up to A Level, the flight deck in the warship's nose.

"Seems like your FTL drive checked out okay, Captain," Jackson observed. "Or else you wouldn't be here and we'd be sucking vacuum right about now."

"Your message took us by surprise just as we were getting ready for a shakedown cruise out to Alpha Centauri. It didn't take much to alter the coordinates to Batuun, though we could only hope we'd get here in time."

"You did. The very nick of time, it's fair to say," the lieutenant replied gratefully.

"What happened back on Mars?" Carstairs asked. "We got a message from MS1 saying you guys all piled onto a mysterious shuttle. We saw the shuttle dock with the *Gladiola*, which didn't respond to our hails. Before we knew it, they were bugging out of the star system at maximum power, and we couldn't have caught them even if we had wanted to."

"We made kind of an unplanned departure," Jackson explained to the naval officer. "The bastards infiltrated MS1. They had an agent there, an Eluoi disguised as a human with nothing more than some language fluency and good contact lenses. And more of them hijacked that Shamani ship, the *Gladiola*, that we saw on arrival."

"What were they after?" Carstairs asked.

Jackson shrugged. "Information, it seems. They heard about us from the Shamani and wanted to see what kind of threat we might pose to them—or what kind of opportunity, for that matter. Apparently, they do a lot of traffic in slave labor."

The captain frowned, glancing through the porthole at the planet that was still sprawling, green and verdant, below. The sun was rising over the eastern part of the planet, though Batuu City was still experiencing the middle of the night. That great metroplis was in view near the black horizon, a blazing splotch of brightness against the vast wilderness that was the rest of the planet.

"These Eluoi, you call them," Carstairs remarked. "Sounds like they could be trouble."

"Yes, sir," Jackson said sincerely. "But I think they're going to remember my Team and our unofficial visit for a long, long while. Might even give them a little pause before they come looking for us or take the chance of having us make an official military stop on their planet. They have no idea how many SEALS there really are."

"I would think there may be a few more assigned to your unit when this report makes the rounds," the captain said with a grim smile.

Consul de Campe Char-Kane emerged from the hatch into the chaos that was H Deck, where the Teammates were taking it easy, relaxing and recovering. They had just enjoyed a hot meal, and several of them were in the process of changing. Teal, Rodale, and Marannis, in their skivvies, hastened back between a pair of lockers as the Shamani woman stood awkwardly, looking around the piles of equipment, dirty clothing, and disassembled weaponry.

"Is the Chief Harris here?" she asked.

"Yes, ma'am," replied the chief, who had just finished cleaning his G15. He stood up and crossed the room to her, ignoring Ruiz's low whistle as he passed the master chief.

"Maybe we can take a climb up the transport shaft," Harris suggested, flashing a murderous look at the rest of his gawking Teammates. Falco, about to make a wisecrack, somehow found a way to bite his tongue.

"Yes, that would be most nice," Char-Kane replied. He followed her into the hatch, and they climbed up to H Deck. There was no one in the central passage outside the goat locker, so they leaned against the railing and looked out the solitary porthole at the dazzling stars.

"Some of the constellations—most of 'em—look just the same as they do on Earth," Harris noted.

"Yes. That is because, in terms of the galaxy, we have traveled only a tiny distance between Sol and Batuun," Char-Kane declared seriously. "The orientation of your view of the universe has changed very little."

"Uh, yeah, that must be it," Harris agreed. "Um, listen. Are you going back to our system? Are you going to be there for a while?"

"Not terribly long," she said, and he allowed himself to think that she sounded a little sad about that fact. "I am due for rotation back to the Spider cluster after two more of your Terran years."

"Two more years," Harris said. "Hell, a lot can happen in two years."

"Yes," she said. "It can."

She was very close to him, so close that he could feel the heat of her body emanating from the golden bodysuit. He reached out, and she came to him. Their kiss was about to enter its second minute when Master Chief Curt Swanson, the COB of the *Pegasus,* emerged from the goat locker and stopped in shock. He gaped for a second, shaking his head, then turned back to his compartment, muttering something about submarines.

The frigate remained on the far side of Batuun, away from the city, and was in a fixed orbit when the hulk of the Assarn destroyer started to come around again. Jackson, Carstairs, and Olin Parvik watched the hulk as it drifted near, the Assarn complimenting the skill of the navy helmsman as *Pegasus* gently maneuvered into a matching orbit.

"Do you want to have a look at my ship?" Parvik asked. "I'd like to get aboard again for some personal effects. There's no chance of finding survivors, but there might be clues as to what happened. I'd reckon it's likely that you could find something useful to salvage. She took a lot of hits in the engine, but some of the weaponry might be intact."

Carstairs all but leaped at the chance and quickly assembled a salvage Team of men in pressure suits. Eight sailors, led by the COB of the *Pegasus,* Master Chief

Swanson, would make up the work party, and Jackson, Ruiz, and Olin Parvik would come along as observers.

With some nimble maneuvering, the frigate, in her matching orbit to the wreck of the destroyer, moved in even closer to the derelict. The robot arm again was extended and secured, holding the two vessels together, and soon the party drifted across the space between the two vessels, using the arm to carry them safely to the destroyer. In single file, led by Olin Parvik, they entered the *Starguard* through one of the holes that had been blasted in its hull. Oddly, Jackson noted, the metal strips of the hull were bent outward; this breach had been created by something bursting out of the ship, not blasting in.

"The magazine exploded," Parvik said grimly. The whole midsection of the ship was a charred chasm, confirming his diagnosis.

In eerie silence, accompanied only by the rasp of the breathers and the privacy of his own thoughts, each man made his weightless way through the hulk that was all that remained of the Assarn destroyer. Each sailor and observer carried a light, and the beams played through the shadows, emphasizing the ghostly darkness all around them.

"Looks like she was caught in a cross fire—Eluoi particle cannons," Olin Parvik deduced after moving up toward the nose. He indicated a couple of holes that extended through the outer hull and inner bulkhead, where the metal had been sheared off cleanly, as if it had been burned through with a torch.

"Nasty stuff," Jackson agreed.

"It shoots a burst of energy at near light speed," the pilot noted grimly. "Like sending a virtually solid slug of pure heat out to about ten thousand kilometers."

The SEAL officer shook his head, relieved that the Team hadn't come under fire from that particular weapon.

"But here—our own laser cannon is intact," Parvik explained through his comlink. "I think we could pop it out of here if you want a souvenir."

"I think Captain Carstairs would be happy to come back from this vacation with a little keepsake," the COB allowed.

His men set to work with a vengeance, using a mixture of hand tools and plasma cutters. It took a few hours, but they finally worked the large-barreled weapon free. With the help of the frigate's crane, the particle cannon was loaded into the shuttle bay of the *Pegasus*.

Six hours after departing, the members of the salvage party and their prize were back aboard, and the *Pegasus* started for home, bearing a secret of alien technology that went far beyond any military information the Shamani had been willing to share. Carstairs's gunnery officer, Lieutenant Williams, was practically drooling as he looked over the laser weapon. With his first cursory inspection he was able to declare it many generations, perhaps a couple of centuries, ahead of what the most advanced Terran technology had been able to achieve.

Jackson had just shucked out of his pressure suit, using the compartment that the ship's executive officer had lent him on B Deck, when he encountered Dr. Sulati coming up from below.

"How's he doing?" the lieutenant asked.

"Mr. Robinson is recovering well," she said. "Better than I would have expected."

"Smokey always did have the constitution of an ox," Jackson said, relieved. "But he gave us a scare."

"Burns like that, over so much of the body, are often fatal," the doctor replied. "I told your corpsman that he saved Robinson's life. But he's going to be off the active duty roster for a very long time. It takes time to heal, even for a SEALS."

The klaxon warned of imminent acceleration, and the

doctor and the SEALS officer went into the XO's quarters and sat at the little table as the ship started to move.

"You and your Team—that was a pretty impressive accomplishment, rescuing us. And then getting your whole Team off the planet alive. You're an amazing commander, and the men are lucky to have you," she said quietly. "I never expected to see anyone from home again. Thanks for coming after us."

"I'm lucky to have those men. And we never leave our own behind," Jackson said. "And out here, that includes you." He hesitated, then asked a blunt question. "Are you going back to Mars?"

"That's my plan. I was in the middle of some important research, and I think they need a doctor up there."

"Yeah," he said. "I guess they do."

"So, Lieutenant," she said with a smile that brightened her dark eyes, "if you're ever in the neighborhood, you might give a girl a call."

"You know," he said, "I was going to do that even if you didn't ask."

The engines powered up with a thrumming whine that could be felt throughout the long, sleek vessel. *Pegasus* pulled away from Batuun with steady acceleration, the inertia dampened to the comfortable weight of 1 G. As soon as they got used to the pressure of gravity again, the two went all the way down the transport tube to L Deck, the Aft Con.

Consul Char-Kane, Chief Harris, Master Chief Ruiz, Olin Parvik, and Ensign Sanders were already there, watching the green planet slowly shrink. The CO had ordered the frigate to plot a course back to the solar system, and the steady press of 1 G allowed the seven of them to look straight "down" through the Plexiglas deck at their feet as the frigate sped away.

"You mentioned something about the Spider War—the Second Spider War, if I recall correctly," the lieutenant said to the Shamani woman. "When was that? What was it about?"

"The Spider cluster is a group of nearly a thousand stars, perhaps twenty light-years from here. It is so named because the stars are grouped in eight 'legs' that spiral out from a core. Some forty of the systems have livable planets, which is a very high percentage compared to the galaxy as a whole. It is one of the ancestral homes of my people, but we were driven out centuries ago by an Eluoi incursion.

"Then, when I was a young woman, being held as a slave there, the Shamani came back and reclaimed all the worlds of the cluster. The Eluoi presence in the cluster was shattered, the survivors driven out. It is a loss that rankles them to this day."

"Will you go back there?" Chief Harris asked.

"Someday, certainly. But there are many other places I would like to see first. If I may be of further service to your people . . . to you SEALS . . . I should very much like to do what I can."

"We couldn't have survived this mission without you," Jackson said, remembering how she had piloted the shuttle that had carried them down to Batuun and the invaluable information she had given them as they negotiated the perils of that alien world. "Thank you, on behalf of the SEALS, the U.S. Navy, and, I daresay, the whole of planet Earth."

Char-Kane's red eyes widened slightly in response to this, and she appeared momentarily flustered. Harris took her hand, and she smiled almost shyly. "You're welcome," she said. She looked at the chief, and her expression warmed. "I owe you all thanks, as well, for you have helped me understand that there are many ways for people to work, and talk, and live with others. We Shamani sometimes feel as though our way is the only way, and I know that is not the case."

Jackson looked at the void, and he remembered the four men, brave SEALS all, who had perished on Mars. They wouldn't be coming back with the Team, but neither would they be forgotten. Almost unconsciously, he raised his hand to his brow in a solemn salute.

"You *will* be remembered," he whispered.

Harris, Ruiz, and Sanders seemed to understand exactly what he meant, for they, too, saluted the darkness of space. Char-Kane watched solemnly, and Olin Parvik, his eyes moist, nodded.

For a long minute they all stood in silence. Not surprisingly, it was the ensign who finally spoke.

"Do you think we'll be back here, to Batuun?" Sanders asked rhetorically. "It's one of the closest stars to our own sun, after all."

Jackson could only shrug and gesture to the vastness spreading beyond the Plexiglas windows.

"Maybe," he allowed. "But it's a damned big universe out there."

Read on for a sneak peek
at the next exciting installment
in the Starstrike series,

# *Operation Orion*

# The **Lotus**

The drop boat had barely come to a halt in the huge hangar of the *Lotus* when *Mikey*'s gunner opened up with the chain gun in its bow-mounted turret. A stream of depleted uranium slugs chewed across the hangar floor, tearing up a bank of metal cabinets—and perforating the body of the hidden shooter just beyond that cover. The barrage of fire was strangely soundless in the vacuum of space, but Jackson could feel the stuttering vibration—more of a *zip* than a chatter because of the high rate of fire—through the drop boat's hull. The body of the target floated into view, a torn spacesuit leaking crimson-tinted vapor from a number of obviously lethal bullet holes. An ugly looking firearm floated out of his lifeless hands.

The vast space of the hangar deck was cluttered with several shuttles and miscellaneous debris floating in the zero-G environment. Emergency lights glowed eerily from many bulkheads, creating a kind of washed out, shadow-free dim. The massive passenger ship drifted, crippled and disabled, but somewhere within the great hull the SEALS knew that some of the Shamani crew remained alive. The unknown attackers, meanwhile, had blasted their way into that interior, and now controlled an unknown number of compartments within the massive *Lotus*.

Even as the gunner swiveled the boat's weapon around, seeking potential targets, the overhead Plexiglas hatches swished backward on each drop boat. The sixteen SEALS sprang upward and away from their landing craft. Each man used the mobility jets on his suit to guide his trajectory, so the Teammates scattered in a haphazard and unpredictable pattern. Fortunately, the chain gun seemed to have dealt with the initial threat. The SEALS came to rest at various places in the hangar without drawing any more fire.

Jackson took stock of their initial deployment. His men had remained together in pairs, each fire Team intact and ready. Rodale and LaRue had their heavy weapons readt, while the gunners on the two drop boats continued to swivel the bow turrets, the multi-barrelled chain guns pointing around the hangar with dull menace. In the zero gravity space the men floated all over the place, some near the upper bulkhead, others close to the deck. Each SEALS had his weapon trained, and between the eight fire Teams they covered all directions, in all three dimensions.

"L.T. Over here sir—take a look." It was one of the new men, Keast, and he gestured to Jackson from his position near the ruptured airlock the officer had noticed earlier. Now Keast gestured toward the far end of the hangar, beyond the two destroyed shuttles.

There were several other small spacecraft over there, the lieutenant saw: low and sleek, with outboard engines and bubble canopies. At least three of those canopies were open, and Jackson allowed himself to drift upward to get a better view over the wrecked transport ships. These mysterious boats were scuffed, stained, and dented—they looked nothing like the sleek boats used by the Shamani. Jackson guessed this was how the pirates had come aboard.

He was still studying the small shuttles when he saw movement, observed another canopy popping open. Three manlike figures, wearing supple spacesuits and carrying small assault guns, flew upward from the cockpit and immediately opened fire. Tracers zipped through the hangar, terrifyingly close. Jackson squeezed off a burst from his G-15 at the same time as a dozen other

SEALS opened fire. Almost instantly the three attackers were killed, their bodies twisting and tumbling crazily as the pressurized suits vented freely from the many bullet holes. The firefight occurred in eerie silence, the vaccum snuffing out any suggestion of sound—though his own breathing was loud in his earpiece as the lieutenant caught his breath and looked around for additional threats.

"Anybody hit?" Jackson asked over the local communicator. He was relieved as all of his men checked in; no one had so much as a tear in his pressure suit. "All right—in pairs, let's secure this hangar before we move in to the ship," he ordered.

The men moved like the precision-trained commandoes they were. As half the SEALS started out, one moving along each wall, several checking the overhead deck or poking around behind the hulks of the battered shuttles, the other half of each fire Team kept his weapon ready and his eyes open, watching for any threat. When the first group had moved halfway across the hangar—which was large enough to hold three or four good-sized jetliners—they halted and took up firing positions so that the second members of each fire Team could advance.

"Got a varmint runnin' over heah!" barked Gunner's Mate Dobson, his thick Alabama accent unmistakable over the com-link. The SEALS snapped off a shot at a suited figure who dived between a pair of metal crates, but the slugs skipped off the cover in a shower of sparks. Dobson and his partner Robinson shot past the crates, weapons trained on the place where the pirate had disappeared.

"Damn, Skipper. Sum'bitch made it through the air-lock!" declared Dobson in a disgusted tone.

"Well, we know where they are then," Jackson noted, using his jets to propel him over to the fire Team. He saw the secured hatch, smaller than some of the other passages out of the hangar, leading toward the interior of the ship. Of course, there was no way to tell how many bad guys were on the other side of that barrier, or what kind of reception they were arranging for the SEALS.

"Want me to blow the door, L.T?" asked Harry Teal who, despite his medical skills as a corpsman, was also a whiz at just about every kind of explosive. "We could make it pretty hot for them."

"I know," Jackson replied, thinking. He looked to the right, where the gaping black hole of the blasted airlock provided another way into the ship. The passageway obviously continued the vacuum of the hangar deck, and was utterly lightless. A quick check of the IR scanner shower no specific signs of heat, nothing that would indicate a power source or living body. He knew that within that dark chamber they would eventually come up against some kind of closed hatch, but he was considering the possibility of taking these fellows by surprise.

"Tell you what, Harry. Why don't you rig a charge. Set it for remote detonation so you can set it off with your clicker. The rest of you men, regroup over here."

The Team formed up outside the blasted airlock as the two scouts, Sanchez and Marannis, probed into the shadowy confines and Harry Teal set his C-6 charge. The corpsman drifted over to the CO after two minutes, holding a small detonator in his hand. "I can set it off from up to a kilometer away, L.T," he said.

"Good."

At the same time, Sanchez glided back out of the airlock to make his report. "Got a short corridor inside sir. It T's after about twelve meters. The branches go twenty or thirty meters right and left. Each ends in another airlock, closed and secured. There's also a hatch just at the base of the T. That one's open. The control panel looks dark—I think it's disabled, Skipper."

Still moving in combat formation, half the men stationary to cover their companions who were moving, the

Team moved through the blasted hatch, some SEALS high, others low, all of them alert. The metal of the framework was peeled and twisted, indicating that a considerable force had been used to force the entry. Fortunately, the inner lock, though currently open, did not look to have been physically twisted out of alignment.

As Sanchez had described, there was a second, undamaged airlock hatch a short distance inside the blasted barrier. The hatch was open, but if they could seal it they would secure this T shaped corridor section from the vacuum of the hangar deck and outer space, beyond.

Jackson gestured to Baxter, who in his short time with the Team had displayed a remarkable skill with mechanics and electronics. "Fritz, can you see if you can get that airlock operable?"

"Aye aye, sir. It's just a matter of hooking up a power source," Baxter reported. He shrugged out of the ungainly battery pack he wore on his back and pulled out a pair of wires tipped with alligator clips. With a quick slice of a hand torch, he cut away the faceplate of the hatch control panel. In a few seconds, he identified a pair of contacts and affixed the stout terminals of his Mark 21 battery pack. Jackson knew that the compact unit could generate enough electricity to run a small town, if necessary. It shouldn't take that much to close and seal the airlock.

And it didn't. Fritz fiddled with the controls, adjusted the output of his powersource, and waited for Jackson's signal. The lieutenant checked to see that his entire Team was positioned inside the corridors, and gave the thumb's up. Baxter pushed the button and the door slid down and nested into its gasket with a smooth, soundless glide. Of course, the corridor they occupied was still in a vacuum state, but now that vacuum wasn't connected to the whole gulf of space outside.

"The rest of you, follow me."

It was time to move. Jackson found Teal and Harris

near the front of the formation. The officer studied the shape of the corridor, and tried to picture the adjacent airlock where the lone surviving pirate had escaped from the hangar.

"I want another C-6 charge on the bulkhead, right here," he ordered. "Set it to go off ten seconds after the first one."

"Gotcha, L.T," Harry Teal replied. In less than a minute he had affixed a small packet of plastic explosive to the wall Jackson had indicated.

"Stand to, Team," Jackson ordered. "We move in as soon as the pressure equalizes—but remember, we don't know if we're tapping into a vacuum or not."

The men nodded, understanding the crucial difference: if the target proved to be pressurized, they would be faced by a quick blast of air as soon as they breached the bulkhead. Because the airlock was closed behind them, however, the wind would quickly ceased, as their own passageway achieved an equal pressure. If the compartment beyond the bulkhead was in vacuum, of course, there would be no exchange of air, and they could move in at once.

The Team backed into the other dead-end corridor, as far away from the explosive as they could get—and out of the direct line of the blast effect. Jackson didn't need to explain the plan in any more detail. Each man understood that the first blast, on the outer airlock, was to distract the enemy. The second explosion would create the breach for the Team's attack. Teal held his clicker at the ready, watching Jackson, and finally the officer nodded his go-ahead.

The first blast was a distant crump, barely felt through the metal of the surrounding bulkheads. The small hatch connecting the hangar to the ship's interior should have been blown off its hinges by the charge, but of course they couldn't see that. The ten seconds seemed to last for half an hour, but when the nearer explosive blasted it sent a flash of light and debris through the corridor where the SEALS were waiting.

The first men, Marannis and Sanchez, were blown back but a gust of air—they had obviously tapped into a pressurized compartment—but almost immediately the pressure equalized, since the T-shaped corridor had been sealed off from space and quickly filled with the air spilling in through the breach.

"Go! Go! Go!" Jackson shouted the unnecessary encouragement as his men, using their jets to move through the weightless environment, started for the breach torn by Teal's second explosion. The first two SEALS tumbled through, snapping off shots against vaguely seen targets in the murky interior. Two by two, the rest of the Team followed.

"Damn!" snapped Falco, dropping his long sniper rifle and tumbling backward, head over heels. Jackson saw a jet of air puffing from his shoulder, where his suit had been punctured; but the quickly equalized atmosphere served to stop the leak. The lieutenant was relieved to see no sign of blood emerging from the tear in the suit, and the self-sealing material was already closing over the breach.

Meanwhile, the rest of the SEALS took the adjacent corridor by storm. Several of the G-15s ripped out their streams of slugs, while one man launched a flash grenade that sparked brightly in the midst of the enemy fighters. Bodies floated, pirates bleeding and motionless where the initial bursts of fire had caught them. Jackson saw three men drifting grotesquely over a heavy machine gun, the weapon propped behind a half-bulkhead and trained toward the airlock where the first blast had occurred. There was a second, interior, hatch behind the first, and the pirates had been covering that entry with a dozen weapons. Clearly the diversion had worked—the enemy had expected a frontal attack, but the Team had taken them in the flank.

With devastating effects, the CO saw as he powered himself forward, through the debris of the brief, violent clash. At least a dozen pirates, all of them in space suits and armed with a miscellany of very deadly looking weaponry, had been prepared to defend against the breaching of the airlock. Some of them had been blasted by the force of the breaching charge, and the others had been too stunned to aim when the SEALS had come pouring through the hole.

"A few of 'em got away," Sanchez reported. "They were heading farther into the ship."

"Let's not let them catch their breath," Jackson admonished. "Full pursuit, Team."

Even in their haste, the men did not forget their training, or their partners. Two fire Teams—Sanchez with Marannis, and Dobson with Robinson, probed down the corridor in a coordinated advance, one man covering while his partner moved. Sanders took several men down a side passage, while Master Chief Ruiz and the new man, Gunner's Mate Mirowski, settled in to guard the rear.

"Permission to take off the helmets, L.T?" asked Chief Harris, as he and Harry Teal accompanied Jackson deeper into the ship. The two SEALS were propelling themselves along near the upper deck, while the officer flew steadily forward just above the "floor".

"Denied, Chief. There are too many ways these bastards could surprise us," replied the CO. He checked the readout on the interior of his Plexiglas faceplate, confirming that the air in the corridor was in fact quite breathable. Even so, he worried about a sudden breach—accidental or planned—that could result in an almost immediate vacuum. Nor could he afford to ignore the threats of poison or disabling gas.

A burst of gunfire ripped out before him, still silent but bright with muzzle flashes and tracer rounds. Marannis sprayed a juncture in the corridor before them, and Sanchez lobbed a grenade from his under barrel launcher. The device exploded twenty meters ahead, concussion and flash punching through the compartment where the enemy seemed to be making a stand.

"I got six or eight hostiles up here, L.T," reported one of his point men. "They got cover, and don't look to be backing up any more."

As if to punctuate the point, a barrage of tracer fire erupted from the large compartment ahead of the SEALS. Immediately the Teammates flowed toward the edges of the passageway, taking cover behind arches, chairs, and within the closed doorways that occasionally dotted the bulkheads. They returned fire, adding a few more grenades to the party, but even after the explosions the enemy returned a heavy volley, keeping the Team pinned in place.

"Sanders—do you copy?" barked Jackson into his helmet mic. He knew that his subordinate had embarked down a side corridor twenty meters back from their position.

"Loud and clear, Boss," came the junior lieutenant's reply.

"See if you can take a right turn. We've got a tough nut in front of us and could use a little flank support."

"Aye aye, sir."

More fire spat from the large compartment before them. Through the smoke Jackson could make out a collection of tables and chairs, like a mess hall deep within the *Lotus*. He couldn't see how wide the space was, but from the firepower there were a good number of hostiles forted up there.

"Grenade!" someone shouted, and the men instinctively pulled flat against the walls or hunkered deeper into their doorway niches. Jackson saw the flash and felt the explosion at the same time, the blast knocking him hard against the floor. A number of red lights flashed on his HUD, and he knew his suit had been breached—but when he pushed himself up again, he was certain he hadn't taken any significant wounds.

"I've got an access route—we're going in, L.T." This was Sanders' voice, sounding very confident. "Look for us to come from your left."

Abruptly Jackson saw the tracers of his men's counterattack, streaking across his field of view into the compartment. They had found a side door and looked to be opening up with everything they had.

"Take it to the bastards!" shouted the officer, activating his jets, shooting forward along the floor. Guns blazing, the rest of the SEALS attacked as well, spilling one by one through the hatch.

They were indeed in a large mess hall, with signs of damage—broken chairs and tables, soot-blackened bulkheads and decks—all around. Junk floated in the air, while several fires burned and smoked in what looked like the galley. Several pirates snapped shots at Sanders and five men as the lieutenant (j.g.) led the aggressive flank attack. Jackson drew a bead, shattering the helmet—and head—of one of these shooters. The enemy's suits looked as shabby as their shuttles, dirty and patched together, and they moved now in sheer terror, trying to flee into a corridor to the right.

Abruptly, a series of blasts—red bolts of directed energy—erupted from that corridor. The fleeing pirates were simply shredded by this new attack. More fighters, wearing battery packs and carrying those beam weapons like compact assault rifles, came charging in from that direction. These newcomers wore white suits trimmed in red stripes.

"Wait—hold fire!" Jackson shouted, as chaotic bursts of beam and projectile gunnery fire ripped into the compartment where the pirates were holed up. The shooters were new arrivals, not SEALS, but they seemed to share them same enemy.

The surviving pirates in their redoubt were shooting wildly now, under attack from three directions. Jackson saw a burst of that energy weapon—definitely not Terran in origin—tear through one of the hostiles, cutting his body almost in half. The riddled corpse drifted grotesquely through the air as the SEALS punched home their attack, six orf eight Teammates tumbling into the large compartment at once.

Maraniss had his small axe out and used it to crack the helmet—and the skull—of one struggling pirate. Another was hit while he was trying to shoot, and tumbled over like a child's toy, drifting eerily.

The two attatcking forces converged in the large compartment, and Jackson identified the white and red suits of their allies as Shamani. He guessed, correctly as it turned out, that these were some of the original crew of the *Lotus* who had impulsively joined in on the attack to reclaim their ship.

In less than a minute the firefight was over. Chief Harris and three SEALS used their in-suit fire extinguishers to put out the smoky blazes in the galley. Several of the white-suited crewmen saluted the wary SEALS, and Jackson returned the gesture, encouraged—although not surprised—by the discipline displayed by his men.

"The air pressure is still good," Ruiz reported. "Quality is fair—non-toxic, for sure."

"We got one prisoner, Skipper," reported Baxter as he and his partner, Keast, held the arms of a pirate behind his back.

"Take off his helmet," Jackson ordered, gliding up to have a look at the fellow. Keast unsnapped the bubble hat and pulled it, none too gently, off of the pirate's head.

The man's face was swarthy, needing a shave. His eyes were dark—too dark to determine to which of the three empires he belonged. He glowered at the lieutenant as Jackson halted and stared at him.

"Does he have a translator in his ear?" asked the officer. His suit contained the software to translate any known language into his own earpiece, but he wouldn't be able to communicate with the prisoner unless the fellow was wearing a device of his own. Fortunately, these translators had proved to be very common among space travelers, and Keast quickly confirmed that the pirate was wearing one.

"Your ship is gone," the lieutenant declared bluntly. "We chased it off and they left you and your comrades behind to die.

The pirate merely smirked. "We're all going to die," he spat, after a second.

Abruptly he convulsed, his eyes rolling back in his head. White foam drifted from his clenched jaws, and by the time Baxter pressed a hand to the man's neck, there was no pulse to be found.

"He suicided, L.T," declared the electrician's mate grimly. "Musta had some secrets he didn't want to share."

Only then did Jackson turn his attention to the Shamani crewmen who were drifting through the compartment, checking the bodies of the slain pirates. The newcomers abruptly parted, moving to open a path and saluting a new arrival, an officer who came gliding in to the increasingly crowded compartment.

From the alluring outline of this person's suit, Jackson guessed her to be female. Even so, he was shocked when she removed her helmet to reveal an attractive, olive-skinned face with startling—and unforgettable—crimson eyes.

"Consul Char Kane!" Jackson declared. "This is a surprise!"

"No less for me, lieutenant," said the Shamani consul de campe. It made sense for a high ranking diplomat to be on the ship, of course, but the SEALS officer was nonetheless startled to recognize the alien official who had been their companion for so much of their first mission. "This vessel was my transport. When we were attacked by these pirates, I feared we were doomed."

"Are you on your way to the Centauri conference?" he asked.

"I was," she said. "But we have more pressing problems right now." Jackson gestured for her to go on, and she continued. "I heard what that prisoner said, and it has been confirmed by the reports of my own crew."

"What is it?" the lieutenant asked grimly, fairly certain he wasn't going to like the answer.

"These pirates—they have occupied the hold of this ship for several hours. There are apparently no survivors of their boarding party, but I am certain they have left a powerful nuclear bomb on board. It could detonate at any time."